TARA SUE ME
THE
DOMINANT

headline
ETERNAL

Published by arrangement with New American Library,
a division of Penguin Group (USA) Inc.
Previously published in a Red Publishing edition.

First published in Great Britain in 2013 by
HEADLINE ETERNAL
An imprint of HEADLINE PUBLISHING GROUP

7

Cataloguing in Publication Data is available from the British Library

ISBN 978 1 4722 0810 1

Offset in Perpetua by Avon DataSet Ltd, Bidford-on-Avon, Warwickshire

Printed and bound by CPI Group (UK) Ltd, Croydon, CR0 4YY

Headline's policy is to use papers that are natural, renewable and
recyclable products and made from wood grown in sustainable forests.
The logging and manufacturing processes are expected to conform
to the environmental regulations of the country of origin.

HEADLINE PUBLISHING GROUP
An Hachette UK Company
338 Euston Road
London NW1 3BH

www.eternalromancebooks.co.uk
www.headline.co.uk
www.hachette.co.uk

Tara Sue Me wrote her first novel at the age of twelve. It would be twenty years before she picked up her pen to write the second.

After completing several traditional romances, she decided to try her hand at something spicier and started work on *The Submissive*. What began as a writing exercise quickly took on a life of its own, and sequels *The Dominant* and *The Training* soon followed. Originally published online, the trilogy was a huge hit with readers around the world. Each of the books has now been read and reread more than a million times.

Tara kept her identity and her writing life secret, not even telling her husband what she was working on. To this day, only a handful of people know the truth (though she has told her husband). They live together in the southeastern United States with their two children.

Praise for *The Submissive*:

'I HIGHLY recommend *The Submissive* by Tara Sue Me. It's so worth it. This book crackles with sexual lightning right from the beginning . . . *The Submissive* has exceeded all my expectations. It has heart and the characters are majorly flawed in a beautiful way. They aren't perfect, but they may be perfect together. Step into Tara Sue Me's world of dominance and submission. It's erotic, thrilling, and will leave you panting for more' *Martini Reviews*

'By the end of the first chapter I was hooked on the story and relationship of Abigail and Nathaniel . . . The book is told in first person so we only get Abby's perspective of the relationship, but it's one that I found real and compelling . . . This is one of those books that I will read and re-read' *The Book Reading Gals*

In The Submissive Trilogy

The Submissive
The Dominant
The Training

To my parents, who instilled in me a love of books, and to my in-laws for their support of my writing.
Maybe one day I'll share my pen name with you all.
But probably not.

THE
DOMINANT

Chapter One

The phone on my desk gave a low double beep.

I glanced at my watch. Four thirty. My administrative assistant had explicit instructions not to interrupt me unless one of two people called. It was too early for Yang Cai to call from China, so that left only one other person.

I hit the speaker-phone button. "Yes, Sara?"

"Mr. Godwin on line one, sir."

Excellent.

"Did I receive a package from him today?" I asked.

Papers rustled in the background. "Yes, sir. Should I bring it in now?"

"I'll get it later." I disconnected and switched to the headset. "Godwin, I expected you to call earlier. Six days earlier." I'd been waiting for the package just as long.

"I'm sorry, Mr. West. You had a late application I wanted to include with this batch."

Very well. It wasn't like the women knew I had a deadline. That was something I would discuss with Godwin later.

"How many this time?" I asked.

"Four." He sounded relieved I'd moved on from his lateness. "Three experienced and one without any experience or references."

I leaned back in my chair and stretched my legs. We really

shouldn't be having this conversation. Godwin knew my prefer-
ences by now. "You know my feelings on inexperienced submissives."

"I know, sir," he said, and I pictured him wiping the sweat
from his brow. "But this one is different—she asked for you."

I stretched one leg and then the other. I needed a nice, long
jog, but it would have to wait until later that evening. "They all
ask for me." I wasn't being vain, just honest.

"Yes, sir, but this one wants to service only you. She's not interested in anyone else."

I sat up in the chair. "Really?"

"Her application specifically states she will sub for you and no
one else."

I had rules about prior experience and references because, to
be frank, I didn't have time to train a submissive. I preferred
someone with experience, someone who would learn my ways
quickly. Someone I could teach quickly. I always included a
lengthy checklist in the application to ensure applicants knew exactly what they were getting themselves into.

"I assume she filled out the checklist properly? Didn't indicate
she would do anything and everything?" That had happened once.
Godwin knew better now.

"Yes, sir."

"I suppose I could take a look at it."

"Last one in the pile, sir."

The one he'd held the package up for, then. "Thank you, Godwin." I hung up the phone and stepped outside my office. Sara
handed me the package.

"Why don't you go home, Sara?" I tucked the envelope under
my arm. "It should be quiet the rest of the evening."

She thanked me as I walked back into my office.

I got a bottle of water, set it on my desk, and opened the package.

I flipped my way through the first three applications. Nothing special. Nothing out of the ordinary. I could set up a test weekend with any of the three women and probably wouldn't be able to tell the difference between them.

I rubbed the back of my neck and sighed. Maybe I had been doing this too long. Maybe I should try again to settle down and be "normal." With someone who wasn't Melanie this time. The problem was, I needed my dom lifestyle. I just wanted something special to go along with it.

I took a long sip of water and looked at my watch. Five o'clock. It was highly doubtful I'd find my something special in the last application. Since the woman had no experience, it really wasn't even worth my time to review her paperwork. Without looking at it, I took the application and put it on top of my *To Shred* pile. The three remaining I placed side by side on top of my desk and read over the cover pages again.

Nothing. There was basically nothing differentiating the three women. I should just close my eyes and randomly pick one. *The one in the middle would work.*

But even as I looked over her information, my gaze drifted to the shred pile. The discarded application represented a woman who wanted to be *my* submissive. She'd taken the time to fill out my detailed paperwork and Godwin had held up sending everything because of Miss I-have-no-experience-and-want-only-Nathaniel-West. The least I could do was respect that woman enough to read her information.

I picked up the discarded application and read the name.

Abigail King.

The papers slipped from my hand and fluttered to the ground.

I was a complete success in the eyes of the world.

I owned and ran my own international securities corporation.

I employed hundreds of people. I lived in a mansion that had graced the pages of *Architectural Digest*. I had a terrific family. Ninety-nine percent of the time, I was content with my life. But there was that one percent . . .

That one percent that told me I was an utter and complete failure.

That I was surrounded by hundreds of people, but known by very few.

That my lifestyle was not acceptable.

That I would never find someone I could love and who would love me in return.

I never regretted my decision to live the lifestyle of a dominant. I normally felt very fulfilled, and if there were times I did not, they were very few and far between.

I felt incomplete only when I made my way to the public library and caught a glimpse of Abby. Of course, until her application crossed my desk, I had no way of knowing if she even knew I existed. Until then, Abby had symbolized for me the missing one percent. Our worlds were so far apart, they could not and would not collide.

But if Abby was a submissive and wanted to be *my* submissive . . .

I allowed my mind to wander down pathways I'd closed off for years. Opened the gates of my imagination and let the images overtake me.

Abby naked and bound to my bed.

Abby on her knees before me.

Abby begging for my whip.

Oh, yes.

I picked her application up off the ground and started reading.

Name, address, phone number, and occupation, I skimmed over. I turned the page to her medical history—normal liver function tests and blood cell counts, HIV and hepatitis negative,

negative urine drug screen. The only medication she took was the birth control pills I required.

I went to the next page, her completed checklist. Godwin had not lied when he said Abby had no experience. She had marked off only seven items on the list: vaginal sex, masturbation, blindfolds, spanking, swallowing semen, hand jobs, and sexual deprivation. In the comment field beside sexual deprivation, she had written, "Ha-ha. Not sure our definitions are the same." I smiled. She had a sense of humor.

Several items were marked "No, hard limit." I respected that—I had my own hard limits. Looking over the list, I discovered that several of them lined up with hers. Several of them did not. There was nothing wrong with that—limits changed; checklists changed. If we were together for the long term—

What was I thinking? Was I actually thinking about calling Abby in for a test?

Yes, damn it, I was.

But I knew, *I knew*, that if the application were from anyone other than Abby, I wouldn't even give it a second glance. I would shred it and forget it existed. I didn't train submissives.

But it was from Abby, and I didn't want to shred it. I wanted to pore over her application until I had it memorized. I wanted to make a list of what she had marked as "willing to try" and show her the pleasure of doing those things. I wanted to study her body until its contours were permanently etched in my mind. Until my hands knew and recognized her every response. I wanted to watch her give in to her true submissive nature.

I wanted to be her dom.

Could I do that? Could I put aside my thoughts of Abby, the fantasy I would never have, and instead have Abby, the submissive?

Yes. Yes, I could.

Because I was Nathaniel West and Nathaniel West didn't fail.

And if Abby King no longer existed. Or if she was replaced by Abigail King . . .

I picked up the phone and dialed Godwin.

"Yes, sir, Mr. West," he said. "Have you decided?"

"Send Abigail King my personal checklist. If she's still interested after reviewing it, have her call Sara for an appointment next week."

Chapter Two

Abigail made an appointment for Tuesday afternoon at four. All day Monday I waited for Sara to tell me she had called and canceled, but by Tuesday at one, I had accepted the fact that Abigail would probably show up. It made me restless.

I paced from my window to my desk and back again, remembering Abigail as I had last seen her—complete patience as she tutored a high school student, laughing softly at something the teenager said. Then I pictured her as I would now allow myself to—as my submissive, ready and willing to service me. To obey my every command.

I walked back to my desk and sat down. For the third time in the last hour, I pulled out the packet of information I'd prepared for her and reread it. Triple-checked that everything was in order.

My cousin, Jackson, called at three thirty and kept me from going completely stir-crazy.

"Hey," he said. "We still on for racquetball Saturday?"

I groaned. I had forgotten the promise I'd made to Jackson that we would have a rematch on Saturday. If Abigail agreed to a weekend test, did I really want to leave her? On the other hand, maybe it would be good to get away from her for a few hours. Give myself a break from what promised to be an intense weekend.

Jackson picked up on my hesitation. "It's okay if you can't. I can always go skydiving."

The last time he went skydiving, it almost ended his career as quarterback, so I knew he was joking.

At least I hoped he was joking.

"Don't blackmail me," I said. "I wasn't trying to bail out. I was just making sure my calendar was clear. I might have a date."

"A date? Getting back on the horse after Pearl Girl?"

"That nickname is completely disrespectful to Melanie." And he couldn't be further from the truth. I'd had plenty of *horse rides* since Melanie.

"Just saying, I'm glad you dumped her ass."

"Enough of me and my love life," I said, because I didn't think Jackson had any idea what my sex life was really like. "Who are you bringing to your mom's benefit?"

"No one at the moment. Thanks for the reminder," he said with a touch of sarcasm.

We talked a bit more and eventually hung up after agreeing I'd meet him on Saturday for our racquetball rematch.

In many ways, Jackson was the brother I never had. My parents had been killed in a car accident when I was ten. My mother's sister, Linda, raised me afterward.

Todd Welling was the third member of my close-as-family group of friends, along with his wife, Elaina. Todd and his family had lived next door to the Clarks while we were growing up. Elaina had lived nearby, and she and Todd had dated throughout high school and during college. They married the month after she graduated. Todd was now a psychiatrist and Elaina a fashion designer.

I envied Todd and Elaina the companionship they had with each other. The passion and love they felt was palpable. I had long since given up on finding a relationship like theirs, but such was the life I lived.

To have Abigail as a sub would almost make up for it.

My phone gave a low double beep.

"Yes, Sara?" I looked at my watch—three forty-five. Abigail was punctual. Another positive.

"Ms. King is here, sir."

"Thank you, Sara. I'll let you know when I'm ready for her." I disconnected.

I drank some water and looked over the pages one more time. All was ready. I picked up her application and reread it, although I'm not sure why. I had it memorized.

When the clock read five after four, I called Sara and told her to send Abigail in.

I took a deep breath, opened a blank document on my computer, and started typing.

Nathaniel West is the world's biggest fucking idiot.

What the hell do you think you're doing?

Idiot.

Abigail opened the door and quietly stepped inside, closing the door behind her.

Big. Fucking. Idiot.

You have no business having her here.

This will go down as your worst mistake ever.

She walked to the middle of my office, and from my peripheral vision, I saw her stand with her hands to her sides, feet spread to the width of her shoulders.

Damn.

Damn. Damn. Damn. Damn. Damn.

Damn. Damn. Damn. Damn. Damn.

Fuck. Fuck. Fuck.

Damn.

I kept typing while I peeked at her. She took a deep breath. Her eyes were closed.

Pull it together, West, I typed. *She's here for you. To be your submissive. The least you can do is not be a complete pansy ass.*

You've done this many times. She wants to be your sub. You are a dom.
She's nothing new. Nothing special.

It's very, very simple, so stop trying to make it complicated.

Give her what she wants. What she needs.

Take what she'll give.

And some of what she doesn't even know she has to offer.

Typing helped clear my head. Very much like playing the piano. I wrote out a few more lines, took a deep breath, and looked up.

"Abigail King," I said.

She jumped. It was to be expected really. Her head was still down, but a faint tremor ran throughout her body. I wanted to reach out and touch her, reassure her I would never harm her.

Instead, I picked up her application and the packet of papers I would give her if the meeting went well and tapped them together.

Her head was still down.

Very nice.

I pushed back from my desk and walked across the floor. Her tremor intensified, but just barely. I stood behind her and reached out a hand. It was time to touch her and realize she was no more than a flesh-and-blood woman. Nothing more. Nothing less.

I brushed her long, dark hair to one side and leaned in close. "You have no references." Because it was the truth and because I wanted to see the pulse quicken at that delicate spot at the base of her throat.

Yes.

Just. Like. That.

I leaned closer, so my lips were almost to her throat. "I would have you know that I'm not interested in training a submissive. My submissives have always been fully trained."

Would she want to know why I was making an exception in

her case? Would my words have tipped her off that something was different about her?

Probably not. But they should have. This was not the way I normally operated. I was changing all the rules for her.

And she didn't even know it.

I took her hair and pulled. "Are you sure this is what you want, Abigail? You need to be sure."

A small part of me wanted her say no, to look up and leave. Never to return. But the biggest part of me wanted her to stay. Wanted her.

She didn't move. Didn't leave.

I chuckled and walked back to my desk. We were both so stubborn. Maybe this would work after all.

Damn, I wanted it to work.

"Look at me, Abigail."

Our eyes met for the first time. Hers were a deep brown and framed by thick lashes. I saw her every thought reflected in those eyes. The nervousness, the hunger, the frank assessment as her gaze traveled over me.

I drummed my fingers on the desk. Her eyes darkened and she looked slightly embarrassed.

Ah, she was thinking dirty, dirty thoughts. And that made me smile—but enough of that for now.

"I'm not interested in why you decided to submit your application. If I select you and you are agreeable to my terms, your past won't matter." Because the past was no more. What mattered was now. I tapped the two reports together. "I know what I need to."

She still didn't move. Didn't say anything.

"You have no training," I said. "But you're very good."

I turned to the window. Darkness cloaked the street down below, but the light from my office made the window a mirror. I could see everything Abigail did. She met my eyes for a second and then looked down.

We couldn't have that.

"I rather like you, Abigail King. Although I don't recall telling you to look away."

Yes, I thought, when her eyes met mine once more. We were going to move forward.

I had her in my hands and I would not let her go.

"I think a weekend test is in order." I turned from the window and loosened my tie. "If you agree, you will come to my estate this Friday night at six exactly. I'll have a car pick you up. We'll have dinner and take it from there."

I put the tie down and unbuttoned the top button of my shirt. She didn't look the slightest bit uncomfortable—excited maybe, but not uncomfortable.

"I have certain expectations of my submissives." My submissive. Abigail King was well on her way to being mine. "You are to get at least eight hours of sleep every Sunday through Thursday night. You will eat a balanced diet—I will have a meal plan e-mailed to you. You will also run one mile, three times a week. Twice a week you will engage in strength and endurance training at my gym. A membership will be created for you starting tomorrow. Do you have any concerns about any of this?"

She was silent.

Lovely.

"You may speak freely."

She licked her lips, her pink tongue running around the edges of her mouth. The sight made my cock twitch. *Easy, now,* I thought. *Time for that later. Please, God, let there be time for that later.*

"I'm not the most . . . athletic, Mr. West. I'm not much of a runner."

"You must learn not to let your weakness rule you, Abigail." Since she had brought it up, I would help her.

I walked back to my desk and wrote down the name and number of the yoga instructor at the gym.

"Three times a week you will also attend yoga classes. They have these at the gym. Anything else?"

She shook her head.

"Very well. I will see you Friday night." I held out the papers. "These will have everything you need know."

She approached my desk and took the papers. Then she waited.

Perfection.

"You are excused."

Chapter Three

While I had never been a Boy Scout, I agreed wholeheartedly with their "Be prepared" motto. Preparation was half the reason my business was so successful. It was partly why I'd never had a submissive use her safe word. If people were just more prepared, the world as a whole would run smoother.

For that reason, I spent part of Wednesday afternoon at my favorite jewelers. If Abigail's weekend test went well, I wanted to be prepared with a collar. After seeing how well she did during her office test, I felt certain that it would.

I glanced over the offerings in the necklace display. My previous submissives had worn plain silver chokers, but I wanted something more for Abigail.

"Mr. West," the manager said, approaching me. "What can I help you with today?"

I wasn't impressed with anything I saw. "I'm looking for a choker. Platinum. With diamonds, perhaps?"

The manager's eyes lit with excitement. "I have just the thing. Arrived this morning, and I haven't had a chance to put it out yet."

He scurried off, returning moments later with a leather-covered box. Inside was an exquisite choker made of two ropelike platinum bands, intertwined, with diamonds embedded throughout.

I could easily picture it on Abigail.

My collar.

My submissive.

"Perfect," I said to the manager.

I decided to cook dinner for Abigail on Friday night. I wanted her to relax before we started anything. Give her a chance to ask any questions or bring up concerns. I wanted her to be comfortable over the weekend—as comfortable as possible, anyway.

I prepared one of my favorite dishes and went over my plans for the weekend. I would not have penetrative sex with Abigail yet. That could wait while I tried other things. And I would test my own control—to have her so near, so near and yet not touch her.

I also made a new rule—I would not kiss her. It seemed only fair to make a new rule, since I was breaking so many others.

Part of me knew it was silly to think not kissing Abigail would somehow ensure I kept the proper emotional distance. But the truth was, she wanted to be my submissive. She did not want me as a lover. As long as I went into the weekend remembering our relationship would be sexual, and nothing more than that, I would be fine.

The car service pulled into my driveway at five forty-five.

I opened the door to find her on her knees, petting Apollo. I had expected Apollo to keep away from her, since he usually shied away from strangers. How unusual for him to be drawn to her. Though they did say dogs had a sixth sense about people.

The fact that Apollo seemed to like her convinced me that the weekend was a good idea.

"Apollo," I said. "Come."

She hadn't heard me open the door. That much was certain in the way her head jerked up. She smiled as Apollo licked her face.

"I see you've made Apollo's acquaintance," I said.

"Yes." She stood up and brushed her pants. The setting sun made her hair and eyes look darker, more mysterious. "He's a very sweet dog."

"He's not. Normally, he doesn't take kindly to strange people. You're very fortunate he didn't bite you."

Apollo wouldn't have bitten her, of course. I wouldn't have left him outside alone if I thought he would bite. I wasn't sure why I said that. Maybe part of me wanted her to leave.

I led her into the house. "We'll have dinner tonight at the kitchen table. You can consider the kitchen table your free space. You'll take the majority of your meals there, and when I join you, you may take it as an invitation to speak freely. Most of the time, you will serve me in the dining room, but I thought we should start the evening on a less formal basis. Is all this clear?"

"Yes, Master."

I spun around, caught off guard by her slip. "No. You have not yet earned the right to call me that. Until you do, you will address me as 'sir' or 'Mr. West.'"

"Yes, sir. Sorry, sir."

I continued on, still surprised by her mistake. Hopefully, the rest of the weekend would go better.

I took her to the kitchen and waited for her to sit down. Her hands trembled when she pulled out her chair. She was nervous; that was all. I could understand that.

But she was here. Here in my kitchen. Here to be my submissive.

The absurdity of it kept me quiet.

We ate in silence for several minutes. She devoured the chicken. I shifted in my seat at the sight of her at my table, enjoying the food I'd made for her.

"Did you cook this?" she asked.

She speaks. Finally.

"I am a man of *many* talents, Abigail." And I can't wait to share them all with you.

She didn't speak again.

"I am pleased you do not find it necessary to fill the silence with endless chatter," I said when we were almost finished. "There are a few things I need to explain. Keep in mind, you can speak freely at this table."

I stopped and waited.

"Yes, sir."

Good girl.

"You know from my checklist I'm a fairly conservative dom. I do not believe in public humiliation, will not participate in extreme pain play, and I do not share. Ever." As if I'd ever share Abigail with anyone if she were mine. "Although as a dom, I suppose I could change that at any time."

"I understand, sir."

Do you? I almost asked.

"The other thing you should know," I said, "is that I don't kiss on the lips."

She looked puzzled by this. "Like *Pretty Woman*? It's too personal?"

Yes, exactly. It's too personal. And I needed to keep the personal out of this as much as possible.

"*Pretty Woman*?"

"You know, the movie?"

"No. I've never seen it," I said. "I don't kiss on the lips because it's unnecessary." *Unnecessary for us. Ask me why.*

Though she looked upset, she just ate another bite of chicken, so I continued. "I recognize that you're a person with your own hopes, dreams, desires, wants, and opinions. You have put those things aside to submit to me this weekend. To put yourself in such a position demands respect, and I do respect you. Everything I do to or for you, I do with you in mind. My rules on sleeping, eating, and exercise are for your benefit. My chastisement is for your betterment." I ran a finger around the rim of my wineglass and smiled inwardly at the way her eyes followed the movement. "And any pleasure I give you . . ." *I will give you pleasure, Abigail, know that now—much pleasure.* "Well, I don't suppose you would have any qualms concerning pleasure."

Yes. She understood. Her eyes grew dark and her breathing changed. I had her exactly where I wanted her.

I pushed my chair back, ready to proceed with the evening. "Are you finished with dinner?"

"Yes, sir."

"I need to take Apollo outside. My room is upstairs, first door on the left. I will be there in fifteen minutes. You will be waiting for me. Page five, first paragraph."

I took Apollo outside to clear my head, to prepare myself as far as I could for what was about to happen in my bedroom. I ran over my plan again in my mind. Abigail enjoyed giving oral sex—I knew that from her checklist. Since that was typically one of my first acts with a sub, it only made sense to start our weekend out that way.

A submissive was reminded of her position and responsibilities while giving oral sex. On her knees at my feet, being used for my pleasure. While I could use a submissive any way I wished, it was a responsibility I did not take lightly.

I pictured the bedroom the way I'd left it—lit candles everywhere, the pillow in the middle of the room, the nightgown I'd purchased. Would I find her on her knees wearing the gown? That was my hope. Maybe I'd find her in the foyer, waiting to tell me she'd changed her mind. That was my fear.

"Come on, Apollo."

When we made it back into the house, I stopped at the laundry room and stripped off my sweater, placing it in the hamper for my housekeeper to take to the dry cleaner. Abigail wasn't in the foyer, so I walked up the stairs, Apollo at my heels. I pointed to the floor outside my bedroom door, and he plopped down with a sigh, head on his paws.

I stepped into the room and found her waiting. She had the gown on and knelt on the pillow.

Yes.

I closed the door. "Very nice, Abigail. You may stand."

She rose slowly. The gown hit at her upper thigh, and the faint pink flush of her skin through the sheer material betrayed her excitement.

"Strip the gown off and place it on the floor."

She drew the gown over her head with trembling fingers. She was nervous, but her nipples were hard and her lips parted slightly.

"Look at me." Once her eyes met mine—yes, she was as excited as I was—I removed my belt and walked closer to her. "What do you think, Abigail? Shall I chastise you for your *master* remark?"

I snapped the belt and it landed on her upper thigh. I was not yet her master, and she needed to understand that.

One day soon, perhaps . . .

"Whatever you wish, sir," she whispered.

Good answer.

"Whatever I wish?" I wished a lot of things, but for now . . .

I stood before her and unbuttoned my pants, slipped them down with my boxers. My erection sprang free. "On your knees." I waited, knowing she was looking. Which was fine. She needed to see.

"Service me with your mouth."

She leaned forward, and my cock slipped past her lips. Her mouth was hot and wet, and I grew even harder. Fuck, she felt good. I hit the back of her throat.

"All of it." She could do it.

She would do it.

She hesitated, though, bringing her hands up to grasp the base of my cock, and I didn't like hesitation.

"If you can't take it in the mouth, you can't have it anywhere else," I said, because I knew exactly where she wanted it. The thought made me thrust forward, and I slipped deeper into her throat. "Yes. Like that."

I looked down, and the sight of Abigail on her knees, with my cock in her mouth, almost made me come. I wouldn't last long. "I like it hard and rough, and I'm not going to go easy on you just because you're new." I grabbed her hair. "Hold on tight."

She wrapped her arms around my thighs, and I pulled out to thrust immediately back into her mouth.

I moved her head with my hands, fucking her mouth, hard and rough. Exactly the way I liked.

"Use your teeth," I said, and she scraped my length as I moved in and out. Then she got into it, sucking me and running her tongue around me.

"Yes," I moaned, closing my eyes and using her even harder.

Yes.

Fuck.

My balls tightened, and I knew I was close. I held off, wanting to make the feeling last—the feel of her mouth on me, the promise of my release begging me to let go, the high of being so close and not letting myself give in just yet.

She sucked harder, and I knew I couldn't hold off much longer.

"Swallow it all," I said, preparing her. "Swallow everything I give you."

I released in several long spurts, but she took it all. Gulping it down, not missing a drop.

I pulled out, my breathing heavy, because, damn, she was good. "That, Abigail," I said, "that is what I wish." I pulled my pants back on, noting how she waited for my next order.

I wanted to throw her on the bed and fuck her properly. I wanted to hold her hands above her head and pound into her over and over until she was screaming with the pleasure I gave her. I wanted—

Enough!

She'd had enough for one night.

She needed time to get used to it. As much as she wanted this, she was still very new to my world. I could not and would not forget that.

I waited until my breathing had calmed. "Your room is two doors down on the left," I said. "You sleep in my bed by invitation only. You are excused."

She slipped the gown back on and gathered her clothing.

"I will take breakfast in the dining room at seven sharp."

Chapter Four

I never needed a lot of sleep. Most nights I did fine with four or five hours, which was just as well, because after having Abigail's lips wrapped around my dick, there was no way in hell I'd be sleeping anytime soon. I ran my hand through my hair and tried to concentrate on the detailed spreadsheet on my laptop, but the numbers jumbled up in my brain. I cursed in frustration.

Damn it. What had I done?

I'd forced Abigail to her knees and fucked her mouth without asking what she thought or how she felt or even if she wanted to.

But, I argued with myself, it was what she wanted. She had free will. She could have told me to stop at any minute and I would have. I knew that, but the fact was, she hadn't wanted me to stop. She wanted me to dominate her or else she wouldn't be in my house and she sure as hell wouldn't be sleeping two doors down from my bedroom.

I shut down the laptop and walked into the hallway.

Her door was closed and the light off. She was sleeping.

Further proof of what she wanted.

I didn't question it again. I went into the playroom and prepared for the next evening.

I finally made it to bed long after midnight and woke up four and a half hours later, at five thirty. I did a few stretches before walking down the hall to Abigail's room.

The door was closed—she was still sleeping. I wondered if she'd wake up in time to fix breakfast and thought briefly about waking her up myself. Then I decided I didn't want to set a precedent, so I turned and went down the stairs to my home gym.

I finished my jog at six forty and heard Abigail banging around the kitchen. She might have woken up later than she wanted, but she was bound and determined to have my breakfast ready. I left the gym and took a quick shower. At seven exactly, I walked into the dining room and found my breakfast waiting.

I observed her from the corner of my eye while I ate. She was dressed casually and her hair was pulled back in a sloppy ponytail. She probably hadn't showered. Her breathing was just the slightest bit heavy, but she worked to control it, as if she didn't want to let on how she'd rushed through making breakfast. She'd worked hard this morning.

Which meant the rest of the weekend looked very promising.

I took my time eating. There was no need to hurry, and I wanted Abigail to have the time necessary to calm her thoughts.

"Make yourself a plate and eat in the kitchen," I said once I finished. "Come to my bedroom in an hour. Page five, paragraph two."

I called Jackson while I took Apollo outside.

"You aren't calling to cancel, are you?" he asked.

"No. I was calling to see if you wanted to have lunch after we played."

"Lunch would be great." His voice dropped. "Did the date not work out?"

I laughed. Little did he know. "The date worked out fine. More than fine, actually—we made plans for tonight."

"All right!" he said. "Score one for you."

If you even knew the half of it.

"So what's she like?" he asked. "Is she pretty? Does she have a sister?"

I reached down to pet Apollo. "I'll tell you all about her at lunch."

As much as I tried to imagine what it would be like to have Abigail spread out on my bed, the sight still left me stunned. The late-morning sun cast a bright glow over the bed—illuminating her body, making her shine.

Her eyes were closed, allowing me a few seconds to observe her unnoticed. I started at her mouth, at the way her lips parted slightly—almost as if she were talking to herself. My gaze continued traveling, skirting over her delicate neck. I watched as she swallowed, how her muscles stirred under her skin. The movement of her hands caught my attention, but she only brushed her fingers over the bedspread. Her eyes were still closed.

Her breasts were the perfect size to fit in the palms of my hands, and as I watched, she took a deep breath, lifting her chest. Her nipples were a dusky rose color, pebbled in obvious excitement. I ached to take one in my mouth. To taste her—

Later.

I clenched my fists and moved my eyes downward, along the gentle slope of her belly, down to where she had her knees spread. My eyes dipped lower, and I saw that she was already wet.

Wet for me.

Ready for me.

My cock hardened at the thought.

Later, West, I told myself. Learn some control.

I knew if I didn't move forward with my plan, I'd tear my clothes off and take her right then and there. But that was not my plan, and I always did everything according to plan.

Almost.

Having Abigail in my house broke damn near every rule I'd ever had and every plan I'd ever created.

This is not about you, I told myself. Not much anyway. Just give her what she needs.

I unclenched my fist and walked to the bed. "Keep your eyes closed."

She jumped. She'd been so inwardly focused, she hadn't heard me enter.

"I like you spread out like this. Take your hands and pretend they're mine. Touch yourself." *Show me what you like, what you want.*

She hesitated. Again.

"Now, Abigail." I had to be more patient than usual. She was new to this, after all.

She moved her hands to her breasts and, while she was gentle at first, her touch grew rougher, harder, as she rolled the tip of one nipple and then the other. She took one and pinched it, eliciting a small gasp of pleasure in the process.

Fuck, yes. She liked it rough.

One hand trailed down her belly, while the other kept working her nipples. She slipped a finger between her legs.

Just one?

"You disappoint me, Abigail." I moved so close, I could feel her breath on my face. Her eyes fluttered. "Keep your eyes closed."

I glanced down, watching the rapid beat of her heart. Could I make it beat even faster?

"You had me stuffed in your mouth last night and now you use a single finger to represent my cock?"

Why, yes, I could. Just look at that heart race.

She slipped another finger inside.

"Another."

Her breath hitched, but she added a third and slowly started moving them.

And slow just wouldn't do.

"Harder. I'd fuck you harder." Because it was the truth. One day soon, I'd show her just how hard.

A faint blush spread across her chest. Yes, she liked it when I talked dirty to her. She liked it dirty and rough and dominating. I felt myself grow harder as I imagined myself in the place of her fingers. My cock pumping in and out of her. My cock being the cause of her moans.

She was close. Her breathing got rougher and the flush on her chest darkened. Her lips opened and closed.

I leaned in closer. "Now."

She let herself go and, damn, there wasn't a sight on this earth as beautiful as Abigail when she climaxed—the concentration of her face, the taut lines of her body as release washed over her, the soft moan falling from her lips . . .

Next time, I promised my straining cock. Next time she climaxes, you'll be inside her.

She opened her eyes and looked over at me. Her gaze dipped down to my pants.

See? I wanted to say. See what you do to me?

"That was an easy orgasm, Abigail," I said instead as her eyes came back to mine. "Don't expect that to happen often.

"I have a previous engagement this afternoon and won't be here for lunch. There are steaks in the refrigerator you will serve me at six in the dining room." I looked over her still-flushed body, now covered with a faint hint of sweat. "You need to shower, since you didn't have time this morning. And there are yoga DVDs in the gym. Make use of them. You may leave."

Not to brag, but I completely smoked Jackson on the racquetball court. I chalked it up to immense sexual frustration.

"Damn," Jackson said as we slipped into the booth at his favorite sports bar. "What's gotten into you?"

"Abigail King."

"Abigail," he mused while looking over the menu.

"Abby to you. She lets me call her Abigail, but everyone else calls her Abby."

He raised an eyebrow.

"Just a little thing between us." I looked at the menu, wanting to change the subject. "You having your usual?"

"Yeah. Why change a good thing?"

The manager came by to make small talk with Jackson. Sometimes it was annoying being related to a celebrity. I checked my phone, scrolled through a few e-mails. Nothing urgent.

"So," Jackson said when the manager had left with our orders, "tell me about this Abby. Where did you meet?"

"She works at the Mid-Manhattan Library."

"A librarian? I never knew you had a librarian fantasy."

"There's a lot you don't know about me."

He laughed as if he didn't believe me. "You bringing her to Mom's benefit?"

"If she agrees. Who are you bringing?"

"I can't think of anyone to ask. You find someone, you let me know."

As if I knew so many available women. I thought back to the woman I'd been with right after Melanie—a submissive with the need for hard-core pain. Needless to say, that had been a short relationship.

"Sure, Jackson. I'll make sure to call you."

After lunch, I drove by the office. For some reason, I didn't want to be in the house. I wanted Abigail to have time to acclimate herself to my home and thought she would stand a better chance if I wasn't around.

At six, I walked into the dining room to find Abigail waiting with a mouth-watering steak on the plate at my seat.

"Fix yourself a plate and join me," I said, cutting into the steak. It was the first real meal she had cooked for me, and it didn't disappoint—the steak was juicy and tender.

She joined me, but we ate in silence. She looked deep in thought, and that worried me a bit. I wondered what had her in such a contemplative mood. Maybe she was thinking about leaving. Maybe she'd had enough. Maybe she didn't want this after all.

There was only one way to find out.

"Come with me, Abigail," I said after we finished.

We went out of dining room, up the stairs, and into the playroom. I stepped to the side of the door and waved for her to enter first.

She took three steps inside and spun around to gape at me—exactly the reaction I'd expected.

"Do you trust me, Abigail?"

She glanced from me to the shackles. "I . . . I . . ."

I breezed past her and unbuckled one of them. "What did you think our arrangement would entail? I thought you were well aware of what you were getting yourself into."

I didn't expect her to answer, of course. I just wanted to bring the point home that we were not lovers.

"If we are to progress, you must trust me." *Trust me, Abigail. Please.* "Come here."

She hesitated again, and I knew I would have to do something about that sooner or later.

"Or," I said, wanting to give her another option, "you can leave my house and never come back."

She walked toward me. She didn't want to leave.

"Very good. Take off your clothes."

Her body trembled as she removed her shirt and bra. Without looking at me, she slid her jeans and panties down her legs and stepped out of them.

I took her arms and chained them above her head. I moved slowly, wanting to savor every minute. Wanting her to savor every minute. I stood before her to undo my shirt, and she watched me with excited, wild eyes.

No, I didn't want her watching yet.

I went back to the large table to my right and opened a drawer. There it was—a heavy black scarf. That would take care of her watching me.

I held it out so she could see, so she would know what I planned. "Your other senses will be heightened when I blindfold you."

I tied the scarf around her head, making sure her eyes were covered. Yes, that was better. I ran my eyes over her vulnerable form. She was now completely at my mercy. Bound and waiting for what I would do to her.

Oh, Abigail, the things I want to do to you. The things I will do to you . . .

I went back to the table and took my favorite crop.

With soft steps, I walked behind Abigail and brushed the hair from her neck. She jumped at my touch. I wondered when she would stop jumping every time I touched her.

"What do you feel, Abigail?" I asked. "Be honest."

"Fear. I feel fear."

Of course she felt fear. What reasonable person wouldn't?

"Understandable, but completely unnecessary," I tried to reassure her. "I would never cause you harm."

I moved to the front of her. Her breathing was heavy; she was trying so hard to hear what I was doing. But she didn't trust me yet.

I circled the tip of her breast with the crop. She gasped at the sensation.

"What do you feel now?"

"Anticipation."

Much better. I circled her breast again. "And if I told you this was a riding crop, what would you feel?"

It's one of my favorite toys. Let me show you what I can do with it. How it can make you feel good. Let me show you the pleasures of my world.

She took a hard intake of breath. "Fear."

I brought the crop back and flicked it gently with my wrist so it landed sharply on her breast. Some things were better explained without words.

She gasped, but it wasn't a gasp of pain. More like one of surprise.

"See? Nothing to fear. I won't cause you harm." I slapped her knees lightly. "Spread your legs."

No hesitation this time. She obeyed immediately.

Excellent. I studied her face—excitement, wonder, and eagerness.

I brought the crop from her knees to her wet sex, never letting the leather tip leave her skin. "I could whip you here. What do you think about that?"

Her brow wrinkled in confusion. "I . . . I don't know."

Let me help you find out.

My wrist snapped, flicking the crop against her swollen, ready flesh.

One.

She sucked her breath in again.

Two.

She released the breath in a moan.

Three.

"And now?" I asked, although I really didn't need to—her face was an open book. But I wanted her to know I cared about how she felt, that I would always keep her thoughts and wants in mind.

"More. I need more."

I circled the crop around her again and then slapped it against her clit. She couldn't hold her response back, and she cried out, pulling against the chains.

Her reaction surprised me. I never would have guessed how responsive she would be. How much she enjoyed what I was doing. How she seemed to crave it.

I wanted to keep her in chains all night, to bring her to the edge of pleasure again and again before allowing her to fall over. But I reminded myself how new she was to this, how she might question her response in the morning, and I knew I shouldn't push her too much.

"You look so good chained before me, pulling against my restraints, in my house, moaning and crying for my whip." I trailed the crop back up to her breast. "Your body is begging for release, isn't it?"

"Yes," she moaned.

"And you'll have it." I slapped the crop against her clit once more because I couldn't help myself. "But not tonight."

I walked away and put the crop back on the table, took some salve from the drawer and placed it in my pocket. I heard the chains rattle behind me.

Someone was just as sexually frustrated as I was.

"I'm going to unchain you now," I said, walking back to her. "You will go straight to bed. You will sleep naked and you will not touch yourself at all. There will be severe consequences if you disobey." I undid the chains and removed the scarf. "Do you understand?"

She swallowed. "Yes, sir," she said, and I saw that she did.

"Good." I took the salve from my pocket and opened it. I gently rubbed the ointment on one of her wrists and then the other.

I didn't think she'd pulled too hard on the chains, but it was best to err on the side of caution.

"All done," I said, once I finished. "You may go to your room."

I watched her slim, nude figure walk out the door and knew I was done for. I'd do whatever it took to keep her with me.

Chapter Five

I was going to do a bad thing.

And while I hated myself for it, I knew I'd do it anyway.

I was going to give Abigail a fake safe word.

I got up from my bed and started pacing. It was wrong. So very wrong. With my previous submissives, I had used the standard green/yellow/red safe-word system. The relationship-ender safe word I planned to give Abigail was deceptive. And it was wrong. So wrong, I'd be ostracized from the community if word got out.

But how would word get out? Abigail wasn't going to tell anyone.

I sure as hell wasn't going to tell anyone.

I'd never had a submissive use a safe word before. I told myself I could read Abigail's signs easily, so I'd never push her too far. I'd check in with her often. If you thought about it that way, who needed safe words anyway?

Safe, sane, consensual people.

But I could be safe, sane, and consensual without a safe word. I knew I could. And Abigail would think twice about using the safe word if she thought she'd have to leave. It was the perfect way to ensure she stayed with me.

Yes, I decided, we'd be fine without safe words. Perfectly safe.

I walked over to my nightstand and opened the top drawer.

The leather box looked up at me and I lifted the lid off. The next day, I planned to offer Abigail my collar.

That would be another rule broken—I never collared a submissive before taking her. Never. What exactly was I doing by offering my collar to Abigail without having her first?

I couldn't answer that question. I only knew I was.

I held the choker in the palm of my hand and tried to imagine how it would look on her. How her long, delicate neck would look with my collar around it. She would wear it all week, and even though the world would see it as just a pretty necklace, she and I would know the truth—she was mine. I could treat her as I wanted. I could pleasure her as I wanted. She would pleasure me as I wanted.

I set the collar back in its box and closed the drawer. To collar a submissive . . .

It had been more than a year since I had collared anyone. My relationship with Beth had ended right before I decided to date Melanie. Beth had wanted more and I hadn't. In the end, we'd decided to part ways. Not long after she left, Melanie called and I thought, what the hell? Give a normal relationship a try.

As if anything with Melanie could be called normal. But by some odd twist of fate, Melanie decided she wanted to be dominated. Or at least she thought she did.

"Tie me up, Nathaniel."

"Spank me, Nathaniel."

Our relationship was doomed from that first phone call. Melanie was as much a submissive as I was.

Collaring someone was significant to me. I was always monogamous once I collared a submissive. Monogamous for however long the relationship lasted. I never shared my collared subs with other doms, and my subs never had to worry about me playing with anyone else.

I sighed and sat on the bed, picked up the leather-bound vol-

ume of *The Tenant of Wildfell Hall* by Anne Brontë and flipped
through it. My eyes fell on a random passage:

> My painting materials were laid together on the corner table,
> ready for to-morrow's use, and only covered with a cloth. He
> soon spied them out, and putting down the candle, deliberately
> proceeded to cast them into the fire: palette, paints, bladders,
> pencils, brushes, varnish: I saw them all consumed: the palette-
> knives snapped in two, the oil and turpentine sent hissing and
> roaring up the chimney. He then rang the bell.

How Helen must have felt when Arthur burned her painting
supplies. Much as I would feel if Abigail were to leave.

Turpentine.

Turpentine in a fire.

I saw them all consumed.

As absurd as it was, it was the perfect safe word.

I was wide-awake at five thirty the next morning and, after a
quick shower, I went down to the kitchen to make breakfast. Abigail had an important decision to make, and I would do what I
could to make that decision easier.

At six thirty I heard her walking around upstairs. No doubt
she wondered what I was up to.

Oh, Abigail, if you only knew what I have planned . . .

I probably should have told her the night before that I'd cook
breakfast this morning, but I had been thinking of other things
and breakfast had not been one of them.

I set two places at the kitchen table, because I wanted Abigail
to speak freely. I was certain she had questions. Questions about
the kissing, why I hadn't had sex with her, what my thoughts and
expectations were.

At seven o'clock she rushed into the kitchen to find me sitting at the table.

Today's the day, Abigail. Today you become mine.

"Good morning, Abigail." I waved at the seat across from me. "Did you sleep well?"

Her eyes were dark-rimmed. She hadn't slept well at all, but she looked me squarely in the eyes—she'd obeyed my last command.

"No. Not really."

"Go ahead and eat."

She looked over the spread on the table and then looked at me with a raised eyebrow. "Do you sleep?"

"On occasion."

I watched her eat, enjoying the play of her jaw and the look of delight when she bit into a muffin.

Talk to me, I wanted to say. Ask me questions.

But if I asked her to talk, would she think me pushy? Would she be talking only because I was a dominant and I asked her to talk?

Who knew? I'd have to try a different tactic.

"I've had a nice weekend, Abigail. I'd like to proceed with our relationship."

She choked. "You would?"

Why did she find my words surprising? How could she not know how much she pleased me?

"I'm very pleased with you. You have an interesting demeanor and a willingness to learn."

"Thank you, sir."

I slipped back to yesterday, the way she looked spread out on my bed. Naked, flushed, and panting.

Once she wore my collar—

Stop it!

You have to ask first.

"You have an important decision to make today," I said. "We

can discuss the details after breakfast and your shower. I'm sure you have a few questions for me."

"Can I ask you something, sir?"

Had I not just told her to ask me questions?

"Of course," I reassured her again. "This is your table."

"How did you know I didn't take a shower yesterday morning or this morning? Do you live here during the week, or do you have a place in the city? How did——"

"One question at a time, Abigail," I said and almost laughed. She *could* talk. "I am an extraordinarily observant man. Your hair didn't look like it'd been washed yesterday. I guessed you didn't take a shower this morning because you rushed in here like you had a demon chasing you. I live here on weekends and have a place in the city."

"You didn't ask if I followed your instructions last night."

Right. I probably should have, even though I knew she had.

"Did you?"

"Yes."

I took a sip of coffee. "I believe you."

"Why?"

"Because you can't lie—your face is an open book." She had to know that, though. "Never play poker. You'll lose."

"Can I ask another question?"

As many as you want. "I'm still at the table."

"Tell me about your family," she said.

Really? I wanted to ask. *Of all the things you could ask, you're asking about my family?* But that was what she wanted, so I talked a bit about my parents, their deaths, and my aunt Linda. Abigail mentioned her friend might be interested in Jackson and it caught me off guard. I'd assumed she'd read all the paperwork and had understood that she wasn't to discuss our arrangement with anyone, even her family or closest friends.

"How much did you tell your friend about me? I believe the

papers from Godwin were very clear concerning my stance on confidentiality," I said in as even a tone as I could manage.

"It's not that." Her words rushed out. "Felicia's my safety call; I had to tell her. But she understands. She won't tell anyone anything. Trust me. I've known her since grade school."

"Your safety call?" That explained how her friend knew. "Is she in the lifestyle?"

"Quite the opposite, actually, but she knows I wanted this weekend, so she agreed to do it for me."

I thought about the type of friend Felicia must be to support Abigail even though she didn't agree with her decision. "Jackson doesn't know about my lifestyle and, yes, he's single. I have a tendency to be a bit overprotective—he's had to deal with his share of gold-diggers."

By the time she'd finished telling me about Felicia, I'd decided I would pass her name and number on to Jackson. He'd asked if I knew of anyone, and Abigail's friend sounded like she might be a good fit for him.

I didn't want to discuss Jackson or Felicia, though. I wanted the conversation to return to us. "Getting back to what I said earlier. I want you to wear my collar, Abigail. Please consider it while you shower. Meet me in my room in an hour and we'll discuss it further."

After she left the kitchen, I cleaned the dishes and went to my bedroom to prepare. When I heard Abigail in the shower, I laid out a bathrobe with a matching bra and panty set on her bed.

She walked into the bedroom right on time. The silver color brought out the pale beauty of her skin, making her look luminous. Her dark hair fell softly around her shoulders and her eyes glanced around the room.

She was nervous again.

"Have a seat," I told her, and she sat down on the cushioned bench like a regal princess.

I took the collar from the box and faced her. "If you choose to wear this, you'll be marked as mine." I held the collar out, wanting her to see. "Mine to do with as I wish. You will obey me and never question what I tell you to do. Your weekends are mine to fill as I wish. Your body is mine to use as I wish. I will never be cruel or cause permanent harm, but I am not an easy master, Abigail. I will have you do things you never thought possible, but I can also bring you a pleasure you never imagined."

I want you, I was saying. And I want to be yours.

"Do you understand?" I asked.

"I understand, sir."

Even though I knew she didn't, not completely, excitement started to pound through my veins. One more question to go . . .

"Will you wear this?"

She nodded again.

Fuck, yes. She wanted it.

I moved behind her, not wanting her to see how excited her answer made me. She was mine. She had agreed to be my submissive. I fastened the collar around her neck and brushed her hair out of the way.

Damn, she looked good in my collar.

My collar.

I wanted to turn her around and crush my lips to hers, to tell her how much she pleased me, but again, I didn't trust myself to meet her eyes—and I had made that kissing rule.

"You look like a queen," I said, and pushed the robe from her shoulders.

Damn, she felt good. Her skin was silky smooth, still a bit damp from her shower.

"And now you're mine." Wanting to prove my words, I slipped my hands into her bra and palmed her breasts, rejoicing in the way her nipples hardened. "These are mine."

My hands continued their course southward, sliding along her sides. "Mine," I said, because her entire body was mine. Pure lust shot through me, and I leaned in to kiss her neck and delight in her taste.

I bit her. She moaned and trembled under my touch. "Mine," I said. *Never forget it.*

My fingers reached their destination, and I pushed aside the flimsy satin material of her panties. "And this?" I slid a finger into her. "All mine."

Hell, yes, this was mine.

She was tight and wet and felt even better around my finger than I'd hoped. My cock hardened, and I slipped another finger inside her. Tight and hot. I moved my fingers deeper—as deep as I could. She moaned and threw her head back.

Yes, Abigail. Feel what I can do to you.

I kept stroking until I felt her start to tighten around me; then I pulled out. "Even your orgasms are mine." She might as well understand that sooner rather than later.

She moaned in frustration.

"Soon," I whispered. "Very soon. I promise."

She reached up and touched the choker.

"It looks very nice on you." I turned and took a pillow from the bed. Would she call me out on this next part, or would she accept it? "Your safe word is *turpentine*. Say it and this ends immediately. You take the collar off, drive away, and never return. Otherwise, you will come here every Friday. Sometimes you will arrive at six and we'll have dinner in the kitchen. Other times, you'll come at eight and head straight to my room. My orders for sleep, food, and exercise remain. Do you understand?"

I held my breath.

She nodded.

"Good. I'm often invited to society functions. You will attend these with me. I have one such function next Saturday night—a benefit for one of my aunt's nonprofits. If you do not have a ball gown, I will provide you with one. Is all this clear? Ask me if you have any questions." Or tell me how crazy I was with that safe word.

She bit her lip. "I have no questions."

Mmmm. Her lip. I leaned close. "I have no questions . . ."

Say it. Let me hear you say it.

I need you to say it.

But she didn't know what I was talking about.

"Say it, Abigail," I whispered to her. "You've earned it."

She leaned forward in understanding. "I have no questions, Master."

Master. I could have groaned with the pleasure of hearing that word fall from her mouth.

"Yes. Very nice." My cock was unbearably hard and pressed uncomfortably against my pants. I unbuttoned them. "Now come and show me how happy you are to wear my collar."

She slipped from the bench and knelt before me on the pillow. Her tongue darted out and ran around the outside of her lips.

Damn, she wanted this as much as I did.

With a sound that was a cross between a sigh and a moan, she leaned forward to take me in her mouth. I placed my hands on her head to steady myself as she took me deeper.

"All of me, Abigail. Take all of me." And I knew it wouldn't be difficult for her to take more than just my cock in her mouth. She alone had the power to take both my body and my soul.

But I couldn't think about that. All I could focus on was the feel of her mouth as she engulfed me. I reached the back of her throat and started to move in and out.

"Do you like that?" I asked. "Do you like me fucking your hot little mouth?"

She gave a muffled groan from low in her throat that caused vibrations to spread throughout my body. I held her hair tighter.

She sucked me harder, and I looked down to watch my cock

slide in and out of her mouth. Her eyes were cast down, and I shivered at the sight of her taking the whole of me. She moved her lips to let her teeth slide along my length.

She remembered.

"Damn, Abigail."

I tried to hold on to the feeling growing deep in my balls, closed my eyes to block the sight of her mouth on me. But the image was burned into my memory and it was useless to deny what she did to me.

"I'm coming," I said as my cock jerked inside her mouth. "I can't—"

I thrust inside one more time and held still deep within her as I released into her mouth. She swallowed, moving her throat around my head, and I hissed through my teeth in pleasure.

When she finished, I withdrew and pulled my pants on. "You may go put your clothes back on."

She stood up, her face flushed with excitement.

I know, I wanted to say. I feel the same way.

She left that afternoon after I instructed her to return on Friday evening at six o'clock. I did my best to contain my excitement when I spoke to her about the next weekend. After all, she wouldn't know what I had planned. Only I knew how long the week would stretch as I waited impatiently to finally claim her body.

I asked her if she had any questions before she left, and she mentioned that if it wouldn't be too much of a bother, would I mind providing a gown for next weekend. My childhood friend Todd Welling's wife, Elaina, was a fashion designer, and I knew she would have something perfect.

"Of course. I'll have something here for you to wear on Saturday. I have your measurements from your application."

"Thank you, Master."

"Think nothing of it—and if you have any concerns or questions for me this week, feel free to call my cell phone."

I really hoped she would call, but I knew she probably wouldn't. Call me, Abigail. I want you to.

Chapter Six

"Elaina," I said when I called on Monday. "My date needs a gown for the benefit on Saturday—can you bring something?"

"You have a date?" she asked. "Really?"

I glared at my cell phone and then gave up. It's not like she could see me. "I've decided not to take that as an insult," I said.

"I just didn't know you were dating anyone since you and Melanie broke up. Besides, you normally show up to these things alone."

She was right. I couldn't argue with her on that one. But I normally didn't have Abigail as my collared submissive. I didn't typically take submissives with me to family functions, even when they were wearing my collar. Paige and Beth were the only two I had ever introduced to my family.

"Well, get your jaw up off the floor and find a gown," I said, "because I have a date."

"About time."

I almost hung up. It just wasn't worth it. But Abigail had asked for a gown, and a gown she would have, even if I had to withstand a few not so funny comments. I knew Elaina meant well. She just liked to tease.

"The gown," I reminded her.

"Right. Right," she said, and I heard papers shuffling in the background. "What does she want?"

She wants whatever I provide, I wanted to say. I didn't, though—
Elaina was clueless as to my life's finer details. "Something sexy,
but not too revealing. Sophisticated sexy."

"Oh, Nathaniel, say it again."

"Say what?"

"Sexy. I want to hear you say *sexy.*"

"Shut up. Do you have something or not?"

"What size?"

"Four."

"Hold on."

I heard more rustling. She was moving around her office now,
probably sifting through material or dresses or whatever.

"I have just the thing," she said finally. "In black."

"Silver." I thought back to the satin bathrobe. "Silver looks
good with her skin tone."

"Did she request silver, or did my CEO workaholic friend actually notice the way a color looks with a woman's skin tone?"

I tapped my pen against my desk. "Okay, you found me out.
I'm a CEO workaholic who finally discovered what color could
do to a woman's skin tone." I sighed. "Do you have it in silver or
not?"

"Sorry. Only black. But I promise if I weren't on deadline, I'd
do a gown in silver for your date with the beautiful skin tone."

"Thanks, Elaina." I wondered how quickly this tidbit would
make it back to everyone. I was sure Elaina would call Todd as
soon as we hung up.

"Does she need shoes and a bag to match?" Elaina asked.

"That would be lovely. Size seven shoe."

More rustling. "Size seven black heels coming up."

"Thanks, Elaina."

"When do I get to meet her?" she asked.

"Saturday night, along with everyone else."

We talked more about the upcoming weekend and Todd's

practice. When we hung up, I tried to concentrate on the report in front of me and quickly gave up. I wasn't going to get anything done—I might as well accept it.

I dialed my cousin.

"Jackson," I said when he picked up the phone. "Let's do lunch."

"Today?"

"Yes." I looked at the clock—it was only eleven. "Can you meet me at Delphina's in an hour?"

"Sure. I'll be there."

I picked Delphina's because it was a favorite of mine and it wasn't a sports bar. As much as I loved Jackson, sometimes it was nice to eat at a place that didn't have games blaring from ten different televisions.

"Hey," he said, sliding into the booth an hour later. "What's happening?"

"The usual. The economy's headed south. My employees are worried. I have a date for the benefit."

"You having a date for the benefit isn't the usual." He picked up the menu and glanced at it. "They only got sissy food in this place?"

"Some of us like sissy food," I said. "The occasional salad won't kill you."

"Hell, yes, it will." He turned the menu over. "Ah, yes, they do have red meat."

The waiter walked over to take our orders, but before we could resume our conversation, my phone buzzed.

I turned the ringer off and sighed. That particular business associate could wait. I wasn't in the mood to deal with Wall Street at the moment.

"I don't mind if you need to take that," Jackson said at my frown.

"I'm not going to ruin lunch by discussing the downward movement of the stock market."

"Economy really sucks, huh?"

"Not everyone makes millions of dollars a year, you know."

"Don't make me feel bad," he warned. "You make just as much as I do. Probably more."

"Not this year."

"What?"

"I'm not pulling a salary this year." I shrugged. "It's not like I need to get paid, after all. And my annual salary will go toward ensuring my employees are taken care of."

He looked at me with disbelieving eyes. "Hell, you're serious."

"Yes, I am."

"Do your employees know what you're doing?"

The waiter returned with our drinks and I took a sip of water.

"No," I said. "Although I'm sure they'll see it when the annual report comes out later."

"Is the company in danger?"

"No," I said. "Not in any way. We're actually doing better than most. I'm just being cautious."

"Mr. Prepared, that's you." He laughed and then looked up at me. "So, Felicia?"

"Yes?"

A grin broke across his face. "I know it's early, but thanks. She sounds like a dream on the phone."

"You called her?" I asked.

"Last night. I asked her to go with me this weekend."

"Abigail said she was a redhead and a kindergarten teacher."

"What else could you want in a woman?"

"I'm glad I could help out."

He leaned back in the booth. "Tell me about your Abby."

Your Abby, he called her.

My Abby.

I cleared my throat. "She's a beautiful, intelligent woman who cooks a mean steak."

"She's already cooked for you?" Jackson watched me with a curious look in his eye. "Serious?"

And sucked me off twice. Serious.

My cock twitched just thinking about it, and I shifted in my seat. "As serious as it can be after one weekend."

The waiter brought my grilled chicken salad and Jackson's hamburger. I put my napkin in my lap and looked up to Jackson. He was staring at me with an odd look in his eyes.

"Fuckin' A, man."

"Something wrong with your burger?" It looked good from where I sat, but you never knew.

"Dude," he said simply, like he knew something I should.

"What?"

He looked at me again, then shook his head. "Never mind."

I frowned and started eating. Jackson didn't normally get weird on me. Maybe he'd gotten hit in the head too many times at the game the day before.

On Thursday afternoon, I left the office earlier than normal and told Sara on my way out not to expect me on Friday. Her jaw dropped slightly, but she recovered quickly and simply nodded.

I spent part of Friday morning walking around my grounds with Apollo, trying to decide what I wanted planted come spring. It was too late to plant tulips, but my gardener had suggested lilies. I'd been hesitant, afraid the exotic-looking flower wouldn't match my more muted plants. On the walk, however, I grew energized thinking about the night to come. Muted was boring. My garden needed more of the exotic. Just like how collaring Abigail had brought the exotic into my life.

She hadn't called me and, as much as I wanted to check up on her, I held back. I didn't want to overwhelm her, and I wanted to give her time to reconsider.

I heard a car pull up the circular drive around two o'clock, and I walked to the front of the house. Todd and Elaina must have arrived. Apollo hung back behind me.

"Nathaniel," Elaina said, rushing forward to hug me. "How are you?"

"Good, Elaina," I said. "Thanks."

Todd held a garment bag and a box of shoes. "Nathaniel," he said, smiling.

"Hey, Todd." I took the bag and box. "I assume these are for me?"

"Sure, man," he said. "Silver's your color."

Fuck. Elaina told him.

"I've heard it does wonders for your skin tone," he said.

Elaina punched him on the arm. "Be nice."

"Come on in," I said, walking inside, ignoring the skin tone comment.

I hung the bag in the coat closet. I would take it up to Abigail's room later. We walked into the kitchen and sat down at the table. I tried to push from my mind that in a few hours, Abigail and I would be sitting here. And that shortly after that, we'd go upstairs—

"So," Elaina said, interrupting my thoughts. "What are you doing at home today?"

I got up and poured us all a glass of tea. "I'm taking the day off."

"You don't take days off," Todd said.

"Sure I do." I set their glasses down. "I took New Year's Day off. I took Christmas off." I wrinkled my forehead like I was in deep thought. "And I'm quite positive I took Thanksgiving off. Day after, too, now that I think about it."

I put the tea pitcher back in the refrigerator.

"You know what I mean," Todd said.

I shrugged my shoulders. "I just wanted to take a day off. Hang out with Apollo, you know?"

Todd and Elaina exchanged a look. Damn. It was the same look Jackson had given me earlier in the week. Was everyone in on something?

"What?" I asked.

"Nothing," Todd said. He winked at Elaina. "Round of golf still on for tomorrow?"

Before I'd collared Abigail, I'd agreed to play golf with Jackson and Todd this weekend. I couldn't very well get out of it. "Sure thing," I said. "Golf tomorrow."

Who could talk about tomorrow? Who could think past tonight?

How much longer until six o'clock? I looked at my watch. Too damn long.

"Everything okay?" Elaina asked. "You look distracted."

Damn right I'm distracted, I wanted to shout. Who the hell wouldn't be distracted?

Instead I sat down and took a sip of tea. I was calm. I could do calm. "Not at all," I said. "Whatever gave you that impression?"

I didn't think they believed me.

I opened the door when I heard the car service in the drive. Abigail's eyes darted to the front door as she got out of the car and she gave me a timid smile.

"Abigail," I said. "It's good to see you this evening."

"Thank you."

She was nervous. I could tell by the way her gaze flickered over everything. Yet the few times she looked my way, her eyes grew dark with yearning and desire. Perhaps her week had been just as long as mine. I could tell without asking that she had followed the command I gave her before she left last weekend—she was not to touch herself during the week.

I led her to the kitchen, and we sat down to eat the clam sauce

I'd made after Elaina and Todd left. Cooking had calmed me down.

"How was your week?" I asked after she started eating.

A smile tickled the corner of her mouth. "Long. How was yours?"

I couldn't tell her it had been the same for me. That I'd spent too much time planning the night, imagining it. To do so would give too much of me away. So I just shrugged, playing it cool. She needed me to be in control.

We continued eating. "Apollo killed a gopher," I said.

She looked slightly taken aback, and her cheeks bore the faintest of pink flushes. She wasn't expecting that, for me to make normal conversation. It made her even more needy, got her more worked up. Playing Abigail was going to be an absolute treat. I would savor every second.

Sex didn't start in bed. Sex started in the way you moved, the way you talked. It was whispered, conveyed with a subtle look.

"My friend Todd's wife, Elaina, brought a gown by earlier," I said, because we wouldn't have another chance to talk about the benefit after dinner. "They're looking forward to meeting you."

"Your friends? Does everyone know about us?" Her voice was anxious.

I took my time twirling a bite of pasta. *I'm in control of this, Abigail. Trust me.* I ate a forkful before answering. "They know you're my date. They don't know about our agreement."

I leaned back and watched her eat. She compulsively cut her pasta up and took several small bites. At one point she looked up, saw me watching, and went back to studying her pasta.

A few more seconds and I'd have her right where I wanted her.

She suddenly put down her fork. "So do you plan to touch me this weekend or not?" she blurted.

Yes.

"Ask me the question in a more respectful manner, Abigail.

Just because this is your table doesn't mean you can talk to me any way you choose."

Her gaze fell to the table. "Will you touch me this weekend, Master?"

"Look at me," I said, because I wanted to see her eyes.

Her expression was conflicted—she knew she'd misspoken—but I'd overlook it this one time. And since she'd asked . . .

"I plan to do more than touch you. I plan to fuck you. Hard and repeatedly."

Her lips parted and her eyes grew wide with excitement, dinner forgotten.

Yes . . .

I pushed back from the table. "Let's get started, shall we? I want you naked and on my bed in fifteen minutes."

Chapter Seven

It was time.

I took my time climbing the stairs, wanting to prolong the moment. I left Apollo outside the door and stepped into the candlelit room. Abigail waited for me on the bed. Naked, just as I'd asked.

I'd realized early in the week I wouldn't be able to take her the first time without covering her eyes. It would be too much—I would give something away. Nor did I want her to touch me. Again, it would be too intimate. I needed to take her bound first, to allow myself to grow accustomed to her body. There would be time later for her to touch me. To watch me.

Her eyes followed me as I approached the bed, and I knew I'd made the right decision. I walked to the edge of the bed and lifted a shackle. Her eyes grew wide and, for a second, it appeared as if she would turn and leave the room.

Something inside told her this was wrong, that she should not be allowing me to do this. But the bigger part of her knew what she wanted and she let that side of herself win.

"I wasn't going to do this tonight," I said as I bound her spread-eagle to the bed, "but I can see you still don't understand completely. You are mine, and you are to do and behave as I tell you. The next time you speak disrespectfully to me, I will spank you. Nod if you understand."

It seemed as good a reason as any to bind and blindfold her, and I really meant the part about spanking her. I'd let her slide too many times as it was.

She nodded in agreement, and a faint smile crossed her face.

"My last submissive could make me climax three times a night." I wanted Abigail to outdo her. "I want to try for four. And I want you totally at my mercy."

I drew a black scarf from my pocket, and again the internal battle raged behind her brown eyes.

Trust me.

I covered her eyes and stepped back.

She'd just allowed me, an almost perfect stranger, to tie her up and blindfold her. She was offering herself to me in the most intimate way there was. She trusted me.

I didn't deserve her trust.

My eyes swept over her naked form. I wanted to make it good for her, to give her what she wanted. What she'd been searching for.

I undid my zipper, and my erection sprang free. Damn, I was so hard, it hurt.

I climbed up on the bed and sat beside her. She was mine to touch now. We were both ready. Finally. I placed my hands on her shoulders, noting the way her heart beat. Rapid.

Exactly like mine.

I dragged my fingertips down her sides, running along the outer edges of her breasts, bringing my hands back together at her belly. So much better than last week. I had been limited then by her sitting down in the bathrobe, but now . . . now she was spread naked before me.

I let one finger skim her pussy—she was already wet. "How long has it been, Abigail?" How long since another man claimed what was now mine? "Answer me."

I brought my finger to my lips and tasted her.

So sweet. I wanted to bury my face between her legs and taste her completely, and I would have, but my cock had other plans.

"Three years."

Three years?

Shit. No wonder she felt so tight. I slipped a finger into her again and leaned in to whisper, "You're not ready yet. You need to be ready, or else I won't be able to ride you as hard as I want."

I took a deep breath and lowered myself to her, allowed myself to taste her neck. Her skin was smooth against my mouth. I parted my lips and nibbled down to her collarbone. The candle-light winked off the diamonds on her collar and I pushed it out of the way to swirl my tongue around the hollow of her throat. I went lower, watching the steady rise and fall of her chest, how her breasts pushed upward, nipples hard. I kissed my way to one breast, circling the nipple.

Oh, God. Her taste.

I sucked at her breast, drawing her into my mouth, enjoying the way she filled me.

Mm.

I licked her nipple, flicked my tongue over it. Her hips shifted on the bed and she moaned. I gave her a gentle tug with my teeth, moved to the other side and sucked at her other breast. I drew her deeper into my mouth, bit her harder.

She writhed against me. Desperate.

I gave her some of what she craved, dragging my fingers roughly across her body before plunging them into her. I smiled to myself when she lifted her hips again. She was ready. Finally.

I tore myself away from her breast and straddled her, moving up her body so my cock rested between her breasts, right where her heart pounded.

"Do you think you're ready, Abigail? Because I'm tired of wait-ing. Are you ready? Answer me!"

"Yes, Master. Please. Yes."

I pushed my cock to her lips, wanting her to feel it. "Kiss my cock. Kiss it before it fucks you."

Her lips came up and gently brushed me, but as I watched, her tongue came out and she licked me.

I nearly came all over her face.

Fuck.

She couldn't go off doing things like that, disobeying me. I lightly slapped her cheek. "I didn't tell you to do that."

I slid down her body to the apex of her legs. With one hand, I lifted her hips, and with the other, I placed myself at her entrance.

I took a deep breath.

Abigail held hers.

Ever so slowly, I pushed myself into her. She was tight and wet and hot and felt better than any woman should feel. I pushed farther, wanting to close my eyes to enjoy the sensation and simultaneously wanting to keep them open so I could watch as I finally claimed Abigail King.

Tight. She was so tight.

Fuck.

The angle was wrong. I couldn't fit inside all the way.

"Damn." I rocked back and forth, sliding in a bit deeper, but it wasn't enough. "Move with me."

She lifted her hips and, yes, that was it. I slipped in deeper.

I looked down—I was almost completely inside. I closed my eyes and thrust hard. A groan ripped from my throat as I entered her fully. I stayed still for a moment, enjoying the feel of her, trying to sear into memory the feel of her hot and wet around me. I looked down to our joined bodies and allowed my eyes to take in the sight of Abigail bound to my bed.

Better than any fantasy I'd ever had.

Except, I told myself, it was really happening. I pulled out and watched my cock slide back into her. She lifted her hips under me. Hungry. Needy.

And all at once, I was hungry and needy as well. "You think you're ready?" I pulled almost all the way out, steadied myself, and slammed into her, pulling out just as quickly.

I glanced down to make sure she was okay and she was. She pulled against the restraints.

That's my girl. My naughty, naughty girl.

I let loose then, thrusting into her, letting my body lead. She answered in kind, lifting her hips and meeting me. Drops of sweat beaded on my forehead, and I knew I wouldn't last much longer.

Under me, Abigail's lips were parted. She was close. I thrust harder, picked up my pace, wanting to bring her to the edge with me. She started making a little panting noise.

"Come when you want," I said, and her muscles constricted around me as she climaxed.

I pushed inside her and held still, back arched against the pleasure of releasing into her. But I knew I could give her more, so I thrust again and again and was rewarded with the feel of her second climax.

I dipped my head and struggled to catch my breath.

When I could breathe, I lowered myself to her and whispered in her ear, "One."

Her body was flushed with the pleasure I'd given her and a smile danced on her lips. She shifted her body, and I checked to make sure her restraints were okay. That she wasn't too uncomfortable. She looked fine.

And by fine, I meant totally fuckable fine.

I rolled off the bed and went to the dresser. From the top, I took the hand salve and walked to the foot of the bed. I unshackled her right leg, took it gently in my hands and rubbed salve where the restraints had been. I took my time, making sure she wasn't injured and ensuring nothing was sore. I repeated the action on her left.

"Do you know why I'm releasing your legs?"

She shook her head.

I put the salve back, making sure she could hear as I walked to stand by her head. "Because when you wrap those legs around my waist, my cock will go so deep inside you, you'll fucking feel me in your throat."

She mumbled something, but her face flushed and her heart pounded.

"Stretch your legs," I said and stood by her side, giving her time to work out any soreness.

After I climbed back on the bed, I ran my hands up to her shoulders, rubbing them, making sure the restraints weren't hurting or pulling too tightly. I glanced down at her face and watched as her lips parted. I brought my mouth down to the crook of her neck and kissed her gently, tasting the faint salty sweat that glistened on her body. Closing my eyes to better concentrate, I nipped the tender skin right at the edge of her underarm.

She sucked in a breath.

"Does it feel good, Abigail?"

She whimpered.

"Want me to make it feel better?"

"Yes, Master," she said so low I could barely hear.

I took one nipple between my fingers and rolled it, pleased with the way it reacted to my touch. "Does this feel good?"

"Yes, Master," she said again, arching her back.

"Tell me if this feels good," I said, biting her tender skin gently.

She gasped, and I bit even harder, sucking as I did so, licking the very tip of her nipple.

"Ah, ah, yes," she stuttered.

I slid a hand down her side and eased a finger into her. She lifted her hips up, trying to take me deeper.

"Ready to see how deep I can go?" I asked.

"If it . . . pleases you."

"Oh, Abigail," I said, straddling her body. "You are pleasing me." I thrust my hips so my erection pressed against her belly. Even I was surprised at how quickly I'd recovered from our first time. "Feel just how much you please me."

She whimpered again and lifted her hips.

I took a hand and brought my cock to her wet slit, easing inside. "Your legs. I want them wrapped around me. Take me all the way inside you."

She obeyed, and I pushed myself into her tight warmth. I worried briefly that it might be too soon after our first time, but her head fell back and she let out a moan. I pushed farther inside and heard myself moan.

I pulled out and started a steady rhythm, not as urgent as the first time, but still steady. I wanted to go slower, deeper. Wanted her to feel just how deeply we were connected. She lifted her hips and tightened her legs as I thrust.

Fuck.

I increased my pace. Damn, what she did to me. I felt my control slip as her heels hit my ass in time with every thrust. I started going faster.

She groaned, and I stopped long enough to check her expression. Complete pleasure. I went even faster, and when she started circling her hips, I almost lost it.

"Come for me, Abigail."

I thrust as deep as I could and felt her muscles tighten around me.

"That's it," I said, thrusting again. "Now."

She released around me and I followed seconds later. I dropped to her side, making sure I didn't put my entire weight on her.

I rested for a few minutes, enjoying the feel of her at my side, before I got up. I took the thick comforter and cotton sheets from my dresser's bottom drawer and placed them on the floor beside my bed, then put one of my pillows on top. It was as comfortable a pallet as I could make.

"You'll sleep in my room tonight, Abigail," I said, unbinding her arms and removing her scarf. She watched my every move. "I'll take you again at some point during the night, and I don't want to be troubled with walking down the hall. I made you a pallet."

She cocked an eyebrow at me. Eventually, I'd have to put a stop to that.

"Do you have a problem with my order?"

She shook her head, and I was thankful she didn't choose to challenge me.

Still . . .

She slipped off the bed, carefully testing her legs as she stood, swaying slightly before she curled up on the comforter and slid between the sheets. I remained on the bed until I heard the heavy, steady breathing that told me she had fallen asleep. Then I climbed down and blew out all but one candle.

It was almost midnight and she needed to sleep for a few hours. Not everyone could function on the small amount of sleep I lived on. I crawled into my bed and put my arms behind my head, staring up at the ceiling. Only then did I allow myself to think about the fact that Abigail King was sleeping in my bedroom. That I had just taken her.

Twice.

I leaned over to watch her. Her lips were parted and her hair was splayed across her pillow in wild disarray. She was the most beautiful woman I'd ever seen.

She started moaning in her sleep.

At first, it was faint, almost a whisper of a sound, but it gradually grew louder. Then she started moving and the sheet slipped from her shoulders, baring her breasts.

I rolled over onto my back and closed my eyes.

You will not wake her up yet.

You will not wake her up yet.

You will not wake her up yet.

I tried running through the day's stock quotes in my head. Just until two o'clock. You can wake her up at two o'clock.

I sighed. It would be a long two hours.

"Wake up, Abigail."

It was two fifteen. I had waited more than two hours while she slept. Two hours of listening to her soft "fuck me" moans, two hours of lying in bed in the near dark, her barely clad body on the floor beside me.

I was harder than I had any right to be, after releasing inside her twice.

"Hands and knees on the bed. Quickly."

She blinked a few times, but crawled on top of the bed, not even making eye contact.

I got even harder at the sight of her on all fours, waiting for me.

"Lean on your elbows."

She dropped immediately to her elbows so her ass and sweet pussy faced me.

This would not be soft. This would not be gentle.

I ran my hands down her back and pushed her legs apart. "You were tight the other way, but you'll be even tighter like this."

My hands made their way back up her body, cupping her breasts. I palmed and played with them. She was already wet when I dipped a finger in her.

Sweet dreams, Abigail?

I gathered some of her wetness and trailed my finger up to her ass. "Has anyone ever taken you here before?"

No. No, they had not. I knew as much from her checklist, but I still wanted her to tell me.

She shook her head.

"I will."

She tensed beneath my hands and that surprised me. Anal sex was not one of her hard limits. I ran over her checklist in my mind. No, it wasn't a hard limit.

"Soon," I said, dropping my finger and watching her relief as she exhaled shakily.

She was scared. That was fine. I could work with scared. I would be gentle and patient as I pushed through this fear. She would end up loving it.

But for tonight—

I guided my cock to her wet pussy and wrapped her hair around my wrists. The hair that had been splayed across my pillow for the last two hours. The hair I'd been wanting to reach for and run my fingers through. It was softer than I remembered. With a pull of her hair, I pushed myself inside her for the third time.

Would I ever get tired of the way I felt sliding into her?

Damn, I hoped not.

She moaned.

Did it feel as good for her?

Damn, I hoped so.

I pulled back and thrust into her. Fuck, she was tight. My head fell back as I moved. Tight and hot and wet. When she started pushing herself back toward me, I groaned. I feared I was being too rough on her, but the sounds she made told me differently. I kept going, pushing harder.

She thrust back into me with a grunt.

Oh, yes.

I slammed into her once more, holding still as she yelled with her release. Her clenching muscles triggered my own climax and I gasped with its force.

She collapsed onto the bed once I withdrew from her. I watched her for several long moments and wondered if I'd planned too much for this evening. But she'd climaxed every time, I reminded myself. Enjoyed them all.

I thought back to how she'd looked just moments before—her hair in my hands, my cock buried deep inside her. Those last few seconds when she'd actually screamed with her pleasure.

Fuck, I was getting hard again.

But I knew I couldn't take her again. She would be sore enough as it was.

Change of plans, then . . .

I rolled her onto her back, and her eyes flew open.

Had she been asleep?

I wasn't sure, but she was wide-awake now. I pushed my hips toward her face. "Round four, Abigail."

She looked around the room. What was she doing?

"Look at me." I took her head in my hands and turned it back to me. "I'm your concern right now. Me and what I tell you. And right now I want you to serve me with your mouth."

She opened her mouth obediently—willingly—and I dropped to my knees, straddling her, while I leaned my head against the headboard.

She dropped her head back, taking me deep into her mouth. Her hands came up to my balls and stroked me as I thrust in and out.

Damn.

Her hands, fuck, her hands were magic. Stroking and teasing while her mouth worked its own kind of magic. I let out a groan as I thrust in time with her sucking, her lips creating the sweetest friction possible on my cock.

All too soon, I felt my release building.

"I'm going to come," I warned as I pushed into her one last time. I rammed myself deep to the back of her throat and held still as I released in several long streams.

Damn, that shouldn't even have been possible. Not after coming three times already. I fell beside her in a breathless heap. She turned to me, and I moved closer. "I think you just broke my record," I said.

She smiled and waited.

"You may go back to the floor." I felt a little bad, but while I wanted her in my room, I wasn't quite ready to have her share my bed. It would be too much, too soon. I needed to keep some sort of control.

She rolled off the bed and curled up on her pallet.

I crawled under my covers and fell into a deep sleep almost immediately.

Chapter Eight

I slept in the next morning, not waking until seven o'clock. I got out of bed and stretched, feeling great. The night before had granted me some of the most restful sleep I'd ever had.

I'm sure the four climaxes had something to do with it.

Abigail slept soundly, curled up in a ball on her side. She hadn't moaned any more that I'd heard. As I watched, she smiled in her sleep. I wondered what she was dreaming of, what caused her to smile so. Maybe she wouldn't even remember when she woke.

Sometime in the night, the sheet had slipped off her shoulders, and her perfect breasts were exposed once more. I reached down and tucked the sheet under her chin—I didn't want her to get cold. She mumbled something and rolled over.

Though I needed to shower and get ready for the golf game, I decided to make a fresh batch of blueberry muffins first. Abigail had liked them last week.

It was almost nine by the time I heard her upstairs. I didn't begrudge her the extra sleep—I'd kept her up late and woken her in the middle of the night. The charity benefit this evening would mean another long night, so she needed her rest.

I boiled two eggs while she showered and, once they were done, I put them in the warming oven for her.

Jackson sent me a text right as I heard Abigail's footsteps on the stairs. I glanced down at my phone—he was stressing over meeting

Felicia. Frankly, I thought it funny that my world-famous-athlete cousin was stressed out over meeting a girl, but I knew it was hard on Jackson. He always worried whether women were genuinely interested in him or just his bank account and celebrity status.

I replied, telling him I was certain she was just as nervous as he was. That we'd all be with him tonight, and honestly, she was Abigail's best friend—how bad could she be?

How's the librarian fantasy girl? he texted.

I will kick the shit out of you if you mention that to her, I warned, right as Abigail shuffled into the kitchen.

She looked tired, and part of me cringed. After all, I'd been the cause of her lack of sleep, the reason she walked so carefully. But I was still feeling the high of incredible sex.

"Rough night?" I asked, keeping my eyes focused on my phone.

"You could say that again."

I smiled. I couldn't help it. She was tired, sore, cranky, and she still had her sense of humor.

"Rough night?" I asked again.

She took a muffin from the counter and sat down across from me.

Good thinking on the blueberry, West—but she needed more than a muffin.

"You need protein," I said.

"I'm fine," she said, before I could tell her I had eggs waiting for her.

"Abigail," I warned. Damn, I didn't want to punish her. Not after the previous night.

She stood up, moved gingerly to the refrigerator, and took out a pack of bacon. That pleased me. Even though she was in pain, she would still cook protein because I told her to.

"I put two boiled eggs in the warming oven for you," I said. Relief covered her face as she put the bacon away. "The ibuprofen is on the first shelf, second cabinet beside the microwave."

"I'm sorry." She took the bottle from the shelf and shook two pills into her hand. "It's just . . . been a long time."

"What a ridiculous thing to apologize for. I'm more upset over your attitude this morning. I didn't have to let you sleep in."

She sat, head down, with her hair hanging over her eyes.

"Look at me," I said. "I have to leave. Meet me in the foyer dressed for the benefit and ready to leave at four thirty."

She nodded, and I wondered what she would look like in the dress Elaina had dropped off. I wished, not for the first time, that I hadn't agreed to golf and lunch with my family. Wished that I could spend the day with Abigail.

Wished I could be normal.

But what was the point in normal? She didn't want it and I couldn't do it.

I sighed. "There's a large tub in the guest room across the hall from yours. Make use of it." Maybe a long soak would make her feel better.

As suspected, lunch was long and golf was longer. I usually enjoyed time with my family and Todd, but knowing Abigail was at home, alone, made the day drag.

Yes, I told Todd, my date was a librarian.

No, I told Jackson for the fifth time. I didn't have a strange librarian fantasy going on.

I made it back home at three thirty and went straight to my bedroom, noting as I went that Abigail's door was closed. By four fifteen I was in the foyer waiting. I turned when I heard her heels on the stairs and almost dropped the wrapper I held.

The dress hugged her curves in all the right places, and the low neckline showed her delicate collarbones. Her hair had been gathered up in a simple knot at the back of her head with a few strands hanging low and brushing her neck.

"You look beautiful." Stunning, actually.

"Thank you, Master."

I held the wrapper out. "Shall we?"

She walked over to me and stopped at my side. I dropped the wrapper around her shoulders, taking time to brush her soft skin with my fingertips, breathing in her soft floral scent. If only we could stay home . . .

But no. She was probably still sore. I had to remember that. I must remember that.

As we walked to the waiting car, it struck me that we could be any normal couple on a normal date on a normal night. For this evening, I decided, that's what we'd be. Normal.

Driving along in silence, Abigail by my side in the passenger seat, I thought back to the two other collared subs I'd introduced to my family. Beth and Paige had both met my aunt Linda, and Jackson, Todd, and Elaina too, but I'd introduced them as girlfriends—nothing more—and if anyone suspected there was anything different about my relationship with them, they kept it to themselves.

Before they met my family, I'd given them a long list of expectations—how they were to talk to my family, what was acceptable behavior, what was not. I didn't give any such instruction to Abigail.

I wanted Abigail to be herself. To watch as she met the people I cared about. I wanted to see her talking and joking with her best friend.

I wanted a piece of normal.

I turned the radio on. One of my favorite piano concertos played, a piece I'd been working at mastering on my own piano. I wondered what type of music Abigail listened to. I knew very little about her outside of what she'd put in her application. "What kind of music do you like?"

"This is fine."

I wanted to ask her more questions—what she was like as a child, how she had learned to cook, what her favorite color was. Details that didn't mean anything, but when taken as a whole, created the woman that was Abigail.

If I asked questions, would she answer honestly or would she answer the way she thought I wanted her to?

This is why you don't do normal, I told myself. It's too confusing. Too many gray areas.

I didn't like gray—life was better in black-and-white.

After we arrived and dropped off my coat and Abigail's wrapper, I saw Elaina making her way toward us.

"Nathaniel! Abby! You're here!" Elaina said, dragging Todd behind her.

"Good evening, Elaina," I said, surprised at the way she hugged Abigail. I raised an eyebrow. Had they met recently, or were they past acquaintances? "I see you two have met already?"

"Oh, lighten up," she said and knocked me in the chest. "I had a cup of tea with Abby when I stopped by your house earlier today—so yes, Nathaniel, we've already met."

Abigail hadn't mentioned her stopping by, but then again, we'd been apart for most of the day. Plus, she wasn't the most forthcoming with her thoughts. Instead of saying anything further, I stood back and watched her with my old friend. She chatted politely with Todd, smiling and seeming at ease with everyone. While Todd had heard me talk about Abigail in the past, he had no idea she was the same woman he was meeting tonight.

Linda approached us, and I introduced her to Abigail, who insisted that my aunt call her Abby. I had to smile at that.

While Linda and Abigail chatted about books, I noticed Todd and Elaina giving each other strange looks, just as they had yesterday at my house.

But it was Linda, my dear sweet aunt who loved me like her own son, whose expression confused me the most. It was a look of the sweetest relief and joy, and I couldn't make sense of it. I mean, they were talking about books, of all things.

I took a step closer to Abigail. Nope, just books. I still didn't understand the look.

Wine. The night needed wine.

"I'll get us some wine," I said to Abigail. "Red or white?"

Her body tensed, and I looked at her in surprise. It was such a minor question.

Then it hit me. *You're not normal. You're her dom. She probably thinks she's supposed to answer in a certain way.*

Damn it.

"I don't have a hidden agenda," I whispered to reassure her. "I simply want to know."

"Red."

There, I thought, was that so hard?

Yes, damn it, it was. The question of red or white wine should not be the cause of angst. It should be a simple getting-to-know-you question.

But what about us was simple? I asked myself.

Not a damn thing.

As I walked off to get the drinks, Kyle ran up to me. I'd been on the Bone Marrow Registry since college, and a few years prior, I'd received a call telling me I was a match for an eight-year-old boy who needed a transplant. It had been a difficult procedure, but a year ago, I met Kyle—the recipient of my bone marrow—and knew the trouble had been worth it. He was now alive and well. It was all very, very humbling.

"Nate," he said, throwing his arms around me.

"Kyle," I said with a laugh. "How are you?"

"Great, man. Just great." He pulled at the neck of his suit. "Even though I have to wear this getup."

"You look very handsome. If only the girls in your class could see you now."

He chuckled and looked down at his feet. I remembered all too well the difficulties of being a young teenager. I wouldn't want to go back to that time in my life for anything.

"If you see Jackson," I said, "make sure to bug him about the Super Bowl. I think I just might be able to score us some tickets if New York makes it."

He smiled and ran off to find Jackson. I retrieved two glasses of wine and made my way back to Abigail. She took the glass with a quiet "thank you" and took a small sip.

During dinner, I watched as she joined in the conversations around her—sometimes talking animatedly; other times just sitting back and listening. She shared a close relationship with Felicia—I could tell by the way they subtly teased each other.

The only time she appeared uncomfortable was when she stood to go to the bathroom and all the men at the table stood up along with her. It angered me that none of the men in her previous relationships had treated her like a lady.

Yeah, my conscience said sarcastically, because you definitely treated her like a lady last night.

I couldn't argue with that, but I was raised to treat a woman right in public. Fortunately, Elaina stood up and went to the restroom with her. I made a note to myself to thank Elaina later.

"Felicia," I said, turning to Abigail's best friend. "I understand you're a kindergarten teacher?"

"Yes." She barely looked at me.

"Is it trying to work with such young children?"

"Sometimes," she said in a frosty voice.

I wondered why Felicia was so cold. She appeared to genuinely like Jackson, and the two of them had spent much of the night in close conversation. Even when she talked with Linda or Elaina, she was friendly.

I didn't have long to think about it—Abigail and Elaina returned to the table moments later. A slight flush colored Abigail's face. I wondered what Elaina had said while they were gone. What could have possibly caused Abigail embarrassment?

I held her chair out while she sat down. It was hard not to touch her—her dress dipped low enough at the back to show glimpses of her soft, feminine shoulders, and I wanted nothing more than to stroke the delicate skin there.

Later. You can do it later.

We finished dinner, and after the plates had been cleared, the band started playing. I wasn't typically a dancer. I could count on one hand, with fingers left over, the number of times I'd asked a woman to dance. It just wasn't my thing.

But this night was different. Abigail was different. I felt different.

And I wanted to dance.

So when a slow song started, I pushed back from the table and faced Abigail. "Will you dance with me?"

I wasn't asking as a dom. I was asking as a date, and that was uncomfortable territory for me. What if she said no?

What if she said yes?

I heard Linda gasp across the table, and Elaina leaned over to whisper something to Todd.

Damn, crazy people.

But then Abigail took my hand and I didn't care what anyone said or did anymore.

"Yes," she said.

I slipped an arm around her once we reached the dance floor, pulled her close, and took her hand in mine. She trembled against me.

"Are you having a nice time?" I asked to calm her down.

"I am. Very nice."

"Everyone is quite taken with you." *And so am I.* I pulled her closer as the song continued. When we returned home, I'd show her just how much.

Later, I went with Todd and Jackson to get the coats while the women waited at the table. Todd punched me on the shoulder. "I like her," he said.

"Abigail?" I asked.

"Felicia was nice as well," he said. "But yes, I was talking about Abby."

"Thanks," I said, oddly pleased.

"Thanks, man," Jackson said, coming up to me. "Felicia's great."

"Really?" I asked.

He just smiled. "And your Abby is something else as well."

That she was.

Apollo ran up to us as I opened the front door. Abigail jumped back and I sighed. I needed to take him out before I could focus on Abigail.

"Keep the gown on and wait in my room," I said. "The way you did in my office."

Ten minutes later, I entered my bedroom to find Abigail standing with her head down. I got hard just looking at her.

I circled her slowly. Walking around her, noting the faint tremor of her body. I walked to her back and lightly traced the top of her gown, running my fingers over the very spot I'd wanted to touch earlier.

"You were spectacular tonight." I leaned in and smelled her hair. Mmm. Ever so slowly, I took the pins from her wavy curls, watching as they bounced down to brush her shoulders. "And my family will talk about nothing but you now."

She was still trembling. Was she scared?

"You pleased me tonight, Abigail," I said, my lips so close to her skin, I could almost taste her. "Now it's my turn to please you."

I took her zipper and slid it down, then pushed the dress from her shoulders. I let myself kiss her, tasting the skin of her back. It was sweet, with just a hint of salt. She was trembling still, but I knew they were tremors of anticipation now.

The gown dropped to the floor and I carried her to the bed. "Lie down."

She did as told, and I crawled to her and slipped off her shoes. I met her eyes before I bent down to kiss her ankle. She gasped.

As I trailed kisses up her leg, I remembered that no one had ever done this to her before. What the hell kind of men had she dated that never took the time to give proper attention to her pussy? How had they contained themselves?

I reached up to remove her panties.

She put a hand on my head. "Don't."

I gritted my teeth, but reminded myself that this was new and she was scared. "Don't tell me what to do, Abigail."

With one move, I slid the panties down her legs and settled my-self between her knees. She was already wet. Wet and swollen.

I stared at her, ready to show her just how much she'd pleased me. Show her how she'd be rewarded when she pleased me.

I started with a kiss on her clit and she nearly jumped off the bed. Steady. I blew gently across her clit and then placed soft kisses up and down her slit. I took it slow and easy, waiting for her to get used to me. Wanting to savor the experience. Wanting to bring her pleasure.

Gently, I took my fingers and spread her, opening her com-pletely for my tongue. With one long sweep, I licked her entire opening. She was delicious. Sweet as honey. I licked her again.

Mmmmm.

I pulled my lips from my teeth and nibbled on her gently. She was still sore—I needed to be gentle. Her legs started to close around my head and I pushed her knees farther apart. "Don't make me tie you up," I told her.

I continued with my mouth, lapping up her wetness, drinking every drop she had. I shifted my eyes upward and saw her clutching the comforter. Her legs shook as I nipped her swollen clit. She was enjoying herself—finally.

I doubled my efforts, slipping my tongue inside her while moving my hands up her body. I stroked her belly and made my way up to her breasts, brushing her nipples. She let out a startled gasp—her body taut.

Yes, my lovely. Come for me.

I sucked her clit into my mouth, grazing it gently with my teeth as I did so, licking right where I knew she wanted it most.

"Oh . . ." She arched her back, pushing herself toward me.

I ran my hands back down her torso and wrapped my arms around her thighs, holding her to me as her orgasm shuddered throughout her body.

She stayed motionless for several minutes, and I would have felt smug except I was hard as a rock. I sat up slowly and adjusted my pants.

"I think it's time for you to go to your room," I whispered.

"What about you? Shouldn't we . . ."

"I'm fine."

"But it's my place to serve you."

She wanted to please me. How did she not know that she had pleased me all evening long? That I wanted this moment to be about her? I wanted to show her our arrangement was more than her doing things for me—it was me taking care of her. She'd given me the responsibility of knowing what she needed, and tonight she needed unreciprocated pleasure.

"No," I said. "It's your place to do as I say, and I say it's time for you to go to your room."

She didn't argue again, but slid off the bed and made her way out, closing the door behind her as she went. I groaned. Apollo was still out in the hall.

I stripped off my tux and made my way to my bathroom, where I turned the water on as hot as I could stand. I stood for several long minutes just letting the water wash over me, replaying in my mind the sight of Abigail climaxing. I turned my face to the showerhead and remembered how it had felt the night before when she came with me deep inside her.

I took myself with both hands and closed my eyes.

She was bound in the playroom, bent over the padded table. We had been playing for hours and were both panting for release.

"Are you ready, Abigail?" I asked, brushing her backside with my cock.

"If it pleases you," she said, voice strained with need.

I moved away from her so she would feel the cold air rush between us. "It pleases me for you to tell me what you want."

"I want . . ."

"Tell me."

She pushed her butt toward me. "I want your cock."

I chuckled and leaned over her, pressing my chest to her back. "Of course you do. Tell me where you want it."

Still silence.

I slapped her thigh. "Tell me or I'll send you to your room with nothing."

"In my ass," she whispered.

"Louder." I slapped her thigh harder. "I didn't hear you."

"Please, Master." She spoke louder this time. "Please, fuck my ass."

"As you wish," I said, taking the lube and spreading it over my fingers. I lightly traced her opening before sliding first one and then two fingers deep inside her. She pushed back, wanting more. Wanting me.

"Patience." I stretched her gently. "You have to have patience."

When she was ready, I slowly slid the slick head of my cock into her, pushing against the resistance and entering her fully. She moaned.

"Do you like my cock up your ass?" I withdrew and entered her again. "You're so fucking tight this way." I pulled out. "You feel so fucking good."

She pushed back against me, bringing me deeper into her, and threw her head back.

"*Just like that, Abigail,*" I said, moving faster. "*So deep. Feels so good.*"
She panted in pleasure.

"*Fuck.*" I thrust harder. "*I'm coming. I'm going to fill up that pretty ass.*"

I released into my hand with a grunt.

After I dried off, I crept into the hallway, where Apollo was still sitting quietly. Abigail's door was closed. I walked down the stairs and to the library, Apollo by my side.

The library was one of my favorite rooms. It had been my parents' favorite place in the house and I'd left it untouched since their deaths. Something told me Abigail would like the library as well and I decided to show it to her next weekend.

But right then I needed to play the piano. I sat down at the bench and let my fingers run up and down the keys, playing scales. Once I'd finished, I closed my eyes and imagined Abigail as she looked earlier—soft and yielding in my arms as we danced. Back arched and head thrown back as I pleasured her. I imagined her and let my hands play out the melody that swirled around in my head.

Abigail's song.

Abby's song.

Chapter Nine

Before I headed down to the gym the next morning, I took a minute to bring the whipping bench out of the playroom and into my bedroom. I felt it necessary——thinking of Abigail as Abby last night had confirmed for me that I needed to set the relationship right. I had been too generous——ignoring her slipups, hesitations, and attitudes. I'd never done that before and didn't like what I was allowing Abigail to get away with.

I decided to give her a subtle warning. I'd show her the whipping bench——a reminder that I was her dominant and of my expectations. Perhaps it would be enough and a chastisement wouldn't be necessary.

I took a plug from the playroom as well. My fantasy in the shower had further cemented my desire to show her the pleasure I could bring her. Pleasure she would not expect. I put the plug in my dresser along with a bottle of lube.

At seven o'clock, Abigail served me breakfast in the dining room. She poured a delicious-looking sauce over perfectly cooked French toast. I couldn't wait to try a bite.

"Make yourself a plate and have a seat." I ate while she went into the kitchen. Mmm . . . bananas. Damn, she could cook.

She sat back down at the table and started eating her own breakfast.

"I have plans for you today, Abigail. Plans to prepare you for my pleasure."

For your pleasure.

"Yes, Master."

"Eat, Abigail. You can't serve me on an empty stomach."

She ate a bit more then, but not a lot. Not nearly enough. I slowed my eating down to match her pace. We both finished around the same time, and she hopped up almost immediately to clear the table.

Yes, this will work fine. Just the sight of the whipping bench will be enough.

She walked back into the dining room and stood at my side. Her body trembled slightly.

"You have far too many clothes on," I told her. "Go to my room and take them all off."

While she went upstairs, I took Apollo outside. He nosed around the yard, caught the scent of something, and ran toward the woods. I went back to the house. He would be fine outside for an hour or so.

When I walked into my room, Abigail stood naked, looking at the bench.

"It's a whipping bench," I said. She jumped at my voice. "I use it for chastisement, but it has other purposes as well."

Don't make me use it for chastisement.

She kept staring at it, perhaps trying to decide what my words meant.

"Step up," I said. "And lie on your stomach."

Get the feel of it, Abigail. Understand that I don't want to use it for punishment, but that I will. Touch it. See that my rules are real. That disobedience has consequences.

Then I will let you step down so I can pleasure you on my bed.

"Abigail," I said with a sigh. "This is getting tiresome. Either do it or say your safe word. I won't ask again."

She wouldn't use her safe word, would she? What if she did? I'd expected her to hesitate before stepping up to the bench, but I assumed she would follow my order. What if I'd miscalculated? What would I do?

Before I could decide, she took a deep breath and stepped up, lying down as I'd commanded.

Yes.

I went to the dresser and took out the plug. I squirted lube on it and placed it beside her.

"Do you remember what I told you Friday night?" I looked over her naked body, laid out and waiting for me. My cock grew hard against my pants.

I didn't expect her to answer, of course, but I wanted her to know where I was headed. I watched her, looking for a sign or movement to show she understood. But there was nothing. Perhaps I needed to refresh her memory. I put my hands on her waist and ran them down to her ass. She tensed.

Yes, she understood.

"Relax." I ran my hands up to her back, gently massaging her. She didn't relax, of course. I stepped back and took my own clothes off. As expected, she grew even tenser.

My experiment with the whipping bench was over. Perhaps she understood and I wouldn't have to bring it out for chastisement. Now it was time to move on to stage two of my plan.

But for a brief moment, as I looked her over, naked and bent over my whipping bench, I allowed myself to fantasize.

The rabbit fur flogger.

I would start with something simple for her first time. Soft and airy, it would lightly brush her thighs, her buttocks, her lower back. I would ignite the fire within her, bring her to the very edge of pleasure, leave her there, and then finally, finally, we would tumble over the edge together.

I took my cock in one hand and stroked it roughly, letting the fantasy play out a bit longer in my head; then I let out a sigh. Someday. Someday soon, perhaps.

"Move to the bed, Abigail."

She stumbled off the bench. Yes, she understood. She wouldn't want to be on the bench again soon. I watched as she scrambled, trembling and nervous, up on the bed.

I followed, taking her in my arms, dropping the plug beside her. "You have to relax. This won't work if you don't."

I kissed her neck, and she grabbed on to me tightly. I worked my mouth down her neck, across her collarbone, and down her torso. Slowly, the tension left her body as I trailed my lips over her. In this, I felt powerful—that I could affect her so.

I used my hands to ease her fear and my mouth to stoke her passion to a burning flame. She threw her head back.

Yes, like that.

I moved back up her body. "What I do, I do for your pleasure as much as mine. Trust me, Abigail."

I will never lie to you. I need your trust too much. I need your trust to bring you the pleasure you crave. The pleasure you deserve.

"I want the best for you," I said against her belly. "Let me give it to you."

She sighed as I brushed a finger against her, testing her wetness.

"I can bring you pleasure, Abigail." I pushed her knees apart and settled between them. "Pleasure like you've never imagined."

I wanted to see her eyes this time. Wanted her looking in mine as I entered her. This was important. She needed to understand this lesson. Needed to know that her pleasure and well-being were always at the forefront of my mind. And that when we were together on my bed, there would be nothing but pleasure involved.

Though her eyes held too many questions I didn't have answers for, I forced myself to look into them as I pushed into her. It would be so easy to close my own eyes, to shut everything off except the feel of her, tight and hot around me. But I couldn't. She needed this link between us, this closeness as we became one.

Her arms tightened around me and she looked up in wonder, running a hand down my back.

Yes.

"Let it go, Abigail." Damn, she felt good. Felt good as she ran another hand down my back and felt good as my cock slid deeply into her. "Fear has no place in my bed."

Ever.

I drew her closer as my hips moved faster. "Yes, Abigail." I thrust into her harder. "Feel what I can give you." She started to tighten around me. "Doesn't it feel good?" I thrust again.

It was working. She left the fear behind, probably already forgetting what my plans were. I sat up and lifted her hips, thrusting even deeper. She wrapped her legs around me, drawing me closer.

I took the plug from beside her knees and, as I entered her again, I slid it into her backside. She screamed through her climax, setting off my own, and we fell into a tangled heap on the bed.

When my heart slowed down, I sat up and looked into her wide, questioning eyes.

"It's a plug," I said, still a little out of breath. "Wear it a few hours every day. It'll stretch you. Help prepare you."

She bit her lip.

"Trust me," I said. She nodded, but I could see she didn't quite believe me. I couldn't do any more—the trust would have to come in time.

I rolled off the bed and pulled on my pants. "I need to let Apollo inside. Let's have lunch at the kitchen table."

She didn't talk much at lunch, but she had a better appetite than she'd had at breakfast. Perhaps my lesson had worked. I looked ahead to the next few weeks and saw us falling into a comfortable routine. The start of any relationship had a few rough patches, as the parties gradually grew more comfortable with each other, as they learned more about each other.

So Abigail didn't talk much—that would come with time. I knew as time passed that it would only get easier for me to see her as Abigail, to put aside my vision of Abby.

It had been a long time since I'd had to work through the details and hardships of a new relationship. I'd gone straight from a long-term relationship with Beth to Melanie, whom I'd known forever. I didn't see the need to count the pain-loving sub I'd played with after Melanie but never collared—that relationship ended before it ever really started.

"Friday at six o'clock," I told Abigail as she left. She nodded in understanding.

I invited Jackson over for dinner that night. The house seemed too quiet and I wanted some noise. Jackson was always good for noise.

He talked incessantly as we ate, causing me to smile several times over little tidbits he shared about his team. Normally, I zoned out when he talked about football, but this time I listened. Something was different about him, and I had a feeling it was Felicia.

"How's Felicia?" I asked as we sat down on my couch after dinner. Jackson flipped through the channels, trying to find the day's scores.

"Great." He reached into his pocket and took out his phone. "That's her now." He read the message she'd texted. "She's watching a movie with your librarian."

"Jackson, I swear to—"

"I know. I know." He held up his hand. "Don't worry. I won't say it to her face."

My eyes fell on the clock above my television as he texted Felicia back. Ten thirty-three.

Ten thirty-three?

I calculated the time in my head. Abigail normally woke at six o'clock to get ready for work. I knew that from her application. If the movie stayed on until eleven, she would get only seven hours of sleep.

Fuck.

I felt my anger rise. The day I brought out the whipping bench to warn her, she reacted by breaking a rule and getting less sleep than I demanded? What the hell?

I groaned as I thought ahead to the coming weekend, suddenly glad I had five days to prepare. Five days to prepare myself.

Chapter Ten

"Nathaniel," Jackson said, breaking my concentration. "You okay? You spaced there for a minute."

"What?" I blinked a few times. "I'm fine, just a bit tired."

"You? Tired?" He didn't look convinced. "Nah. Can't be."

Suddenly, I didn't want noise anymore. I wanted quiet. Quiet so I could think. "Actually, Jackson, I think I'm going to head on upstairs. Good luck at the game tomorrow."

He looked at me funny, but stood and gathered his coat. "Okay, if you say so."

I walked him to the door, took Apollo out one last time, and made my way upstairs. The whipping bench still stood in my room. I might as well leave it there. Odds were good I would have need of it Friday night.

Damn it, Abigail.

Maybe, just maybe, she would end up getting eight hours of sleep somehow. Doubtful, but I could still hope.

I sat on my bed and thought back to my time with Paul, the dominant who had been my mentor. The only person I'd ever subbed for. He'd given me several instructions on punishment, the first rule being not to punish out of anger. Thus far I'd never done so, and I felt certain that by Friday night I'd be calmer.

My packet of instructions to Abigail listed the consequences for disobedience. Beside "lack of sleep," I'd listed spanking, twenty strokes per hour lost.

At the time it'd made sense; looking back it seemed a little high. A little too much. Should I change it? Would Abigail notice?

No. I couldn't change it and keep any of the respect I needed as her dominant. Twenty strokes it would be.

I remembered something else Paul told me—make the first punishment memorable and you wouldn't be doing it again anytime soon.

Yes. I would make it memorable, and in doing so, perhaps straighten out the rest of her behavior as well—no more raised eyebrows or hesitations.

The voice in the back of my head warned me I could not punish her for those things. They were in the past. I'd let them slide and that was my fault. To bring them up would be wrong.

But if I made the punishment memorable enough, it would have a deterrent effect.

I sighed and made my way to the playroom, where I chose a leather strap. Back in my bedroom, I placed it on my dresser. If I looked at it and the bench all week, maybe I'd feel ready by Friday.

I could do it. I knew I could.

I was Abigail's dominant, after all, and it was time I started acting the part.

Paul had taught me three kinds of spankings—erotic, warm-up, and chastisement.

I'd given Abigail a taste of an erotic spanking with the riding crop during our first weekend together. Erotic spankings tantalized the recipient, heightened their pleasure—took them to a new level.

Unlike the next two spankings.

The warm-up would be very important with Abigail. Her skin was pale, fair, and fine. She bruised easily. I needed to take that into account, make certain I didn't leave any lasting marks.

Twenty strokes with the leather strap would bruise her if I didn't properly prepare her backside first. Even with the warm-up, I would have to walk a fine line, gauging her skin, her reactions, and her emotions. Her emotions . . .

She would cry.

I was going to make her cry. Could I do it?

I had to if our relationship was to progress. If I couldn't handle the sight of her tears, I had no business keeping her as a submissive. That was a cold, hard fact of our relationship.

I had Sara call Abigail on Wednesday. The coming weekend, unlike the others, would not start with a meal at the kitchen table. For one, I doubted my ability to eat with Abigail right before I punished her. Second, having her arrive at eight o'clock and head straight to my bedroom would set the tone for the night.

I called the local kennel to make arrangements for Apollo to stay overnight. If Jackson and the team made the play-offs, I'd have to board him the next weekend anyway. It'd be easier on him if he could get a trial run in beforehand. And, I admitted to myself, I wanted him out of the house.

I stood at the window overlooking the drive on Friday night, waiting for Abigail to arrive. Finally, I heard the sound of the hired car. I closed my eyes.

You can do this.

You have to do this.

My body tensed as I listened to the car door slam. Was she surprised Apollo didn't meet her? Did the change in time tip her off that I knew she'd disobeyed me? Would she look remorseful as she walked into the house?

The doorbell rang.

I opened the door, and she stood there looking confused but not remorseful. Maybe she'd slept in on Monday and gotten eight hours.

"Abigail," I said, waving her into the foyer.

She stepped inside and looked around.

"Did you have a good week?" I asked, wanting her to tell me. "You may answer."

"It was fine."

Maybe hers had been fine. Mine sure as hell hadn't been. Mine had been a horribly confusing week as I'd tried to work out the best way to handle what had happened on Sunday night.

"*Fine?*" I asked, slightly irritated at her response. But maybe, just maybe, she hadn't broken any rules. I would give her one more chance before I asked straight out. "I'm not entirely sure *fine* is the appropriate response."

Confusion clouded her expression.

Yes. It was fine. She hadn't disobeyed me. The punishment wouldn't be needed. For the first time in five days, I felt like I could breathe.

She gasped, and my hopes plummeted.

"Abigail." I took a deep breath. "Is there something you wish to tell me?"

She looked to the floor. "I got only seven hours of sleep on Sunday night."

I closed my eyes.

Damn Jackson for dating Felicia.

Damn Abigail for breaking a rule.

Damn me for stating that twenty strokes for a lost hour of sleep was appropriate.

And damn me straight to hell for ever thinking being Abigail's dominant was a good idea.

But . . .

I had given her the rules, I had written down the punishment, and damn it all, I was her dom.

I straightened my shoulders. "Look at me when you speak."

"I got only seven hours of sleep on Sunday night," she said, clearly this time. Abigail was a woman who owned up to her mistakes.

"Seven hours?" I stepped toward her. "Do you think I put together a plan for your well-being because I'm bored and have nothing better to do? Answer me." Maybe that was it. Maybe this was all a joke to her. She would never take us seriously if I didn't punish her.

"No, Master."

Apologize for breaking one of my rules.

But she just stood there, flushed and fearful.

"I had plans for this evening, Abigail," I said. "Things I wanted to show you." And now the library would have to wait. "Instead we'll have to spend the evening in my room, working on your punishment." I wanted her to know this was not how the weekend should have gone. Her disobedience changed everything.

Would she apologize?

"I'm sorry to disappoint you, Master."

Yes. Thank you. That's what she'd done. She'd disappointed me.

"You'll be sorrier still when I finish with you. My room. Now."

I watched as she climbed the stairs and headed to my bedroom. Then I checked myself to make sure I wouldn't act rashly or out of anger and gathered myself together. Abigail would be frightened enough—I needed to be in control.

I rolled my sleeves up and headed for the stairs.

She waited, naked, on the whipping bench. The prior weekend, the sight of her bare ass had fueled my fantasies. This weekend it reminded me that as nice as fantasies were, our relationship had rules and Abigail had broken one. Broken rules led to consequences. As the rule maker, I enforced the rules and handed out the consequences.

I ran a hand through my hair. I didn't have to like it and I didn't have to enjoy it, but I had to do it.

I went to the bench and gently brushed Abigail's ass. She jumped.

Nerves.

That made two of us.

"I use three different types of spankings," I said, wanting to explain my methods. "The first is an erotic spanking. It's used to heighten your pleasure, to excite you. The riding crop, for example." I trailed my fingers over her buttocks to her warm sex, all the while measuring her bottom, planning how and where to strike when the time came. As bad as tonight would be, I wanted her to know that spankings could feel good, that I could excite her with a spanking as well as punish her.

My touch grew rougher, and I watched her skin for any change of color. I pinched to see how red her skin would become. I didn't know her body well enough yet, and doing this would help me judge how her skin reacted. "The second spanking is for chastisement. You won't feel any pleasure. The purpose is to remind you of the consequences of disobedience. I make rules for your well-being, Abigail. How many hours of sleep are you supposed to get Sunday through Thursday? Answer me."

"Eight," she sputtered.

"Yes, eight. Not seven." Disrespecting my rules meant disrespecting me. "You obviously forgot, so perhaps a sore backside will help you remember in the future."

Perhaps we have both forgotten a few things and this will help us both.

"The third spanking is a warm-up spanking. It's used before a chastisement spanking." I bent down and picked up the strap from the floor. "Do you know why I have to use a warm-up spanking?"

Silence.

I put the strap on the bench, right next to her face. She needed to see it.

"Because your ass can't handle the chastisement spanking first."

Because you might bruise otherwise.

"Twenty strokes with the leather strap, Abigail." But I needed to remind her she had an out. She could use her safe word. Neither of us had to do this. "Unless you have something you'd like to say."

If she had entered into this arrangement for any other reason than to be my sub, if she wasn't one hundred percent certain she wanted to be dominated, I would find out now. She had only to say the word to bring our relationship to an end.

She was silent.

"Very well." If she could handle it, so could I.

I drew myself up straight and started spanking her. I began softly, making sure my hand landed in a different place each time, gradually warming the areas I would use the strap on— not too high, focusing more toward her sweet spot, right where her thighs met her butt.

I could tell when the strokes moved from pleasurable to painful because she started cringing before each one landed. Her ass turned pink and I started spanking a little harder. After a few minutes, I stopped. I ran my hand over her skin, testing, feeling the warmth, making sure it was okay to continue. She didn't flinch at my touch. The skin looked red, but I knew it could handle what was to come.

I only hoped I could.

I took the strap from beside her. "Count, Abigail."

I raised my arm and let the strap fly. It landed with a solid thump.

"Ow!"

"What?" I asked, raising my arm again.

"One," she said quickly. "I meant one."

I brought my arm down again.

"Shit!" she said, and then corrected herself. "I mean, two."

"Watch the language," I said with the third stroke.

"Th-three," she stuttered.

I moved so the fourth stroke landed on a different patch of skin. I concentrated on her backside, planning ahead to where the next few would land.

"F-four," she said, but moved her hand to cover herself right as I brought my arm back for five. I stopped and looked closely at the red skin before me. She was still fine. She knew better than to move. Damn it. Would she not learn?

I moved to her side and whispered, "Cover yourself again and I'll tie you up and add an additional ten." I was tired of her defiance. It would stop. Today. Now.

I brought the strap down for five, six, and seven. Quick and businesslike. She counted each time.

Eight landed on a new spot.

She started sobbing.

"Ei . . . eight."

Why had I ever decided twenty strokes was an acceptable punishment? I took a second to run my hand over her skin. Still fine. Still wasn't going to bruise.

I did my best to shut my brain down for nine, ten, eleven, and twelve, but I couldn't. I had to concentrate on her, on her responses, to make sure I wasn't being too hard on her. Was she crying out of shock? Was the pain really too much?

"Thir . . . teen."

I stopped again. Fuck. Seven more.

Should I stop?

Should I use the safe word?

No, not yet. She was fine. I needed to go on.

"Fourteen."

At fifteen she stopped counting.

"Abigail," I choked out.

"Sorry." She gasped for breath. "Fif . . . te . . . en."

Five more. My concentration was shot to hell. And there before me was Abigail King, the woman I'd longed for and admired for too damn many years to count.

I made her cry. And I would make her cry more.

Just get through it.

My strokes were lighter now, but I knew she was beyond noticing. Just a tap would hurt her after what I'd already put her through.

"Oh, God. Sixteen." She took a ragged breath. "Please."

I stopped and rested with my hands on either side of her body. I wasn't sure of anything anymore. Wasn't sure I could continue. Wasn't sure I needed to. Would she finally use her safe word? Is this what would break her? Twenty lashes with a leather strap?

Over a lost hour of sleep?

I stepped back, brought my hand up and back down.

Her body jerked. "Seventeen. Oh, please," she sobbed. "Better. I'll do better."

Just get through it.

Once more I ran my hand over her, judging. Could she handle three more? Maybe. If they were light.

"Eighteen," she whispered. "I'll get ten hours."

Two more, West. Get through it.

"Quit begging." I couldn't bear her to beg.

I struck again. Softer than ever.

"Nine . . . nine . . . teen."

I straightened my back again. Would this ever end?

I cleared my throat. Forced myself to speak. "How many hours of sleep are you to get, Abigail? Answer me."

Her body shook, jerked on the bench. "Ei . . . ei . . . eight," she half choked, half snorted.

One more, I told myself. *One more. Surely you can handle one more.* And I knew I spoke for myself, because there was no longer any doubt in my mind that Abigail was stronger than I was. That she could handle what I gave her.

I brought the strap down one last time.

"Twen . . . ty."

Her sobs filled the air.

My God, West. What have you done? Look what you've done to that beautiful creature.

I was sick.

Sick at myself and sick at what I'd done.

I had to get her out of the room. I couldn't look at her. Couldn't look at what I'd done.

I pulled deep for the sternest voice I could manage. "Clean your face and go to your bedroom. You have sleep to catch up on."

I waited until she hobbled from the bedroom, and then I fell against the bench, burying my face in my hands.

Chapter Eleven

The sound of running water gradually trickled its way into my consciousness and I slowly pulled myself upright. Once again, it seemed, Abigail had proved herself stronger than me. When told to clean her face and go to her bedroom, she went with no hesitation. Unlike me. I had languished in my room, wallowing in self-pity.

An inner voice whispered that I should go to her. To give her the aftercare she so desperately needed. But my pride kept me where I was.

If I went to her and broke down, as I feared I might, she would want to know why a dominant of so many years' experience would fall apart after punishing her. One thing would lead to another and she would discover the truth—that I knew of her long before her application crossed my desk.

I waited until the water in her bathroom stopped running, then paused, listening, a few minutes longer before walking into the hall.

She was crying.

Again.

I walked to her door and the crying stopped.

I put my hand out to turn the doorknob, but guilt prevented me from turning it. I knew what she would look like.

Runny nose. Wet eyes. Tear-streaked cheeks.

But worst of all, what would her expression hold? Hatred? Fear? Pain?

If I reached for her, would she shy from my touch? If I talked, would she listen?

I sighed.

I couldn't do it. I couldn't face her.

I reached and placed my hand flat against her door.

I can't, Abigail. I'm not strong enough. Forgive me.

It was too early to go to bed—not even nine o'clock—and the house was too quiet. I started to regret my decision to kennel Apollo for the night.

I walked into the kitchen and picked up my phone to check on him.

"Hello, Mr. West," the receptionist said after I introduced myself. "How are you?"

Not in the mood for small talk.

"How's Apollo?" I asked.

"He's doing very well, sir. So much better than last time."

I couldn't even muster up the energy to be happy.

"You'll be picking him up tomorrow at ten thirty?" she asked.

"Yes."

"And you'll be dropping him off again next Friday." I could hear the smile in her voice. "Assuming we win this weekend, of course."

This was where I was to engage in witty banter about football. Unfortunately, I had no witty banner in me.

"I'll see you tomorrow," I said and hung up.

I walked through the house, double-checking locks and security codes. I listened for footfalls from upstairs, but none came. Which was fine. If only one of us slept that night, I wanted it to be her.

Without thinking, I made my way to the library and my piano. I felt a stab of pain as I thought about how I had wanted the weekend to go. If I was lucky and Abigail stayed with me, maybe I would show the library to her later.

I sat at the piano, trying to decide what to play. The song I'd composed last weekend, the one inspired by Abigail's beauty, mocked me. How dare I play about her beauty? What right did I have after what I'd done?

I had no right.

Anger surged through me and I let my frustration out on the piano keys, playing the furious notes that pounded through my head. For a long time, I was lost in the anger, but as always, playing helped restore my calm. Eventually, the sweetness, the very essence of her took over, and I found myself unable to do anything but allow it to overtake me.

I wasn't a coward, I told myself the next morning. I was giving Abigail time. Time for what, I couldn't say. I only knew I wasn't ready to face her, and I suspected she felt the same.

I left the house shortly after six and drove into the city to my office. Three hours later, I had accomplished nothing. I thought back to the note I'd left in the kitchen. Would Abigail have found it? Would she still be at my house when I returned at noon?

I had to talk to someone, someone who would understand. I looked at the clock, grabbed my phone, and did something I hadn't done in months—I called Paul.

"Hello," a cheerful feminine voice said on the other end of the line.

"Christine, hello," I said. "It's Nathaniel." Christine and Paul had been married for three years. She was also his submissive.

"Nathaniel. It's been too long."

"I know," I said, still not ready for small talk. "Is Paul around?"

"He's right here. Hold on."

I heard muffled speaking and then the unmistakable sound of a kiss.

"Nathaniel," Paul said. "What's going on?"

It all came out then. I talked at length about Abigail, that she was inexperienced, that I'd taken her on as a submissive, and finally I went into the details of the previous night—the rules I had, how she'd broken one, the punishment.

The entire time, Paul let me talk and made appropriate comments. Yes, the punishment had been needed. Yes, it was always hard to punish a sub. Yes, I was normal. Yes, I would get over it. Yes, our relationship would only grow from here.

Trust Paul to know exactly what I needed. I felt better within minutes.

"What did you do for aftercare?" he asked.

"I'm talking to you," I said without thinking. I realized my mistake as soon as the words left my mouth.

"I got that," he said. "What did you do for her last night?"

I couldn't talk. For the first time in my life, I had no words.

"Nathaniel," he said as the silence dragged on. "Please tell me I'm interpreting your hesitation the wrong way. How did the aftercare go?"

"I didn't . . . I mean . . . I couldn't . . ."

"Aftercare, Nathaniel," he said more forcefully. "What did you do?"

I closed my eyes. "Nothing."

"You took a leather strap twenty times to an inexperienced submissive and did nothing for aftercare?"

"I couldn't face her . . . I didn't think she'd want—" I stopped. There was no excuse for my behavior.

"I, I, I," Paul said, mocking me. "This is not about you, Nathaniel, and if you don't understand that, you have no business having a submissive."

He was right. I couldn't argue with him.

"That woman gave you her submission, and it's your responsibility to treat that submission with the respect it deserves." I heard him slam a fist on a table or countertop. "Fuck, Nathaniel. I trained you better than this. Have you treated all your submissives with the same lack of care? Forgotten that your needs are second to theirs?"

"No," I whispered.

"I want you to understand something," he said in the cool, calm voice I knew he used to convey his displeasure. "The only reason I'm not hopping on the next plane to New York to strap your ass forty times with a leather paddle is that Christine is days away from delivering our first child."

He would have done it. I knew he would have. And though he had never been my master, I'd have let him. It would be preferable to the pain eating away at me. Forty straps with a leather paddle would have been over and done with. It wouldn't leave a gnawing ache.

"I can't believe you. I really can't." He stopped for a minute. "Where is she? Let me talk to her."

"She's not here. I'm at my office in the city."

"You left her alone? By herself?"

"Yes."

Silence on the other end of the phone, then finally: "Part of me hopes she's not at your house when you get back. That she leaves you."

My biggest fear.

"But part of me," he continued, "thinks that would be entirely too easy for you. I want her to be there, and I want you to have to deal with her."

I remained silent.

"What are you going to do?" he asked. "How are you going to make this right?"

I took a deep breath and described my plans for the day. After detailing everything, I finally hung up, promising to call back later in the day.

I picked Apollo up from the kennel and drove home, relieved when I pulled up to the house and saw movement from the kitchen window. I let myself into the house quietly, but Apollo nosed his way past me and ran down the hall to the kitchen, toenails scraping on the hardwood floor. A muffled shriek came from down the hall, followed by a loud "woof," and I smiled in spite of myself.

She was still in the house. In the kitchen, even. Making lunch. Bread, if I'd identified the smell wafting down the hall correctly. That alone told me what I'd feared—she probably hadn't sat down all day. And she needed to. She needed to sit down and see that her backside wasn't as sore as she made it out to be in her mind.

I walked into the living room and took a pillow from the couch. From the downstairs linen closet, I took a pile of towels and set them to warm in the dryer. Then I went into the dining room and set the pillow on the chair next to mine.

I needed to get my focus back on her. Immediately.

My heart plummeted when she walked into the dining room at noon. Plummeted because I knew suddenly that there were worse things in life than Abigail's face showing pain, fear, or even hatred.

The worst thing was Abigail's face showing nothing.

Her hands shook slightly when she put my plate in front of me, but her eyes were empty.

See what you did? You killed her light.

"Eat with me," I said, because it was the only thing I could force out.

She walked back to the kitchen, and I took a second to close my eyes and gather my thoughts.

She was still here. She wanted to stay. She still wanted me to be her dominant.

She returned to the dining room and stopped for just a minute when she pulled the chair out and saw the pillow.

Sit down, Abigail. You need to see that it's not as bad as you think it is.

She took her seat slowly, testing herself. I could almost hear her sigh of relief as she sat.

If I had been the dom I needed to be, I would have been home for breakfast and had her sit down then.

We ate in silence. Of course, we ate in silence—she wasn't going to speak at this table. Why had I chosen to eat here instead of the kitchen?

Because you're a coward. Because you didn't want her to speak her mind. Now, suck it up and talk to her.

"Look at me, Abigail."

She jumped.

Fuck. We were back to that.

Her empty eyes looked at me, and I mustered the strength to continue. "I didn't like chastising you." Understatement of the year. "But I have rules, and when you break them, I *will* chastise you. Swiftly and soundly."

As much as last night hurt us both, she needed to understand that point if we were to continue. "And I don't give gratuitous compliments, but you did well last night. Far better than I thought you would."

My words struck a chord, for something flickered in her eyes for the briefest of seconds.

I didn't deserve the flicker.

"Finish eating and meet me in the foyer in half an hour in your robe."

I left the table, took the towels outside, and turned on the hot tub. Once I made it back inside, I changed into my robe and waited for Abigail to join me.

"Follow me," I said when she met me.

Her eyes were full of questions, but she didn't say a word as we walked through the living room and made our way outside. She didn't even hesitate when I opened the door—she just walked through as if it were completely normal to be outside in a bathrobe in January.

She stood and waited for instructions when we reached the hot tub. I took a step close to her and inhaled her wonderful scent. Yes, she was still here. Yes, we could make this work.

I untied her robe, anxious to see if the punishment had left any lingering marks.

Please don't let there be any marks.

"Turn around," I said.

She turned slowly, almost embarrassed.

"Good," I said, running a hand over the pale skin of her backside. She didn't flinch. "It won't bruise."

I slipped off my robe and took her hand, leading her down into the tub.

"It'll sting a bit," I warned her. "But that should disappear soon." I needed to get her in the water, needed her to relax a little.

She gasped as she entered the pool. I could imagine the brief sting it might cause, but I knew what her body needed. Knew she'd feel better after.

"No pain today. Just pleasure," I said, drawing her to sit crossways on me, so there was no pressure on her backside.

Her sitting on my lap was more than I deserved. More than I had any right to. But I was a greedy bastard and I wanted more. I wanted her to touch me. Wanted her hands on me.

I nibbled her neck. "Touch me," I whispered. Touch me. Tell me we're okay. Tell me we can move past last night.

Please.

A tentative hand ran down my chest, and I groaned with pleasure.

Yes.

Her hands brushed lower, and she grabbed me. I sucked in my breath. "Two hands."

She took my cock with both hands then and gave me a tight squeeze. Fuck, she knew me well.

"You learn fast." I spun her gently so she straddled me, careful to make sure the position didn't put unnecessary pressure on her bottom.

I felt heady with delight. Delight that she was still with me and delight that we could once more be together like this.

I stroked her arms. "Are you okay? We can just sit here if you want."

She shook her head.

"Talk to me," I begged. She was positioned right above my cock and it was too damn hard to think straight. If she just wanted to sit, she better tell me soon.

"I want—" she started, and I rejoiced at the sound of her voice. "I want you to touch me."

She wouldn't have to ask twice. I ran my hands down her back, rubbing and massaging as I went. Her muscles were tense and tight, and I wanted nothing more than to feel her relax under my hands. To bring her body pleasure.

Her lips parted as I slowly circled her breasts and stroked the outline of her rib cage. She looked at me questioningly.

"What is it?" I asked. "Talk to me."

She licked her lips. "May I touch you?"

I smiled and brought her hands from the side of the tub to my chest. "All you want."

For the next several minutes, we explored each other with our hands using gentle caresses, both above the water and under. I took my time, and slowly her body relaxed for me. Eventually, the tension and the pain left, leaving only the burning ache of need. And as her body responded to my touch, I felt my own pain dissolve. Felt my own need rekindle.

I could do this, I told myself. I could be her dominant. We had made it through her first punishment and could move on.

I slipped a finger inside her, and she bucked against my hand. "Ready, are you, Abigail?" I teased.

"Yes, please," she whispered.

I took her hips and slowly lowered her onto my cock. She felt even warmer than the water. I raised and lowered her with my hands, making sure I didn't touch her backside. She wrapped her hands around my neck and pushed herself farther onto me. I held her hips so she wouldn't have to move and thrust gently in and out of her.

"Let me do the work, Abigail. You just feel."

She dropped her head forward, digging her hands into my hair and whispered a soft "Okay."

I worked my hips up to hers, teasing her, taunting her. Making sure she felt every ounce of pleasure possible. She felt weightless in the water. I saw the sweat start to break out on her face, and I thrust harder, wanting to bring her release. Wanting nothing more than to replace the pain of the night before with pleasure.

"Come for me," I said as I shifted my hips and slid in deeper. "Let me see you come."

She bit her lip in concentration and let out a moan as she contracted around me. I thrust into her again, feeling her release trigger my own, and I emptied myself into her.

Her head rested on my shoulder as we relaxed. I finally took her and sat her across my lap once again, enjoying the steam and heat of the tub, relishing the aftermath of our joint pleasure.

"Let's just sit here for a little while and rest," I told her, suddenly tired from both the emotional turmoil of the previous night and the conflicting emotions of the morning.

We sat in silence, neither one of us ready for any deep conversation, both of us needing only the reassurance that we were still okay.

After we sat for some time, I noticed her face heating and I knew she needed to get out of the tub. I rose first, grabbing a towel and holding it out for her. "Abigail."

I wrapped her in the towel after she stepped out of the tub and dried her gently. Then I took my own towel.

"How are you feeling?" I asked, drying off my legs and working up my body.

She yawned. "Tired."

Of course she was tired—she probably hadn't slept much the night before, and any sleep she had gotten was probably restless.

"Would you like to take a nap?" I asked.

A look of surprise covered her face, and she smiled. "Yes."

I led her back to the house and held the door open for her. "Go rest, then, and don't worry about dinner tonight. I'll cook."

Chapter Twelve

On Sunday night, I thought back to how the remainder of the weekend with Abigail had gone. How rested she'd appeared to be Saturday night. Her delight at the dinner I'd prepared. Most of all, I thought back to the conversation I had with Paul Saturday night. He was calmer and no longer threatened me with the forty lashes. But I still knew I deserved them.

After Abigail left, I went to Linda's house for dinner. Once a month, Jackson, Todd, Elaina, and I all met at my aunt's for dinner. That particular night, we'd be discussing the upcoming weekend in Philadelphia.

I wanted to surprise Abigail, so I hadn't mentioned Philadelphia to her. When she arrived on Friday evening, I'd drive her to the airport and we'd take off on my private plane. We'd spend the weekend in Philadelphia, watch the game on Sunday, and jet back to New York on Sunday night.

A perfect weekend.

Elaina was waiting for me inside the foyer of Linda's house.

"Where's Abby?" she asked as I hung my coat in the closet.

Just the sound of her name made me smile. "She had other plans tonight." *I didn't ask her,* I wanted to say. *Didn't want to make her feel obligated.* "Did Jackson bring Felicia?"

She rolled her eyes. "Jackson's not back yet."

"Well, then," I said. "It would have put Abigail in an uncomfortable position, right? Knowing she was with us while Felicia stayed behind."

"How is Abby this weekend?"

"Doing well." It was the truth. She'd looked more like herself when she left my house earlier. I thought back to our goodbye.

"Have a nice week, Abigail," I'd said, brushing her arm with my fingertips.

"Thank you." She looked down.

"Look at me," I commanded. When she met my eyes, I smiled. "Six o'clock Friday?"

Her eyes grew wide. "Six o'clock."

"I'll see you then," I said, opening the front door and then watching as she climbed into the waiting car.

Five more days.

"Nathaniel?" Elaina asked.

"Hmm?" I said. "Sorry. I was, uh, just thinking about Abigail's French toast."

"Uh huh. French toast. Is that what the single people call it these days?"

I blinked. "No, real French toast. Abigail's a great cook."

"I was kidding. Jeez, lighten up."

We went through into the dining room. I hugged Linda and kissed her cheek.

"Nathaniel," she said. "I was hoping you'd bring Abby."

"Maybe next time. Do you need any help?"

"No. Todd's helping me."

Todd walked in carrying a platter of delicious-looking Cornish game hens, and we made our way to the massive dining room table.

"Nathaniel." Elaina sat down. "Didn't you say Abby worked at the midtown branch of the city library?"

"Yes."

"Good." She put her napkin in her lap. "I'm going to invite her to lunch on Thursday. Do you think she'll come?"

Some part of me wondered how much Elaina knew about my lifestyle. I thought I'd kept it well hidden, but there was something in the way Elaina looked at me. Some of her comments made me wonder.

"I'm sure she'd love to have lunch with you," I said. "Would you like her number?"

"No. I'll just surprise her."

Elaina called me on Thursday afternoon. "I just talked to Abby. We're meeting at Delphina's in half an hour. I'm going to tell her all your deep, dark secrets."

"You do that." I laughed, certain there was nothing Elaina could tell Abigail that would scare her away. Not after the previous weekend. "Tell me how it goes."

I sat at my desk and thought about taking Abigail to Delphina's. Had I locked myself into a relationship with her that would always be defined by our sexual natures? Could I ask her out and expect her to want me as a man? As well as a dominant?

Paul and Christine made it work, but Paul and Christine didn't have the history I had with Abigail. They had started out clearly defined as dominant and submissive, and their relationship gradually grew into more.

As opposed to what? I asked myself. Mooning over some girl you never had the balls to approach as a regular man?

But I wasn't a regular man. I knew I could never be a regular man. I would always be a dominant. Maybe I could one day mesh the two desires together, but did I really want to try it with Abigail?

Would she want me to mesh them?

No, I told myself. It was better to think of Paul and Christine's life as something out of a storybook—something I could never have. It was safer to imagine what could be instead of trying and failing.

I had failed with Melanie. The experience still haunted me.

I told Melanie early in our relationship about my sexual nature. She knew all about my past submissives, both collared and uncollared. She was fully aware of my past experiences and thrilled that I wanted to try something more traditional with her.

Sex with Melanie was just sex. It was there. It happened. There wasn't much to say about it. I chalked it up to my dominant nature and told myself sex would grow better with time. I just needed to get used to being more normal.

I never mentioned to Melanie how our sex life left me unfulfilled, but I suspected she knew. At times, she'd urged me to tie her up or spank her. I always smiled and said maybe later, knowing full well "later" would never come.

For five months, I tried to deny myself, and for five months, the need became more pronounced. I found myself growing restless. More short and unkind.

I waited for a Thursday. On Thursday nights Melanie always ate dinner with her parents and spent the remainder of the evening at the assisted-living facility her grandmother lived in. I waited until seven o'clock and then took the key to my playroom and entered the room I'd avoided for five months.

I'd walked around, touching my equipment. Remembering. I'd felt tempted to call someone over and scene with them—just once—but I couldn't do it. Couldn't do that to Melanie. And playing again would make me a failure. I had told Melanie my past was behind me and I'd meant it.

Then why did I still have a playroom? Why hadn't I thrown everything away?

Because I knew I couldn't give it up.

I'd taken a suede flogger from the wall and run my fingers through the strands, remembering the last time I'd used it . . .

I had invited a close dominant friend and his collared submissive over to my playroom shortly after my breakup with Beth.

Hours later, we were deep into the scene. Jen was on her knees before Carter, his cock in her mouth. At Carter's request, I was flogging her with a suede flogger. I timed the strokes with each thrust of Carter's hips, my eyes and concentration focused on Jen—her breathing, her movements.

My cock grew hard as I waited for him to release into her mouth. He was taking his time, his hands buried in her hair, holding out for as long as he could.

"Damn, Nathaniel," he said. "Her mouth is so hot. If you want her to service you, I'll have no problem with it."

I knew many dominants who shared their submissives and, while it never bothered me, I had never been one to share my collared subs with others. Would I be a hypocrite to accept Carter's offer?

I refocused my attention on Jen. Her body strained with the effort of controlling her own lust.

Fuck. I was turning her on with the flogger. Exciting her. My cock strained against my jeans.

Would I do it?

"That's it, my Jennie," Carter said. "Nice and hard."

Jen moved her body, and we were all in sync—Carter's hips, Jen, and my flogger.

"I can't hold out anymore," Carter panted. "Let me know, Nathaniel. You really should fuck her mouth."

I unzipped my pants.

"Nathaniel!"

Melanie's voice broke through my memory, and I opened my eyes. The flogger dropped to my side. Somehow during my daydream, I'd undone my pants and had been stroking myself.

"What the hell?" Melanie screeched.

She stood in the playroom door with her hands on her hips, all the blood drained from her face.

"Wait downstairs," I said, buckling my pants.

"Not until you tell—"

"Now!"

She turned with a huff and stomped away. I walked out of the room and closed the door behind me.

Melanie waited in the living room, pacing.

"You want to explain to me what the hell I just saw?"

I collapsed onto the couch. I felt a hundred years old. "You knew. I never made a secret of who I was."

"You told me you'd try. That you weren't going to do it anymore." She paced to the fireplace.

"I wasn't doing anything, Melanie."

"That's not what it looked like to me. What was that . . . that . . . thing in your hand?"

"A flogger."

"A flogger?" she asked in disbelief. Her pacing stopped. "You flog people?"

"Don't look at me like that. It feels quite nice if the flogger knows what they're doing."

"Which you do, I suppose?"

"Of course I know what I'm doing." I felt anger start to boil deep within me. "I've been doing it for a long time."

She huffed one more time and turned from me. "That room. That room with all that stuff . . . I didn't know . . ." Her shoulders hitched. "I thought I'd come by tonight and surprise you. Mom's sitting with Grandmother. I guess I'm the surprised one, huh?"

I got up and put my arms around her. "I'm sorry. I thought you'd be away. I just wanted . . . I just wanted to remember. I thought it would help me. Help us. I never wanted you to know."

She was crying. I hated knowing I had caused her tears.

"Melanie," I whispered. "This is why I never wanted to scene with you. You wouldn't like it. It just . . . it wouldn't work." *Like we don't work,* I'd wanted to add.

She turned to look at me, her eyes filled with tears. "I can try, Nathaniel. Please, let me try."

"Don't. Please. It's not your fault. It's me." I stroked her back as she cried. "It's all me."

We went through the motions for another month. Pretended we were okay. We slept together, went out, tried to put that Thursday night behind us.

It didn't work.

I was who I was and Melanie was who she was.

I'd told her she deserved better than me. Deserved a man who could love her the way she needed to be loved. Who wouldn't need the crazy lifestyle I needed. She'd begged me to collar her, to try to scene with her, but I couldn't do it. I knew deep down that Melanie would never be a submissive.

And I knew that I would always be a dominant.

My phone rang, dragging me back to the present. I checked the caller ID. Elaina.

"Hey, Elaina," I said. "What's going on?"

"I told Abby all your deep, hidden secrets and she said she didn't care."

"Silly woman, I could have told you that."

"I really like her. You better hang on to her."

"I plan on it. Where are you?"

"We just left Delphina's. I'm heading back to see Linda, and Abby just got a . . . Abby!" Elaina screamed suddenly. "Stop!"

I jumped to my feet, sending my office chair sliding across the floor. "Elaina!"

I heard a terrific crash through the phone and then a low moan from Elaina: "Oh, God. Abby."

"Elaina!" I shouted into the phone. "Where's Abby? What happened?" She didn't answer. "Elaina!"

"Oh, God. Nathaniel," she said. "It's Abby. It's . . . it's not good."

My heart felt like the world's strongest man had it in his grasp. I couldn't breathe, and only one thought kept running through my head.

Abby.

Abby.

Abby.

Chapter Thirteen

"Elaina!" I shouted again, but she didn't answer. From her end of the phone, I heard frantic voices and the sound of a car door slam. "Elaina!"

What had happened to Abby? What did Elaina mean, it wasn't good? Was Abby involved in the crash I'd just heard?

Then I heard yelling.

"Call 911!"

"Is she breathing?"

"Can you find a pulse?"

Breathing? Pulse?

Abby?

"Elaina!" I shouted.

Nothing.

"Abby," I finally heard Elaina say. The tone of her voice didn't comfort me. I strained to hear more. "Abby, wake up. Wake up, Abby."

"Don't move her," someone else said. "Her neck could be broken."

My body shook and my knees threatened to give out. Broken? Abby? I reached for my keys with fumbling fingers. A cab or the car?

"Elaina!" I tried again. I picked the keys up and they fell to my desk. "Elaina! Damn it. Talk to me!"

I picked the keys back up, held on to them this time. The car.

"She's alive, Nathaniel," Elaina sobbed.

The keys dropped again. Alive? Had there been a doubt? I swiped the keys and shoved them in my pocket. "Where are you?" I asked as I stumbled out of my office.

"Mr. West," Sara said, jumping up from her desk.

"I'm leaving! Don't know when I'll be back." I turned once more to the phone. "Where, Elaina?"

"Lenox," Elaina said with a shudder in her voice. "I'll have them take her there. I'll call Linda."

I don't remember much from the drive to the hospital. I tried calling Elaina several times on the way, but she didn't answer her phone. Linda didn't pick up her phone either.

I pulled into the parking lot, stumbled out of the car, and ran to the ER. Had she made it here yet?

Why hadn't Elaina picked up her phone?

Because Abby was worse.

I felt sick.

She was worse. Or else her neck had been broken. Or else her pulse—

I couldn't think that. Couldn't do it.

I burst through the hospital doors, and the receptionist looked up and smiled. Thankfully, she was someone I recognized from visiting Linda before.

"Mr. West," she said. "How are—"

"I'm here to see a patient." My eyes darted frantically around the room.

"Patient's name?"

"Abigail King."

"I don't see her here," she said, looking at her computer screen. "Maybe they just brought her in."

"Yes!" I shouted in spite of myself. Damn it, when would she let me through the doors? "They just brought her in."

"Hold on." She picked up the phone.

Hold on? Hold on? Had the entire world gone crazy?

She spoke low into the phone, having a conversation that took damn near years. She looked up. "She's in trauma room four. I'll send you through, but you'll have to wait outside the room."

The door to my right finally buzzed open, and I ran through.

I'd been in the ER before, mostly to visit Linda. I sprinted down the corridor and turned left. Doctors and nurses rushed around, but my eyes focused on the room at the end of the hallway.

Abby!

If I could just reach the room. Just get there. Had a hallway ever been so long?

"Nathaniel!" Elaina jogged toward me. "She's okay. She's going to be okay."

I pushed her aside and opened the door. "Abby! Abby!"

Then I stopped short.

The trauma team worked frantically, moving around the room, all of them talking at once. The center of their attention was Abby. She lay naked, still as death, and the blood from her head drenched the white sheet of the bed. Only when someone touched her did her body move. So vulnerable. So very fragile.

Abby?

I grabbed on to the doorframe to hold myself upright.

Mumbled voices. Something metallic.

"Got the call hours ago," a deep male voice said. "Took a long time to get down that ditch. Can't imagine anyone's still alive."

I couldn't open my eyes. It hurt too much. Where was Mommy? Where was Daddy? Why had they stopped talking?

"Probably hit the ice. Had no chance once he hit the ditch."

"Man and a woman. Look to be DOA. Damn, all that blood."

"There's a child in the backseat!"

The voices weren't Mommy or Daddy. Who were they? What happened?

I cracked my eye open. Didn't hurt too much if I just moved my eye.

"Hey! You can't be in here!"

I shook myself and looked back to Abby. Was she breathing? They were checking her IV, taking her blood pressure, and hooking her up to monitors. That was a good sign, right? It was only bad when they stopped.

"I'm Nathaniel West," I managed to say. "Linda's nephew."

"I don't care who you are. You can't be in here!"

I stood where I was, unable to take my eyes off of Abby and the blood. All the blood.

"Why won't you—" I started.

"Don't make me call security!"

Two gentle hands grabbed my shoulders. "Nate."

"Linda!" I spun around. "Is she okay? Why won't they stop the bleeding?"

"She's okay. Let them work." She pushed me to the door. "You can't be in here. I'll be out in a few minutes."

The door closed behind me and I faced Elaina. Mascara smudged her eyes, and she sniffled. "Is she still okay?"

I turned back to the closed door. "I don't know."

Time stood still. I measured its passage by my breaths. Willing Abby to keep breathing. No one else entered the trauma room. But no one left either. Was that good?

What would I do if something happened to Abby?

Surely nothing would happen to her. Not now. Not when she finally had a place in my life.

If I never saw her again—

Stop it!

I bent over and grabbed my knees. I couldn't think like that. Wouldn't think like that.

Finally, the door opened and they wheeled her out.

"What's going on?" I asked, running to her side. She was still out, but the blood had been wiped away. Most of it, anyway. "Is she okay?"

Why wouldn't anyone answer?

"Abby," I said, starting down the hall after her.

"Nathaniel. Elaina," Linda said, coming up behind us. "Let's sit down."

I pointed down the hall. "I want——"

"I know, but you can't go." Linda sat on a bench, patting the spot beside her. "Sit down."

"Oh, God." My knees felt weak again, and I struggled to breathe. "It's bad. It's really bad."

"Nathaniel!" she said more forcefully. "She's going to be fine. Sit down."

I sat.

"Nothing's broken," she said as Elaina sat on her other side. "We think she has a concussion, but we need a CAT scan to see the extent of it."

"Why won't she wake up?" Elaina asked.

"The brain is a remarkable organ," Linda said in a soft, soothing tone. "It knows what the body needs, even when we don't understand. I'm sure she'll wake up soon. She's going to be on the fifth floor, G hall. Why don't you go up and wait for her?" She stood up to leave. "And someone needs to call Felicia."

An hour later, they wheeled Abby into her room. I followed, anxious to see and touch her. A nurse remained behind, checking her vitals.

"Is she awake?" I asked.

"Not yet, Mr. West." She tucked a sheet under Abby's arms before turning to leave. "I'll be back later to check on her. Call me if she wakes up."

I slowly approached her bed. The sheet moved up and down with her breathing. Her head had been bandaged in one place. Small cuts marked her face. I reached out and brushed hair back from her forehead. She moaned.

"Wake up, my lovely," I begged. "Wake up for me."

Nothing.

"What the hell are you doing here?"

I spun around.

Felicia.

"She's fine," I said, smiling. "Abigail is going to be fine."

"Abigail," she spat. "Her name's Abby. She's lying there in a hospital bed and you can't even call her by her name. I always knew you had the heart of a fucking animal." She put her hands on her hips. "I don't even know why you bothered showing up."

I clenched my teeth. "You don't know what you're talking about!"

She took a step closer to me. "I know all about you and Abby. About your little weekend games. She scratches your kinky itch, that's all."

There was no need to argue—to try to justify my life. We were wrong to argue in front of Abby, whether she was conscious or not.

"You don't know anything about us," I said.

"Fine then!" She stamped her foot. "Why don't you explain it to me!"

I stepped away from Abby's bed. "I refuse to stand here and explain myself to you." I glared at Felicia. "I answer to no one, but just in case it's not clear, I care deeply for that woman and you will not—"

"Mr. West!" A nurse interrupted. "I can hear you down the hall. I'm going to have to ask you both to calm down and for one of you to leave the room. You're disturbing the patients. This commotion isn't good for Ms. King."

Felicia pointed at me. "You leave. I just got here."

I nodded. "You have twenty minutes."

I went out to join Elaina and Linda in the waiting room.

"What did the CAT scan show?" I asked.

"Nathaniel," Linda said. "If you and Felicia can't control your-selves, I'll have to ask one of you to leave." She looked at me sharply. "And she is Abby's emergency contact."

I sighed. "I understand."

"Good. The scan showed a moderate concussion. We just need her to wake up now."

"How long will that be?" How long until those beautiful eyes opened?

"Shouldn't be too much longer. I'll go check on her as soon as Felicia leaves." She clasped my shoulder. "She's going to be fine. I promise."

"Thanks."

She walked off and I turned to Elaina. "Tell me what happened."

The damn driver ran a stop sign.

I was still fuming when Felicia left Abby's room.

She curled her lip up. "Twenty minutes. I'll go call her dad."

Linda chuckled behind me, and we pushed against the door to enter the room.

Abby lay still. I focused on the movement of the sheet.

She was breathing.

She was fine.

I stepped back so Linda could examine her.

But when would she wake up? Why wouldn't she wake up? What if her brain was hurt worse than the scan showed? What if she never woke up?

I started chanting in my head, matching my words to the up-and-down movement of her chest.

Wake up.

Wake up.

Wake up.

Her eyelids fluttered.

Oh, please.

"Abby?" Linda asked.

Her eyes opened. I almost dropped to my knees in thanks.

She licked her lips. "Dr. Clark?" Her voice sounded scratchy.

"You're in the hospital, Abby. How are you feeling?"

She tried to smile, but winced in pain. *Don't move, Abby. It's okay. You're okay.* Relief flooded through me. *Take it easy, Abby.*

"I must be badly off to have the chief of staff in my room."

"Or else you're very important." She stepped to the side so Abby could see me.

Excitement filled her eyes. God, she was beautiful. Bandages covered her face, she'd be a mess of bruises for weeks, but she was still the most beautiful person I'd ever seen.

And she was happy to see me.

"Hey," she said.

I walked slowly, trying to contain all the emotions coursing through me. I took her hand. It felt so good to touch her. "You scared me."

"Sorry." She wrinkled her forehead. "What happened?"

She didn't remember. What if she'd lost her memory? But she knew me, knew Linda. She was fine. I had to keep telling myself that.

"Your cab was hit by a dump truck," I said. "Damn driver ran a stop sign."

"You have a moderate concussion, Abby," Linda said. "I'm keeping you overnight. You were more deeply unconscious than we'd usually expect in concussion cases. But there's no internal bleeding. Nothing broken. You'll be sore for the next few days."

"Did I hear Felicia?" Abby asked, and I cringed. Not yet. I wasn't ready to hand her over to Felicia yet.

My aunt smiled at her. "New hospital regulation. Nathaniel and Felicia aren't allowed within twenty feet of each other."

Keep it light. Good thinking, Linda.

"We had a slight misunderstanding," I said. "She's with Elaina. They've been talking to your dad."

"Can I——?" Abby asked.

What? What did she want? What could I do?

"You need to rest," Linda said. "I'll go let the others know you're awake. Nathaniel?"

She would tell Felicia that Abby was awake. I had a few moments. That was all.

Abby waved me over.

What did she need? I'd do anything for her.

"I missed yoga class this afternoon," she whispered.

Was she serious?

Did she think I'd punish her for missing yoga?

I tucked a strand of hair behind her ear. "I think I can overlook it this one time," I said, just in case she was serious.

"And I'll probably miss my jog tomorrow morning."

The medication. It had to be the medication.

"Probably," I teased.

"But on the upside," she said with a yawn, "I seem to be getting lots of sleep."

She was serious. She was seriously telling me she was getting enough sleep.

I didn't know whether to laugh or cry.

"Shh," I whispered instead, brushing her forehead. Her eyelids fluttered, and she drifted off to sleep.

I sat for several long minutes, watching her. Had there ever been a more perfect creature? My heart swelled. She was fine. She was going to be okay.

I ran my hand down her arm, cupped her hand in my palms, and studied it. The soft, pale skin. I raised her fingers to my face and kissed the inside of her wrist, right where her pulse surged strong and steady.

"Abby," I whispered.

The door pushed open.

"I heard she was awake," Felicia said. "When were you planning to let me see her?"

I wiped my eyes. "I was just leaving."

"Sure you were."

"She went back to sleep."

Felicia walked to the bed and took Abby's other hand. "She's okay, then?"

And for that moment, whatever our differences, whatever our personal lives, Felicia and I were united.

"She'll be fine."

An hour later, we all sat inside Abby's room. Linda and Felicia chatted by the door. Elaina and I stayed by Abby's bed.

"I have Abby's necklace," Elaina said in a matter-of-fact voice. "It's in my purse."

"Thanks," I said. "You can give it to me later."

Did Elaina know? Did she know it was more than a simple necklace? Did I care?

No.

"Just wanted you to know." She fingered a loose thread on the sheet. "She wears it a lot, so I know it's important to her."

I nodded, unable to think about the collar. I just wanted Abby to wake up again.

We all looked to the door when a hospital employee entered the room with a tray.

"Wait a minute," I said, after he set the tray down. I lifted the lid. "What is this?"

"Chicken broth."

"This isn't chicken broth." I lifted the spoon and let the liquid dribble back into the bowl. "This is water with salt and pepper thrown in." I put the lid back down and handed him the tray. "I wouldn't feed this to my dog."

"I just deliver," he said, not fazed by my words. "I'm not taking it back."

"Then I'll take it back," I said.

Elaina giggled. Felicia rolled her eyes.

"I'll be right back," I said, walking out the door.

Someone, probably Linda, had alerted the kitchen staff to my arrival.

"You're not cooking here," a chef said, arms crossed, standing in front of his stove as if guarding a fortune.

I held up the tray. "I'm not letting her drink this."

"An impasse."

"No. I talk and you cook." The chef sighed, but I continued. "First take two pieces of chicken, with the meat still on the bone . . ."

I heard the difference as I neared Abby's room. Voices. Excited voices. But more important—Abby's voice.

She was awake!

"Did Sleeping Beauty wake up?" I said with a smile as I entered the room. I set the tray down and pushed it over to her. "You should see what they call food in this place. They serve chicken broth out of a *can*."

"Did you make this?"

"No. They wouldn't let me. But I dictated."

She smiled. I swore that smile could light up the heavens.

I looked to Linda. "Did you tell her?" We had decided while Abby was out that she would spend the weekend with me, while everyone went to Philadelphia. Felicia had fussed for a bit, but finally agreed.

Linda shook her head. "No. She just woke up. Come on, Elaina. Let's get something to eat. Felicia, would you like to come?"

"I'll be down in a minute."

I went to work setting up the tray, getting Abby's spoon and napkin ready, adjusting the bed, making sure she was upright enough. "Eat."

"Damn, Nathaniel," Felicia said. "She's not a dog."

I narrowed my eyes at her. "I know that."

"Do you?"

Did I treat Abby like a dog? What had I ever done to deserve such criticism?

"Felicia," Abby said.

Felicia glared at me once more and stomped out the door. Jackson was going to have his hands full with that one, but I was glad Abby had such a caring friend.

"I'm sorry about that. Felicia is . . ." Abby sighed. "Felicia."

I sat on the edge of her bed, wanting to be near her. Needing to be near her. "Don't apologize. She cares for you and is looking out for your best interests. There's not a thing wrong with that." I pointed to the bowl. "You do need to eat."

She took a sip. "This is good."

"Thank you."

I sat and watched her. Enjoyed the sight of her awake. Alive. Moving. Breathing.

Being Abby.

"Elaina has my collar."

Okay, it wasn't enough to be near her. I needed to touch her. "I know. She told me. We'll get it later."

I made lazy circles on her leg, then stroked from her ankle up to her knee. Touching her. Reassuring myself she was fine, that she was alive.

"What did you mean earlier—had they told me?" she asked.

"Told me what?"

"About the weekend." I looked into her eyes—they were intelligent and alert. "Tomorrow, Felicia and everyone will head on to Philly as planned. But since you shouldn't be alone this weekend, you'll stay with me."

"I'm sorry. You'll miss Jackson's game because of me."

Like I cared about Jackson's game with her in the hospital.

"Do you know how many times I've watched Jackson play football?" I asked.

"But this is the play-offs."

"And I've seen him in the play-offs too many times to count. I don't mind missing this one. We can watch it on TV." I smiled. She didn't know about my surprise. "But I am disappointed you'll miss it."

"Me?" She looked endearingly confused.

"You and I were going to take my jet to Philly tomorrow evening. Spend the weekend in the city. Watch the game on Sunday." I patted her leg, still not wanting to stop touching her. "Now we'll have to make do with the couch and takeout."

Still the confused look.

"Don't worry," I said, laughing inwardly. "If they pull this off, there's always the Super Bowl."

She started eating again. I thought back to her comments earlier about the yoga and jogging and suddenly I wanted to make myself clear.

"And, Abigail. All you're going to do this weekend is rest."

Chapter Fourteen

She finished eating and pushed her tray away from the bed. "Is there a mirror around here?"

"I don't know," I said. She wanted to see herself. Was that a good idea? Should I let her? I thought she was beautiful, but what would she think? "I don't think . . ."

She ran a finger over her cheek and winced. "Is it bad? Do I look that awful?"

I stood up and walked to the sink. Felicia would get her a mirror if I didn't. I found a small mirror and handed it to her, watched as she examined herself.

"Poor kid was stuck in that car for the better part of three hours, just watching and listening to his parents die." The voices were low and soft. They didn't know I was listening. Didn't know I was awake. "Makes you wonder how something like that will affect him."

"Ugh," Abby said. "I'm going to have a black eye. It'll look like I've been beaten."

"Makes you think it might have been better if he——"

Where am I? Are Mommy and Daddy here?

"Wait, look. I think he's awake."

"What is this? What happened?" Abby asked.

I looked over to her. She lightly touched her bandage.

"Head wound," I said. "There was blood everywhere. It

wouldn't stop and they weren't trying. They were too concerned with whether you had a broken neck or internal bleeding."

They were lifting Mommy and Daddy from the car. Why were they covered in red? Was all that blood?

"Head wounds bleed a lot. I remember."

"Get the boy! Get him out of here!"

Abby said something, but I missed it.

"What?" I asked.

"My bleeding. It stopped."

Yes, for Abby the bleeding stopped. She was okay. She was alive and she was with me.

"Yes. Once they decided you hadn't broken your neck, they bandaged your head." I took her tray. "Let me put this outside."

Linda stood at the nurse's station, talking with Abby's nurse.

I put the tray down and walked toward her. "She's doing well. She ate all the broth."

"Good." She smiled. "Are you going to stay here tonight?"

Where else would I go? "I was planning on it."

"I'll round you up some scrubs. They'll be more comfortable than that suit."

"Right." I'd forgotten I still had my suit on. "How long will she be here?"

"Anxious to get her to your house?"

"Do you know how many people die of hospital-acquired infections each year?"

She set down the papers she'd been looking over. "As a matter of fact, I do. But Abby's extremely healthy. She's not going to die of a nosocomial infection."

"I can feed her properly when she's at my house."

"Take it easy on my kitchen staff. It's hard to find good help."

"How about you go find those scrubs?" I growled.

"It's all going to be fine. Just wait and see."

I wished, not for the first time, that I shared Linda's optimism.

Elaina and Felicia returned not long after. I moved from my place at Abby's bedside to allow Felicia to sit next to her.

"Did you eat, Abby?" Felicia asked.

"Mmm." Abby nodded. "Best chicken broth ever."

Elaina tapped me on the arm. "Come outside for a minute."

We walked outside, and the door closed softly behind us.

"I have to leave, but I wanted to give you this." She took out her purse and handed me Abby's collar. "I'll let you give it back to her."

And in that minute, I was certain Elaina knew. "Thank you."

"I'll come by tomorrow with some clothes for her." She kissed my cheek. "Are you staying here tonight?"

"Yes."

She laughed. "Good luck with that. So is Felicia."

I groaned. Of course Felicia would be staying.

Felicia stood by the bed talking with Abby when I reentered the room. I watched as she squeezed Abby's hand and whispered in her ear.

I walked over and stroked Abby's cheek. "I'll stay tonight."

Felicia huffed.

"Do you have a problem?" I asked.

"I'm staying with Abby tonight."

"Really?" I countered. "So am I."

She waved to the large bag in the corner of the room. "I already brought an overnight bag with a change of clothes and a toothbrush."

She was fighting with me. Again. In front of Abby. Fortunately, I didn't care this time. "Linda's bringing me a set of scrubs."

"I think that's improper use of hospital equipment." She pointed at me. "Maybe I'll report it to the board."

She was fighting *and* threatening me. Or, at least, trying to threaten me.

"Linda's *on* the board," I said.

A nurse entered the room to check Abby's vitals again, point-edly stepping around us as Felicia sank defiantly into the recliner by the bed.

"We'll both stay." I could spend one night in a room with Felicia. It wouldn't kill me.

"Sorry, Mr. West," the nurse said. "Only one visitor in the room overnight. It's a rule."

A rule. I couldn't very well go against hospital rules. Not after punishing Abby for not following mine.

"I see." I glanced at Abby, and her face was flushed. "Felicia, you can stay." I walked to Abby's bed. "I'd better leave before they call security. I'll see you first thing in the morning." I leaned over and whispered in her ear, "Sleep well."

By ten o'clock, everyone had left the hospital except staff and overnight visitors. Abby's night nurse was a short, stocky woman with friendly eyes and a warm smile. When I saw her pass the door of the waiting room, I took my scrubs and followed her.

She stayed in Abby's room for about five minutes. The door was slightly ajar and I peeked inside. A groggy Abby lifted her arm for the nurse to take vitals. Felicia sat huddled on the reclin-ing chair in the corner. Our eyes met briefly.

I stopped the nurse when she left Abby's room.

"Is she okay?" I asked, blocking the hall.

"You're Nathaniel West. Nice to meet you."

"Yes, sorry." I held my hand out. "It's just . . . I'm worried."

"Abby's fine. I bet she'll go home tomorrow."

"Thank you," I said.

She winked. "I'll check on her again soon."

As the nurse walked away, Felicia opened the door. "Visiting hours are over."

"I'm not visiting." I pointed to the waiting room. "I'm waiting."

"You're staying here all night?"

"Here in the hallway? No. Here in the hospital? Yes." I held up my scrubs. "I was just getting ready to change into my board-approved scrubs."

"Fine. Just make sure you don't bother Abby tonight. She needs her rest."

"Hell, Felicia, do you think I'm going to bust into her room and have my wicked way with her? Force myself on a woman who's been unconscious for the better part of the afternoon?" I took a step closer to her. "Is that what you think of me? That I care only for myself? My needs? I hold her above all. Do you understand? Whenever we're together, Abigail is at the forefront of my mind. What she wants. What she needs."

For the first time, I felt a change in Felicia. Nothing major. I knew she still didn't like me, or what Abby and I did, but maybe, just maybe, I was changing her view of me. I wondered why the thought made me happy.

She lifted her nose. "I don't believe you."

"I didn't expect you to."

I didn't sleep well that night. The waiting room couch didn't fit my frame, and the blankets Linda had found for me were scratchy. But, of course, the real reason was three doors down the hall.

Abby.

I could no longer think of her as Abigail. Not after today. Not after almost losing her.

Abby's nurse walked down the hall, and I got up from the couch to follow. Once more, Abby was half asleep and Felicia sat huddled on the recliner.

The four of us replayed the scene several times during the night. By six forty-five, the nurse was preparing for a shift change and Felicia dozed uneasily. I walked down to the kitchen to see to Abby's breakfast.

"Not you again," the chef said when I walked into the kitchen.

"I came to oversee breakfast."

"Breakfast today is turkey sausage, scrambled eggs, or waffles."

"Ham and cheese omelet," I said. "Real eggs, freshly shredded cheese, and that ham over there." I pointed to the large ham I'd noticed when I entered the kitchen.

"That's for lunch."

"And a small slice or two can be used for breakfast."

He sighed. "If I make the omelet, will you promise to order lunch from a nearby restaurant?"

"And miss our little chats?"

"Lunch from a nearby restaurant and I make an omelet so light and fluffy, you'll cry." He picked up a carton of eggs. "Your call."

I was a smart enough businessman to know a good deal when presented with one. "I accept. Lunch from a nearby restaurant."

Fifteen minutes later, I walked toward Abby's room carrying the tray. Her other breakfast was about to be delivered.

"Here." I shoved the tray into the employee's hands. "She gets this one instead."

He looked at the tray, but didn't question me.

"Breakfast time," I said, entering the room and preparing Abby's table. She looked tired, dark circles under her eyes, bruises more pronounced. I couldn't wait to get her out of here. "Ham and cheese omelet this morning."

"I've got to run, Abby." Felicia kissed Abby's cheek, completely ignoring me. "I still have to pack. You take it easy. I'll call you when I can." She spun around and stared at me. "Hurt her and I cut off your dick and feed it to you for *your* breakfast."

"Felicia Kelly!" Abby chided.

I actually found Felicia's outburst amusing.

"Sorry," Felicia said, but I knew she wasn't. "It just came out." She pointed to me. "But I mean it."

Felicia picked up her bag and left the room.

"I don't know what's gotten into her," Abby said.

I sat down next to her, pleased to have her to myself. "She was pretty upset yesterday. She just doesn't want you to get hurt."

"Are you going to tell me what you two argued about?"

"No."

She took a bite of omelet. "Are other hospital patients eating ham and cheese omelets for breakfast?"

"I find myself rather unconcerned with what other hospital patients are eating for breakfast." I found myself unconcerned with anything besides the fact that Abby was safe.

While Abby went down for what I hoped was her final CAT scan, Elaina dropped by with some clothes.

"Going home today?" she asked.

"That's the current plan."

"We'll miss you in Philly."

"Maybe we'll get together in Tampa."

She hugged me, pulling me tight to her chest. "Take care of Abby."

"Make sure Felicia doesn't call all the time. I want Abby to rest."

We left a little before eleven o'clock. When the hospital insisted on taking Abby out the door in a wheelchair, her protests fell on deaf ears. I went to the parking lot to retrieve my car and pulled it around to meet her. I hopped out to ensure she made it into the car comfortably and adjusted the seat so she leaned back more than normal.

"What happened to the cabdriver?" she asked as I pulled onto the street.

I'd known she'd ask about him at some point, so I'd called and spoken to Linda earlier. I'd also made a few other decisions.

"Minor scratches. He was released yesterday. I don't like cabs. I'm buying you a car."

"What? No."

No? Had Abby just disagreed with me? Did she finally feel comfortable enough to actually talk to me?

"What's wrong with me getting you a car?"

"It feels wrong." She sniffled, and I looked over to her. Were her eyes wet? Damn.

"Are you crying?" I asked.

"No," she said, but the sniffle gave her away. She was crying over a car? Really?

"You're crying. Why?"

"I don't want you to get me a car."

I started to protest, but she spoke again. "It'd make me feel . . ."

"Make you feel what?"

"Make me feel dirty, like a whore."

I clutched the steering wheel tightly to keep the car on the road. A whore? She felt like a whore?

"Is that what you think you are?" Good God. What had I done to her?

"No," she finally said. "But I'm a librarian. You're . . . you're one of the wealthiest men in New York. How would it look?"

I forced myself to remain calm, to resist the urge to call Felicia and have her cancel the Philly trip, to ask her to take Abby home. Abby was not a whore. I'd break our relationship off immediately to ensure she never felt like one.

"Abigail." There, I could talk. I even sounded reasonable. "You should have thought about how things would look long before now. You wear my collar every day."

"That's different."

I shook my head. "It's the same. My responsibility is to take care of you." How was it she didn't know that?

"By buying me a car?"

If need be. "By making sure your needs are met."

It was what I told Felicia in the hospital—it was my most important responsibility. Didn't Abby understand that?

She didn't argue any more. After a while, she closed her eyes, but I knew she wasn't asleep. Still, the silence gave me time to think. Somehow, her accident had made her more comfortable talking to me. The Abby who showed up at my office weeks ago would not have argued over a car. I was pleased she felt more comfortable around me.

I didn't understand her refusal, though. I was her dom and I had the means to help her. Why shouldn't I?

Because it would look like I was paying her for sex. Like she was a whore.

I stifled a groan.

Did she feel cheap because of what we did? She had never been in a relationship like ours before. It was new to her. I thought back to our kitchen table conversations—she'd never quite opened up to me.

If I could only ensure she felt comfortable sharing her mind with me as well as her body . . .

We pulled up to my house, and once I stopped the car, I got out and opened her door. "The car conversation is not finished, but you need to get inside and rest. We'll talk later."

I led her inside, trying my best to keep Apollo from jumping on her, and settled her on the couch. Then I went into the kitchen. I'd called my housekeeper from the hospital earlier in the morning and instructed her to stock my refrigerator and pantry for the weekend.

I made a turkey, cheese, and avocado sandwich for Abby and filled her plate with grapes and apple slices. I grabbed a bottle of water from the refrigerator and joined her in the living room.

She took the plate from me. "This looks delicious. Thank you."

I resisted the urge to stroke her forehead. "Just eat what you feel like." I glanced down to where Apollo sat beside her on the couch. "You can either rest here or in your room. I'll put Apollo outside if he bothers you."

She patted his head. "He's fine."

I turned the TV on and gave her the remote. "I'm going to make myself a sandwich. I'll join you in a minute."

Minutes later, I sat down at my desk with my lunch and turned on my laptop. I sent a short note to Sara, telling her I'd be back on Monday, and quickly scanned the rest of my e-mails.

I read a message from Yang Cai and sighed. I'd probably have to schedule a trip to China for later in the year. I sent back an e-mail, promising to follow up with more details after the weekend.

When I looked up, Abby was asleep. I stood, took her plate, and set it on the table, tucked a blanket around her curled body.

Then I sat back down and watched Abby sleep.

The weekend before, I'd wanted to show her the library. What if I took it a step further? What if I gave her the library? She rarely took advantage of her freedom at the kitchen table—if I gave her an entire room, would she feel more at ease?

There was only one way to find out.

She woke up at three thirty, blinking awake, glancing around and smiling when she saw me.

"Feeling better?" I asked.

"A little." She reached out and swallowed the pain pills I had set out while she slept, then stood and stretched.

"Come with me." I got up and walked toward her, held out my hand. "I want you to see the southern part of the house."

She took my hand without question, and I ran my thumb over the tops of her knuckles. We went down the hallway toward the library.

Would she like it?

I dropped her hand, pushed the double doors open, and stood back so she could enter first.

She gasped.

"I want this to be your room," I told her. "When you're in this room, you are free to be you. Your thoughts. Your desires. It's all yours. Except for the piano. The piano is mine."

Use it, Abby. Please, be yourself. Open up to me.

She walked around the room as if in a daze. Trailing her fingers along the book spines, stopping here and there to read a book title. The sunlight bounced off her hair, illuminating her.

But what was she thinking?

"Abigail?"

She turned around. Silent tears fell down her cheeks.

Was that a good sign?

"You're crying," I whispered, overcome by the emotions she could evoke from me. "Again."

"It's so beautiful."

She liked it. I smiled. "You like it?"

Without a word, she walked back to me and threw her arms around me. "Thank you."

"You're welcome," I whispered into her hair.

Chapter Fifteen

I spent the next two days caring for Abby. Watching her as she rested and making sure she stayed comfortable. She passed time lounging in the library, even eating a few meals sitting on one of the couches, engrossed in one book or another. I joined her occasionally and tried to start a conversation, but she never spoke freely.

Perhaps I'd read too much into her whore comment. If our relationship worked for her, it would work for me. Her needs. Always hers.

On Sunday afternoon, I sat at the small desk in the library, waiting to see if Abby would join me.

Then, there she was. "Everything all right?" I asked. "Do you need something?"

"Yes. You."

She slipped her shirt over her head.

Fuck.

"Abigail," I said, trying to ignore the twitching of my cock, "you need to rest."

She didn't listen. Instead she slipped her pants down and stepped out of them.

I swallowed a moan.

She wanted me. She was asking for sex.

I'd had submissives ask for sex before. Sometimes I agreed. Sometimes I didn't. I walked the line between fulfilling their needs and ensuring they knew I could and would turn them down if I wanted to.

I didn't want to turn Abby down.

But was she ready?

Did she feel obliged to do it because I was taking care of her?

I knew I should probably turn her down. She needed to rest, and I didn't want her to offer sex out of obligation.

If I turned her down, would she ever ask again?

She reached behind her back and unhooked her bra, slowly slipping it off her shoulders. It fell to the floor, exposing more of her body to me—more than she probably meant to expose. There was a purplish blue bruise on her right shoulder.

I decided to turn her down. Explain it wasn't her—that I wanted her badly, but she needed to rest.

She hooked her thumbs into the waistband of her panties and slipped them over her hips.

I stood up. I couldn't turn her down. Not when I'd given her this room and told her to be herself in it. Not when she stripped herself naked before me. If she wanted me, wanted the pleasure my body could give her, she would have me.

I opened the desk drawer and took out a condom. Slowly, I walked over to where she stood. We would have to take it easy. I'd let her take control and set our pace.

I placed my hands on her shoulders, careful of the bruise, and trailed my fingers down to her hands, delighting in the goose bumps that rose to meet me. My eyes took in the soft angles of her form—the curve of her neck, the swell of her breasts, the slope of her belly. I gently took her hands and slipped the condom inside her fist. Her eyes questioned me.

Oh, Abby. I could never turn you down. Not for anything. My body is yours. Take it.

I brought her hands to my chest, showing her I wanted her to lead this time.

"Okay," I said simply.

She opened her hand, glanced at the condom, and gasped. A smile lit her face.

She'd thought I would turn her down.

You almost did.

Idiot.

The condom fell to the floor and she worked to unbutton my shirt. When she took it off and ran her hands down my chest, I had to bite the inside of my cheek to keep from moaning. As much as I'd wanted to touch her in the hospital, I hadn't thought about how much I needed her to touch me. To have her hands on me.

She walked around and cupped my shoulder blades. I closed my eyes to better focus on her hands and sucked in a breath when she kissed my back.

Then she licked, *fucking licked*, her way down my spine, ending with a gentle kiss, right at the spot above my pants.

I clenched my fist to keep from grabbing and throwing her on the couch.

Her way, West. Let her do it her way.

Her way would kill me.

She dropped to her knees before me and stroked the front of my pants. I couldn't hold back the moan that escaped from my lips. She unbuckled my belt and, very deliberately, stroked me again before working on the button of my pants.

I dropped my eyes to watch as she unzipped me, dragging her fingers roughly over my hardened cock. My eyes damn near rolled back in my head and I wasn't even naked yet. I forced myself to watch, to enjoy her response, her actions. She licked her lips right before she pulled my pants and boxers down. Then she took me in her mouth.

Holy shit.

Her mouth.

Her mouth on me.

She wrapped her arms around my backside and pulled me toward her so I went deeper. I nearly fell over, but steadied myself by resting my hands on her head.

Gentle, I reminded myself. She's still sore.

She sucked me a few times. I hoped fervently that she'd stop soon or else I'd come in her mouth. I wanted to be buried inside her when I came. Deep inside, with my arms wrapped around her, bringing her the pleasure she deserved.

Right when I thought I might have to pull her to her feet, she released me and ripped open the condom. With sure hands, she rolled it onto me, giving my cock a hard squeeze. She stood up, smirked, and pushed on my chest.

The couch. She wanted me on the couch.

And, fuck it all, I think she's going to ride me.

My cock grew so hard, it hurt, but I walked backward and fell onto the soft leather of the couch. Abby straddled me.

Hell, yes.

Her breasts bounced right before my eyes. I couldn't help it. I leaned over and sucked one into my mouth. Umm. I'd forgotten how damn sweet she tasted. I swirled my tongue around the nipple, feeling it grow hard in my mouth.

She reached up with her hand and pushed on my chest, bringing me back down to the couch and pulling herself from my mouth. Then she rested one hand on either side of me and lifted her hips.

My cock ached with the need to be inside her.

She moved slowly, too damn slowly, lowering herself so I felt every inch of her as she took me inside her tight heat.

"Abigail." I rocked my hips, wanting her deeper, but she held back, continuing her slow descent. Finally, though, finally, I was buried inside her and she held still.

She groaned and my eyes flew open. Was she hurt? Her eyes were closed, her mouth open, and her head slightly back.

She was fine.

Thank the sweet heavens.

She started moving, and I knew nothing but the feeling of her above me, riding me, working herself on me. I couldn't keep my hands off her, couldn't keep from touching her, from making sure she was fine. Her slender waist, the strength of her spine, her beautiful breasts—she was more than fine, and—for that moment—she was mine.

She was mine.

I took her by the waist and helped her move, thrusting harder. I wouldn't last much longer, but I wanted her to come first. My balls ached with the need to release, but I held back, urging her on, until she moved faster.

I thrust quicker then, pushing her toward the release I knew was close. She held still, muscles clenching around me as her orgasm swept through her body. I gave one last thrust and held deep within her as I released into the condom.

Her body shook, and I wrapped my arms around her. Sex had probably not been a good idea. I rolled us over so she was sandwiched between me and back of the couch—if one of us fell off, it would be me.

I ran my hand down her back and her eyes opened.

"Are you okay?" I asked.

She still breathed heavily, but she smirked at me. "I am now."

She was a vixen.

Then she ran a hand down my chest and I knew vixen didn't come close to describing her. So, just in case she had any other ideas and her hand decided to continue its way south, I stopped her. Took her hand and held it to me. "I want you to take it easy the rest of the day."

She agreed, but with a smug little satisfied grin.

I had to get away from her or else I'd be tempted to keep that satisfied grin on her face by taking her again. I pulled away and stood up. Then I made the mistake of looking at her again—naked and sprawled out on my couch.

Her couch.

Damn. Think of something. Quickly.

I glanced at the clock. The game. I needed to prepare for the game. "What type of pizza do you like?" I asked, keeping my attention focused on the buttons of my shirt.

She didn't say anything, but I could see that she was hesitating.

Right. Pizza. Not exactly on the meal plan.

"The Clark family has to eat pizza and hot wings during every play-off game," I explained. "If we didn't and the Giants lost, Jackson would disown us."

She took her time rolling off the couch. "I've heard of crazier superstitions. Just don't tell me if he wears the same unwashed underwear."

I almost laughed, but then remembered the player who *did* wear the same unwashed underwear. "My lips are sealed."

"Mm." She ran her fingers through her hair. "Mushroom. I like mushroom pizza. And bacon."

"Mushroom and bacon it is. Picnic on the floor sound good?"

Her fingers stopped and her eyes got a faraway look.

Was she thinking of us? On the floor?

"Abigail?"

She blushed. "Yes?"

Fuck. She was thinking of us on the floor.

"Picnic on the floor would be great," she said.

In more ways than one, I wanted to say, but knew we had already done more than we should. "You will take it easy the rest of the day," I told her.

Before the game started and right before the pizza and wings were due to be delivered, I went up to my bedroom to get Abby's collar.

The locked box I'd put it in on Friday held several pieces of my mother's jewelry. I unlocked it and slipped the collar into my pocket, but instead of putting the box away, I took out a few pieces.

Nestled together sat a pair of diamond earrings I remembered Dad giving to Mom one Christmas. Santa brought me a bike that year, so I didn't remember much of the earring exchange. I closed my eyes and thought back, trying to remember. They kissed. I remembered that. But I thought kissing was gross, so I'd turned back to the bike.

I put the earrings away and picked up Dad's wedding band. Strong and sturdy—just like him. Would he have been proud of the man I turned out to be? Of how I'd built his company? I slipped it onto my left ring finger. It looked odd, so I took it off and placed it back in the box.

Next I lifted Mom's wedding band and held it between my thumb and forefinger. So tiny. I slipped it on my pinkie and it didn't go halfway down. Funny. I remembered Mom being so much bigger than me. But of course she would have seemed big to a young boy.

I took the ring off and was about to place it in the box when something caught my eye—there was writing inside the ring. I brought it close and squinted.

But I send you a cream white rosebud.

I spun the ring around, looking for more, but that was it. Nothing else.

A cream white rosebud?

I picked Dad's ring back up. Yes, there was writing inside it as well.

With a flush on its petal tips.

I set it down. What did that mean?

The doorbell rang.

I sighed and left the box on my bed. The rings would have to wait.

———

Abby knew nothing about football, so in between bites of pizza and wings, I did my best to give her a tutorial.

She finally shook her head and sighed. "I'm a lost cause. I'll never understand football."

I wanted to tell her that she'd have plenty of time to learn the rules of football, that football was huge to my family, but I didn't want to make any assumptions. She might not want my collar back. She might look at it and tell me to go hang myself.

Or she might be like Beth and tell me she didn't want the collar because she wanted "more."

I broke into a cold sweat.

What if Abby wanted more?

Could I give her more?

I watched as the clock ran down on the TV. When it hit zero, I got up and turned it off. I didn't even know who was winning.

Abby sat on the floor, propped up by a mountain of pillows. I stood by her side and took the collar from my pocket.

"Elaina gave it to me at the hospital," I said.

She looked me in the eye. "Elaina knows. But it wasn't me. I didn't tell her."

I'd been right. I wondered how she knew.

But Abby was so honest; she couldn't lie.

Unlike you. Lying bastard.

"I thought as much. Thank you for being honest." I hesitated, worked up my courage. "I want to make sure you still want this. I wasn't sure . . ." I looked into her eyes. "You know more now. Maybe you don't . . . want it."

"I want it."

She rose to her knees and dropped her head.

She wanted it? No questions asked? Nothing?

"Look at me, Abigail."

She lifted her head and I dropped to my knees before her— something I'd never done to a submissive before.

Relief surged through me. She wanted the collar. She wanted me. I fastened the collar around her neck, then ran my fingers through her hair.

Damn. She looked so good wearing my collar.

My cock twitched and I moved toward her.

One kiss. One little kiss wouldn't hurt anything.

I stopped myself. She didn't want more. She wanted what we had, and because of that, I couldn't kiss her. I needed to hold myself back.

I sighed.

Damn it all.

I stood back up and turned on the game.

Chapter Sixteen

It was Wednesday and therefore a fitting day to drop by and see Abby at work. The first time I ever saw Abby had been on a Wednesday. Outside of a library to be exact.

I told myself over and over again that this was just part of my Super Bowl plan. Maybe if I said it enough, I'd start to believe it. Having sex in public, much less a football stadium, was a huge deal. I needed to ease her into it slowly. First step: having sex in the just-as-public-but-much-less-likely-to-get-caught-there Rare Books Collection of the New York Public Library.

But it wasn't just step one in my plan. I knew that. All I had to do was slip a hand inside my coat's inner pocket to know my Wednesday visit meant more. For there, tucked away where no one could see, was a perfect cream-colored rose. Just a hint of pink on its tips.

After Abby left my house on Sunday, I'd Googled the inscription I found inside my parents' wedding bands. The lines came from a poem by John Boyle O'Reilly. Fascinated, I'd walked down to the library and found a slim volume of the poet's work.

I spent the evening reading over several of his poems, but I found myself going back so often to the poem "A White Rose" that by the end of the evening, the book fell open naturally to that page. I pondered the meaning of the poem, wondered if Abby would have heard of it.

If I gave her a cream-colored rose tinged with pink, would she guess the meaning behind it? Would she know that my feelings were growing beyond what I'd ever imagined I could feel? For anyone?

Did I want her to know that?

Fear pounded through me. It was so new. So unexpected. But as scared as I was, I had to know. Had to know if Abby might possibly feel the same.

In the end, I'd decided to bring a rose to the library with me. I would keep it hidden in my coat pocket. Determine later if I wanted to give it to her.

I stood inside the library for a few minutes, watching Abby work. Her back was to me and she had a stack of books by her side. She worked diligently. A man approached her at one point, and she laughed at whatever it was he said. When he left, her hand trailed absentmindedly to her throat and she fingered my collar.

A wild and shocking spurt of jealousy shot through me.

He'd made her laugh. Had I ever made her laugh? I thought back to our short time together. No, I never had.

With renewed determination, I walked to the front desk.

"I need to see something in the Rare Books Collection," I said to her back.

She didn't even turn around. Didn't even acknowledge it was me. "I'm sorry. The Rare Books Collection is open by appointment only and we're a little short-staffed at the moment. I really don't have time this afternoon."

Maybe she didn't recognize my voice.

"That's rather disappointing, Abigail."

She spun around at my use of her name. Her mouth hung open and her eyes were wide with shock.

"Is this really such a bad time?" I asked.

"No. But I'm sure you have the exact same books at your house."

Yes, but you aren't there. You're here. I thought that much would be obvious.

"Probably," I said.

"And," she said, not really listening to me, "someone will have to escort you the entire time."

Which is my entire point, Abby. I want you and I want to have you in the public library. Right now.

"I certainly hope so. It'd be rather boring in the Rare Books Collection all by myself." I took a glove off and shoved it in my pocket. "I know it's not a weekend. Please feel free to tell me no. There will be no repercussions." *You can turn me down.* I gave her a weak smile. "Will you escort me to the Rare Books Collection?"

"Ye-ye-yes," she said, as understanding dawned in her eyes.

"Excellent."

But she didn't move. She stood staring at me. Like I'd disappear.

"Abigail, perhaps that lady right there"—I pointed to another librarian—"can work the front desk while you are . . . otherwise occupied?"

I wanted there to be no misunderstanding—if she left the front desk for me, I'd be buried inside her in less than ten minutes.

"Abigail?"

"Martha?" she said, slipping out from behind the counter. "Watch the desk for me, will you? Mr. West has an appointment to see the Rare Books Collection."

That's my girl.

We walked toward the stairs. Abby stayed slightly in front of me, and I took a minute to admire her very fine ass.

"Just for my education," I said, focusing my attention on the curve of her backside, the way it moved as she walked, "does the Rare Books Collection room happen to have a table?"

"Yes."

Of course it did.

"Is it sturdy?" I asked.

"I suppose so."

"Good. Because I plan to have more than books spread out for me."

We reached the top of the stairs and walked down the hall to a set of double doors. She reached into her pockets and then fumbled with the keys she withdrew. Finally, she found the correct one and unlocked the door.

"Oh, no. After you," I said when she pushed the door open.

I locked the door behind us. While taking off my coat, I glanced around the room. In the middle of the room stood a waist-high table.

That one.

But I took my time and walked around the room, running my fingers over the other tables, pretending to read a few titles. I did everything deliberately, giving Abby more time to think about what we were going to do.

"This one," I said, pointing to the table I'd picked out. The one standing at just the right height. "This one is exactly what I had in mind."

Abby had a sly grin on her face.

"Strip from the waist down, Abigail, and hop onto the table."

She moved quickly, and I watched her bare ass as she climbed onto the table. Damn, I couldn't wait to bury myself deep inside her. My erection grew just thinking about it.

I unbuckled my belt. "Very nice. Put your heels and ass on the edge of the table and spread those pretty knees for me."

The sight of her, legs spread and waiting, made my balls ache.

I grabbed the condom from my pocket and slipped my pants off. I took my time, making sure Abby watched everything. Again, very deliberate. I rolled the condom on, resisting the urge to stroke myself.

"Beautiful," I said, because she was. Because she was beautiful in her submission and beautiful offering herself to me.

I slowly made my way to the table and spread her knees farther apart.

"Tell me, Abigail," I said, wrinkling my brow, studying our positions as if in deep concentration. "Have you ever been fucked in the Rare Books Collection before?"

Her body shook with anticipation. I grabbed her hips tighter.

"No."

I looked up at her. "No, what?" I wanted to hear it—either *Master* or *sir*. Either one.

"No, sir."

I pushed forward, entering her slowly. "Much better."

Her eyes closed when I held still. She bit her bottom lip with a small moan, and I knew I couldn't wait any longer. I thrust roughly, entering her deeply.

I took her hips and pulled her to me. "Lean back on your elbows, Abigail. I'm going to fuck you so hard, you'll still be feeling it Friday night."

She leaned back, hair falling to the table as she did so, arching her back and taking more of me inside.

I pulled out and thrust again. The overhead light caught the diamonds on her collar and the stones winked at me.

Mine.

She was mine.

She wore my collar.

Mine.

I thrust again and she lifted herself up to take me deeper.

Maybe I never made her laugh, but I could do this to her— make her needy and aching, then fill her, build her need before finally letting release overtake her. Bring her to the mountaintop and watch as she flew.

"You're mine," I growled, thrusting into her again.

She spread her legs wider, taking me farther inside.

"Mine. Say it, Abigail."

Tell the world.

"Yours."

I kept a steady pace, thrusting into her as she repeated it over and over.

Yours.

Yours.

Yours.

Mine.

Mine.

Mine.

She let out a little moan and pushed up on her heels again and I knew she was close. I thrust again and felt her explode around me. I kept driving into her, pressing toward my own release. Then I held still and allowed it to wash over me, coming hard into the condom.

I pulled out of her, pressing my forehead to her abdomen and catching my breath. Sweat glistened on her body. I kissed a drop away.

"Thank you for escorting me on my tour of the Rare Books Collection," I said, in between kisses to her belly.

She dug her fingers into my hair and I stifled a groan.

"Anytime," she said.

I kissed her belly one more time, wanting to kiss her lower, but not wanting to tempt fate.

Later this weekend, I told myself. You'll have plenty of time.

I slowly pulled back and slipped my clothes on. Abby hopped down from the table.

Once we were dressed, she took the condom from my hand. "I'll take care of this," she said as we headed out into the corridor.

"I'll see you Friday at six." I slipped a hand inside my coat pocket, making sure the rose was still there.

"Yes, sir."

The front desk was vacant when I reentered the main section of the library. I took the rose from my pocket.

Should I leave it? Would she even get it? I was a man leaving a rose for a woman. It was no big deal.

Except that it was.

"Find everything you needed, sir?"

I spun around. Martha stood before me, smiling.

"Uh, yes," I stammered. "Everything."

Martha looked down at the rose and raised an eyebrow. "Oh, you shouldn't have."

"It's for Abby."

"Of course it is."

Did she know what we'd been doing?

"I was going to leave it right here for her." I set the rose on top of the books Abby had been working with.

"John Boyle O'Reilly?"

Caught.

It was too late to take the rose back. Abby would know.

But what would she know? That I left a rose? That it matched one described in a poem? So what?

My knees trembled.

I could always play it off. Pretend it was nothing. Unless . . . Unless she wanted it to mean what I wanted it to mean. What did I want it to mean?

Acting far calmer than I felt, I plucked a petal from the rose and winked at Martha. "Of course."

Chapter Seventeen

On Friday night, Apollo started barking at the sound of the cab pulling up the drive. I shushed him and looked out the window. "Ready to see Abby?"

He cocked his head to the side and whined. I carried the dinner plates to the table and went outside to meet Abby.

I opened the front door and watched her walk up the stairs. She wore a thick brown sweater that matched the brown of her eyes. Her gaze locked with mine and I smiled. Did she get the rose? Would she say anything about it?

Probably not.

But I wanted so badly to know what she thought about it.

"Happy Friday, Abigail."

Her eyes lit with excitement. A good sign, surely.

I led her inside and pulled a chair out for her. This was her time. Her time to ease into the weekend, to voice any concerns, ask any questions.

She didn't say anything, but occasionally her eyes would glaze over with a faraway look. What I wouldn't give to know what went on inside that beautiful head of hers. Maybe one day I'd ask what she was thinking. But for tonight, it was time to move upstairs.

I hated that Abby's first taste of a spanking from me had been for punishment. Earlier in the week, I'd thought back on our first weekend—to our time in the playroom. She'd thoroughly enjoyed the riding crop. I knew I needed to spank her again. For fun this time—the pillows were already out on my bed.

"How are you feeling today?" I asked. She would take the question one of two ways—she'd either assume I was asking about the accident or that I was referring to my statement on Wednesday about how sore she'd still be this evening.

"Sore in all the right places," she said, smiling.

Excellent.

"Abigail," I said with mock surprise. "Have you been a naughty girl this week?"

She blinked at me in confusion.

I looked at her, gaze unwavering. "You do know what happens to naughty girls, don't you?"

Her mouth opened a bit and she shook her head.

"They get spanked."

Fear clouded her face. "But I did the yoga and I got my sleep and did the walking instead of jogging, just like you said." She stopped talking and chewed her lip.

Damn it. Of course she was scared—which was why this was so important.

"Abigail," I said as soothingly as possible. "How many types of spankings are there?"

She didn't answer. She just continued to look at me with a confused expression.

"Three," I said, wanting her to understand my logic. "What was the first one?"

Come on, Abby. Remember for me.

I knew the second she remembered the word *erotic* because her eyes lit up with anticipation, replacing the fear and confusion.

Oh, yes. This would be fun.

"Get your ass upstairs."

She bolted from the table.

I took our plates from the table and set them in the dishwasher. Since Apollo had been outside before dinner, I let him follow me up the stairs, leaving him outside my bedroom and closing the door behind me as I entered.

Abby stood naked by the bed, waiting for me. Her hands hung by her side, and I noted the faint tremor running through her body. Again, her obedience struck me. I'd expected it, of course, but somehow, coming from her, it always meant more.

I unbuttoned my shirt. "On your stomach over the pillows."

Pillows tonight. No whipping bench. Neither one of us was ready for the bench to be brought out again just yet.

She climbed onto the bed, showing her beautiful bare ass to me. I took a condom from my pocket and set it beside her on the bed.

Damn, she looked hot. Lying there. Waiting for me.

I slipped out of my pants and walked to the head of the bed. Making sure she watched, I pulled out a tie-down and took her hands. "We can't have you trying to cover yourself, can we?"

I secured her wrists, gave a gentle tug to position her on her elbows, and stepped back. Sheer fucking perfection, I thought, letting my gaze travel across her vulnerable form.

I climbed up behind her on the bed and cupped her ass. "Have you been using your plug, Abigail?"

She didn't tense up like she had before. She simply nodded.

"Good," I said, taking her legs and spreading them to give her a more stable stance. "I want you open for me." I ran a finger along her exposed slit. "Look at this, Abigail." I licked the evidence of her arousal from my finger. "So slick already. Does the thought of me turning your backside red excite you?"

She didn't answer, but the same tremor I'd noted earlier was still evident. She wanted this. I rubbed the sweet spot of her ass, brought my hand back and smacked her three times in quick succession. She moaned.

I struck her again, watching as my hand left a faint pinkish tinge on her skin. "The good people of New York pay your salary so you will work in the library, not sneak off into the Rare Books Collection." I moved my hand each time, making sure I didn't cause any unnecessary pain.

Only pleasure this time, Abby. Only pleasure.

She moaned again and thrust back against me.

I grabbed her ass and squeezed, feeling her arousal as my fingers dipped lower. "You're so wet."

I licked the tips of my fingers again and then pulled back to slap her pussy.

She moaned harder.

Hell, yes.

"Do you like that, Abigail?" I asked, smacking her again.

I didn't expect her to answer. I struck the soft flesh between her legs one more time. Any more might cause pain, and I didn't want that for her. With firm strokes, I worked on her backside again, spanking until the skin before me was an even shade.

"Your ass is a beautiful shade of pink." I shifted so she could feel my hardness. "Soon I'll do more than spank it. Soon I'll fuck it."

I couldn't wait anymore and I doubted she could either. I ripped the condom open and rolled it on my erection. With one move, I pushed into her.

She moaned.

I pulled out, aching to slam into her. "No noise tonight or you can't have my cock." I spanked her again. "Do you understand? Nod if you do."

She nodded frantically.

"Good." I thrust inside her once again, just as she pushed back to take me deeper. "Greedy tonight, aren't you?" I asked, entering her wet heat. "Well, that makes two of us."

I grabbed her hips and began a steady rhythm—thrusting as

hard and as deep as possible. She responded in kind, working her inner muscles to clench my cock with each stroke into her. I looked down to where we were joined, watched as I slid in and out of her.

Wonder what she would do if I . . .

I slipped a hand between our bodies and rubbed her clit. She arched her back, her massive orgasm triggering my own.

She slumped off the pillows and I lowered myself to her side, taking the condom off and placing it on the floor. I ran a hand up her torso, skimmed her breast, and rubbed her shoulder to make sure she wasn't putting undue pressure on her arms.

She was fine.

"I don't believe I saw everything I wanted to on Wednesday. Perhaps you would be so kind as to set up an appointment for me to visit the Rare Books Collection again this coming Wednesday?" I looked up to her. "One thirty?"

"Yes, Master," she agreed with a wicked grin.

"Oh, Abigail. How very, very naughty." Her face flushed, and I rose to my knees to untie her. "I think that calls for a little reward. What do you think?"

I pushed the pillows out of the way and shifted her body so she rested on her back. "I asked you a question, Abigail—what do you think of a reward?"

"Whatever would please you, Master," she whispered.

I stretched her arms above her head once again and retied them. "Whatever pleases me," I mumbled under my breath.

I moved down her body, trailing my hands as I went. First along her arms and across her collarbone, down to her breasts, rubbing her pebbled nipples, then skirting her stomach until I came to her thighs. I spread them apart. "Guess what would please me now, Abigail."

She bit her bottom lip.

"This, my naughty girl." I blew on her clit. "It would please me to have you come on my tongue. Show me how much you love your reward. Don't hold back."

I licked her hard and deep, working my tongue into her. She lifted her hips from the bed with a small cry. I nibbled on her tender skin, alternating between tiny nips and rougher bites. With my fingers, I rubbed her clit, starting slow, but eventually getting faster. Her breaths came quicker and she lifted her hips against me.

"Oh, please," she moaned as I sucked her clit into my mouth, swirling my tongue around it.

I lifted my head. "Louder, Abigail. I don't have any neighbors."

To help her along, I thrust two fingers inside her and twisted them. She cried out in response.

"Better," I said, lifting her hips to my mouth once more and licking her again as my fingers worked themselves deeper.

Her lower body tensed, and I looked up to watch as she came. Her back arched. I switched so my fingers caressed her clit, while my tongue slipped inside. The sudden change of sensation sent her over the edge, and she came hard against me.

I set her thighs back onto the bed, watching her pant. I blew on her sensitive flesh, and she moaned as aftershocks shook her body.

"I trust you enjoyed your reward?" I asked, crawling up her body and releasing her arms.

"Yes, Master, thank you," she said, eyes closed, still trying to calm her breathing.

I rubbed her arms, starting at her shoulders and making my way to her wrists. I leaned down to whisper in her ear, "You can thank me soundly next Wednesday."

After my shower, I turned the light in my bedroom off and waited. I wasn't sure what I was waiting for—Abby hadn't mentioned the rose all night. Maybe Martha hadn't said anything to her. I felt like a teenager working up the courage to ask a girl out on a first date.

Fucking send her a note, West. Do you like me? Check "yes" or "no."

I listened for noises down the hall. Nothing.

What do you think she's going to do? Bust into your bedroom and say, "Uh, excuse me. Did you mean anything by the rose you left?"

I sat up and punched the pillow.

Idiot.

What I needed was a nice, long jog. Or the piano. Either one. I got up and started pacing, walking from my bed to the window and back again. Apollo lifted his head from the floor, sighed, and jumped up to rest on the bed.

That's right, even your dog thinks you're crazy.

I knelt beside the bed and ruffled his fur. As I stood up, I heard the faint creaking of Abby's door.

I held my breath. Counted.

She wasn't coming to my room. Where was she headed?

The answer knocked the breath from my body.

The library.

Chapter Eighteen

She was headed toward the library. I was willing to bet anything. For four seconds, I contemplated staying in my room,
but I couldn't. I knew I had to join her. Just to see. To see if I
would find her curled up asleep on a leather couch or standing in
the poetry section with my John Boyle O'Reilly volume open in
her hand.

If she found the poem, she would find the rose petal. I'd stuck
it inside, marking the exact page, on Wednesday night.

Would I see confusion or longing in her eyes?

I stood by the door and took a deep breath.

Right before I left my room, I stuck a condom in my pocket. It
never hurt to be prepared, I decided, remembering the last time
Abby and I were in a library.

I walked down the stairs slowly. Taking my time and trying to
decide what I'd do and say once I entered the library.

But that was silly, wasn't it? What I did would depend upon
what Abby was doing. So I decided that for once, I'd go with the
flow. Fly by the seat of my pants.

Hope and pray I didn't crash and burn.

My eyes went directly to the poetry section when I walked
into the library.

And there she was.

She stood in front of a window, and I saw every curve of her body through the sheer material of her gown. She might as well have been cloaked in moonlight, for nothing was hidden from me—not the dusky hue of her nipples, nor the faint flush of her cheeks.

Not the wondrous amazement covering her face.

She knew.

My heart gave an unsteady thump.

I turned on the small lamp by a corner table. "Abigail."

She tucked a strand of hair behind her ear. "I couldn't sleep."

Okay, she didn't want me to know she knew.

"Decided poetry would knock you right out?" I asked and then, in the next minute, I decided to try something new. "Let's play a game, shall we?

> 'She walks in beauty, like the night.
> Of cloudless climes and starry skies;
> And all that's best of dark and bright
> Meet in her aspect and her eyes . . . '"

I gave her a sly smile. "Name the poet."

She tilted her head and crossed her arms. "Lord Byron. Your turn.

> 'I sleep with thee, and wake with thee,
> And yet thou are not there;
> I fill my arms with thoughts of thee,
> And press the common air.'"

She thought of me. She dreamed of me. She wanted me.

Though the hour was late, those thoughts made my body buzz as if I'd consumed a pot of coffee. Unfortunately, I had no idea who the poet was and, judging by her self-assured expression, Abby knew it. "I should have known better than to suggest such a contest with a librarian and English major," I admitted. "I don't know that one."

"John Clare. One point for me."

I closed my eyes and tried to think of a poem, any poem, and grinned when one came to mind. "Try this one," I said.

> " 'Let not thy divining heart
> Forethink me any ill;
> Destiny may take thy part,
> And may thy fears fulfill.' "

Give me time, Abby. I want to try, but I'm so scared I'll screw us up. I don't know what I'd do if I screwed us up.

She narrowed her eyes, and looked . . . worried?

"John Donne," she said.

"Your turn," I said with a nod.

She quoted a John Boyle O'Reilly poem. I recognized it from my Wednesday-night reading.

> " 'You gave me the key of your heart, my love;
> Then why do you make me knock?' "

Her eyes were soft and filled with longing. And I was done for. In that minute, I knew. Whatever happened next. Whatever I did or we did or whatever I screwed up, I was gone. I was hers and hers alone. It scared the shit out of me.

I would have to take it slow. We would take it slow. I had no experience here and didn't know what to expect, or what to do. But we had time, right? We had all the time in the world. Surely we could figure it out.

"John Boyle O'Reilly," I said. "I give myself a point for knowing the next line:

'*O, that was yesterday, Saints above!*
And last night—I changed the lock!' "

Thank goodness she stood across the room. Maybe from there she couldn't see my heart beat. I should have put a shirt on. At least tried to cover myself.

"A tie, then." She walked around behind the couch, slow and calculating, trailing a finger along its leather back. "So, why *are* you visiting my library this time of the morning?"

I came to see you. Just like Wednesday. It's you. It's always you.

"I came to play," I said, nodding toward the piano. I would play, try to calm myself down, make sense of the situation with music.

She sat on the couch. "May I listen?"

"Of course." I walked to the piano bench and took a seat. Closed my eyes and took a deep breath. Abby's song. It was the only tune I could hear, the only tune I could play. The only thing that made sense in that crazy, confusing, what-the-hell-do-I-do-now moment.

As always, I got caught up in the notes, focusing on expressing my feelings. I thought about the softness of Abby's skin, the sweetness of her personality, the delicate gracefulness of her body, the haunting ache she left in my heart—and let it all come pouring out. I knew I'd never be able to put into words what I could say through music, so I let the piano speak for me.

While I played, the clear-cut lines of black-and-white that had always dictated my world started to melt and blend, becoming the most alluring and beautiful shade of gray. For the duration of the song, gray was exquisite. Gray was two people from different worlds coming together unexpectedly and creating something new. Gray took the best parts of us both and fit them together into something larger than we were apart.

The music ended and I sat silently. This was her room. I'd told her to be herself here. I would do no less. In this room, I'd give myself free rein and damn the consequences.

"Come to me," I whispered.

She stood up and walked toward me. "It's my library."

"It's my piano," I said, for we were both giving something up in that moment. Both letting the other see inside the deep secret places of our souls.

My arms slipped around her when she stood before me, and I pulled her into my lap. She felt so delicate and small. I touched her hair, caressed her shoulders, dipped my hands to rest along the curve of her waist. I sighed and dropped my head to her chest, inhaling the delicious scent of her.

She dug her fingers into my hair and, for the smallest second, tried to pull my head up. I wanted nothing more than to lift my head and crush my lips to hers. No, not crush—to savor. To taste her mouth and explore her lips.

But I'd made that rule and I wasn't ready to break it. Too much was on the line to do so. Instead, I turned my head and drew her nipple into my mouth, running my tongue over the gauzy nightgown.

I pulled back and looked into her eyes. "I want you. I want you here. On my piano. In the middle of your library."

Right now, Abby. It's the only way I know to express these feelings I don't understand. And right here, in the one room where we can both be ourselves.

"Yes," she whispered with her eyes closed.

It was the only word I needed. I helped her to her feet and drew the nightgown over her head. Her hands ran down my chest and she untied my pants.

"My pocket," I whispered before she could take them off.

"Pretty sure of yourself, aren't you?" She took the package and ripped it open.

No, I'm not. I used to be sure of myself, but now I'm not. When I'm with you, I'm not sure of anything anymore.

She rolled the condom onto me, her hands confident as they squeezed the base of my cock, right near my balls. I sat us down at the piano bench and she faced me, wrapping her legs around me.

"Play for me," she said as her arms came around me.

Her room. Her desires.

The melody that flowed from my fingers to the keyboard was new—teasing and sensuous, just like Abby in her library. Any other night, I would have pulled paper from the notebook in my bench and written down the notes, but with Abby in my lap, all I could do was play.

In one slow motion, she took my cock inside her.

"Keep going," she said, as my fingers threatened to stop. She rode me slowly, taking me deeper with each pass of her hips. Drawing me farther into the gray that we were becoming.

She nibbled my ear. Her hot breath sent shock waves throughout my body, and then she whispered, "I love the way you feel inside me."

Holy fucking shit. She was talking dirty.

"During the week, I fantasize about your cock—how it tastes." She thrust downward, squeezing her inner muscles around me. I moaned.

She thought about me during the week.

Just your cock, I told myself. *Not you.*

"How it feels," she continued, and it took all my strength to hold on to her. "I count the hours until I see you. Until I can be with you like this."

Forget playing. The music stopped as I wrapped my arms around her, wanting nothing more than to touch her.

She held still. "Keep playing."

I restarted the song. Faster. Desperate.

"I've never felt this way before," she said. "Only you. Only you can do this to me."

It was too much. I couldn't do it anymore. Could no longer deny myself. No longer deny us. No longer wanted to.

I've never felt this way before, she'd said.

She was confused too. This was new to her.

Of course.

My hands dropped from the keyboard and I finally, *finally,* had her in my arms.

"You think it's different for me?" I asked. How was it she didn't know what she did to me? I slipped my arms up to hook them around her shoulders and thrust upward with all my might. "What makes you think it's different for me?"

I count the hours until the weekend. I think about you during the week. It's the exact same for me. I've never felt this way before either.

Stay with me, Abby. Bear with me while I sort this all out.

Please.

She moved faster and my body took over, meeting her downward thrust by lifting my hips to her. Wanting. Needing. She tightened around me, and I slipped a hand between our bodies to bring her the climax she craved. Her hands grabbed and pulled at my hair.

I rubbed her clit faster, desperate to feel her release around me. She lifted her hips, and when I thrust up to meet her, I felt her climax shake her body. I buried myself as deeply as possible and held still as I came hard into the condom.

We didn't move. Reality crashed down on me as my heart slowed.

What had we done? What had I done? Where did our actions leave us? And how did we move forward? A bigger man would have talked about it with her.

I was not a bigger man. And I didn't want to talk just yet. We had plenty of time, I reasoned. I would think about us, about this, later. Later in the week when she wasn't right before me. But for now, I had to get us back on track. Get us ready for the remainder of the weekend.

"Breakfast at eight in the dining room, Abigail," I said, setting her on her feet. I wasn't ready to eat at the kitchen table with her again. Not until I had time to process what had just happened.

"French toast?" she asked, pulling her arms through the gown.

"Whatever you prefer." I discarded the condom and watched as she left the library for her room.

Chapter Nineteen

I spent the next hour in my bedroom, pacing. Again. Whatever had just happened, whatever had just passed between Abby and me needed to be set aside and explored later. After I was better able to wrap my mind around it.

For now, we had the weekend to get through and I had the Super Bowl to plan for. Those plans required I get myself back into the proper mind-set.

More important, Abby needed to get back into the proper mind-set. Eating breakfast in the dining room would be one step toward ensuring that happened. I had changed breakfast time to eight o'clock instead of our normal seven. Had she noticed I wanted her to sleep later than she normally did? To make up for our late night?

I probably should have said something about it. Made it clear what I was doing.

Probably should have said a lot of things.

I wondered, not for the first time, how Paul and Christine did this. How they went from dominant and submissive to . . . *more*. Was it confusing? How did they mesh the two together?

I knew married dominant and submissive couples, of course, but had never questioned the hows and whys before.

Not tonight, I told myself. Later. You have plenty of time.

Proper mind-set.

We both needed a reminder.

Our current relationship had to be the focus at the moment.

I set a pillow on the floor and a tube of lube on my dresser before crawling into bed.

She walked proudly into the dining room the next morning, carrying a plate of her delicious French toast. Still wanting to serve and please me.

I smiled at the thought.

"Make a plate and join me." I ate a piece of sauce-covered toast while waiting for her to return.

Proper mind-set. Get there.

Get her there.

"Last night doesn't change anything," I said once she sat down. "I am your dom and you are my sub."

I kept my voice even and calm. I was a master of control, and this was no different from anything else.

"I do care for you," I said. An utter and complete understatement. "It is not unheard of. It's to be expected, actually."

I had, after all, cared for my previous collared subs. Hell, I'd even cared for Melanie, but what I felt for Abby was . . . intense. Too intense. But I couldn't tell her that at the moment. It was too much, too soon, too overwhelming, and too damn confusing.

"But sex is not the same thing as love." Love? The thought shocked me. Is that what I felt? "Although I suppose many people confuse the two."

As planned, she didn't say a word during breakfast. She sat quietly at the table and ate. I could tell her mind was elsewhere. I felt better about the pillow waiting in my bedroom. Best to remind her of her reason for being here and to do it quickly.

I watched as she finished her breakfast.

"Clear the table and go up to my bedroom," I told her. "I'll join you soon."

She carried our plates into the kitchen. When I heard water running, I took Apollo outside.

My phone rang and I looked at the display. Kyle.

"Good morning," I said.

"Nathaniel," Kyle's mother said. "I'm so sorry to bother you, but I wanted to let you know that Kyle has been running a fever for the last few days. I'm not sure the doctors will let him go to the game this weekend."

My stomach clenched. He'd been looking forward to the Super Bowl all season.

"I'm so sorry to hear that, but let's not do anything hasty. We have tickets in the box, and if he's able to go, your family is more than welcome to fly with me on the jet."

"Thank you. I'll keep you posted."

"You do that." I motioned to Apollo, and we walked back inside. "Tell him I've got tickets to the Yankees headed his way."

"You're too good to him, Nathaniel," she said with a sniffle. "Thank you."

Once inside and up the stairs, I left Apollo outside the bedroom door. Abby knelt on the pillow, watching me.

Yes, last night had been strange, but we were still here. We could still do this. She still wanted this.

The rest would follow in time, perhaps.

I walked to stand before her. "Very nice, Abigail. It pleases me that you anticipate my needs."

I took my pants down and let my erection spring free. With no hesitation, she leaned forward and took me in her mouth.

I slipped my fingers into her hair and slowly worked her mouth. Taking my time. Wanting to get us both back to where we needed to be.

She moved her head in time with my thrusts, matching me as I pulled on her hair. I hit the back of her throat and felt her relax around me, taking me deeper. A tentative hand reached up to cup and stroke my balls.

She felt so good. I knew I didn't deserve her. Didn't deserve the gift of her submission.

But I was a greedy bastard and I was going to take it anyway. Take it for as long as she allowed me to have it.

I moved faster, hitting her throat, and my lips parted in pleasure. It surprised me that I'd been clenching my teeth.

Her tongue slipped around me as I thrust into her mouth. My hands tightened in her hair and I drove faster toward my climax.

I wouldn't warn her of my impending release. I'd wait and see how she reacted, if she picked up on my body's clues. I thrust deeply, ejaculating down her throat.

She didn't miss a drop.

I loosened my grip on her hair and sighed. Yes, this was good. We were still good.

I reached a hand down to help her up, wondering if she'd noticed the lube when she entered the room. Did she have any idea what I would do next?

I unbuttoned her shirt, throwing it to the ground. Her pants went next, and she gracefully stepped out of them. Her eyes darted around the room and her body tensed when her gaze fell on the lube.

"Look at me, Abigail," I said calmly, running my hands down her arms to take her hands. "I want you to answer my questions."

It would help her to answer out loud. I pushed her back toward the bed and grabbed the lube from the dresser. "Where are we?"

She scrambled up onto the bed, looking at me with her deep brown eyes. Wanting so much to trust me. "Your room."

I joined her on the bed. "Where in my room?"

"Your bed." She sat down on her heels.

I grew hard again, but I ignored my erection. This was about her. Relaxing her. Preparing her. My desires would have to wait.

"What happens in my bed?" I trailed a hand down her side, watching as her skin broke out in gooseflesh.

Her eyelids drooped in anticipation. "Pleasure."

"Yes." I took her in my arms and gently lowered her onto her back. *Yes. Only pleasure in my bed. Nothing else. Ever.*

I bent my head, nibbling along her neck, while my hands paid homage to her breasts. I gently cupped them and brought my hands up, barely applying friction to her nipples. Her back arched upward.

I moved my lips lower, swirling my tongue into the hollow of her throat, nipping gently. She drew a hasty breath.

"Just feel, Abigail," I whispered. I ran my hand back over her chest and felt her heart racing. Yes. It was working.

I brushed my fingers lower, slipping into her folds, testing her readiness.

More. She needed more.

I slid down her body, my lips moving effortlessly across the smooth skin of her belly. Her hands ran nervously across the bedspread, and I licked her belly button.

So sweet. Every part of her was sweet.

I traced the line of her abdomen, dipping my fingers lower to flit gently over her swollen flesh. Slowly, I pushed a finger inside her; she rocked against my palm.

"Yes," I said, against the expanse of her belly. "Just feel."

I settled myself between her legs and pushed her knees up and out, opening her to me. Her hips bucked off the bed in anticipation.

"Wait," I said, placing kisses up her thigh, making my way to where she wanted me the most. She groaned. "Wait."

I pushed my tongue inside her and licked. I brought my hands under her legs and slid underneath, so her knees rested on my shoulders.

She whimpered.

Oh, yes.

I went back to licking her, tasting the delicious evidence of her arousal while my finger circled her clit. I glanced up. Her hands fisted the bedspread and her body arched as she tried to get closer to me.

I grabbed the lube from beside us. I licked around her clit, almost touching, while squeezing lubricant on two fingers.

This was new, and she had been uneasy every time I'd brought it up. I wanted to make the experience as pleasurable as possible for her. Show her just how much pleasure I could bring her when she trusted me.

I went back to nibbling her pussy. Slowly, I brought my fingers to her lower opening, just enough for her to realize they were there. Stroked her. I took a long lick at her clit, finally giving her the friction she craved while at the same time I pushed a fingertip inside her anus.

She gasped.

"Pleasure, Abigail. Just pleasure," I reminded her. My fingertip moved slowly in and out, going deeper with each push.

I matched my finger to my tongue, working her two ways. My teeth nipped a bit harder, and once more, her body climbed near release. I heard her choppy breathing and saw her legs tremble.

"Relax," I whispered, because what came next would hurt a bit. I gently slipped a second finger inside, making sure never to stop with my tongue.

"Oh." Her body tensed.

I lightly drew my teeth over her clit, and she rocked her hips in to me. Both my fingers moved inside her now, gently going deeper, gently stretching.

"Oh, ah," she panted.

"That's it, Abigail," I encouraged. "Let it go. Let me make it good."

Trust me.

She wouldn't last much longer. Her entire body trembled. Just another pass or two, I decided, licking her clit. On my next lick, I pulled my lips back and grazed her with my teeth, pushed my fingers inside as far as I could.

She gave a startled yelp as she climaxed around me.

I gently placed her body on the bed and watched in satisfaction as the aftershocks of orgasm rippled through her.

I'd done that.

I'd brought her that pleasure.

Me.

Her eyes slowly opened and she gazed at me in wonder.

"Are you okay?" I asked. Of course, she didn't need to answer; it was obvious just how okay she was.

"Mmmmm," she mumbled, rolling onto her side.

I gathered her to me. "Can I take that as a yes?"

She gave a weak nod and tucked her head into my chest.

Something I'd never experienced swept over me, and I pulled her tightly to me. I never wanted to let her go.

Chapter Twenty

On Wednesday when I arrived at the library, Abby stood at the front desk, but this time she faced the door. Dare I hope she waited for me?

"Good afternoon," I said.

"Good afternoon, sir," she said with a seductive grin.

Damn. Just hearing her call me *sir* made me hard.

"Is this still a good time?" I didn't want to assume anything. Wednesdays were outside of our original agreement, and I wanted her to feel free to turn me down. I hoped beyond hope she wouldn't turn me down, but the choice was still hers.

"One thirty." She pointed to the computer screen. "Says so right here."

I looked deep into her eyes, unable and unwilling to hide what I felt, but certain it didn't come across. "Will you accompany me to the Rare Books Collection?"

"Yes," she whispered.

I held out my hand. She took it and walked around the desk to stand before me. I stood for just a second, staring at her.

She wore a long-sleeved dress today. It hugged her curves, showing the outline of her breasts, the swell of her hips.

"You look very nice," I said.

She smiled at the compliment. "Thank you."

It felt odd. Standing there, making normal everyday conversation while we both knew where we were headed. What we would be doing in just a few minutes.

I looked around for Martha. She stood by the newly released biographies.

"I've got you covered, Abby," she said, waving from her post. "You go on."

Abby dropped my hand. "Follow me."

Like I could do anything else.

We walked up the stairs, Abby leading the way. When we reached the room, she opened the door and entered first. I closed and locked the door behind us. She waited.

"Take your shoes off," I said.

She obeyed, slipping off one shoe and then the other. Fuck. Even Abby taking off her shoes was sexy. She reached down and, with one finger, slipped off the tiny socks that had been hidden by her shoes. I swallowed a moan. Abby taking off her socks was even hotter.

"Turn around," I said, and she turned to face the table from last week. I came up behind her and placed my hands on her shoulders, feeling how she trembled in anticipation. "To the table," I said, gently pushing her.

She walked forward until she stood before the table. I pressed up against her, making sure she felt my erection.

I bent her over, running my hands down her arms as she complied. I pushed her to her elbows and pressed my cock harder against her.

"I like this dress you're wearing," I said, stepping back and running my fingers across her backside. "Just a simple little piece of fabric between us."

She pushed back against me and I grinned.

Naughty.

"Know what else?" I asked, slipping my hands under the hem of her skirt and lifting it up, exposing the pale pink panties underneath. I slid them down her legs. "We don't need to use a condom anymore."

My middle finger skimmed her entrance. She was already aroused. "I'll be able to feel everything when I slide into you." I unbuckled my pants and pushed them down. With one step, I pressed against her again. "And you'll feel all of me."

She moaned.

"You like that, don't you, Abigail?"

"Yes, sir. Please."

I pushed two fingers into her, testing her arousal again. "Have you thought about me all day? Imagined me doing this to you?"

She gasped and nodded.

I pumped my fingers slowly. "Tell me. Tell me with words."

"I've thought about you all day, sir. Imagined what you would do."

"While you were supposed to be working?" I asked in mock surprise, pulling my fingers out.

"Yes, sir."

I spanked her once. "Shame on you." I spanked her again and she moaned. "You're such a naughty girl, Abigail." I spanked her one last time and leaned over her back to whisper in her ear, "Do you know what happens after naughty girls get spanked?"

"No, sir."

I gave her ass another slap. "They get fucked."

She mumbled something under her breath.

"Reach out, grab the end of the table, and brace yourself." I watched as she wrapped her fingers around table's edge. "You have no idea how fucking hot you look like this."

I took my cock in one hand and teased her, pressing it against her, but never going further. She whimpered. With one smooth stroke, I slid into her and we both moaned.

It had never been like this. Never. With my previous subs, I had been fine with our weekend arrangements. Never before had

I felt the need to seek them out during the week. Why was every-thing so different with Abby? Why couldn't I last from Sunday afternoon to Friday night without seeing her? Without touching her?

I began thrusting, blocking everything out of my mind except her. The feel of her around me. The way her muscles clenched each time I plunged into her.

Our bodies slammed against the table. We really shouldn't have been doing this. It could get her in trouble. But I couldn't stop.

As I drove us both toward release, I knew. I could never get enough of her and I could never stop. I should have realized it years ago when it became impossible to stay away from her. Rec-ognized it when she walked into my office weeks ago. Admitted it when I took her for the first time. I was in too deep. Her scent, her touch, her very essence. They were part of me.

Afterward, while we collected our clothes and straightened ourselves up, I brought up the subject of the car again.

"I've been giving some thought to what you said about the car issue."

Fierce determination colored her face, but her voice was calm. "You have?"

I matched her calm tone, knowing I'd made the right decision. "I've decided not to press the issue."

"What?"

"The idea made you extremely uncomfortable, and though part of me still thinks it'd be safer for you to drive, your mental well-being is just as important to me. I won't have you ever think-ing you're a whore."

She looked shocked. "Thank you."

"Give and take, Abigail, that's what relationships are." I turned so she wouldn't she what the next admission cost me. "I appreci-ate you being honest with me about your feelings. I have difficul-ties with that myself."

She jumped from the table. "Maybe we can work on that to-gether."

A cold chill ran through me, but I shrugged it off and opened the door. "Maybe."

I led her down the stairs to the main floor. "We need to be at the airport at four on Friday. If that time doesn't work for you, let me know. You have my number."

"Four o'clock should be fine. I'll call you if there's a problem."

We stood at the front door.

"Until then," I said, lifting a hand to stroke her cheekbone.

Abby didn't call, but Kyle's mom did. His fever hadn't gone down and, as a result, he wouldn't be able to come to the Super Bowl. I talked with him on Thursday afternoon, told him there was al-ways next season and that if the Yankees made it to the World Se-ries, I'd do anything I could to get tickets.

On Friday at four, Abby met me at the terminal where I kept my jet. Her eyes swept over the plane.

"Good afternoon, Abigail. Thank you for making arrange-ments to leave work early."

She took my hand and we walked up the stairs into the cabin. The pilot waved from the cockpit. "We'll be ready for takeoff shortly, Mr. West."

I led her to our seats and she sat beside me, with her hands in her lap. Every once in a while, she glanced around the cabin and then smoothed out nonexistent wrinkles from her pants.

Of course she felt anxious, I thought. All this was new to her. I needed to reassure her, let her know what to expect. After all, we would be in public and with my family and close friends for most of the weekend.

We had a few minutes before the flight attendant entered the cabin.

Abby took a deep breath and closed her eyes.

"I want to discuss the weekend with you," I said, and her eyes opened. They were full of gratitude. "Your collar will remain on. You are still my submissive. But my aunt and Jackson have no need to know of our private life."

I wondered if Felicia had told Jackson anything, but then decided she must not have. Her boyfriend's cousin's sex life probably wasn't too high on the list of topics Felicia wanted to discuss.

"Also, you will not address me as *Master*, *sir*, or *Mr. West*. If you try, you can avoid using my name at all." I met her eyes. It was a delicate balance, living as we did, but it was doable. "You will not call me by my given name unless it is unavoidable."

She nodded.

"Now, today," I said, unable to keep the excitement from my voice, "you're going to learn about control."

The flight attendant walked into the cabin. "Can I get you or Ms. King anything, Mr. West?"

"No. We'll page you if we need anything."

She smiled. "Very good, sir."

"She'll spend the remainder of the flight with the pilot unless we need her," I said, unbuckling my seat belt and holding out my hand. "Which we won't. Come with me."

I took her into the plane's small bedroom and closed the door. "Remove your clothing and get on the bed."

Abby had marked wax play on her checklist as "willing to try." Wax play with real candles could become very intense, and I didn't want to move too fast by using my usual soy or paraffin candles. Instead, I'd ordered a special candle wax for her. This one turned to body oil when heated. Its melting point was lower than either soy or paraffin. It would be the perfect way to start her out.

As Abby undressed, I went over to the small dresser and

took out the battery-operated warming bowl I'd turned on earlier. The candle had melted nicely. I dipped a finger in the wax to test the temperature. Just right. I slipped a blindfold into my pocket.

Abby lay naked on the bed. Perfect submission. Not a bit of hesitation. Even with a flight attendant within calling distance.

I set the bowl on the floor, then took Abby's arms and stretched them out so they were spread wide. "Stay like this and I won't tie you up."

I took the bowl and sat on the edge of the bed. "This is a battery-operated hot plate. Normally, I'd use a candle for this, but the pilot won't allow it. And rules are rules."

And, most of the time, I followed the rules.

A tremor of excitement ran down her body and her nipples hardened. Her breath hitched. Just for a second.

Oh, yes. She wanted this.

I took the blindfold from my pocket. "This works better blindfolded."

I secured the blindfold around her head, once more gauging her reaction, making sure she was willing to proceed. Her body shook with anticipation. "Most people find the sensation of the heat very pleasurable."

I tipped the bowl so a drop of wax landed on her upper arm. Just a drop, on a safe area of her body—the best place to test both the wax and Abby's response. She hissed, but it was a sound of pleasure. I rubbed the oil into her skin, explaining what it was and how it worked.

As I tipped the bowl again, another drop fell on her opposite arm, and I gently rubbed it in, massaging her. Her skin felt soft and supple under my fingers. I slowly dribbled more oil onto her, always gentle, always taking my time, making her body more relaxed, slowly igniting the fire within, rewarding her trust with every pass of my hands. Showing her how absolute submission would be rewarded. It was an important step in my plan for the evening—to work her body into an absolute frenzy so she would enjoy what would happen after dinner.

I glanced at the clock. We had another ten minutes before she needed to get dressed. How would she react to this next part? I dipped my finger into the bowl, collecting melted wax, and dropped it on her nipple. A half gasp, half moan escaped from her.

I rubbed the oil in, palming her breast in the process. "Do you like the heat, Abigail?" I whispered in her ear, flicking another drop on the other nipple.

She moaned.

Yes, she liked it. She craved it.

I tipped the bowl a little more, and a stream of wax dribbled over her breasts. Then I set it down and straddled her, massaging her body with long, firm strokes. Up and over her breasts, along the line of her torso, rubbing the oil in thoroughly. Once more doing my best to relax her, to build her anticipation.

"Control, Abigail. To whom do you belong? Answer me."

"You," she whispered.

"That's right. And by the end of tonight, you'll be begging for my cock." If I did everything right, that was. "If you're good, I might just let you have it."

I slipped off the bed to give her time to relax and to anticipate the night to come. I walked to one of the windows and looked outside. We were approaching the Tampa airport—Abby needed to get dressed. My flight crew had stocked the plane's refrigerator before we took off. I took out a cold bottle of water and returned to the bedroom.

Abby was still on the bed, arms stretched out, eyes covered.

I sat beside her and ran a finger over her shoulder. "Abigail."

She turned her head to me.

I untied the blindfold and she looked at me with her trusting eyes. "It's time for you to get dressed." I took her arms, brought them close to her body. "I brought you some water."

She licked her lips and I smiled.

We checked into our suite at the hotel and I showed Abby her room. We had an hour before we met everyone for dinner, plenty of time for us to get ready.

She appeared in the suite's living room later, dressed and looking absolutely beautiful.

"Very nice, but go back and remove the hose." Her eyes questioned me. "I want you totally bare beneath that dress. I want you to go out knowing I can lift your skirt and take you anytime I want."

I wouldn't, of course, not tonight. Not with my family with us, but Sunday . . . All bets were off in the football stadium.

She turned and went back to her room, returning moments later.

"Lift the skirt."

Her fingers fumbled, but she pulled the hem of the skirt up to her waist and I saw that there was nothing but Abby beneath the dress.

"Now we're ready," I said, holding out an arm to her.

Jackson had secured reservations at a downtown steakhouse. An excellent plan, considering how crowded the downtown area was. We pushed our way through the mass of humanity, finally making it inside the restaurant.

Everyone sat at a large table in the middle of a large room. Many of the patrons ogled Jackson, but no one approached him. After Abby and I sat down, she made polite small talk with Linda and Elaina. While she talked naturally with everyone, I sat back and watched her, joining in the conversation to tease her only when she told them our flight had been "fine."

The waiter poured us both wine. Excellent. Abby needed to be very relaxed by the time we made it back to our room. I, on the other hand, would limit myself to one glass. I made it a point never to drink more than a glass of wine before a scene. Besides, what I planned tonight would take my utmost concentration; I didn't need alcohol clouding my judgment.

I glanced to my side. Abby read over the menu with a troubled look on her face. I rebuked myself for not thinking of the menu beforehand.

"The lobster bisque is excellent," I told her. "So is the house Caesar. I would also recommend either the filet or the strip steak."

Relief washed over her face and she closed the menu. "Lobster bisque and filet, then."

Conversation carried on easily and everything went smoothly until Todd discovered that Abby had graduated from Columbia. For several minutes, they compared favorite hangouts and memories. A warning bell sounded in my head. I needed to change the subject and change it quickly. What if Todd remembered my obsession with a Columbia coed? Would he bring it up to Abby? I wasn't sure. Elaina and Todd loved to tease me. He just might. I interrupted the conversation, contributing stories about my favorite Dartmouth haunts and memories. Elaina joined in the conversation, and slowly but surely, talk drifted away from the powder keg of Columbia.

I breathed a sigh of relief and turned my attention to Abby. It was time for part two of my plan.

Chapter Twenty-one

The conversation around the table continued as I slipped my hand under the table and brushed Abby's kneecap. Caressed. Stroked. Teased.

"Abby," Linda said, "I keep meaning to call you for lunch. This coming week isn't good. How would the next Wednesday work for you?"

I kept caressing her knee, interested in her answer.

"Wednesdays aren't good for me," she said. "There's a patron who comes in every Wednesday to see the Rare Books Collection— and we don't let researchers in unaccompanied, so I have to be there with him."

I almost laughed.

My aunt sighed. "That must be a bit tiresome, but I suppose that's what customer service is all about."

"I don't mind," Abby said. "It's refreshing to find someone so thorough."

I slipped my hand farther down her knee. She thought I was thorough? I couldn't wait to show her just how thorough I could be.

"How would that Tuesday work?" Linda asked. "He doesn't come on Tuesdays, does he?"

My heart leaped with the knowledge that my aunt wanted to spend time with Abby. I rejoiced at how my family accepted her.

"Tuesday will be fine," Abby said.

"It's a date then." Linda smiled.

I slipped my hand back under the table and stroked Abby's knee again. Todd asked me a question about the upcoming local election. He knew I couldn't keep out of a political debate. I didn't mind, though—it kept everyone's attention away from where my left hand was.

You're mine, I told her with my fingers. Even at this table. I can do anything I want.

And she'd let me.

I passed the bread to Felicia. I wouldn't call her attitude toward me warm, not by any stretch, but she wasn't as cold as she had been at the hospital. Maybe she'd come around eventually.

I dropped my hand back to my lap and inched closer to Abby. Working up to her thigh this time. Just to remind her. Elaina asked me a question and I picked my silverware up when I answered her. I wanted to remind Abby not to draw attention to herself. What we did was between us. In the eyes of my family, we would be just another couple eating dinner.

But below the table . . .

I reached my hand down to touch her knee again, but her legs were crossed. We couldn't have that. I pushed on her upper leg and she spread her knees for me.

Much better.

I inched my way up higher, drew up the hem of her skirt, and went back to eating my salad.

I glanced around the table—Felicia laughed at something Jackson said; Linda was talking with Elaina.

I let my mind wander to my plans for the remainder of the night. I'd left instructions for the hotel to—

Abby's choking brought me back to the present.

I slapped her back a few times. "Are you okay?"

"Fine," she said, her face flushed with embarrassment. "Sorry."

"You know," Todd said from across the table. "You're not supposed to pat people on the back when they're choking. It could be dangerous."

"Thank you, Dr. Welling," I said.

"Just trying to help."

"Don't try so hard next time."

He gave me a teasing grin. "What's the fun in that?"

The waiter cleared our dishes. Abby's wineglass was empty, so I poured her a bit more. I wanted her completely relaxed.

"What do you read besides poetry?" I rubbed her upper thigh. We were just any other couple showing affection.

Sure we were.

She took a sip of wine. "Just about anything. Classics are my favorite."

I smiled. Because I'd enjoyed our poetry game in the library last weekend, I spent some of my lunch hour this past week reading quotes from famous authors. I couldn't wait to show off.

"A classic," I said, "is a book which people praise and don't read. Mark Twain."

Abby smiled an evil grin. Her eyes flashed with delight. "I cannot think well of a man who sports with any woman's feelings. Jane Austen."

Yes, I supposed I was sporting with her a bit. But Jane Austen to my Mark Twain? She did know about the animosity between the two, right?

I smiled at her. "But when a young lady is to be a heroine, the perverseness of forty surrounding families cannot prevent her." *Take that.* "Jane Austen."

She didn't even blink when I slid my hand up her dress, but calmly quoted, "Truth is more of a stranger than fiction. Mark Twain."

Oh, she got me. She got me good. I laughed, drawing the attention of the table. "I give up." I set my hands back on the table. "You win. But only this round."

"Hey, you two," Elaina said to Abby and Felicia. "Linda and I are hitting the spa tomorrow for massages and facials and to get our nails done. We made you both appointments as well. Our treat. Will you come?"

I had called Elaina earlier in the week to suggest it. She'd surprised me, though, by saying she'd already booked treatments for Abby and Felicia.

"How very thoughtful." I stroked Abby's knee again. I hated to spend the day apart from her, but I did want her to get to know my family. "I suppose Todd and I can amuse ourselves with golf. Would you like to go with the girls, Abigail?"

"Sure. I'd love to."

Of course she would. What woman wouldn't want a spa day? I looked across the table to Todd.

Todd winked at me. *You're going down, West*, he mouthed.

I'm going to kick your ass all over the green, Doctor, I mouthed back.

"Try it," he said.

Linda coughed.

"Sorry," I said.

I went back to eating, keeping watch on Abby from the corner of my eye. She smiled throughout dinner and talked with everyone at the table. Nothing shy or self-conscious about her. She was beautiful.

She was also strung so tightly, it wouldn't take much to make her pop.

I didn't want that. Not yet.

I left her alone as we ate our entrées. I was next to her. It was enough. I could damn near feel every time she took a breath—the slight shift of her body, the gentle rise and fall of her chest.

She laughed at something Felicia said, pushing her hair back with an elegant sweep of a hand. My mind wandered, and I pictured those hands on me.

I wanted those hands on me.

I poured her more wine and watched as she took a sip.

I wanted that mouth on me.

I reached for her hand, placing mine on top, and brought them both to rest on my erection. Very slowly, so as not to capture the attention of anyone at the table, I lifted my hips and thrust into her palm.

See? I wanted to say. *See what you do to me?*

She did. She bit her lip and left her hand against me. It was too much. I gently squeezed her hand and placed it back on her leg.

Soon, I promised. *Soon.*

I hoped we would both last.

I teased her more in the car—flipping her skirt up to her waist to expose her bare sex to me.

"You're going to mess up the interior of the rental." I ran a finger along her slippery entrance and thrust inside. "Wet as you are."

From the corner of my eye, I saw her bite the inside of her cheek. Yes, my plan was working. I bet she'd beg me right now if I asked her to. I played with her for few more minutes, gliding my fingers through her folds, toying with her clit.

I pulled up to the valet and slipped Abby's skirt down before anyone came to the car. After handing the keys over, I went to the passenger's side and opened the door for Abby. She took my offered hand and once more we became any other couple.

We rode up to our suite alone in the elevator. I squeezed her ass, just because I could, and she responded with a moan.

"Not yet," I told her.

I kept my hand at the small of her back while we walked to our door. She trembled with anticipation.

Oh, Abby, I thought. *You have no idea what I have planned for you tonight.*

Or maybe she did.

I opened the suite door and let her enter first. The hotel had followed my directions—all the lights had been turned off except for a dim light in the living room. I led Abby down the short hall to my bedroom, where one lamp gave a dull light. The bed had been turned down.

Excellent.

I left her at the foot of the bed and unzipped my duffel bag. I removed the warming gel and vibrator and placed them on the bed.

Her eyes grew large.

On second thought, maybe she didn't know what I had planned.

"I've been patient, Abigail," I said, speaking firmly, but in a low, soothing voice. "And I'll be as gentle as I can, but tonight's the night. You're ready."

Trust me. I wouldn't do this if I didn't think you were ready.

I walked to the edge of the bed, where she stood—still frozen in shock.

"Undress me," I told her, in part to get her mind on something else.

With fumbling fingers, she slipped my jacket off and ran her hands down my arms. Fuck, I loved her hands on me. She rushed through the buttons on my shirt and threw it to the ground. Then her hands dropped, pushing my pants and boxers down with one shove.

"All for you," I said as my erection sprang free. "Because you did so well at dinner tonight, I'll let you have a little taste."

She dropped immediately to her knees and took me in her mouth. I felt her moan as I thrust into her warmth.

On her knees, she would focus on me. Not so much the items I had on the bed. I hoped she would, anyway. If nothing else, it would remind her that I had the entire night under control. I could lead us both through this. I closed my eyes and turned my attention to her. The feel of her mouth around me, the way I hit her throat, the silky strands of her hair between my fingers.

After a few minutes, I pulled back, not wanting to come just yet. I reached a hand down to help her stand. She wobbled a bit and I hoped she hadn't had too much wine.

"Undress for me," I said. "Slowly."

She stepped out of her shoes, one at a time. Fuck. Why was that so sexy? With her eyes on mine the entire time, she reached behind and undid her zipper. Her left hand came to the top of her right shoulder and slowly pushed the sleeve of her dress down.

I needed to have her strip for me more often.

Once the dress hit the floor, she reached behind her back again and unclasped her bra. Taking it in one hand, she lifted it up and dropped it.

She absolutely glowed in the moonlight. Her body swayed slightly, throwing shadows across the bed.

I sat down. "Touch yourself."

She moved, uninhibited, palming her breasts, rolling her nipples into hard peaks. Pinching one first and then the other. Her eyes closed and she moaned in pleasure, swaying once more.

One hand skimmed down her side and over her belly until she was touching herself, while the other continued playing with her breast. It was the most erotic thing I had ever seen.

"Enough," I said, when she started rocking into her palm. "Come here."

She sashayed toward the bed, and I reached out when she approached me, grabbing her around the waist. She let out a little sigh as I flipped her to her back and straddled her.

I nuzzled her neck, inhaling the scent of her, smelling the sweetness of her breath as she sighed again. My teeth nibbled along the line of her jaw, and she buried her hands in my hair.

My exploration of her body grew bolder. I tasted the hidden skin under her jaw while my hands circled her breasts. Lower, my hands went, pinching a nipple, squeezing her hip as they dipped even lower.

My mouth followed, savoring, as I lapped at the circle of her belly button and teased her swollen clit. Her head thrashed and I knew she was ready.

I moved my way back up her body, still dragging my hands, but softer this time. Gently. Reverently. I nibbled even more softly. She groaned under me. Anxious and wanting.

I slowly turned her to her side, trailing my hands up and down her arms.

You're fine. You'll be fine. Trust me.

I spoke the words with my touch, and she pushed her head back in to me, arching her back.

I took the warming gel at my side and squeezed the slippery lube onto two of my fingers. I dribbled more along the length of my aching cock.

Slowly, so damn slowly, with one hand I made small circles around her clit while my other slid in between her ass to press against her anus. She startled briefly. I assumed it was the temperature of the gel; I hadn't used the warming gel the previous weekend.

Just in case, I slowed down even more and took my time pushing my finger inside, making sure I paid proper attention to her clit. I concentrated on her response, looking for any signs of discomfort. There were none, only a sigh of pleasure as my finger slipped all the way inside.

I repeated my actions with the second finger, wanting to stretch her slowly, prepare her for my cock. She thrust against the finger at her clit, pushing my fingers deeper into her as she thrust back toward me. Still I went slowly.

We had all the time in the world. All night, if need be. I would move at a snail's pace to ensure she enjoyed herself.

She thrust again against my fingers.

Stay with me, Abby.

I removed my fingers and lifted her leg. With one hand, I held my cock against her. My other hand still circled her clit, fingers dipping into her wet folds. I pressed forward slightly, letting her know where I was, what I was getting ready to do.

She held still. Accepting me.

Her body didn't hitch, didn't tremble. She gave no outward signs of distress.

I pushed forward so just the very tip of my cock entered her.

Slowly, I told myself. The urge to shove into her was strong, but I held back, knowing I had to focus entirely on her. I shoved my needs to the back of my mind. Abby had trusted me in this so far, and I would do all I could to reward that trust.

I pushed harder and she gasped. I redoubled my efforts on her clit, holding my lower body still, working her back to an aching need. Pushing forward again as she relaxed. Stopping again. Teasing her once more with my fingers.

I pressed against her natural resistance and, with one gentle push, slipped the head of my cock inside. Again, I felt the urge to thrust the rest of the way in and again I resisted, focusing on the woman in my arms, on the trust she had in me. I would not destroy that trust.

She sucked in her breath.

Damn, she was hurting.

I removed my hand from her clit and found her hand. Took it in mine.

"Are you okay?" I asked.

It was painful, but while I could not totally ease the pain, I could show her I knew. That I would be gentle. That she was cherished.

She sucked in another breath. "Yes."

She wouldn't lie. If she wanted me to stop, I would. If she told me she wasn't okay, I would put an end to the night.

I squeezed her hand and leaned close to kiss the nape of her neck. "You're doing great," I whispered.

The tension left her body with one large sigh, and she melted against me.

I took the vibrator and turned it on. With one arm, I pulled her closer to my chest, leaving my hand between her breasts so I could feel her breathing.

With the other hand, I ran the vibrator down her body, so she would be aware of what I was doing. My body shook with the need to press forward, to thrust entirely within her, but instead, I slipped the vibrator inside her. Her breath hitched as I slowly entered her both ways, pushing my cock farther inside at the same time as the vibrator.

I held her tightly to me, both our bodies strained with effort.

Just a little more. Stay with me, Abby.

Almost.

Then, finally, I was inside.

I let out the breath I'd been holding.

"Still okay?" I asked, surprised at the hoarseness of my voice.

"Yes," she replied in her own hoarse voice.

I held still once again, allowing her time to adjust to the feeling of being filled so completely.

It was utter and complete hell.

Separated by only a thin piece of skin, the vibrator buzzed against my cock, driving me mad with the urge to begin thrusting. The need to thrust. Anything to relieve the burning ache inside.

But her heart pounded under my fingers and her breath came in sharp gasps.

And I would not, *would not*, hurt her.

So I gritted my teeth and waited for her to relax.

I pulled the vibrator out slightly while holding my own body still. Then pushed it inside again as I pulled my hips back. Back and forth I worked the vibrator and my cock—one thrusting in as the other pulled out.

She felt so fucking tight. I groaned as I thrust and the vibrator struck me again. I held her even tighter against me. Her heart raced.

I moved a bit faster, working my body and the vibrator opposite each other. She held still and groaned. I angled the vibrator so it pressed against her clit and was rewarded with a tiny whimper.

I began thrusting faster, pushed the vibrator deeper. She squeezed her muscles around me, and I almost lost it.

Sweat ran down my face as I pushed us both toward climax. Wanting her to draw every conceivable bit of pleasure possible.

She tossed her head and moaned.

I couldn't hold back anymore. I thrust again, and she screamed as her climax threw her back against me. Her muscles clenched around me, drawing me deeper, forcing the vibrator against my cock.

Fuuuuuck.

My release shot through me, and I thrust harder and bit into the tender skin of her back. She screamed again, her second orgasm just as intense as her first.

She didn't move for several seconds, but her heart pounded steadily under my hand and her breathing came in heavy pants.

"Abigail?"

"Oh, God."

"Are you okay?"

She mumbled something but didn't move. I wanted nothing more than to stay exactly where I was and never move again, but I had to attend to Abby. Had to help bring her down, relax her so she wouldn't be quite so sore in the morning. Let her know just how much it meant that she'd trusted me.

"I'll be right back," I whispered, rolling off the bed and walking toward the bathroom.

I turned the dimmer switch on in the bathroom, casting the room in a warm, soft glow, and padded over to the tub. I'd brought Abby's toiletries from my house, and as warm water filled the tub, I poured her body wash in. Within minutes, the bathroom was filled with wet, steamy, Abby-scented heat.

I walked back into the bedroom and found her still lying on the bed in the same position I'd left her in. I slipped my arms under her body and carried her into the bathroom, where I placed her gently in the tub.

She sighed as the warm water enveloped her body. I took a washcloth and dipped it into the water, then squeezed it over her shoulders, washing her gently. Cleaning first one arm and then the other.

I leaned her forward and washed her back. Reverently, I lifted her hair to one side and rubbed her neck, placing soft kisses against the mark I'd left. When I finished with her back, I drew the washcloth over her breasts and watched the soapy bubbles slide between them.

I washed her abdomen next, remembering how it had clenched in pleasure under my hands. Then I dipped my hands lower and pulled her knees up so I could wash her legs.

The entire time, she lay against the back of the tub with her eyes closed. A small smile played along her lips.

I slipped the washcloth between her legs, being as gentle as I could.

"Lift up for me, my lovely," I said.

She raised her butt, and I drew the washcloth lower, washing away the last traces of my release and the lube. Then I pulled the plug from the tub and let the water drain out.

I picked her back up and sat her on the edge of the tub. I draped one towel around her shoulders while I took another and dried her feet. Slowly, I worked my way up, drying every inch of her perfect body.

When I finished, I took a brush from the countertop and brushed her hair with soft, gentle strokes. "You were wonderful. I knew you would be."

She smiled again.

I took the nightgown I had hanging on the bathroom hook and slipped it over her head. Then I picked her back up and carried her to her bedroom.

She was already asleep when my lips brushed her forehead.

Chapter Twenty-two

I woke at five thirty and slipped quietly out of the suite to hit the exercise room downstairs. Before leaving, I stopped by Abby's room. She was sleeping soundly and probably wouldn't wake up before my return.

My thoughts ran back to the previous night, the way she'd melted against me, her complete and absolute trust. The night had been a turning point in our relationship. Now we could start to delve more deeply into our play. I would show her even more pleasure. Make her scream out in delight more often.

When I returned to the suite more than an hour later, I called for room service and took a shower. Before walking back to the living room, I stopped once more in Abby's room and left a cold bottle of water and a couple of ibuprofen. She might be sore when she woke.

The knock on the door sounded as I left her room, and I went to let room service in.

After the deliveryman left, I heard the water running in Abby's bathroom.

Excellent.

While I waited, I sat at the table and ate my own breakfast. Not that I counted, but she stepped into the living room twenty minutes later.

"Come sit down and have breakfast, Abigail."

She sat at the table and started eating.

"Linda and Elaina want you and Felicia up in the spa at nine thirty," I said. "I'm not sure what they have planned, but apparently you won't finish until sometime this afternoon."

She ate silently while I drank another cup of coffee. I wondered what she was thinking. I thought briefly about asking her to spend the day with me instead of going to the spa—I'd beg out of the golf game and we could do something together. But I remembered how I wanted her to spend time with my family and changed my mind.

"Come here," I said, when she finished eating. I walked into the living room and she followed.

I moved behind her. "Elaina and Felicia know of our lifestyle. I'd like to think my aunt doesn't, but even if she does"—I unhooked her collar—"there's no reason to flaunt it in her face." I circled her and stood before her. "You'll get your collar back this afternoon."

Her head dropped.

Was she upset I took it off? Had she wanted to wear it to the spa? Where people might ogle her? Where my aunt would wonder why she insisted on wearing a necklace?

Or maybe . . .

Maybe she didn't want to take it off because of what it represented.

I lifted her chin and stared into her eyes. "You're still mine," I assured her. "Even with this off."

Jackson sat downstairs in the lobby. At least, I thought it was Jackson.

He wore a hooded sweatshirt, dark sunglasses, and a wig made up of dark dreadlocks.

"Hey, man," he said. "There you are."

"What the hell are you wearing?"

"I'm in disguise."

I glanced around the lobby—we were drawing all sorts of stares. "I don't think it's working. You just look like a football player in disguise."

"Yeah, but which football player?" His eyebrows waggled. "No one knows and no one has asked for an autograph yet."

"That doesn't mean the disguise is working. It just means you're scaring people off." I smiled. "But now that I've approached you, maybe everyone else will work up the nerve."

"Damn it." He pushed his hood back, exposing more dreads.

"Did you get hit in the head too many times at practice? What are you doing hanging out here on your own?"

"I wanted to talk to you before I left with the team and you went off with Todd."

I glanced around the spacious lobby. A small cluster of chairs sat in a far corner.

"I've got twenty minutes." I nodded toward the corner. "Let's go over there."

"What's going on?" I asked once we sat down.

"Last night, Felicia and I—"

"Take off the sunglasses. I can't concentrate on a word you're saying when you look like that."

He slipped off the glasses. "Felicia and I . . ."

I could not for the life of me decide where this was going. Had Felicia said something? Did she and Jackson break up? How would it affect my relationship with Abby if they broke up?

"Yes?" I said.

"It was like nothing I've ever done. I mean, we just talked, you know? Talked. Then we walked and we talked some more." He shook his head, like he couldn't believe it either. "She's unbelievable. Like no one I've ever met. 'Course she's smokin' hot as well."

I nodded. I supposed she was hot. If you liked redheads. I thought back to Abby—her lush brown hair, the graceful curves of her body. Felicia Kelly had nothing on Abby King.

"I grew up watching Mom and Dad," Jackson said. "Watched Todd and Elaina fall in love. I mean"—his expression grew serious—"I just never thought I'd find what they had."

I knew exactly what he meant.

"But now," he continued, "whenever I'm with her, I feel like it's there. Like I can reach out and touch it." He shook his head. "I don't know. Maybe I should talk to Todd. But I thought if you understood, if you thought it was possible to find . . ."

Why would he think I knew anything? Me? I was in no position to offer any sort of advice. Especially on that subject. Surely he knew as much. I had no knowledge, no expertise whatsoever on relationships. Which is why the next words out of my mouth surprised us both.

"Of course I think it's real," I said. "That you can find it. And if you've found it with Felicia, I couldn't be happier for you."

Todd beat me at golf. It was a close game, but in the end, as I told him, everyone knew doctors didn't really work. They just played golf all day. Of course he won.

After the game, I asked him if he wanted to go find a drink. I wasn't sure why I'd decided to talk to him—maybe I still felt something of a natural high after the previous night.

Or maybe it was because Todd knew about my lifestyle and I finally felt like I could talk about it with someone close to me. I didn't know. I think I just wanted someone to talk to.

Abby and I were to have dinner with Todd and Elaina later, but dinner was hours away and I didn't want to spend those hours alone in the hotel room. Looking back, that drink with Todd would be both the best and the worst decision I ever made.

We sat down and I thought for a few minutes about how to approach the subject of my lifestyle with Todd. I finally decided to be direct.

"Abby told me you know about our lifestyle," I said after the server took our order.

Todd's eyes bulged out. Obviously, he hadn't planned on me taking the direct approach.

I shrugged my shoulders. "I wanted to get it out there. I don't want it to become the elephant in the room."

He sat back in the booth. "That's some elephant, Nathaniel. Are you sure you want to talk about this?"

"Why not? I have nothing to hide. But let me ask you—how did you find out?"

"Melanie visited a few months ago." He paused briefly and I nodded. "I think it was hard on her, the breakup with you. She wanted to see some familiar faces and, once she saw us, she broke down."

"I knew dating her was a bad idea."

"Why did you do it?"

I raised an eyebrow. "You aren't going to psychoanalyze me, are you?"

He laughed. "You're my best friend. It would be unethical for me to psychoanalyze you." The corner of his mouth lifted. "Although it would be fun."

"Shut up."

"Sorry. I couldn't help it." He grew serious. "Why did you do it?"

"I wanted to see if I could do a 'normal' relationship. It had been a long time."

"How long?" He glanced around the nearly empty bar. "Listen, man, you don't have to answer anything you don't want to. I get too close, you tell me to shut the fuck up, okay?"

I nodded. "Okay. I was in graduate school at Dartmouth. I'd

had a few relationships, nothing serious, nothing too exciting. I wasn't a girl magnet like Jackson. I didn't meet the love of my life in the sandbox like you. Linda never said anything, but I knew she didn't like me being alone all the time."

"You never did bring anyone home."

"I never found anyone I wanted to bring home. I had this friend, Paul, who was a dominant. I went to a few parties with him, hung out some." I closed my eyes, thought back to the early years. "I never looked back. I enjoyed the lifestyle—grew to where I needed it. I've wondered, over the years, if my childhood had anything to do with it."

"Probably not."

"I thought you weren't going to psychoanalyze me."

Todd threw his hands up. "No analysis. Just my thoughts."

"You have a lot of experience in this?"

"No, but I don't think your parents' deaths have anything to do with it. I don't think it's just one thing. I mean, why do some people like green and others blue? It's just the way your brain works."

"You don't think it comes from some overwhelming urge to control everything?"

"Do you?"

I thought about the question. Thought back to my time with Melanie, and to Paige and Beth. And Abby. "No," I said honestly.

"Okay then. There's your answer."

I let out a sigh of relief. "I always thought maybe there was something wrong with me."

"You know better than that."

"I know. I know." I picked through the peanuts the server had brought. "It's just hard sometimes."

"Doesn't look too hard lately." He smiled. "You and Abby, huh?"

I ducked my head, images of the night before running through my mind. "She's . . . not like anyone I've ever been with."

"And that's a good thing?"

"A really good thing." After last night, our relationship would only grow better.

"A really good permanent thing?"

"Hell, Todd, we've been together for only a little over a month. Give me a break."

"Right, right, right." He popped some peanuts in his mouth. "But the potential's there?"

"I don't know. I don't know if I'm cut out for that."

"See that?" He pointed at me. "That right there? I think that's due to your childhood."

"And this—" I pointed at him. "This right here? I think this is when I tell you to shut the fuck up." I smiled so he would know I hadn't taken offense, but that I meant every word.

"Sorry. It's the job. Hard to quit, you know?"

"I don't need a head shrink."

He wasn't paying me any attention. "It's just that when my workaholic best friend brings a new woman around, walks with a spring in his step, and smiles all the time . . ."

"Knock it off, Todd."

"And are those diamonds in her collar?" He wrinkled his brow. "I don't remember any of your other girlfriends wearing diamonds."

"I mean it."

"And you've known her how long? A few weeks?"

I stood up.

"Okay, okay," he said. "I'll stop. Sit down and finish your beer."

I took a long swig and looked at my watch. Still too early for the women to be finished at the spa. Damn. Why had I thought it a good idea for Abby to spend so much time away from me on a weekend?

My mind went back to the night before. How I'd held her in my arms and given her so much pleasure that she screamed.

"I meant to ask you," Todd said, dragging me away from my pleasant thoughts again. "What ever happened to that girl you liked at Columbia? Wonder if Abby knew her."

My mind was still hazy with thoughts of the previous night. That was the only reason I could come up with later to explain my unplanned admission.

"It was Abby."

He set his beer bottle down and leaned close. "Really?"

"Really."

"Wow." He took a drink of his beer, swiveled the bottle. "What did she say when you told her?"

I broke out in a cold sweat.

Fuck.

"I—uh—I—" I stammered.

He raised an eyebrow. "You did tell her you've been somewhat obsessed with her, right?"

"Not exactly."

"What do you mean, not exactly?"

"I couldn't tell her while she was still at Columbia," I said. "I was already a dom and didn't want to corrupt her. I knew we couldn't have a normal relationship. That's why I never approached her."

"But that was six years ago. You must have told her when . . . when she became your submissive."

"I didn't exactly tell her then, either."

"What?"

I had already admitted everything—there wasn't any reason to lie. "I haven't told her." I didn't add a "yet." I wasn't sure I'd ever tell her.

Todd's jaw clenched. "You haven't told her?"

"No. And don't you go trying to be the morality police."

"Wait a minute." He held up a hand. "You followed this woman around for years—"

"I never followed her."

"You damn well might as well have." He sighed. "I knew you were up to no good, but now . . . fuck."

"Stay out of it."

"The hell I will. I won't pretend to know or understand everything involved in this lifestyle of yours, but from what I do know, honesty and trust are two of the most important aspects."

"Exactly," I said. "You don't know, so don't try to act like you do. What have you done? Read a few books? Googled it?"

"I understand this," he said, voice rising slightly. "You've deceived Abby."

"I've never deceived Abby."

"You deceive her every second you don't tell her the truth."

He was right. He was right and I knew it. He spoke my worst fear. Voiced the worries that nagged me as I fell to sleep every night.

You're wrong, the worries said.

Tell her, they insisted.

I'd ignored them and pretended I couldn't hear, but I no longer had that ability.

So I did the only thing I could do—I took the anger I felt at myself and turned it on Todd.

"Shut the fuck up," I said. "You know nothing. Nothing. Everything is going just fine—"

"Fine?" he interrupted. "*Fine?* You think Abby will think what you've done is fine? I've seen her, Nathaniel. I've seen you. That woman is in love, and if you think she's going to be fine when she finds out what you've done—"

"Who's going to tell her? You?"

"I damn well might."

"You wouldn't dare."

"Try me."

We stared at each other for several long seconds, peanuts and beer left untouched at our elbows.

"I can't do it," I finally admitted. Not now. Not anymore. If I told her, she might hate me. And was she in love with me? Damn. I had to get out of the bar. Had to think.

"You don't have a choice," Todd said.

"The hell I don't."

"I love you, Nathaniel. You know that. But I can't stand by and watch you harm her. I was wrong six years ago to remain silent. I won't do it again."

"Give me time," I begged, feeling my world start to crumble around me.

"How much?"

"I don't know."

"You better decide." He slid out of the booth and threw a handful of dollar bills on the table. "Or else I'll do it for you."

"Damn it, Todd."

"It's the only way." He stood by the table. "But I'll keep your secret. I won't tell Elaina."

"Thanks for the small favor," I said with a sneer.

"You'll thank me one day," he said, and turned to leave the bar. "See you at dinner."

I dropped my head to my hands when he left.

Chapter Twenty-three

I eventually made it back to the suite, and since it was still too early for Abby to be back from the spa, I sat on the couch and stared at her collar.

Todd knew.

Todd knew and he would force my hand and Abby would be upset. How else could she react to the news that I'd been watching her? I had lied to her. A lie of omission, true, but a lie all the same. Would she ever trust me again?

I would have to tell her of the way I'd watched her. That would lead to the ridiculous safe word and how I'd deceived her about the lifestyle. She would know I'd misled her.

No, she would never trust me again.

I wouldn't blame her, but . . . I didn't have to tell her. Whatever Todd decided, so be it. Let him do it.

After the previous night, my relationship with Abby had changed, taken a turn for the better. I would not, could not, destroy it. Not after all we'd been through and not over something as silly as a crush.

What did it matter anyway? So I'd watched her. I'd never approached her. I didn't manipulate her. It was no big deal.

Except it was.

Our relationship, perhaps more so than any other, demanded

complete trust and honesty. I knew that. I'd lived that. Abby deserved that.

But I couldn't do it. I thought back to the absolute trust she had given me the previous night and I knew I couldn't look her in the eyes and tell her. I was too much of a damn coward.

After dinner, I'd find Todd and tell him. Abby would remain in the dark. Bottom line.

I picked up the newspaper and skimmed over the first page. Nothing newsworthy. The second page was even worse. I glanced at my watch. She would be arriving any minute.

I couldn't wait to see her.

Finally, I heard the key in the door.

She walked into the suite looking totally and completely beautiful. The spa day had been a wonderful idea—she glowed. Her soft curls brushed her shoulders and her expression was luminous.

"Did you enjoy your day?" I asked.

"Yes, Master," she said and her head dipped slightly.

Fuck. I loved it when she called me *Master*. Why did hearing it from her always make me hard?

I stood up and held out the collar. "Miss something?"

She nodded.

I walked toward her. "Do you want it back?"

She nodded again.

"Say it." I wanted to hear it. Needed to hear it. "Say you want it."

"I want it," she whispered. "I want your collar."

My collar. Damn straight. She wore my collar. She was mine. And I'd be damned if Todd would take her from me.

I slipped her shirt over her head, the bite mark from last night visible on her shoulder. I pushed her hair to one side and kissed the bruise where I'd bitten her. "I marked you last night. Marked you as mine and I'll do it again." I ran my teeth over her tender skin. "There are so many ways I can mark you."

I slipped the collar around her neck. Fuck. The sight of my collar on her made me even harder. I wanted nothing more than to push her over the arm of the couch and fuck her senseless.

Instead, I fastened the collar. "Unfortunately, we have to have dinner with Todd and Elaina. Go change. I have your clothes out on the bed."

I stood by the couch when she returned wearing the cotton dress I'd laid out after she left this morning. "Bend over the arm of the couch, Abigail."

She lowered her body over the couch, resting on her arms, and I lifted her skirt. No panties. I chuckled. "How well you read my mind." I ran a hand over her soft skin. "Too bad. I was looking forward to giving you a spanking before dinner."

Elaina had made reservations for the small waterfront bistro earlier in the week. As we drove to the restaurant moments later, I remembered Abby had eaten red meat the night before. A nice serving of fish would be good for her, so I instructed her to order fish for dinner.

Todd and Elaina were nowhere in sight when we arrived. I waved Abby into the booth while we waited. She picked up her menu and started reading. I looked toward the door, waiting.

Todd entered first and spotted us immediately. Elaina looked troubled. She knew, then, that something had happened. I glanced over to Abby—she was still reading the menu.

I'm not telling her, I mouthed to Todd as he came closer.

His expression grew darker. "Abby," he said in a rough voice.

Abby looked up warily. Shit. Now she knew something was wrong. Todd didn't take his eyes off me when she answered; he kept his stony glare on me.

We all sat down, and the waiter came to take our drinks order.

You need to tell her, Todd mouthed while Abby and Elaina chatted quietly.

I shook my head.

Todd slapped his menu on the table when the waiter left.

"So, Nathaniel," Elaina said, obviously desperate to keep some sort of peace at the table. "Where's Apollo this weekend?"

"At a kennel," I said. I could talk normally. Keep the conversation reasonable. This was possible.

"He's better, then?" she asked. "You can leave him there?"

See? We were talking about my dog. Perfectly reasonable.

"He's made marginal improvements," I said.

"Glad someone has," Todd mumbled.

So much for reasonable.

Fortunately, the waiter arrived with our drinks. "Everyone have a chance to look over the menu?"

Right. The menu. Probably would have been a good idea to decide what to order.

And then I noticed the way the waiter leered at Abby. Fucking leered. At Abby.

"Ma'am?" he asked her. Like he wasn't imagining her naked at that very moment.

"I'll have the salmon." Because I told her to order fish and she always did as she was told. She handed the menu to me.

"Wonderful choice," the obnoxious waiter said. "The salmon's one of our best sellers." Then he fucking winked at her. Fucking winked. At Abby.

I cleared my throat.

"Yes, sir," he said. "What would you like?"

"The salmon," I said, handing him our menus as he wrote Todd's and Elaina's orders down.

He would leave now.

But instead he rocked back on his heels. "You guys in town for the game?"

He said *you guys*, but he looked straight at Abby.

She scooted closer to me.

That's right, loser, I wanted to say. *She came with me. She's sitting with me. When we leave, she'll be leaving with me. And when you're alone tonight, she'll still be with me.*

"Of course. Giants all the way," Elaina said, once more trying to bring peace to the table. Poor woman had her work cut out for her.

The waiter smirked.

"You know," I said. "If you put in our order, we'll get our food faster and get out of here quicker."

Waiter guy finally left after shooting Abby one last glance.

The tension was so palpable when he left, I almost wished he'd return. If for no other reason than to move some of the attention off Todd and me.

Elaina pushed out her chair. "I need to hit the restroom. Abby?"

"Sure," Abby answered, the relief in her voice obvious.

Todd and I stood up as the women got up from the table and we both watched as they walked to the bathroom.

"You're making a damn big mistake," he said when they were out of earshot and we'd sat back down.

"It's my mistake to make."

"Maybe, but when that mistake hurts Abby, it's not just about you anymore."

"The mistake will never hurt Abby, because she'll never find out."

He leaned across the table. "Don't bet on it. When she does find out, and she will, it will go easier if you're the one to tell her. And if you tell her sooner, rather than later."

"Leave. It. Be," I said, leaning across the table myself.

"You're an intelligent, well-respected man," he said. "You built your business on principles of honesty and integrity. You live your entire life by those values. You demand it of your employees. What would you do if you knew I was keeping something from Elaina?"

"I'd trust you to make the right decision. About your personal life."

"The hell you would," he said, voice rising. "You'd tell her yourself."

I slammed my fist on the table. "You won't take her from me."

"Damn it, Nathaniel," he said. "I don't want to take her from you. I want her to stay with you because you deserve the trust she's placed in you." His eyes shot to the side. "I suggest you calm yourself down. They're coming back."

I had steadied my breathing by the time Abby and Elaina made it to the table. While I was certain Abby knew something was up, I also knew she would never question me about it. My friends were, technically, not her concern.

I couldn't remember a bite of anything I ate, though at the end of dinner, my plate was clean. I remembered only arguing with myself.

Tell her.

Don't tell her.

Lose her.

Keep her.

The choices went around and around in my head. I didn't know what to do. Couldn't decide.

Later, as we rode up the elevator to our room, I knew one thing—in this one moment, for this one night—she was mine.

I slammed the door behind us as we entered the room. Grabbing Abby by the arm, I spun her against the door and slipped my hands up her dress.

"Damn it. Damn it. Damn it." I breathed in the scent of her. She was mine. Her smell was mine. Her body was mine. Her damn soul was mine. I jerked the dress over her head and ripped her bra off.

She stood naked before me.

I pushed my pants off with one move and then ripped my shirt open and off, not caring that buttons flew everywhere. Abby stared at me with wild, wide eyes.

I picked her up and pushed her against the door. "Next weekend, you're not wearing a bit of clothing from the time you arrive until the second you leave my house."

I was so far gone, we weren't going to make it to the bedroom. I was going to take her there. Against the door.

I slipped two fingers inside her. Thank goodness she was already wet. I wasn't in the mood for foreplay. "I'll take you whenever and wherever I want." I twisted my fingers and she moaned. "I'll fuck you five times Friday night alone."

Because I fucking can.

"I want you waxed bare next weekend, Abigail. Not a bit of hair left."

She blinked.

"Spread your legs and bend them," I told her. "I'm not waiting any longer."

With no hesitation, she parted her knees and bent them. I dipped below her, guiding my cock into her in one smooth motion and thrusting up at the same time.

Fuck. Yes.

I pulled back and thrust into her again, slamming her into the door. She gave a small hop and wrapped her legs around my waist.

My eyes rolled back into my head.

But still it wasn't enough. Over and over, I sent us both pounding into the door—working myself deeper and trying my damnedest to possess her completely.

Her arms dipped from their place around my neck to my back.

"Yes," I shouted as her nails scratched me. *Mark me. Possess me.* "Damn it. Yes."

I knew then that as much as I might possess her, she also possessed me. That thought, the thought of her owning me, sent me into more of a frenzy. I thrust into her again, wanting to force myself deeper.

She groaned in my arms.

"Not yet, Abigail." I pounded her into the door again, slipped even deeper inside. "I'm not finished."

I would never fucking be finished with her.

She groaned again as her muscles tightened around my cock.

"You better not come before I tell you," I said, thrusting into her again. "I brought the leather strap."

Her nails ran down my back again, and I felt the marks she left behind. Knowing she'd marked me increased my fury and we hit the door again. She moaned once more. I knew I was being unfair not letting her release. She just felt so fucking good. I bent my legs lower and angled my hips to hit a different place inside her on my next thrust. She groaned in response.

That's right, Abby. Your moans and groans are for me and me alone.

I thrust into her three more times and I knew I couldn't hold on anymore. Not to her. Not to myself.

She whimpered again, the strain of trying so hard not to climax evident in her expression.

"Now," I said in a whisper.

She let her breath out in a sigh of relief, her orgasm causing her to spasm around me. Over and over, her muscles constricted my cock. I dropped my head and bit into her shoulder as I came deep within her, unable to hold out any longer.

With trembling arms, I held her pressed again the door while I struggled to get my breathing under control. She leaned her body against me and I pulled back to look at her, brushed the hair away from her face.

She looked thoroughly and completely fucked.

I propped her up and staggered into the closest bathroom. Several towels and washcloths hung from the sink's towel bar. I took one and soaked it in warm water.

When I made it back to the doorway, Abby hadn't moved. I parted her legs and washed away the traces of her arousal and my release. Gently. After last night and what had just happened, I was certain she was sore. Or would be.

I washed her, looked into her soft, trusting eyes, and knew what I had to do.

I had to tell her.

"I'm sorry," I said, and I wasn't sure what I was sorry for—the rough sex, the truth I hadn't told her, the pain she would feel when I did tell her. All of it, maybe. All of it and then some. "I have to go out. I'll be back later." Because in that moment, I couldn't look her in the eyes knowing I'd lied to her.

Chapter Twenty-four

As I jogged the next morning, I thought back to the previous evening and my conversation with Todd. I'd knocked on his door after leaving Abby. He had looked surprised, but agreed to talk with me in one of the hotel's lounges.

He had seemed relieved at my decision to tell Abby, but I knew the hard part would be the actual telling. Todd had talked with me for several hours, saying repeatedly that I'd made the right decision. He even seemed content with my timeline—I'd tell her within three weeks.

The entire time, the thought that ran through my head most was *I no longer have all the time in the world. I have three weeks.*

Three weeks.

I'd left Todd and gone down to the lobby to play the hotel piano. Of course, the only song that came to mind was Abby's song. I'd counted as I played:

Three weeks.

Twenty-one days.

Five hundred and four hours.

I still wasn't sure how to tell her, but I knew one thing—I sure as hell wouldn't be telling her anything this weekend.

I'd played for hours, letting the music take over my mind, just as Abby had taken over my soul. With each note I played, I felt myself grow calmer and calmer. By the time I'd returned to the suite, I'd felt more like myself than I had in weeks.

I told myself I was still the same man I'd always been. The same exact one. Except now I had Abby in my life. I would tell her the truth sometime in the next few weeks and . . .

Well, I didn't know what would happen then. I didn't want to think about that yet. We still had this weekend to get through.

I finished my jog and returned to the suite. Stepping into Abby's room, I noted she was still asleep. Good. I probably had time to shower before she woke up.

By the time she made it into the suite's living room, I had showered and dressed for the day. She stood in the doorway between the dining and living room, wearing pants, a gray sweater, and a devilish grin.

I let out a sigh of relief. At least she didn't appear scared after the rough sex of the night before. She looked . . . refreshed . . . replete . . . and totally fuckable.

She danced over to the coffeepot, poured a cup of coffee and, God help me, wiggled her ass.

I almost spilled my coffee.

The panty lines, idiot. She's showing you her panty lines.

Abby wanted a spanking.

My cock went hard in less than three seconds.

"Abigail," I said calmly. "Do I see panty lines?"

She held still for just a second. Just stood there and let me admire her ass.

I placed the coffee cup on the table in front of me. "Come here."

She turned, devilish grin still in place.

"You're wearing panties." I walked behind her. "Take them off. Now."

With trembling hands, she undid her pants and pushed them to the floor. Her panties joined her pants.

"Over the arm of the couch, Abigail."

She draped herself over the couch and lifted her butt in the air.

I gave her ass a sharp slap. "No more panties the rest of the weekend." I slapped it again. "When I finish, you will go to your room and bring them all out to me." Another one. "You'll get them back when I say." Another slap. "Which won't be next weekend either." Slap. "I told you last night what will happen next weekend."

I slapped her ass again. Her skin was turning such a lovely shade of pink. I slipped a hand between her legs. Fuck, she was wet. Her butt pushed back toward me.

"Not this morning." I spanked her again. *Believe me, I wish we had time.* "Put your pants on and bring me what I asked for."

She stood slowly and redid her pants. Her expression was one of intense longing.

Next weekend, Abby. I promise. We'll have all the time in the world.

At least for the next three weeks.

She gave an impish grin and trotted back to her room, returning moments later with an armful of panties.

"Planning on staying in Tampa long, Abigail?" I said, taking them from her.

"I like to be prepared, Master," she said with lowered eyes.

Fuck.

When we entered the ballroom for brunch, I glanced around the room. Many of my business associates were present. Several of Jackson's friends stood together talking and, in one corner, Felicia talked with Linda. Another couple stood nearby.

I sighed.

Melanie's parents. And they had seen us come in.

I didn't want to leave Abby's side, but I knew I had to at least chat with them and I preferred to do so without Abby present.

Abby knew I'd dated Melanie. I suspected she also knew Melanie was not my submissive. But Melanie's parents didn't know of my lifestyle. At least, I didn't think they did.

"We're a bit early." I dropped my hand to Abby's lower back. Just in case the Tompkinses had any doubt, I wanted them to know I was with Abby. Word would get back to Melanie, of course. Perhaps she would find some closure in that.

"I need to go speak with a few people," I told Abby. "Should I take you over to Felicia and Linda or are you okay here?"

"I'll be fine here." She glanced over to where Elaina and Todd stood.

She wanted to talk to Elaina. Probably to see if Elaina would tell her anything about last night. It was a nice try, but it wouldn't work. I knew Todd would not betray my confidence.

I brushed my finger along the top of her arm. "I won't be long."

The Tompkinses watched as I approached and I swallowed my grin. I hadn't spoken to them face-to-face since I broke things off with Melanie.

"Ivan," I said, shaking her father's hand. "How are you?"

"Nathaniel." He spoke far more civilly than I would have, had the situation been reversed.

"I'm so glad you were able to come," I said with a sideways glance at Melanie's mother, Tabitha.

"Well." He slapped my back. "We decided to let the past stay in the past. Sometimes things don't work out."

I noticed Tabitha didn't seem to share the sentiment.

"How is Melanie?" I asked.

"She's still in New York," her father said.

Yes, of course she was still in New York. Had she not been in New York, she wouldn't have told Elaina and Todd about my lifestyle and perhaps I wouldn't have the three-week deadline staring me in the face.

"I wish her every happiness," I said.

Tabitha gave a *humph* in reply.

"We know you do, Nathaniel," Ivan said. "Our families have had a long and happy relationship. That won't change just because things between you and Melanie didn't work out."

"Ivan, look," his wife said. "Isn't that Samuel over there?"

"Why, yes. Yes, it is." He turned back to me. "You will excuse us, won't you, Nathaniel?"

"Of course, sir."

He winked at me. "I'll come by later to meet your new lady friend."

I felt relieved at that. Tabitha would tell Melanie and then she could move on with her life. Find someone who could love her the way she deserved.

After they left, I chatted for a few minutes with some colleagues who had traveled to Tampa for the game. The box was under my name, but Linda had rented the ballroom. It was no accident on either of our parts that Melanie had not been invited to the game or the brunch. I'd told Linda to invite her parents, hoping to make peace between us. Looked like that mission had been accomplished.

Linda approached me as I moved toward Abby. "How did it go with them?"

"As well as could be expected. Ivan was fine, but I think Tabitha is still upset she can't order the monogrammed towels."

"I told her as much weeks ago. I even mentioned Abby—"

"Linda."

"Now, now." She patted my arm. "She might as well learn sooner rather than later. Melanie will never be a West."

"I'm not marrying anyone."

"Why don't you go rescue Abby? Elaina has been chewing her ear off since you walked in."

I collected Abby from Elaina and Todd, and the four of us wandered to the buffet line. Felicia joined our table when we sat down. Jackson, I knew, would be with the other players until the game was over.

"Nathaniel," Felicia said as she sat down. It was the friendliest she'd ever spoken to me.

She'd hate me for what I'd done to Abby. If she ever found out I'd watched Abby for years . . . Even if Abby forgave me, Felicia never would.

"Felicia," I said, acknowledging her greeting. I had three weeks. For three weeks, I could pretend all was well. "How's Jackson doing?"

She chatted for several minutes about Jackson, the game, the players she'd met the previous night, their wives. I could see what Jackson liked about her. She did have a certain . . . something that fit well with him.

But, of course, she was no Abby.

"How long have you worked at the library, Abby?" Todd asked.

My head shot up. What the fuck?

She speared a piece of pineapple with her fork. "At the public library for seven years, but I worked at one of the campus libraries before that."

"You did?" he asked. "I wonder if I ever saw you. I spent a lot of time in the campus libraries."

I kicked him under the table. *What the hell?* I mouthed.

Fortunately, Abby didn't see. "I don't know," she said. "I'd probably remember you."

"One would think," Todd said, and I kicked him harder.

Fuck off, I mouthed.

He raised his eyebrows.

Elaina looked from her husband to me and back again. I schooled my features, knowing Abby would be looking as well.

Todd cleared his throat. "You like the public library better than the campus one?"

"The people are a lot more diverse," Abby said. She smiled, but I could see that she'd picked up on the undercurrent of tension at the table. "Plus, college students can be a bit obnoxious. Did I ever have to tell you to tone it down or to stop ripping pages from the reference books?"

Todd laughed and the tension evaporated. "No. I definitely would have remembered that."

Elaina asked Felicia another question about Jackson, and the conversation drifted seamlessly back to the Super Bowl.

Todd got up to refill his plate and I went with him.

"What the hell was that?" I asked him.

"Just helping you out." He lifted a piece of bacon from the silver serving tray. "This look crispy enough to you?"

"I don't care about the damn bacon." I watched as he lifted another piece and put it on his plate. "Help me how?"

He moved on to the scrambled eggs. "If Abby remembers a pseudo-stalker from years ago, it makes your job easier."

"The hell it does."

"You might want to put some food on your plate, or else she'll know you got up only to bug the shit out of me." He held out a spoonful of eggs. "Want some?"

"Why not."

He spooned the eggs onto my plate. "Look, you want me to stay out of it, I'll stay out of it. Just say the word."

"Stay out of it," I growled.

"I'm out."

True to his word, he didn't bring up Columbia or libraries for the duration of the brunch and I didn't have to step on his foot again.

When I entered the box with Abby, I noticed the duffel bag in the corner. I bent down. Yes, it was the bag I'd requested be delivered. Two blankets, tickets to the upper middle section, a ziplock bag, and a short skirt would be inside.

I closed my eyes and focused on the upcoming plan.

Sex in a public place. Abby had marked it as "willing to try" on her checklist.

She was finally going to get a chance to experience it.

I was thankful for the unusually chilly Florida weather. Had it been a normal February, my plan would never have worked—at least not at the Super Bowl. I'm sure I would have thought of some other way to introduce Abby to the joys of public sex, but this way . . .

Would be unforgettable.

Throughout the first half, she watched the game and chatted with Felicia and Linda. Every once in a while, she'd glance my way, a shy smile playing across her lips.

I couldn't even say what the score was. I was too wrapped up in the beautiful brunette at my side.

Minutes before the second quarter ended, I took her hand and led her to Linda. I explained we had something to do and we'd be back later. Abby didn't even question me. Didn't say a word as I picked up the duffel bag.

"My plan? Starts now."

She looked up in confusion.

I handed her the bag. "Go change. I have an extra ticket in the bag. Meet me there before the halftime show starts."

Without a word, she took the bag and walked off to the bathroom.

I checked my pockets, made sure I had the condom and ticket, and then walked toward our new seats. I went a few rows higher than I needed to—I wanted to watch her as she arrived.

I didn't have to wait long before my wish was granted. She walked to the new seats, shuffling her way through the crowd, looking around as if trying to find me. She had the skirt on. I could have stayed and watched her all night, but it was cold. She needed the blanket around her.

And I needed her.

I sauntered down the stairs, anxious to be back by her side. To have her near me.

I sat beside her and put my arm around her, wondering how she would react to what I would say. "Do you know that three out of four people fantasize about having sex in public?"

She grew still.

I licked the inside of her ear, watching as she shivered. "The way I see it"—I gave her ear another lick—"why fantasize when you can experience it instead?"

She moved closer to me.

"I'm going to fuck you during the Super Bowl, Abigail." I nibbled her earlobe and she rewarded me with a moan. "As long as you're quiet, no one will know."

She crossed and uncrossed her legs, then glanced around us. No one was watching us, of course. No one cared about us. They were too wrapped up in themselves.

I caressed her shoulder, stroked her. A faint smile crossed her face.

Yes, she wanted this.

"I want you to stand up and wrap a blanket around yourself. Open in the back. Put one foot up on the railing in front of you."

She jumped to her feet and wrapped the blanket around herself, just as I'd asked. I looked around and carefully studied the crowd. There was still no one looking our way. We would be just another couple in the crowd, cuddling to keep warm.

My gaze traveled from the crowd surrounding us to the scoreboard. The quarter was in its last seconds. I took the other blanket, stood up, and pressed close to Abby. Jackson and his teammates ran off the field. I draped the blanket around my shoulders and brought the ends around Abby.

My hand found its way up her shirt and I grazed her breast with my hand. Pulled at her nipple.

She gasped.

"You have to be quiet," I told her again. What the fuck would I do if she got too loud and we were discovered?

But it was too late now—we were both too caught up in the moment to care. So I let myself go and enjoyed the present.

I leaned closer to her. "I can't wait to be inside you." My hands explored her body under the blankets, cupped her breasts. "You feel so fucking good. You turn me on so fucking much." I thrust my hips against her. "Feel what you do to me." My hips rocked into her backside. "How hard you make me."

The stadium grew dark then, and I stepped back long enough to undo my pants and slip on the condom. "Lean over the rail just a little."

She looked first to her right, then to her left, but she pressed against the rail and leaned over.

"No one knows." I lifted her skirt up. "People are so caught up in their own little worlds, they don't notice what's going on around them." *Like when you helped someone on your way to a* Hamlet *reading years ago.* "The most life-altering event could be happening right next to them and they'd miss it entirely. Of course, in this case, it's a good thing."

Whistles, claps, and shouts filled the stadium. The main act had arrived. I took advantage of the growing chaos and thrust into Abby. She let out a yelp.

I rocked my hips into her, in time with the music. Fuck, it felt so good to be so deep inside her. I took the ends of the blanket and wrapped my arms tighter around her, drawing her back against me. Without my asking, she spread her legs a bit, allowing me to thrust and enter her even deeper.

I glanced once more to the people nearest us. "All these people and no one knows what we're doing." I pulled back and drove myself into her again. "You could probably scream." I teased her, tried to drive her to make a noise by pulling at her nipple, but she didn't make a sound.

I slowed my movements for the next song. This was good. I could do slow—could take a moment to simply enjoy being inside her. To take and hold in my memory the feel of her right now. How she felt in my arms. How her warmth wrapped around me. How her breathing slowed a bit but her heart still raced beneath my hands. I splayed my hands over both breasts, felt the hard pounding underneath.

And, fuck it all, the next song slowed even more. I hardly moved, but the connection, our connection, was still there. If we had nothing more, we had this and for now, in this moment, it was enough. I could enjoy and take this part of Abby—the submission and trust she gave me for this moment—and not worry about the future.

The rest of the world slipped away as the last song started. My thrusts picked up and I knew I wouldn't last long. I moved my hand to the front of Abby's body and rubbed her clit. She pushed back harder against me and started clenching around me.

I moved even faster into her, slamming her against the rail, driving myself farther into her. My hips circled and rocked as the song reached its ending. Lights flashed around us. I pulled her tightly against me, thrusting in time to the last few beats of the song.

"Come with me," I whispered and thrust into her once more, holding still as I released into the condom and she climaxed around me.

I kept my chest to her back, not wanting to draw any attention to us and waiting for the crowd to die down a bit. But most of all, enjoying the feel of Abby under my hands, under my body. Could she feel the pounding of my heart? Could she feel how she affected me?

As the crowd settled back into their seats, I pulled Abby back from the rail but kept my arms around her. I slipped off the condom, dropped it into the plastic bag I had waiting in the duffel bag, and redid my pants. Then I drew her into my lap—unwilling and unable to let her go just yet.

I ran my nose along her neck. She smelled like sex.

"Now, that," I whispered, "was an amazing halftime show."

Chapter Twenty-five

I felt as giddy as a teenager on his first date. Of course, I'd had plenty of public sex in the past: a deserted park, an empty parking lot, even the ever-popular back row of the movie theater, but I'd never participated in something as brazen as a packed-to-capacity football stadium during one of the most watched sporting events in the country.

What if we'd been caught on television?

I ran my fingers through Abby's hair, and the floral scent of her shampoo surrounded me.

Who the hell cared? It was so dark during the halftime show, no one would have noticed us.

Leaving the stands to return to the box, on the other hand . . .

I'd always had an excellent poker face and could hide my emotions behind a carefully constructed facade, but even I doubted I could hide the I've-just-had-incredible-sex look on my face.

Abby sighed and leaned her head against my shoulder. I knew she wouldn't be able to hide her expression either. Besides, we'd spent too much of our weekend with my family and friends. I wanted some time with Abby, even if we shared that time with the strangers sitting next to us.

So, for the third quarter, we sat. Simply enjoying each other's company. Pretended to watch the game.

Near the end of the quarter, Abby shifted in my lap and I knew if we didn't get back to the box, I'd be hiding more than what we'd been doing. I was already half hard again as it was.

"We should head back to the box," I told her, but held on tightly and wouldn't let her go. "Do you know why we had to wait?"

A serene smile crossed her face. What the hell was she thinking?

"Because your face shows absolutely everything," I answered for her. "You're an open book."

Except now. Now I have no idea what you're thinking.

She laughed and the sound caused me to smile. I'd done it— I'd made her laugh. Finally. Even if I had no idea why.

"You better change." I nodded at her outfit. "Felicia will have my head if she sees you in that skirt."

I didn't pay attention to the game anymore when we made it back to the box. I noticed New York won only when Jackson looked our way and blew Felicia a kiss. I hoped he knew he owed me big-time.

Abby and I left shortly after the trophy presentation. I told Linda I'd see her for dinner on Tuesday night and bade Elaina and Todd goodbye. I hugged Todd, still slightly pissed about his antics at brunch, but wanting to believe he had the best of intentions.

Once Abby and I were seated in my plane, I looked at my watch. It was late. On a typical Sunday, Abby would have already left my house for the weekend. I wanted nothing more than to drag her back to the bedroom and take her again, but I didn't. It would be outside of our agreement, and I'd already assumed too much outside of our agreement.

Which reminded me . . .

"Did you make me an appointment for Wednesday?" I asked, knowing I'd have to wait until at least Wednesday to have her again. "Or were you just saying that to Linda?"

She flashed me a sly grin. "I was hoping you would want to stop by."

She had made me an appointment. I crossed my right leg over my left, wanting to hide my erection, and smiled. "Wednesday, then." I thought back to her comment to Linda. "Research?"

"You do need help with your literature. If you try really hard, I'm sure you can do better than Mark Twain and Jane Austen next time."

"Really?" I thought Mark Twain had been really good. "Who would you suggest?"

"Shakespeare." She leaned back and closed her eyes.

Fortunately, I had many, many volumes of Shakespeare at home.

Todd called on Tuesday afternoon and apologized for his behavior on Sunday. He said he was only trying to help, but that he was wrong to try to jog Abby's memory. I accepted his apology. He thanked me and said he knew it was hard, but telling Abby was the right thing to do.

I thought about calling Paul, but then I remembered how he'd gone off about my lack of aftercare and I knew he'd book a flight to New York if I told him how I'd lied to Abby. He'd be right, of course, but I'd just defused Todd, and I didn't need another person telling me what to do.

That night, I ate dinner with Linda. She was all atwitter about her upcoming lunch date with Abby. She frowned and asked why I never brought her to dinner, but I covered by saying Abby didn't feel comfortable visiting and leaving Felicia behind. Linda shook her head and told me Felicia was welcome to come.

It was the opening I needed: I launched into a discussion of the Super Bowl, and within minutes all talk about Abby joining me for a family dinner was forgotten.

Abby hadn't waxed when I showed up for my Wednesday afternoon appointment in the Rare Books Collection and it made me edgy the rest of the week. What if she didn't wax after I'd told her to? I felt like beating my head against a wall. I'd have to punish her.

Damn it all.

What a way to start a weekend with Abby naked—in my room and on the whipping bench.

There went any hope of anything except punishment. And since there was no penalty written down for failure to wax, I'd have to think of something.

Twenty strokes for a lost hour of sleep was too much. I knew that now. What would be acceptable for another failure to obey a direct command? Not twenty. Fifteen? Ten? Somewhere in the middle? Thirteen?

Could I do thirteen?

Yes.

Yes, I could.

Because this time, I'd provide the necessary aftercare. This time, I'd be better prepared. This time would not be like last time.

I left the city on Friday morning, deciding to work from my estate so I could properly set up for the weekend. The first thing I did was turn up the heat. Abby would be naked all weekend and I didn't want her to be cold. I checked the heat on the hot tub and ensured clean towels were in the nearby cabana. I made paella for dinner.

I pulled the whipping bench into my room.

I took Apollo outside and played catch with him for a few minutes. After having him at the kennel the previous weekend, I didn't have the heart to send him away from home for any length of time.

I made everything as near perfect as I could, and then I paced.

Up and down in the foyer. Down and up. To the front door and back to the entranceway of the kitchen. Straining my ears and listening for the sound of a car pulling up the drive.

Apollo heard her before I did.

"Down, boy," I said as he ran to the door and scratched at it. He looked back at me and whined.

This was not a good idea.

I quickly took Apollo to the kitchen and closed the door. By the time I made it back into the foyer, the doorbell had rung.

I opened the door slowly.

Please, please, please.

She entered the foyer with my favorite grin on her face.

Oh, Abby. This is not the same as wearing panties. I hadn't given you a command last Sunday about panties. I did tell you to wax.

I pointed at her clothes. "Take them off. You'll get them back on Sunday."

She slowly slipped her sweater over her head, turned, and set it down. Then she looked over her shoulder at me and unhooked her bra.

Fuck. She was doing a tiny little striptease.

That meant she'd waxed, right?

The bra dropped to join her sweater on the floor.

Maybe she was trying to distract me with the striptease.

I shifted my weight from foot to foot.

She turned around to face me, and my cock went hard at the sight of her topless. Her hands slid down her body to the button on her jeans.

Yes, take them off. Let me see.

With deft fingers, she unbuttoned her jeans. She peeked up at me and slowly worked the pants over her hips. A little rock or two of her hips and—

Fuck. She wasn't wearing panties.

The jeans slipped lower.

She had waxcd.

The weight of the world lifted from my shoulders. Her jeans dropped to the marble floor, forgotten, and I crossed the hall to take her in my arms. The sight of her bare made me hard as a rock. There would be no punishment. None. It would just be us. Together.

I pushed her back to the plush bench in the middle of the foyer. "How pleased I am you followed my order." She sat down on the edge of the bench and I pushed her legs apart. "I'll admit, you had me just a little worried on Wednesday." I bent down so my face was level with her pussy. "I should spank you for that, and I might just do it later." I looked up and grinned so she knew exactly what type of spanking I meant. "For now, though, I think I need a taste of this deliciously bare pussy."

I placed a kiss right on the tip of her clit. She moaned and dropped back onto the bench. I spread her with my fingers and licked away the moisture gathered between her lips. Fuck. So sweet. Always so sweet. I took my time, overjoyed that there would be no punishment, and concentrated on her. Wanting, once more, to show her just how sweetly obedience would be rewarded.

I took her knees and pushed them up so her heels rested on the edge of the bench. Her position allowed me greater access to her body, and I ran my hands up her sides to play and tease her nipples. She arched her back, bringing her hips closer to my mouth, and I ran my tongue up her slit and gave her clit another kiss.

I slowly felt her relax and give herself over to me as pleasure worked its way through her body. Once more I licked her, wanting to drain her dry, wanting to taste her as she came. I nibbled her playfully, enjoying the way she trembled under me.

I poured my relief into bringing Abby pleasure. Used my fingers and mouth to show her how delighted I was. I stroked with my fingertips, teased with my lips, and nibbled with my teeth. In return, she shuddered under my hands. Her moans echoed in the open room and bounced off the marble floor.

I pushed my tongue deeper into her, feeling her tighten around me. Yes. I quickened my movements, wanting nothing more than to feel her come around me.

"Oh, please . . ." she moaned.

Yes.

Her breathing hitched. I sucked her clit into my mouth and her hips jerked against me. Her body tightened briefly before she rippled around me.

I took her legs and gently placed her feet on the floor, then brought her knees together. She gave a satisfied sigh.

"I like you like this." I ran a hand over her bare skin and another aftershock shook her body. "Bare for me. Did it hurt much?"

"Nothing I couldn't handle."

I preferred my submissives waxed. I didn't typically require it, but often I would request it after a few months. Part of me felt bad for throwing it at Abby the way I had. But all I had to do was look at her and that part of me was forgotten.

I stood up and held out a hand. "Ready for dinner?"

I expected her to be shy. To show some discomfort at her nudity. She surprised me, though, sitting up and running a hand through her hair. My eyes dropped to her breasts.

"Yes, please, Master."

Yes, please?

Yes, please what?

She took my hand and stood up. "What did you cook?"

Right. Dinner. Eating. Food.

I'd never make it through the weekend.

The paella had been an excellent choice. The spicy rice and succulent shrimp and chicken seemed to please Abby. She ate nearly everything on her plate.

Okay, I decided, there would be no deep conversation at dinner. Probably not for the entire weekend. Not with Abby naked.

I'd thought about taking her back into the playroom, had planned on it, even. Of course, that had been before Tampa and Todd. I decided instead to keep things the way they were—playing in the bedroom. At least until I told her the truth and she decided to stay.

Please, please, please let her stay.

But since I'd decided not to tell her yet, I pushed those thoughts aside and focused on the here and now. On Abby, naked and at my table. On what I decided we would do tonight . . .

"Abigail," I said, putting my fork down. She looked up and waited for me to continue. "I'm afraid in my . . . highly, uh, aroused state last weekend, I might have misspoken and, um, overestimated my abilities."

Her fork stopped halfway to her mouth. "What?"

"Five times would be"—I cleared my throat—"quite an accomplishment."

She cocked her head to the side. "I think you've already accomplished one time." She flushed and looked down at her plate.

"Yes, well," I said. "Never mind what it would do to me—five times would certainly take its toll on you." I lifted my wineglass to my lips and took a long sip. "And that would definitely interfere with my plans for tomorrow."

I said the words, but in my mind, I wanted to take her up the stairs, throw her on the bed, and keep her there for several long and sweaty hours. I pushed back from the table, fully intending to carry out my plan for at least two or three times, when I remembered—the whipping bench.

It was still in my room.

"Abigail. Clear the table and meet me in the foyer. I'll be right back."

I left her in the kitchen, ran up the stairs, and moved the bench back to the playroom. I wondered if she heard what I was doing.

When I made it back down the stairs, she stood waiting for me. One delicate hand trailed down the arm of the plush bench. Her back was to me and, at my return, she slowly turned her head to look over her shoulder. Our eyes met.

Time slowed. Then stopped completely.

She belongs here.

My life had been a puzzle with one piece missing and then that piece fell into place.

Abby.

My one percent.

The picture was complete. I stood mesmerized and watched as she turned to fully face me.

Her elegant eyebrow rose, just a bit, and she grinned.

I kept my eyes on her as I slipped out of my shirt and stepped out of my pants. I nearly came as my erection sprang free. She waited.

We weren't going to make it to the bed.

"Come here," I nearly growled, and she glided across the floor to me.

We weren't going to make it up the stairs.

The faint light of the foyer lamps reflected off the diamonds on her collar.

Mine.

I hooked a finger around the collar and pulled her to me. "I want you. And I'll have you. Right here."

"Yes, Master."

"Sit on the third step."

As she settled herself on the stairs, I lazily stroked my cock.

The stairs had not been my plan, but that was okay. Plans could change. Change was good.

Especially when that change meant taking Abby on the stairs.

"Put your feet on the second step and lean back on your elbows." My hand flew over my length, stroking faster. Fuck. This wouldn't be slow. Maybe round three would be slow. Round two would be hard and fast on the stairs.

I lowered myself, careful to keep my weight off her. "Do you like this?" In this position, her chest was pushed out—bare and vulnerable. "Do you want me to take you on the stairs?"

"I want only to serve you." Her eyes were dark and veiled. "In any way you wish."

"Be still." I cupped a breast and flicked her nipple. Her body tensed, but she remained motionless. "Serve me on the stairs, then."

I could have feasted on the sight of her spread for me for hours, but I was hard and ready. I knew it wouldn't take long before she was just as ready as I was. I played her body, using everything I knew she'd love—starting with light, tender touches and eventually moving to rougher caresses and strokes. I tasted her—from the salty flavor of the curve of her breasts to the faint metallic taste of her neck. The entire time she held still—breathing heavily, though, and heart pounding.

I finally lowered my weight onto her and gathered her wrists in one of my hands. "Relax, Abigail." Her body stretched under mine. "Move as you wish."

Her legs wrapped around my waist and drew me close.

"Are you ready for my cock?"

She swallowed and answered in a small voice, "Yes, Master."

But I wanted to tease her a bit more. I ran my free hand over her ass. "One day soon, I'll introduce you to my flogger." Her breath hitched, and I pinched her other cheek. "You'll love it. I guarantee it."

I released her arms and brought my elbows to rest on either side of her head. I shifted my hips and felt her wetness on my length. "Take my cock and place it inside yourself."

Her hand slipped between us and her warm fingers wrapped around me, her thumb rubbing over my tip. She wasted no time guiding me into her, and we both moaned as she lifted her hips to take me inside.

"Yes," I said. "Just like that."

I loved being inside her, but I forced myself to hold still. "Work yourself on me. Show me how much you want my cock."

Her hips lifted in response, taking me deeper, and she started a quick rhythm. I dropped my head to her neck and inhaled her scent as she worked her wet heat over me.

Finally, I couldn't remain still. Over and over, I pounded into her. Her legs fell from around my waist, and as she braced them against the stairs, I knew I wouldn't last much longer. I dropped a hand between us and rubbed her clit.

"Come hard for me," I said, and she tightened around me. "Fuck. Now." I pinched her clit gently, setting off her orgasm.

I pushed inside her once more and allowed my release to overtake me.

She threw her head back onto the stairs, and her body clenched around me for a second time.

I drew her close to my chest as our breathing slowed. "Can you stand up?"

She straightened her legs experimentally. "I think so."

I massaged her hips and ran my hand down to her knees, wanting to ease any discomfort.

"Come on." I stood up and held out a hand. "Let's go upstairs. There's something I want to try."

I kept my hand on the small of her back as we walked up the stairs, enjoying the way her hips swayed. When we reached her room, I turned to her.

"Take a quick break. Meet me in my bedroom in ten minutes."

While Abby used the bathroom, I set up my bedroom—lighting candles, pulling the sheets down. I went down to the foyer and gathered our clothes, putting mine in the laundry room and setting Abby's on her bed.

I wanted to take this next round slower—for us both to enjoy and relish each other. I wasn't sure how much time we had together, but if our time ended, I wanted Abby to have pleasurable memories to look back on.

Some part of me desperately wanted to keep her in my bed all night, to sleep with her in my arms, but I told myself not yet. If, after two weeks, she stayed, then I'd invite her to stay in my bed all night.

She didn't look uncomfortable at all when she walked into the room. She saw me standing there and dropped her eyes to the floor.

"I have pillows on the bed," I told her. "Come get on your hands and knees."

Without a second's hesitation, she walked to the bed and climbed on top.

"Lean your head into the pillow," I said.

She followed my instruction, situating herself with her head sideways and her forearms on either side of her head.

I reached under the pillow. "Do you know what I have hiding under here?" She didn't say anything and I slid the toy out. "The riding crop."

Her skin broke out in gooseflesh.

"*Mmmmm.*" I ran the crop down her spine. Lightly. Just so she'd know it was there. "Remember what I said in the foyer?"

Again. Silence.

"All Wednesday night, all day Thursday, and for most of the day today, I've been worried." I trailed the crop back up her spine. "I think you deserve a spanking for worrying me so." I slipped the crop between her legs. "Spread your knees wider."

She moved her legs apart and grabbed the pillow with both hands.

I lightly tapped her thighs with the crop. "Such a naughty girl, making me worry so." I brought the crop up to her ass and hit her a bit harder. She moaned and closed her eyes. "You like that, do you?" I brought the crop down again and she bit the pillow.

I slid a finger around the outside of her entrance. "So naughty, Abigail." I licked her wetness off my finger. "Getting turned on by a riding crop." I tapped her with the crop. "You want me right here, don't you?"

She still had the pillow in her mouth.

I chuckled and slapped the crop against her pussy a few more times. She mumbled something; I couldn't make out what it was through the pillow. I dragged the crop up over her ass and hit her there a few times. Just enough to leave a faint pinkish mark. Just enough to bring her nearly to the edge.

Then I put down the crop and stepped back. Gave her a few seconds to realize I'd stopped. When her breathing slowed, I got in place behind her and leaned my body over her.

"Tell me, Abigail," I whispered. "Has anyone ever hit your G spot before?"

She shook her head.

"Answer me." I cupped my hands under her breasts. "Would you like to see if I can find it?"

"Yes, please."

I slapped her ass. "Yes, please, what?"

"Yes, please, Master."

"*Mm*." I moved my hand to skim her bare entrance and my cock grew even harder. "Right here, you think?" Nothing. I slipped one finger inside. "How about here?" Still silence. I added another finger. "Here?" Nothing. I hooked my fingers and pressed them deeper. "Right here?"

Her hips bucked back against me and she let out a small squeal. Ah, yes. Right there.

"I think I found it." I stroked the spot with my fingers again and she nearly came off the bed. I took my fingers out and re-placed them with my cock. "Let's see if I can find it again." With one stroke, I thrust into her deeply.

She gave a sigh of contentment.

It took everything I had not to pound into her repeatedly, but I wanted this time to be slow. To take it easy. To make it last.

I pulled back slightly and ran my hands over her back. Spread my fingers over her delicate shoulder blades and dug into the hair at the nape of her neck. "You feel so good under me."

She pushed back against me.

"So greedy." I palmed her breasts. "And we have all night. All weekend." My hands slid to her waist. "I want to memorize every detail of you. To touch every part. See every inch."

I held her hips and started a slow, even pace, making sure I hit the delicate spot deep inside her. "Is that it?" I asked when her hips bucked in response. "Did my cock find it?" I angled my hips and thrust into her again; she mewed at me. "Ah yes, I think I've got it now."

My balls ached and my cock begged for relief, but I kept my movements slow and steady, hitting her with just enough force to drive her to the edge, but not enough strength to push her over. We both teetered there precariously.

I kept the rhythm up for several long minutes, but I knew we both wanted more. I built up slowly, going only slightly faster, pushing only slightly harder. But it didn't take long before both of our bodies took over and I was thrusting into her with all the force I could muster.

And poor Abby. I'd worked her too long and too hard with my previous teasing. Her body tensed and trembled under me, and her head jerked off the pillow.

"That's it," I said, reaching down and pulling her hair as I con-tinued thrusting. "Come hard for me."

Her body responded and she climaxed immediately, her tight

muscles setting off my own orgasm. I pulled her head back as I came hard and deep inside her.

This woman, I thought as we both tumbled to the bed. This woman will be my undoing.

Her confidence grew the next day. I watched her become even more comfortable in her body as she walked around the house. Late Saturday morning, I wrapped her in a thick fluffy bathrobe and took her outside to soak in the hot tub. We sat relaxing in the warm water. The sky looked odd—hard and gray—and it was bitterly cold, but we were too wrapped up in each other to care.

That afternoon, pleased with the way she'd handled herself, I gave her another robe and told her she could spend some time in the library. For the next few hours, she read, curled up on a couch with her toes peeking out of the warm bathrobe. I joined her later, played a bit of piano, and we spent the afternoon in a world of our own.

My cell phone woke me up the next morning. I blinked a few times, rolled over in bed, and picked it up.

"What?" I asked, not even checking to see who it was.

"Tell Abby I picked up Felicia." It was Jackson. "She's with me."

"What?" Damn, I needed coffee.

He sighed. "Tell. Abby. I. Picked. Up. Felicia."

"Jackson." I sat up and rubbed my eyes. "Why the hell are you calling me at"—I glanced at the clock beside my bed—"five thirty on a Sunday?"

A long sigh came from the other end of the phone. "Unless it's slipped your attention, New York's just been hit with the worst blizzard in recent history."

I jumped out of bed and stepped to the window. "What?"

"Happened overnight. Caught everyone off guard."

White. As far as I could see, there was nothing but white and more white falling.

"When . . . What?" I stuttered.

"Didn't you watch the news yesterday? They were predicting snow, but nothing like this."

No. I had not watched the news. I had not logged onto the computer or checked my e-mail. I had been too consumed with Abby.

Fuck.

Well, yes. That too.

"Hello?" Jackson was saying. "Nathaniel?"

I rubbed my eyes again. "I heard you. Yes, I'll tell Abby." My head started to pound. "She's still sleeping."

"Okay. Have her call Felicia when she wakes up."

"I will. Thanks, Jackson."

I slipped into fresh clothes and went downstairs to the kitchen to make the coffee. Snow was piled up against the window— about four feet high—and still falling.

A blizzard.

No way to leave.

When Abby woke up, I'd have her get dressed so she would be comfortable as we discussed this. This meant new rules, new situations, new everything.

Abby and me stuck inside my house for who knows how long.

I couldn't shake the suspicion that this would not end well.

Chapter Twenty-six

Before talking to Abby, I tried my best to plan the week. We would take turns with meals. Outside of the weekend, she was not to serve me. She was my submissive, yes, but we were equals in every sense of the word. I would not allow her to serve me during the week.

Abby didn't seem upset by the situation. She asked a few questions, but overall appeared at ease. I, however, felt on edge all day Sunday. To say the blizzard put a kink in my plans would be a serious understatement. I kept my unease buried just under the surface, though, hopefully hidden away from Abby.

I had no way of knowing how long we'd be stuck—I estimated a week. I could do a week, I told myself. It was a large house and I was able to work from home.

But so much time with a submissive—with Abby in particular—frightened me. I feared I could not keep my feelings buried for an entire week. Something would crack.

Probably me.

After I sent Abby upstairs to dress on Sunday afternoon, I went into the kitchen. Homemade rolls and a hearty beef stew sounded good. The repetitive action of kneading dough helped to occupy my mind. Like playing the piano.

Abby walked into the kitchen at six thirty. She wore a simple outfit of a high turtleneck and blue jeans. I had spent the entire weekend watching her naked body move around my house, but she was no less awe-inspiring fully clothed. I gazed at her and, in my mind's eye, remembered the places hidden underneath her clothes.

"Ready to eat?" I asked, pulling out a seat for her.

"Yes. Thank you." She sat down. "Smells wonderful."

Indeed, the kitchen smelled of freshly baked bread, mingled with hints of garlic, onion, and beef. A perfect accompaniment to the snow falling outside.

I dimmed the lights in the kitchen and turned the lights on outside. The snow still fell and the lighting cast it in a beautiful glow. We sat in silence for some time, simply watching the snow.

Do it, I told myself. I tightened my grasp on my spoon and felt my heart pound. *Do it.*

I cleared my throat. "Did you grow up in New York?"

"Indiana. Felicia and I moved here after high school." She swallowed a sip of stew. "I like the city. The way it's always the same place, but always changing."

I leaned back in my chair. *See?* I told myself. *You can carry on a conversation.* "I like the way you think," I told her.

"Do you ever think about living somewhere else?"

I thought for a second. "No, I once thought about Chicago, just to experience life in a different city, but my roots are here: my home, my business, my family. I don't want to leave." I wondered if she ever thought about living somewhere else. The idea made me sad. "You?"

"No. I can't imagine living anywhere else."

We fell into a comfortable silence and watched the snow. Made small talk about nothing in particular. After dinner, I cleared the table and put away the dishes. Abby wiped down the table and countertops, even though I told her she didn't have to.

Afterward, I headed to the living room and she went down the hall to the library. Just as well, I decided. I needed to catch up on the news. Abby, it appeared, wanted to be alone.

She made breakfast the next morning, her special French toast. The snow was still falling, but had slowed. She told me she'd called Felicia the night before and things seemed to be okay with her and Jackson. I assured her that his penthouse would be completely safe for her to ride out the storm. They would have plenty of company nearby and Jackson would take care of her.

When breakfast was over, I took Apollo outside and then went upstairs to my bedroom. I made a few phone calls, read some e-mails, and sat staring out the window, mindlessly wondering what to make for lunch, when the thumping bass of music came from downstairs.

Abby?

I walked down the stairs, Apollo by my side.

She was dusting. At least, I thought it was dusting. She had a duster in her hand and she twirled to the song coming from the speakers. Her body moved in time to the music as I stood, mesmerized. I'd known Abby was a beautiful woman, but to see her move like that, to see her dance . . . it stirred an almost primal urge inside me.

The song went on for several minutes and she cleaned my living room without ever noticing me. Just as well—had she known I was watching, she'd have probably stopped.

All things must end, though, and the song finally came to its close. She gave my end table one last sweep of the duster and turned.

She jumped when she saw me. Busted.

"Abigail, what are you doing?" It was hard not to laugh.

"Dusting."

Dusting. Like an employee.

"I do employ a housekeeper for such tasks." She was not my employee. She should not be working in my house.

"Yes, but she won't be able to come this week, will she?"

Okay, she had a point. "I suppose not. Although, if you insist

on making yourself useful, you could wash the sheets on my bed."
The sheets did need washing, especially after our weekend activities, even though I rather enjoyed them smelling like Abby.
"Someone got them all messy this weekend."

She placed a hand on her hip. "Really? The nerve."

My cock hardened just thinking about the past weekend. During our talk on Sunday, I'd told Abby I didn't expect anything sexual from her this week—that we'd take things naturally. But the truth was, I didn't think sex would be a good idea. I needed to keep to our original agreement, and that meant no sex while we were snowed in.

"By the way," I said as a new thought came to me. "I'm dropping yoga from your exercise routine."

"You are?" she asked, and I'd never heard her sound so relieved.

"Yes. And adding dusting." I left her there and went to prepare lunch.

I decided to make chicken salad. The same thing Abby had made the day after her punishment. Her chicken salad had cranberries and pecans—mine was more traditional, but not as tasty.

"It's not as good as yours," I told her as I put her plate on the kitchen table. "But it'll do."

"You like my chicken salad?" she asked.

"You're an excellent cook." Had I never told her before? "You know that."

"It's nice to hear every once in a while." Her eyes—they laughed at me.

"Yes," I said, smiling pointedly. "It is."

For a second she looked puzzled, then realized I was teasing her and said in a rush, "You're an excellent cook as well."

"Thank you, but you did compliment my chicken once before."
I thought back to our first weekend and knew I needed to make my honey-almond chicken for her again.

"I was wondering," she said after a bite of salad, "if I could take Apollo outside this afternoon."

I looked up. She had a tiny bit of mayonnaise on the side of her mouth. I wanted to reach out and wipe it away.

Or lick it away.

I could lick the mayo away.

Apollo lifted his head. Right. She wanted to take him outside. "I think that would be a good idea. He needs to get out and he seems to like you."

"What's his story, if you don't mind me asking? Elaina mentioned something in Tampa that made me think he'd been sick." She took her napkin and wiped off the mayo.

Ah, well. Maybe next time.

Focus. She wants to talk about Apollo.

I reached down and rubbed his head. "Apollo is a rescue. I've had him for more than three years. He was abused as a puppy and it made him hostile. Although he's never had a problem with you—maybe some sort of sixth sense about people?"

We spoke about Apollo some more—his problems with being away from me for long periods of time, how training him had been hard, but worth it. Abby surprised me with her unrestrained contempt of people who abused animals.

The discussion about Apollo somehow led us to the Bone Marrow Registry and my decision to donate once I'd been matched. Or, more to the point, how it hadn't really been a decision.

"Some people wouldn't feel the same," she said.

"I like to think I have never been considered *some people*," I said, trying to lighten the mood.

But she mistook me.

"Sorry, sir." She looked horrified. "I didn't mean . . ."

"I know you didn't. I was teasing."

She looked down at her plate. "It's hard to tell sometimes."

"Maybe I should wear a sign next time." She still didn't look up. I stretched my arm across the table and gently lifted her chin. "I'd rather you not hide your eyes when you're talking to me. They're so expressive."

I couldn't look away once I met her eyes. In their depths, I found the answer to every question my heart had ever asked. I saw my own longing and loneliness mirrored back at me.

Oh, Abby. Have you been missing your one percent?

I dropped my hand.

Could I possibly be what she'd been looking for? What could I offer her? How could I complete her?

It was absurd. It was wonderful.

It was frightening.

She looked away first and asked about Kyle.

A safe subject. Kyle wasn't dangerous to anyone.

"We're close," I told her. "I took him to a few baseball games last year. I actually hoped he'd be able to go to the Super Bowl. He'd been looking forward to it."

I felt a sense of accomplishment whenever I spoke of Kyle. Of course, it wasn't anything I'd done—it was simply the luck of my bone marrow being a match for his. Anyone would have done the same.

"Why wasn't he able to go to the Super Bowl?" Abby asked.

"He was sick," I said, remembering the disappointment in his voice when I talked to him the day Abby and I left for Tampa. "Maybe next year."

"Felicia said something about Jackson retiring. Will he play next year?"

"I think so, but it might be his last season." I thought back to a conversation I'd had with Jackson last week. *"Don't tell me it's too soon, man,"* he'd said. *"I don't even want to hear it."*

"He's ready to settle down," I told Abby. "If Felicia is amenable, that is."

"Are you ready to deal with Felicia as a member of the family?"

Not really.

"I will for Jackson's sake." I met her eyes once more. "And she does have the most amazing best friend."

I went back to my bedroom after lunch. I wanted to call my employees, to ensure they were all safe. Not an easy task with the number of people I employed, but the peace of mind it would afford outweighed the time it would take.

I had made a good-sized dent in my list when I heard laughter coming from outside. I got up and went to the window. Abby and Apollo were playing in the snow. As I watched, she made and threw a snowball. Apollo took off after it, only to stop in confusion when it disappeared.

She belongs here, I thought. *She is my one percent.*

Hell, even my dog thought so.

She won't like it when she finds out the truth. She'll hate you.

Maybe not. Maybe she wouldn't care.

I glanced at the list of phone numbers on my desk and then back outside at the embodiment of my every need.

My employees were going to have to wait.

I changed into warmer clothes and started a fire in the library before heading outside. Abby and Apollo still stood by the garage, playing. She looked carefree and uninhibited. I wanted to feel that way too.

"You're confusing my dog," I said when she threw another snowball.

She turned and smiled. "He loves it."

Apollo took off after another ball, determined to get it, and she giggled when he skidded to a stop.

"I think he loves the person throwing them." I decided to try my hand at her new game. It worked—Apollo looked back, saw that I threw the snowball, and danced in circles.

"You've stolen my game," she said. "Now he won't want to play with me."

I watched, delighted, as she balled up a handful of snow and threw it in my direction. I'd grown up with a cousin who went on to become a professional football player—I'd actually expected her to hit me. But the ball went wide and missed.

"Oh, Abigail," I said, moving toward her. "That was a big mistake."

"You wouldn't happen to be wearing a sign, would you?"

I scooped up a handful of snow. "Not on your life."

She backed away from me, holding up her hands as if in surrender.

"You threw a snowball at me." I tossed my own ball from hand to hand. Her eyes followed its movement.

"I missed."

"You still tried." I pulled my arm back, pretending I was about to throw the snowball at her, but at the last minute threw it to Apollo instead.

It was too late, though. She'd yelped and run off before the ball left my hand and, the next thing I knew, fell facedown in the snow.

I jogged the short distance to her, anxious to ensure she wasn't hurt. What if she had broken something?

As I approached, she rolled over and moaned.

"Are you okay?" I held out my hand to her. She looked fine. Wet, but fine.

She shivered. "Nothing hurt but my pride."

The library would be nice and warm by now. The fire had been going for a good while. She took my hand and climbed to her feet.

"Time to go inside?" I asked. "Something warm by the fire?"

I shut down the various images that sprang to mind—Abby and me by the fire, limbs intertwined, the way the firelight would play off her skin.

Remember the plan, I told myself. No sex this week.

The plan was very slowly, but very thoroughly, going straight to hell.

Chapter Twenty-seven

We shuffled into the house, Abby sniffling in wet clothes. I took her into the library and sat her by the fire while I went upstairs to gather something dry for her to put on. I glanced into the kitchen on my way downstairs. She needed something warm to drink as well. Should I make coffee?

I took the clothes into the library, and my eyes fell on the decanters I kept filled and displayed.

The brandy.

While Abby dressed, I poured, and when she settled back in front of the fireplace, I handed her a glass and sat beside her.

She sniffed it. "What is this?"

"Brandy. I thought about coffee, but decided this would warm us quicker."

She swirled her glass. "I see. You're trying to get me drunk."

"I don't, as a practice, *try* anything, Abigail." I nodded at her glass. "But it is more than forty percent alcohol, so you'd better have only the one glass."

She took a tentative sip, choking slightly as the fiery liquid made its way down her throat. She looked at me, shrugged, and took another sip.

"*Mm*," she said, so quietly I could barely hear.

I leaned against the couch and closed my eyes as the alcohol slowly warmed my body. Apollo crossed the room and put his head on my feet. A feeling of contentment swept over me—Abby was at my side, we were safe and warm in my house, and Apollo was well. For just a moment, I could close my eyes and life was damn near perfect.

Abby's voice broke through my reverie. "Did the library come with the house, or is it something you had added when you bought it?"

I opened my eyes. She sat, still swilling her glass.

And she wanted to talk.

Finally.

"I didn't buy this house," I said, watching her. "I inherited it."

Her eyes grew wide. "This was your parents' house? You grew up here?"

"Yes. I've made major renovations, like the playroom."

She moved closer to me. "Has it been hard to live here?"

Linda had asked me the same thing when I graduated from college and told her of my plans to renovate.

"I thought it would be, but I've redone so much, it doesn't resemble my childhood home anymore. The library is very much the same as it was then, though."

Especially with her in it—it was once more the hub of the house. She filled it with light and warmth and life.

"Your parents must have loved books," she said.

I looked around me. My parents had loved this library. I wondered if that was the reason I'd given the room to Abby—to somehow capture for the house some of what had been missing since my parents' death.

Mom and Dad would have loved Abby. They would have gotten along so well. Some part of me knew, even though I had been so young when they died.

"My parents were avid collectors. And they traveled frequently." I waved toward the section of the library that held maps and atlases, remembering my father's joy and my mother's delight whenever they added a new volume. "Many of the books they found overseas. Some had been in their families for generations."

"My mom liked to read, but mostly she just went for popular fiction." She set down her glass and hugged her knees.

"There's a place for popular fiction in every library. After all, today's popular fiction may very well be tomorrow's classic."

She laughed softly. "This from the man who said no one reads classics."

Ah, she remembered.

"That wasn't me." I put a hand to my chest. "That was Mark Twain. Just because I quoted him doesn't mean I agree with him."

"Tell me more about your parents," she said, and my memory shot back to that day in the hospital after her accident.

"The afternoon they died, we were on our way home from the theater." I hadn't spoken of my parents' death in years. Not since I was a boy and Linda sent me to counseling. "It had been snowing. Dad was driving. Mom was laughing about something. It was very normal. I suppose it usually is."

Mommy was so pretty. Daddy looked at her and smiled. She laughed at something he said.

The car jerked . . .

"He swerved to miss a deer," I said. "The car went down an embankment and flipped. I think it flipped. It was a long time ago, and I try not to think about it."

"It's okay," she said. "You don't have to tell me."

But I wanted to tell her. I wanted to share this part of my life with her. This secret part.

"No," I said. "I'm fine. It helps to talk. Todd's always told me to talk more."

The car fell for a long time. When it finally stopped, I wondered why. What caused it to stop? Would it start moving again?

"Nathaniel?"

"Nathaniel?"

Mommy kept screaming.

"I don't remember everything," I said. "I remember the screaming. The shouts to make sure I was okay. Their moans. The soft whispers they had for each other. A hand reached back to me." *Mommy's hand. I couldn't reach it.* "And then nothing."

Daddy wasn't moving anymore. Why was he so quiet?

"They used a crane to pull the car out. Mom and Dad had been gone for some time by then, but like I said, I don't remember it all."

I didn't like the hospital. Everyone looked at me with sad faces and talked outside my room a lot.

Someone brought me a bear. I was ten. I was too old for bears. I didn't want a bear. I wanted Mommy.

"Linda's been wonderful. I owe her so much," I said. "She was very supportive." I swallowed more brandy. "And growing up with Jackson helped. Todd, too. And Elaina, when she moved nearby."

They were always so playful, so much fun.

"Your family's the best," Abby said.

"They are more than I deserve," I said, standing. "You'll have to excuse me. I need to get back to my work now."

And finish the phone calls, for I was no longer ten years old. I was a man. I had responsibilities. My afternoon of play was over.

She stood up, too. "And I need to start dinner. I'll take that for you." She held out her hand for my glass.

I looked deep into her eyes. I'd shared more with her today than I'd ever shared with another person. She'd sat and listened and had just been there.

"Thank you," I whispered.

I finished calling my employees while Abby made dinner, made sure all my workers were accounted for and safe. Before heading down for dinner, I called Jackson. His voice grew excited as he talked about how much he was enjoying his time with Felicia. From his tone, it appeared he no longer had any doubts about whether or not what he felt was real.

Last, I called Linda. She'd been at home when the snow hit and had tried to make it in to the hospital but ended up having to turn around and go home. I could tell from her voice she was still upset at being stuck at home and away from the action.

Mouth-watering smells met me as I walked down the stairs. Abby had made a meat loaf. I couldn't remember the last time I had meat loaf. It was a meal I enjoyed but never thought about making myself. I sniffed again. Mashed potatoes, too.

"Something smells good," I said, sitting down.

"Thanks." She carried our plates to the table. "It's been ages since I've cooked meat loaf."

"It's been ages since I've had one."

She stopped, halfway into her chair. "Do you not like meat loaf?"

"Please." I motioned for her to sit down. "I love meat loaf. I just don't cook it for myself."

She placed a napkin in her lap. "I don't cook it often, but it's my father's favorite."

Her father—the opening I'd been looking for. "Tell me about your parents. What does your father do?"

She finished chewing, and I took a bite of the mashed potatoes—red potatoes, skin on, a bit of garlic mixed with a touch of parmesan. Perfection.

"He's a contractor," she said. "He's been building houses for as long as I can remember."

"And your mother?" I asked, trying to sound as calm as possible. I was treading on dangerous ground.

Abby watched me with careful eyes. "Mom passed away. Heart disease."

I hadn't known that. "I'm sorry."

"It's okay. She was so young, though. And just starting to get her life back on track after breaking up with my dad."

It seemed only natural to ask how her mother had gotten her life back on track, but I was afraid if I did, I wouldn't be able to keep my involvement secret. I took a bite of meat loaf instead and then quickly changed the subject.

Tuesday, after breakfast, we sat in the living room. Abby talked to her dad on the phone and I worked through my never-ending e-mails. Yang Cai had grown more impatient—there was no longer any doubt I'd be going to China. The only question was when. I glanced down at my calendar—June, perhaps. Or July.

Abby must have left the room at some point—I noticed she'd been gone only when I looked up and saw her return. A mischievous grin covered her face.

"Yes?" I asked.

"Will you help me with lunch?"

She was planning something, I felt certain. But whatever it was would be better than worrying about Yang Cai. "Can you give me ten minutes?"

"Ten minutes will be perfect."

She left, and I strained my ears trying to hear something from the kitchen. More dancing, perhaps? Did she really want me to help her cook?

Why had I told her ten minutes? I couldn't concentrate on anything anymore. I sat at my desk staring aimlessly at my laptop, and when eight minutes had passed, I went into the kitchen.

Abby stood at my counter, staring at two cans without labels. "Abigail?"

She didn't move. "I'm trying to decide what someone like you is doing with label-less cans in their kitchen."

"The small one is Italian peppers." I walked to the counter. "The larger one holds the remains of the last nosy submissive who bugged me about my label-less cans."

"Sign?"

"Sign."

"Seriously," she said, and her eyes were dancing, "what are you doing with label-less cans in your cabinets? Doesn't that break about a hundred different rules of yours?"

I smiled, pleased she felt so comfortable in teasing me.

"The small one really is peppers from Italy. The larger one should be tomatoes from the same company. I ordered them on-line."

"What happened to the labels?"

I thought back to the day the cans arrived—months ago. "They came that way. They probably are peppers and tomatoes, but I've been hesitant to open them and never sent them back. What if they're pickled cow tongues?" I sighed. "I don't have enough faith, I guess."

Her expression grew serious. "All of life is faith. Just because something has a label doesn't mean it's always going to match the inside."

Like your label, she was telling me.

"Trust me," she said. "Sometimes it takes more faith to believe the label. Don't be afraid of what's on the inside. I can make a masterpiece with the insides."

I can make a masterpiece with you, she meant—but I knew better.

Oh, Abby. You can't. You just can't.

Part of me wanted to believe her, so I cupped her cheek. "I bet you could," I said, and saw in her eyes that she believed her words.

It was too much—I dropped my hand. "Now, what do you need my help with?"

She knew enough not to push it. Instead, she turned and opened the box at her side. "I want to do a mushroom risotto, but I can't stir the rice and cook everything else at the same time. Can you stir?"

She really just wanted me to cook with her? "Mushroom risotto? I'd be happy to stir."

She set out chicken broth and white wine next to the vegetables already on the counter. "You might want to take that sweater off. It'll probably get hot in here."

She wasn't thinking we were going to . . . ? In the kitchen?

I took the sweater off and draped it over the arm of a chair.

"I'll chop up the mushrooms and onions," she said. "You start the rice."

The nonchalant way she said it. Her offhanded manner. Her command of the kitchen.

"Bossy little thing, aren't you?" I teased.

She cocked her eyebrow and put her hand on her hip. "It's my kitchen."

Her words surged through me, turning me on more than I could have imagined.

I shoved her against the counter and rocked my hips against her. "No. I said the kitchen table was yours. The remainder of the kitchen is *mine*."

Her eyes grew dark, and I knew exactly what her plan was. The only question was, what would I do about it?

"Now," I said. "What was that about the rice?"

I turned on the burner and readied the pan. Abby held up the bottle of wine.

"Yes, please," I said, and she poured us each a glass before setting to work chopping the onions.

I added the rice to the pan, and stirred it a bit, coating the grains with olive oil. I poured in some wine from the bottle.

"You ready for this?" she asked, motioning toward the onions.

"I'm always ready." I just wasn't going to do anything about it. I shifted my hips. Damn my erection that thought differently.

She dipped under my arm and scraped the onions into the pan. "There you go." Her ass grazed my cock and I grew even harder.

Then she was gone, dicing mushrooms, while I was stuck in front of the oven, stirring. I glanced over to the chicken broth. Was it time to add some?

She noticed. "Want me to get that chicken stock for you?" Without waiting, she dipped under my arm again and got the pitcher. Her arm brushed me as she poured.

Fuck. What was the plan?

No sex. Not during the week. Right. Back to the plan.

Maybe she saw my resolve and gave up—she spent the next few minutes dicing the rest of the mushrooms.

Until one dropped to the floor and rolled to where I stood.

"Oops," she said. "Let me get that."

She squeezed between me and the stove while I kept stirring and bent down to retrieve the mushroom, brushing against my thigh and then grabbing me around the waist to steady herself as she stood up. I knew exactly what she was doing.

But the plan, I reminded myself. Not during the week. But if Abby wanted it . . . No. Not during the week.

I argued with myself as the risotto simmered away. Thinking one thing and then deciding on another. Thinking that kitchen sex wouldn't be so bad and then reminding myself that I needed to keep sex out of our weekday relationship.

Again, Abby must have somehow picked up on my hesitation, because she didn't try anything else. Instead, she prepared the chicken breasts and passed me the mushrooms once they were finished.

Then she stripped off her sweater, and I knew she hadn't picked up on what I was thinking at all.

She lifted the pitcher of chicken broth again. "Need more?"

It was okay. I could resist her. "Just a touch."

She had a white tank top on under the sweater. I stared at her as she poured broth into the pan—was she wearing a bra?

Somehow, she poured more broth on her than she got in the pan. And, no, she didn't have a bra on.

"Damn," she said. "Would you look at that?"

Her nipples were hard beneath the thin white material. I wanted to taste them . . . wanted to taste her . . .

"I guess I need to take this off before the stain sets. It could be a problem." She walked over to the sink and, damn it, took off her top.

My last coherent thought was to turn the oven and burner off so the house didn't burn down. I strode across the floor and grabbed her by the waist. "I've got a bigger problem for you."

She knew exactly what I was talking about, for her eyes dropped down to where my erection strained against the front of my jeans.

I picked her up and carried her to the counter, shoving anything in my way off onto the floor. Something broke as it hit, but I didn't look to see what was—I didn't care. Instead, I unbuttoned her jeans and jerked them off.

Fuck.

She wasn't wearing panties.

I took a step back and shoved my own jeans off. "Is this what you want?"

Without waiting for an answer, I stepped close and she wrapped her legs around me.

"Yes." Her hands snaked their way under my shirt and I ran my thumb over her nipple. "Please," she said. "Please. Now."

I slid my hands over her body, trying to wrap my brain around the fact that Abby was in my kitchen, naked, on a Tuesday. This really wasn't my plan. I didn't want to push her. To confuse us.

"I didn't want . . . I didn't think . . ." I started, but her lips were on my neck.

"You think too much," she whispered.

Damn straight. For the rest of the afternoon, I wouldn't think.

I took her legs, spread them farther apart, and thrust into her. The angle was a bit off, so I shifted my hips and thrust deeper.

"Oh, hell, yes. More," she said as I withdrew. "More, please."

I pounded into her as she sat on the counter, pushing harder, wanting deeper. Trying to give her what she wanted, taking what she'd give me. Her head hit a cabinet and I slowed my movements.

She would have none of that. "Harder," she begged. "Please, harder."

"Fuck, Abigail." I held her steady and pushed farther into her.

"Again." She bit my ear. "Damn it. Again."

Her words spurred me forward, and I worked my hips harder and faster. She felt so damn good. I wanted more. Wanted more of her. I angled my hips and hit deep within her.

"Yes," she said, breathless, head hanging back. "Right there."

Her talk turned me on even more. "Here?" I thrust, hitting the spot again. "Here?"

I knew I hit it, because she started whimpering. I worked my hips harder, driving us both toward our release, and slid my hand between us to rub her clit.

"Harder," she moaned. "Almost there."

I drove into her as hard as I could, forcing myself not to climax until I could bring her hers.

"I . . . I . . . I . . ." she stuttered.

She tightened around me, and I thrust as deep as possible, releasing into her, my muscles shaking as I finally allowed my orgasm to overtake me.

I couldn't talk for several minutes. Around us the kitchen was in disarray, the risotto cooled, and the chicken was probably overdone.

I couldn't care less.

"Damn," I said, after I found my voice. "That was . . ."

Incredible.

Amazing.

Wonderful.

"I know," she said. "I agree."

I lifted her from the countertop and set her on her feet. The drawer next to the oven held fresh towels, so I took one out and gently cleaned her.

Incredible, amazing, and wonderful, yes. But it couldn't happen again.

Chapter Twenty-eight

I hummed that night as I cooked dinner. Maybe being snowed in for a few days wasn't the worst thing in the world. So far, things were going well. Abby and I had watched a bit of television earlier in the afternoon. When we got bored of news and weather, we went into the library. Abby sat in front of the fireplace and I sat at my desk—pretending to work, but really reading a collection of Shakespeare quotes. Apollo followed us wherever we went, and Abby and I took turns taking him outside.

I was going to open one of my label-less cans. I would close my eyes, hope for the best and, if all went according to plan, make a delicious marinara.

Abby sat behind me at the kitchen table, drinking a glass of red wine. I was surprised she'd decided to be in the kitchen while I cooked. Normally, she stayed in the library.

When I picked up the can opener, she rose onto her toes behind me to peek at the contents of the can. "Just checking," she said.

Label-less cans—who would have thought they could entertain and keep our attention the way they had? I set the opener down and slowly lifted the lid.

"Tomatoes," we both said when the red fruit came into view.

"Drat," she said. "I was hoping for pickled cow tongue or some incriminating body parts."

I forked a tomato. "Rather anticlimactic, don't you think?"

"No." She dropped back to her heels. "It's better to know."

It's always better to know. *Tell her*, my inner voice nagged.

"You're right," I said. "And it's going to make us a delicious supper."

I poured the tomatoes into the waiting sauté pan. The smell of juicy tomato joined the aroma of browned onion and mushroom. Abby didn't return to the table, standing behind me instead. I glanced over at the countertop, seeing her there, remembering the words she'd spoken as I took her.

Harder. Please, harder.

"Smells good," she said, looking over my shoulder again.

If I turned around, I would have her naked in less than ten seconds.

"Go sit down," I said. "I'd like to have one hot meal today."

She didn't move. "Breakfast was hot, and lunch was hot." She paused for a second. "At least the part before lunch was hot."

"Abigail."

"I'm sitting," she said, moving away. "I'm sitting."

I reached down to discreetly rearrange my pants while I continued stirring with the other hand. The sauce was coming together nicely, but needed some time to cook thoroughly. While it finished up, I'd get the plates down, maybe grab another bottle of—

"You know," she said, "you had a breakthrough today."

"What was that?" I asked, not sure what she was getting at.

"You opened one of your label-less cans," she said, and my body relaxed. "I think that calls for a celebration."

"What did you have in mind?"

She wore a wicked grin. Trouble. The woman was nothing but trouble. "Naked picnic in the library?"

Like I said . . .

I turned on the burner under the water pot. "That's your idea of a celebration?"

"I should have made bread for dinner," she said.

What? Bread? What was she talking about? Did that mean no naked picnic?

"You've done quite enough for one day," I said. *But let's do more anyway.*

"Yes," she said in a very serious voice. "It is my idea of a celebration."

Thank goodness.

"Okay. Naked picnic in the library. Thirty minutes."

She hopped up from the table. "I'll go set up."

"Extra blankets are in the linen closet," I called as she left.

I added pasta to our plates and then ladled marinara over the pasta.

Naked picnic in the library . . .

There went the plan.

Again.

But did it matter? So what if we had sex? It was her library. We'd had sex there before. Nothing had changed then, why would tonight be any different?

Todd's voice echoed in my head. "A relationship like yours . . . complete honesty and trust . . ."

I ignored Todd's voice.

It was picnic time.

I undressed in the laundry room and walked into the library. Thick blankets covered the floor and half a dozen pillows sat in front of the library. And Abby . . .

Abby sat in the middle of it all—long hair brushing the tips of her nipples, one leg propped up, showing her bare, glistening—

"Do you need any help?" she asked.

I swallowed. Hard. "No. I'm fine. Let me set this down and I'll get our drinks. More wine?"

A trip to the cold wine cellar was just what I needed to cool down a bit.

"Please."

It worked. The short walk down the stairs to the wine cellar chilled my body just enough to keep my cock in line. I returned to Abby and poured us each a glass.

I watched as she brought a forkful of pasta to her mouth and tasted my label-less marinara. She immediately took a second bite and then a third.

"This is superb," she said, twirling another bite. "My compliments to the chef."

"To label-less cans," I said, lifting my fork and trying to keep my eyes off her mouth and other body parts.

"To label-less cans," she repeated, lifting her own fork.

But what the hell? Somehow, label-less can marinara sauce flew the short distance from her fork to my . . .

I stared at it. "You got marinara on my cock."

Her voice held a smile. "Oops."

"Get. It. Off."

I raised my eyes. She wasn't even trying to hide the smile.

"Lie back." She took my plate and set it beside me.

Crazy. Somehow I'd envisioned sex happening *after* dinner. "Abigail."

She pushed on my shoulders. "You want me to use a napkin?"

Hell, no. I wanted her to lick it off.

I dropped my head to one of the pillows and closed my eyes as her hand ran down my chest. "The marinara, Abigail."

Her fingers traced my nipples. "I'm getting there."

"Get there. Faster."

She wasn't listening. She started at my chest and took her time nibbling down, licking and grazing her teeth along the planes of my stomach. Then she bit me, right below my belly button.

I clenched my fists.

She finally made it to where I wanted her—and blew warm air at the head of my cock.

She was fucking teasing me.

My body trembled in anticipation of her mouth on me. Then finally, *finally*, her tongue came out and licked me.

Damn. Don't stop.

She didn't stop, but she didn't take me in her mouth either. Instead, she played me—sucking just my tip in her mouth, licking me and stroking the rest of my length with her hands. She drove me mad with the urge to shove my cock down her throat, but I held still, fists clenched at my side.

Right when I least expected it, she deep-throated me. She took my entire length into her mouth and relaxed as I hit the back of her throat.

"Fuck," I said.

She released me. "I can stop."

"Hell, no," I said. "Swing those legs up here. I want to taste that sweet pussy."

She twisted her body.

Perfect.

I grabbed her hips, moving our bodies into sixty-nine position, and thrust my tongue deep within her, releasing my need by pleasuring her.

"*Mmmmm*." I licked her clit. "Sweeter than the finest wine. And I'm going to drink from you until there's not a drop left."

I started doing just that and she deep-throated me again.

Our movements mirrored each other's—her licks and nibbles matched mine. Her teeth ran down my cock whenever I nipped her clit. I licked her again, and she moved her hips closer to my face.

I rolled us to our sides to give us better access to each other. I could thrust deeper into her mouth this way. She responded by moving herself on my tongue. I pushed three fingers inside her and she moaned around my cock.

Like that, do you?

I licked her clit and moved my fingers inside her. I tried to reach the spot I'd found last weekend, but it was too hard in the position we were in. Then she ran a finger from my balls to my ass and, instinctively, I thrust into her mouth harder.

The friction of her mouth on my cock was amazing. Incredible. Knowing I was pleasing her at the same time—feeling her move her hips against my fingers—only made me push her harder.

She groaned again, sending vibrations along me, and I sucked her clit into my mouth, lightly dragging my teeth against her. She trembled and then tensed as her climax overtook her. I gently bit and she released a second time, drawing me deeper into her mouth. I moaned as my own orgasm hit, coming in her mouth, and she swallowed it all.

I placed soft kisses on her bare pussy and reached down to pull her up to me. With weak arms, I held her.

"Dinner's cold," she said against my chest.

I ran a hand down her back. "Screw dinner."

Eventually, though, I sat us both up. "We need to eat."

The question danced in her eyes, but she didn't verbalize it.

Yes, Abby. Food this time.

I handed her plate back to her and picked mine up. The pasta wasn't bad cold—I could only imagine how it tasted hot. Although, if I had to pick between hot pasta and Abby . . . well, Abby won every time.

Her face knit together with concentration and she scowled at her pasta. Whatever could she be focused on so intently? She glanced up, and I quickly looked at my own plate.

"How long have you been a dom?" she asked.

Ah. She wanted to ask personal questions. A flicker of unease tickled my belly.

"Nearly ten years."

"Have you had a lot of subs?"

Collared or uncollared? And define *had*.

But I took the easy way out. "I suppose that depends on your definition of 'a lot.' "

She rolled her eyes, undeterred. "You know what I mean."

While pleased she felt comfortable enough to ask me questions, I needed to lay a few ground rules.

"I don't mind having this conversation, Abigail. This is your library. But keep in mind that just because you ask a question doesn't mean I'll answer it."

Again, a look of determination crossed her face. "Fair enough."

"Then ask away."

Her first question surprised me. "Have you ever been a sub?"

My time with Paul flashed back to me—the various scenes he'd mentored me through, the few times I subbed for him. Our relationship hadn't been sexual, but he believed a dominant needed the experience of submission.

"Yes," I said, and her eyes grew large. "But not for any extended period of time, only for a scene or two," I hastened to add.

Surprisingly, she didn't question me further about those scenes. "Have you ever had a sub use her safe word before?"

"No," I said, wanting to see her reaction.

"Never?"

"Never, Abigail."

She looked away first.

"Look at me," I said, because I wanted her to hear the truth of what I told her. "I know how new you are to this, and I ask you, have I ever come close to pushing you beyond what you could handle?"

I knew the answer before she spoke, but I wanted her to follow my reasoning.

"No," she said.

"Have I been gentle and patient and caring?" I asked. "Anticipated your *every* need?"

"Yes."

"Do you not think I would have been gentle and patient and caring with my past subs? Anticipated their *every* need?"

Understanding dawned in her eyes. "Oh."

"I am starting you out slowly, because I see this as a long-term relationship, but there are so many things we can do together." I traced her arm down to her elbow, imagining her in my playroom again. "So many things your body is capable of that you don't even know yet. And just as you have to learn to trust me, I have to learn your body."

She swallowed loudly, and her skin broke out in gooseflesh.

"I have to learn your limits, so I'm working you slowly. But there are many, many areas we have yet to explore." I circled her wrist and squeezed. "And I want to explore them all." *That's enough, West.* "Does that answer your question?"

"Yes."

"Any other questions?"

She straightened her back. "If your other subs didn't use their safe word, how did the relationships end?"

Should I really tell her how Beth left because I couldn't give her what she wanted? Or was she calling me out on the safe word?

"They ended as any relationship ends," I said, giving her a safe answer. "We grew apart and went our separate ways."

"Have you ever had a romantic relationship with a woman who wasn't your sub?"

Damn that Elaina. When I got my hands on her . . .

"Yes," I said simply.

Two brown eyes peeked up at me. "How did that go?"

It didn't go. It was a horrific failure.

I was a horrific failure.

I, Nathaniel West, who never failed at anything, had failed Melanie.

"You're here now," I said, playing it safe again. "Was that a rhetorical question?"

"Melanie?"

That was it. I would call Elaina after dinner. She had no business telling Abby everything about my personal life. "What did Elaina tell you?"

"That Melanie wasn't your submissive."

I sighed in relief. Elaina wouldn't have known why Melanie and I split, would she?

"I would prefer my past relationships remain in the past," I said. "What Melanie and I did or did not do has no bearing on you and me."

She looked down, shuffling her remaining pasta from one side of her plate to the other.

I'd upset her.

"Abigail. If I wanted to be with Melanie, I would be with Melanie. I'm here with you."

"Did you ever have a naked picnic with Melanie?"

Naked picnic with Melanie?

I tried to imagine it.

On the floor, Nathaniel? Without clothes on? You're kidding, right? Tell me you're kidding.

"No," I said. "Never."

She smiled in triumph.

"Any more questions?" I asked.

"Not right now."

Thank goodness. For as much as I was pleased Abby felt brave enough to ask me questions, there were some things I wasn't ready to discuss.

And I still had a week and a half before I had to.

Chapter Twenty-nine

Elaina picked up on the second ring.

"Hello," she said.

"Elaina Grant Welling," I said in my best no-nonsense voice.

"What? What'd I do?"

"If I wanted Abby to know the particulars of my relationship with Melanie, I would have told her."

I walked to the window in my bedroom and looked down to where Abby and Apollo were playing outside. She'd wanted to take him outside one last time before going to bed, which was fine—I wanted her out of the house while I talked with Elaina.

"Oh, that."

"Yes, that."

"I didn't tell Abby anything, other than that Melanie wasn't your . . ." She stopped for a second. "Abby told you."

"I don't mind you knowing about my lifestyle. I do mind you interfering."

"How is my telling Abby that Melanie wasn't a submissive interfering?"

Because Abby would want to know why Melanie and I didn't work out. She would want to know why I had gone from being a dom to trying something "normal" and then gone back to being a dom.

"You're interfering anytime you tell my submissive something I've chosen not to tell her."

"Your submissive?"

"Yes, my submissive."

"Is that all she is to you?"

"What the hell does that mean? You have no idea what it means to have a submissive." I glanced back out the window and saw Abby reach down and pet Apollo's head. I sighed; my fight wasn't with Elaina. "I don't want to discuss this with you. You have no clue what my lifestyle entails, and I don't feel like giving you the details tonight."

"I just thought she might be more one day. I thought she might be . . . special."

My something special. I closed my eyes.

"It's my life, Elaina," I said. "Let me handle it."

"I know. I'm sorry. I'll stay out of it."

We hung up after making a bit of small talk about the blizzard. She asked if I wanted to talk to Todd, but I declined.

I opened the window a tiny bit. Just enough to let some cold air rush into the room, but of course, Abby's laughter came drifting in too. Her laugh filled me with warmth, even as the cold air chilled me.

I walked to my bed and sat down. When had everything become so confusing? Why had I ever allowed Abby into my life? It would have been so much easier to have left her as she was— someone I dreamed about but never met. Someone I watched, but never approached.

She approached you. She wanted you.

She wanted me as a dom, and I had just told her in the library that I had met and anticipated all her needs, but I hadn't. I had not always been gentle and patient and caring. I had failed her as much as I'd failed Melanie. Probably more so.

And still, she's here.

Because she doesn't know.

I groaned and fisted my hands in my hair. I couldn't think

straight anymore. Nothing made sense. Nothing. I had a week and a half left to come clean with her, and instead of deciding how best to go about telling her the truth, I was spending my time reading Shakespeare and having naked picnics.

I heard the sound of footsteps coming up the stairs and I stood to meet her at the door. Apollo made it to my room first and pushed his cold nose into my outstretched hand. Abby walked up behind him.

"He got all wet," she said. "I tried to dry him off, but . . ."

He lifted a wet paw to my knee, and I felt the dampness through my pants.

"Can't be helped in this weather," I said. "Thanks for taking him out."

She petted him one last time. "I like playing with him. He's a lot of fun." She turned to leave.

I wanted nothing more than to take her in my arms and tell her everything. To murmur in her ear how much I wanted her. How much I needed her. To tell her she was my one percent—my something special. To fucking kiss her. "Abigail?"

She turned and looked at me with expectation. "Yes, sir?"

Fucking used the wrong name. If you want her to believe she's your one percent, you should have called her Abby. You can't do anything right.

Which was why I shouldn't try.

"Good night," I whispered.

A soft smile came over her face. "Good night."

I stayed in my room the next morning until I heard her in the kitchen. I tossed my book to the nightstand and went to join her.

Sunlight streamed through the kitchen windows, providing perfect light as Abby danced across the floor, a cooking fork in her hand.

I entered the kitchen and propped myself up against the countertop. " 'I'll say she looks as clear as morning roses newly washed with dew,' " I said, and grinned.

She stopped dancing and nonchalantly walked to the stove to flip the bacon. " 'You have witchcraft in your lips.' "

She liked it. She wanted to play.

" 'All the world's a stage,' " I said. " 'And all the men and women merely players.' "

" 'Life's but a walking shadow, a poor player.' " She took the eggs off the stove and spooned them into a bowl. " 'That struts and frets his hour upon the stage, and then is heard no more.' "

It was time to bring out the heavy ammo. I walked to the stove, where she would have to look at me. In the most dramatic pose I could muster, I held one hand to my chest and pointed the other to the window.

> " *'But soft! What light through yonder window breaks?*
> *It is the east, and Juliet is the sun.*
> *Arise, fair sun, and kill the envious moon,*
> *Who is already sick and pale with grief*
> *That thou, her maid, art far more fair than she.'* "

She laughed, and the sound made my heart soar. What was it I had been worried about? I couldn't remember anymore.

With a serious expression, she looked at me. " 'Asses are made to bear, and so are you.' "

The Taming of the Shrew?

" 'Women are made to bear, and so are you,' " I said, quoting the next line, unable to keep the pride from my voice.

She turned the burners off, moved the frying pan to a trivet, and turned to fully face me. "I have no other but a woman's reason: I think him so, because I think him so."

I laughed. Damn, she was good.

And I was running out of Shakespeare quotes.

I had one more. I couldn't find one that called her a vixen, but this one was almost as good. " 'O villain, villain, smiling, damned villain!' "

"You called me a villain."

"You called me an ass."

"Draw?"

I pretended to think about it. "This time, but I'd like the record to show that I'm gaining on you."

She lifted the bacon onto a serving plate. "Agreed. But speaking of gaining on me, I need to use your gym today. I have a few miles to log on the treadmill."

"I need to jog as well." Her bacon looked perfect, just the right amount of crispy without being burned. I took a piece. "I have two treadmills. We could work out together."

After cleaning up from lunch, I headed to the library. As expected, Abby sat curled up on the floor with Apollo beside her and a book in her lap.

I sat down at the small desk. Between mushroom risotto and the naked picnic, I'd gotten very little work done the day before. I flipped my laptop open and started answering e-mail.

A few hours later, my phone rang. I looked at the display. Jackson.

"Jackson," I said, watching as Abby stood up and left the library.

"Nathaniel," Jackson whispered. "Hey."

I dropped my voice to match his. "Why are you whispering?"

"I don't want Felicia to hear."

Oh, no. Had something gone wrong? I looked outside—the snow had melted a little today. If something had happened between Felicia and Jackson, she should be able to make it back to the apartment. I wondered for a minute if Abby would want to stay through the weekend and not go home . . .

"Nathaniel?" Jackson asked.

"Sorry. What were you saying?"

He gave a nervous laugh. "I'm going to do it."

For the life of me, I didn't know what he was talking about. "Do what?"

His voice dropped even lower. "I'm going to propose."

"Propose what?"

"Come on. Get with it. Propose. I'm going to ask Felicia to marry me."

"You are?" I concentrated on the computer screen in front of me as his words sank in. "You are?"

"It's crazy, isn't it?" He didn't wait for an answer. "But it feels so right. I just know it's right. Everyone always says how you'll know. Well, I know."

My heart started to pound. You would know? Just like that? It was that easy? You asked yourself if it was right and then—bam— you knew?

"Uh, Jackson . . . I . . ." I stuttered. "I don't know what . . . congratulations."

"Thanks, man. Listen, don't tell Abby. Let Felicia surprise her."

"You're assuming she'll say yes."

"She'll say yes. I know."

As we hung up, I felt myself gearing up for the battle to come. The part of me that knew I couldn't do a normal relationship and the part that desperately wanted to try. I pulled a stack of papers from my desk and flipped through them, not really seeing what they were.

You aren't normal and you'll never be normal, I told myself. *Accept it and get on with it. You have a good thing going with Abby now. Why ruin it? She's happy. You're happy. Enjoy what you have.*

I thumbed through the papers.

Pull it together, West. Jackson and Felicia getting married doesn't change anything. He's like your brother. You should be happy.

And I was. I was happy for Jackson and Felicia. But why couldn't I have—

"Nathaniel West."

Chapter Thirty

My head shot up.

What the hell?

That was all I needed. As if I wasn't confused enough, Abby had decided *now* was a good time to traipse into the library and call me by my name?

Had I not told her to address me as *sir* during the week? I narrowed my eyes and thought back—yes, yes, I had. It had been one of the rules I gave her on Sunday morning. She had never been one to intentionally disregard a command, so what the hell was she up to?

"I assume you will apologize for that slip, Abigail?" I asked.

"I'll do no such thing." She brought her hands out from behind her back and showed me the box of candy I kept in the kitchen. "What are these?"

The hell? The day just got more and more baffling as it went on. She was calling me by my first name over candy? Really?

Perhaps all the situation needed was a strong look. I set the papers down and glared at her. "They are chocolate bars, Abigail. It says so right on the box."

She didn't move as I stood up. "I know what they are, Nathaniel. What I want to know is, what are they doing in the kitchen?"

Not only was the day growing more and more confusing, it was also going straight to hell. Why the fuck was Abby asking me why I kept candy in the kitchen?

"What business of yours is it?" I asked.

She shook the box at me. "It's my business because these are not on your meal plan."

Not on my meal plan? I didn't have a meal plan. She had a meal . . .

Oh.

Oh.

She wanted to role-play. I knew beyond a shadow of a doubt that Abby would never want to be a domme, but if she wanted to play around a bit. Well . . .

Part of me knew this was dangerous, blurring the lines even further. The other part of me wanted to see how far she'd go. I'd told her my room and the playroom were off-limits for the week. Where would she take this? Had she planned this out?

There was only one way to find out.

"Do you think I put together a meal plan for you because I'm bored and have nothing better to do?" she asked as victory surged in her eyes. "Answer me."

My words from the night I punished her. I uncrossed my arms and dropped them to my sides. "No, Mistress."

She gave a dramatic sigh. "I had plans for today, but instead we'll have to spend the afternoon inside, working on your punishment."

I wasn't sure what she had planned, but for that one moment, I didn't much care. Abby and I working together on anything for the entire afternoon would be delightful.

"I'm sorry to disappoint you, Mistress."

"You'll be sorrier still when I'm finished with you. I'm going up to my room. You have ten minutes to join me there."

She turned and left the room. I glanced down at Apollo and smiled. "Go to the kitchen, Apollo."

He cocked his head to the side and pawed the air.

"I mean it."

With a heavy sigh, he left the library and I was alone. Needless to say, my thoughts were all over the place. What was Abby up to? How far would I allow her to take this? If it were a real scene in which I was a submissive, I would enter her room naked. Since that wasn't the case, I decided to leave my clothes on.

As I walked up the stairs, thoughts swirled around in my head. I needed a plan. I needed to decide how long and exactly what I'd allow Abby to do. Lay out when I'd call a stop to her little game. But how could I plan when I didn't know what she had planned?

Her words from the kitchen came back to me: *You think too much.*

She had been right, of course. I did think too much. So for to-night I wouldn't think. I'd simply allow myself to fly by the seat of my pants—to be spontaneous. I could handle whatever Abby had planned, and if at any point I needed to, I'd call a stop to it.

It was simple when you thought about it.

She stood by the foot of her bed, dressed in the silver robe she'd worn the day I collared her. She looked even more beautiful today, if such a thing were possible.

She crossed her arms and tapped her foot. "What do you have to say for yourself, Nathaniel?"

Nathaniel.

The way she said my name. The way it fell from her lips.

I dropped my head so as not to show how it affected me. "Nothing, Mistress."

"Look at me."

No. Please, no. Anything but that. If I looked at her, she'd know. She'd know everything. I couldn't hide it anymore. Then again, I didn't want to hide it anymore. I was so tired of hiding.

"I am not a mistress," she said. "I am a goddess." She pushed the robe from her shoulders, exposing more of her gorgeous body. "I will be worshipped."

The truth of her words stunned me momentarily. She was right. She had never been more right.

She was a goddess.

She should be worshipped.

Tonight, I would do no less than prove it to her. I would show her exactly what she did to me, what she made me feel. Perhaps, in return, she would show me how I made her feel.

Dropping the role-play completely, I walked to her, closing the distance between us. Gently, I gathered her in my arms and sat us both on her bed.

I stared deeply into her eyes. What was this thing I felt whenever I looked at her? What was it she did to me that no one else ever had? Whatever had I done to deserve what she gave me?

The only things I knew with any certainty were that she was my one percent and I'd be damned if I'd deny it any longer.

Of its own accord, my hand reached out to stroke her cheek. "Abby," I whispered, rejoicing in the freedom her name held. "Oh, Abby."

To say it, to say her name . . . How was it something so simple stirred my very being? As if I'd finally found what I'd spent my entire life searching for? She was mine and I was hers, and if the world ended at that exact second, I'd die knowing that most sacred truth.

And still, I craved more. I needed more. I needed . . .

Her lips.

I traced her mouth with my thumb. " 'A kiss of desire . . .' "

I couldn't finish. It was too much. My body shook with the effort to remain where I was.

As my one percent, of course she knew what I meant. What I had been unable to say.

" '. . . on the lips,' " she finished.

I could contain myself no longer. I had denied myself too much. In telling myself kissing would make our relationship too personal, I'd created a rule that didn't matter and couldn't be obeyed. It hadn't helped anything anyway.

I pressed forward, willing myself to take my time—to enjoy and revere the moment. I was so close, I could taste her—could feel her breath, warm against my lips. I inhaled deeply and then, ever so gently, touched my lips to hers.

Oh, God.

Surely my body couldn't contain the joy that welled up inside. Surely this frail human shell was not meant to feel such deep emotion.

But my heart still beat within my chest, so I steadied myself and kissed her again.

And still I lived—or started to live. I wasn't sure which.

I knew I would never get enough of her. Never would I tire of her lips on mine or the way she felt in my arms. The greedy bastard inside begged for more, and it wasn't enough to simply touch her lips—I had to consume her. Had to let her consume me.

I framed her face with my hands to steady us both and kissed her again. Longer. But still softly—she was a goddess to be worshipped and I was nothing but a lowly disciple longing for the favor of her touch.

My tongue brushed the outline of her mouth, tasting and teasing. She parted her lips slightly, and my heart clenched in amazement. She would allow me this honor. After all I'd taken from her, still she would give me more.

I knew immediately her taste would be seared into my memory for as long as I lived. Her hands ran through my hair, pulling me closer, and I moaned.

She unbuttoned my shirt without breaking our kiss, and just as quickly, she slipped it from my shoulders and ran her hands over my chest.

Oh, God. Yes, Abby. Touch me.

I finally convinced myself to pull away and stood watching her as I stepped out of my pants.

She held out her arms. "Love me, Nathaniel."

Love?

Was that what it was? I loved Abby? Is this what Jackson meant? What Todd and Elaina had? Certainly not. Certainly no one else had ever experienced emotion this intensely before. But if love was the only way to describe it, love would have to do.

Love.

I loved Abby.

I had been such a fool.

"I always have, Abby." I picked her up and gathered her to me once more. "I always have."

I gently lowered us to the bed, kissing her again, allowing the truth of my feelings for her to wash over both of us. This time, unlike the others, there were no words spoken, because no words were needed.

It was as if I touched her for the very first time. Even her hands on my body were new. Touching, teasing, and exploring, yes, but there was a new meaning behind each touch and caress.

I love you, my fingers said as they breezed down her arms.

I love you, her fingers responded, stroking my back.

Her lips danced against mine, our mouths moving together in unbroken and unrestrained love.

Our joining was slow and purposeful. I closed my eyes as emotion surged inside me again for it was more than I could bear. My entire life, I'd seen and used sex as a means to physical pleasure. I had always made certain my partners and submissives had pleasure in return, but that was all it was—meaningless pleasure. Now I knew the truth. Sex could be, should be, so much more. It should be me using my body not just to bring pleasure or to gain pleasure, but to show love, to give love, to give myself.

The truth burst from me as I released, and a tear escaped my eye.

Afterward, I drew her to my chest. I stroked her hair, unable to keep my hands from her. With a sigh of contentment, she turned and put her head above my heart, and within minutes, she fell asleep.

Sleep did not come as easily to me. Instead, the real world crashed down.

What had we done?

What had *I* done?

I closed my eyes and tried desperately to hold on to the feeling I'd had minutes before. But I wasn't strong enough and the demons came back.

She would hate me for what I'd done now. Hate me when she discovered that I had been dishonest with her. She might stay with me for a time, but eventually she would feel nothing but pity, and I knew I could not bear her pity.

Her eyes would grow dimmer with each passing day as she discovered I could not be what she wanted. And what did my earlier epiphany mean? Was my entire life as a dom something less than it should be? How could I reconcile what I was with what I felt?

I tightened my arms around Abby's sleeping body. How could I offer her less than what she deserved?

As the night deepened, I knew.

I loved her. I would do anything, absolutely anything, for her.

I would let her go.

Chapter Thirty-one

I looked over Abby's head to the alarm clock on the nightstand—two o'clock. Roughly four more hours before I needed to leave her bed.

I closed my eyes and tried to commit her entire being to memory. I breathed deeply and inhaled the sweet scent of her hair, dipped my head lower and delighted in the floral smell of her skin. I ran my hand down her back, remembering how she arched against me in an attempt to draw me closer as we made love, how her body shook as wave after wave of pleasure washed over us both.

Now her body was relaxed in the stillness of sleep, though my hand moved up and down with her steady breathing. I ran my hand back up and rested my palm at the nape of her neck. Her skin was so soft, so flawless. Perfect, just like everything else about her.

Her lips formed a perfect *0* as she slept. I brought my head to where my lips nearly brushed hers, but I stopped myself—I didn't have a right to her lips anymore. Not with what I planned to do in a few short hours. Instead, I lightly kissed her neck. She tasted of sex and sweat—a bittersweet reminder of what we had experienced together.

"I'm sorry," I whispered against her skin. "I won't mean a word of it. I only hope . . ."

I stopped.

Hoped what?

That she would understand? I couldn't expect that.

That she would forgive me one day? Perhaps. Perhaps, maybe, years from now.

Did I hope she wouldn't hurt? I wasn't so blind or foolish that I thought I wouldn't hurt her. I knew she would hurt.

Or did some small part of me hope that she would know I didn't mean it? I was certain she would fight me, but in the end, I knew what it would take to make her leave. I hadn't earned my reputation as a hard-ass without learning a few things.

I shut my eyes against the onslaught of hot tears threatening to overtake me. How could I bear to do this to myself? How could I do it to her?

Because it was for the best. I wasn't sure of anything after the previous night—if I should continue my lifestyle, what Abby would do if I told her the truth—told her how I'd tricked her, lied to her, played on her naïveté.

I didn't dare ask her to remain with me as I tried to sort it out. It would be better for us both if she left. If I forced her to leave.

It would be the most despicable thing I'd ever done, but I'd do it for Abby.

She sighed in her sleep and cuddled closer into my embrace. I glanced at the clock again—two more hours. Two more hours to relish the feel of her in my arms.

At six o'clock, I slowly extracted myself out from under her and settled her back on the bed. I stood beside her and watched as she burrowed deeper into the covers.

I brushed my lips against her forehead and choked down the words I desperately wanted to say.

Forget it. You don't have the right to tell her.

But I shouted it in my head.

I love you.

I love you.

I love you.

I walked down to the kitchen and put on the coffee. Not because I wanted any, but because the normal, everyday act calmed me. I took Apollo out the front door and into the yard. My yard crew had been by the day before and had cleared away the melting banks of snow, so Abby should be able to make it home.

The paper had even been delivered. I took it inside and sat at the dining room table, then stared at the front page for half an hour before realizing I hadn't read a word. I closed my eyes and focused on what I needed to do, what I would say.

Not much later, I heard the sound of her feet overhead. I listened as she walked down the hallway, and then, seconds later, descended the stairs. She would go to the library first. Most mornings the past week, that was where I'd started my day—anxious to be in her room and near anything that was hers.

She was closer now. I heard her in the kitchen. Her footsteps stopped. She would be in the dining room next. I opened the newspaper to a random page and pretended to read.

She was seconds away from me.

"Hello," she said from the doorway.

I closed my eyes. Show time.

I turned down one side of the newspaper. "There you are."

The sight of her stunned me. She was even more beautiful in the morning light—hair slightly disheveled, lips full and swollen. I wanted to drop the paper, take her in my arms, and kiss her into oblivion.

"I was just thinking that you should be able to make it home today," I said.

Her forehead wrinkled. "What?"

I set the paper down. "The roads are clear. You shouldn't have any trouble getting to your apartment."

The wrinkle deepened. I could see her trying to work out what I was saying. "But why would I go home?" she asked. "I'll just be back tomorrow night."

I focused on the spot in between her eyes. "About that. I'll be at the office most of the weekend, digging out from this storm. It would probably be best if you didn't come over this weekend."

It was a lie. I had phone calls to make, but nothing that would keep me busy all weekend.

"You have to come home at some point," she said.

"Not for any length of time—" I stopped. *Say it. Make her leave.* "Abigail."

She sucked in a breath as if I'd punched her. "Why did you call me that?" she whispered.

"I always call you Abigail." The words just came out. I was dead inside.

"Last night you called me Abby."

Last night . . .

Oh, God . . .

I braced myself.

"It was the scene."

"What do you mean?" she asked.

"We switched." I'd thought the lies would be easier as I told them, but they were not. Each one struck my heart and killed part of me as it came from my mouth. "You wanted me to call you Abby."

"We didn't *switch*."

Blackness. Blackness and death consumed me. "We did. It was what you wanted when you came into the library with the candy."

"That was my original intention," she said, and I knew she was nowhere near giving up. "But then you kissed me. You called me Abby. You slept in my bed. All night."

End it. Now.

I slipped my hands from the table and clenched my fists as tightly as I could.

Do it.

I took a deep breath. "And I have *never* invited you to sleep in mine."

My words hit their mark. Pain rippled across her face. "Fuck it. Don't do this."

"Watch your language."

"Don't fucking tell me to watch my language when you're sitting there trying to pretend last night didn't mean anything." She balled her fists. "Just because the dynamic changed doesn't make what happened bad. So we admitted a few things. So what? We move on. It'll make us better together."

"Have I ever lied to you, Abigail?" I was lying now. Just calling her Abigail was a lie. But I was winning. The damage had been done. Soon now. Very soon.

She wiped her nose. "No."

"Then what makes you think I'm lying now?"

"Because you're scared. You love me, and it's scaring you. But you know what? It's okay. I'm a little scared too."

"I'm not scared." Another lie. "I'm a coldhearted bastard. I thought you knew that."

Her eyes closed and her shoulders sagged. It was over. She'd given up easier than I thought she would, but in the end, it was probably better that way.

I saw her determination. Her hands went to her neck, and I braced myself again.

The collar fell to the table with a metallic clink. "Turpentine."

The words I read weeks ago echoed in my head.

Turpentine.

Turpentine in a fire.

I saw them all consumed.

Chapter Thirty-two

I had planned it. I'd anticipated it. Still, there was something so final about her removing the collar and the way it looked so broken as it lay on the table.

I couldn't take my eyes off it. Couldn't bring myself to look at Abby with a bare neck.

She's not yours anymore.

I closed my eyes against the pain. I couldn't think about it just yet. I still had a part to play.

"Very well, Abigail," I said, finally looking at her. "If that's what you want."

"Yes," she said. "If you're going to pretend last night was nothing but a damn scene, this is what I want."

She knew. She knew I was pretending. Maybe that would make it easier for her to handle later.

I nodded. "I know many dominants in the New York area. I would be more than happy to give you some names."

The previous night, I had run through various names in my head. I knew she would need a dom sooner or later, but I hadn't been able to decide on anyone good enough for her. I hoped she didn't call my bluff—I had no names ready to give.

"Or I could give them yours," I added.

I intended my offer to be a kind one, but the look she gave me—so hurt, so sad. She didn't understand. Did she not know how much it pained me to offer her the names of my friends? To imagine, even for a moment, her being with someone else?

"I'll keep that in mind," she spat out.

I sat there, silent, not moving.

"I'll go get my things." She turned and left.

When I heard her footsteps on the stairs, I dropped my head into my hands. Oh, God. She was doing it. She was leaving me. Would I see her before she left or would my last sight of her be the pained look on her face as my words cut her open?

Apollo got up from his place by my feet and cocked his head at me.

"Go," I whispered. "Go to her." He remained by my side.

Minutes later, she walked down the stairs. Apollo heard and scrambled out to meet her.

"Oh, Apollo," she said from the foyer. "You be a good boy."

I dropped my head and pulled at my hair. It was worse than my worst nightmare.

"I'm going to miss you," she said to my dog. "I can't stay here anymore, so I won't see you again. But you be good and . . . promise me you'll take care of Nathaniel, okay?"

A sob ripped from my chest. Her last thoughts were of me. The front door opened and closed.

I pulled together all the strength I could and rose to my feet. I had one last task as Abby's dom—to see her safely home.

Hours later, having driven behind her all the way to the city without her knowing, I walked back into my empty house.

It was done. She was gone.

I walked into the foyer, my footsteps echoing in the stillness. Even when Abby left on Sundays, the house never felt so desolate.

It was because she'd never be back. The house would always feel empty now.

I couldn't bear the emptiness; I needed to make it go away.

Apollo looked behind me, as if expecting Abby to enter, but I only gave him a glance as I walked straight to the library.

Various bottles sat on the bar. I went straight for them, didn't even bother to look around at the rest of the library. I couldn't handle looking just yet. The brandy was forty percent alcohol; it shouldn't take too long to do the trick.

The glasses went down easier the more I drank. To be honest, I lost count after three. If I drank enough, got drunk enough, maybe it wouldn't hurt so badly. Maybe it wouldn't feel like my heart had been pulled from my chest.

Of course, it didn't help. It only made the pain worse.

Apollo sat beside me and whined.

"S'kay, Apollo," I mumbled as I poured another glass. "It's better this way. Trust me."

The room spun slightly, so I stumbled over to the leather couch and collapsed. More. I needed more. The brandy didn't even burn as it went down.

I heard the glass fall to the floor and then . . . nothing.

The sunlight coming through the window blinded me and I squinted. Something moved at the curtains. Turned toward me.

"Abby?" I choked out.

Unparalleled joy coursed through my body.

I sat up. "Abby!" My voice sounded stronger.

She smiled at me.

"I knew you wouldn't believe me. I knew you wouldn't. And you came back. Oh, Abby. I love you so much. I'm sorry I didn't tell you before."

I stood up to take her in my arms. Finally. Finally, I would tell her everything.

She walked to me, still smiling.

I watched her, mesmerized. The sunlight shimmered around her. Her dress was beautiful and it floated around her as she walked. She moved so gracefully, it was as if she walked on air.

When she stood before me, I lifted a hand to her cheek. Her skin. So perfect. I stroked it. "You forgive me?"

She nodded.

I fell to the ground before her. "I'm sorry, Abby. So sorry." I stroked her feet and kissed them. "Thank you. Thank you for coming back."

The possibilities of what we could be, how we could be, ran through my mind. However we were together, however we worked it out, would be fine. The important thing was, we were together. In the end, that was all that mattered.

I gave one last sob and wiped my eyes. I peeked up at her, and there she stood—looking down on me and smiling.

I slowly rose to my feet. "Abby."

Our lips came together softly. She tasted even sweeter than I remembered. I moaned and pulled her closer. She melted into my embrace, wrapped herself around me.

Was it odd that she wasn't talking? Shouldn't she be talking? We could talk later, though, right? We had plenty of time to talk.

I kissed her deeper, taking her head in my hands and tangling my fingers in her hair. Why didn't she smell like anything?

Her fingers danced along my back, teasing me. I pulled back.

I took my place on the couch and patted the empty spot beside me. "Here. Sit down. Let me tell you everything."

She shook her head.

"Please, Abby."

She took a step back. "It's too late."

"You said you forgave me. You came back."

"Too late, Nathaniel."

Another step back.

"But I want to tell you," I pleaded. "I need to tell you. Wait. Don't leave me."

She took another step back—almost to the window—and shook her head again.

"Abby?" I asked, but she had disappeared. "Abby?"

The curtains swayed.

"Abby, come back! Abby, I love you!"

Something warm and soft and wet licked my cheek. I shook myself awake and sat up. Apollo whined and licked me again.

I looked around the library.

Empty.

It had been a dream.

A damn dream.

She hadn't come back. She believed me, and she was never coming back.

I pushed Apollo away and reached for my glass. Where was it? I stood up, and my shoes crunched broken shards of glass. Fuck.

I left them and went to pour another glass of brandy. I took a long sip and dropped that glass to the floor too. Watched it shatter into hundreds of pieces.

Just like my life.

Just like my heart.

Just like I'd shattered Abby.

I poured a new glass and drained it within minutes. I looked again to the window—to where Abby had stood in my dream. Like I expected her to be there. To appear out of thin air. Like she'd just breeze into my house and make her way back into the library as if I hadn't ripped her fucking heart out.

It was as if I looked at the library through a thick haze. Everything was blurred and distorted. My mind, though—my mind worked with the utmost clarity, for I remembered every second Abby and I had ever spent in the library.

There, on the floor, where we had our naked picnic.

There, on the couch, where she had stripped herself bare for me.

And there, on the piano bench, where she'd taken me after I played for her.

I grabbed my hair and pulled. Maybe, if I tried hard enough, I could rip the memories right out of my head. The pictures in my mind blurred together—Abby and me in the library, playing the piano for her, Abby reading, standing in the poetry section, the rose I gave her . . .

She had never asked me about the rose.

Why not?

Would it have mattered?

She had to have known something about the rose. She fucking knew everything. She knew about Melanie, for fuck's sake.

My cell phone vibrated. I took it from my pocket and squinted at the screen.

Jackson?

I didn't want to talk to him. I dropped the phone to the floor and my eyes scanned the library. The fireplace was empty.

I saw them all consumed.

The library needed a fire.

Fucking consume everything—the piano, the couches, the fucking poetry. Everything.

I laughed. Wouldn't take much. The brandy on the floor would help.

Now. Where to get matches?

I staggered into the kitchen, not quite sure why the floor kept moving the way it did. Made it hard to walk. I yanked a drawer out and the contents poured onto the floor.

Something pounded in the other room.

I looked up from the mess. Abby?

No. Abby was gone and would never come back.

The ache in my heart would never get better. Had to fix it myself.

Ah, yes. My fingers wrapped around the matchbox. Just what I needed.

I took the matches and started walking back to the library. Just needed a little help from the wall so I could make it down the hall. I heard footsteps behind me.

"Nathaniel?" Jackson called.

I laughed. He could join me in the fire.

I pretended not to hear him and kept walking.

"Nathaniel?"

Damn, he was fast. How'd he make it to me so quickly? I turned. We were right outside the library.

"Con . . . congra . . ." I waved the matches in the air. "Besss wisssses on your . . ." What was the word? "Yeah."

"Holy fuck," the blob that was Jackson said. "You're trashed."

I turned and stepped into the library.

"What are you doing?" he asked.

"Burning."

"Burning what?" He trotted along beside me.

"Lib . . . rary."

He grabbed my shoulders and spun me around. "What the hell are you doing? What have you done to this place?"

I laughed.

"Nathaniel . . . fuck." He shook me. "Stop laughing. You're scaring me."

I stopped laughing and tried to focus on his face. I had to get this next part out. "She . . . left . . . me."

The pain in my heart exploded, and I stumbled toward the couch but ended up slipping on the brandy. The glass cut into my knees.

Yes. That was better. The pain in my knees. Not as bad as the pain in my heart, though.

I pressed my hand to the floor to help me stand, but that just jabbed glass into my palm.

I held my hand up to Jackson.

"Damn it, Nathaniel."

I shook my head. "She'sss not ever coming back." I watched as blood spilled out of my hand. "Never . . . coming . . . baccckkk."

The room dissolved into darkness.

It was dark when I woke again. For a split second, all was well with my world, but then everything crashed down on me again.

Abby was gone. Forever.

I couldn't decide which hurt more—my head or my heart.

"Nathaniel?" Jackson asked from somewhere.

My head hurt like the devil, but my heart was definitely injured worse.

I tried to sit up, but the room spun too fast and I lay back down. Where was I?

I turned my head. The living room. Jackson must have carried me into the living room.

"You awake?" he asked.

"I think that's generally what it means when one has their eyes open." It hurt to open my eyes, though, so I closed them again. "Where's my drink?"

"I put it all away, and I—"

"Why?"

"Why what?"

I opened one eye. "Why did you put my drink away?"

"I think you've had enough."

"I'll decide when I've had enough." I opened the other eye. Ah, yes. There he was—sitting in an armchair.

"When I came inside, you were trying to burn down the library."

"And you stopped me?" Had I really tried to burn down the library? I didn't remember that.

Abby was gone and there was a big gaping hole in my heart. I remembered that.

"That's why I'm not letting you drink anything else." He picked up my remote and changed the channel on the television.

"You ever have a woman leave you?"

He looked out the side of his eye at me. "No more brandy."

"I'll alternate with red wine, then," I said. "It's heart healthy."

He didn't try to stop me. For the next few days, I spent most of my time in a drunken haze. It felt better that way. If I drank enough, I fell into such a deep stupor, Abby didn't visit my dreams.

The worst was when I was awake. When I was awake, I saw her everywhere. Unlike my dreams, I knew she wasn't really in the house, but I could sense her. Could sense her everywhere—in the kitchen, in the living room, in the foyer. She had left her imprint on nearly every room of my house.

I never set foot back in the library after that first day, and I refused to sleep in my bedroom. Since Jackson insisted on staying with me, I let him have my bedroom and I moved into the guest room across the hall from both my room and Abby's room. At least there, I had no memories of Abby.

Jackson called Sara for me on Monday and told her I wouldn't be in for a few days. I wasn't sure what excuse he used. I didn't really care. Fucking company could run itself. I knew he talked to Linda—I heard him sometimes. She never came by, so I could only imagine what he told her.

I hated it when he talked to Felicia in my presence. Hated it and loved it. Loved it because it was a connection to Abby. Hated it because it was a connection to Abby.

I wondered how she was doing. Jackson never said and I never asked. He never mentioned Abby's name to me. When he saw me listening to his conversations, he walked out of the room or hung up.

I wished I could do it all over again.

Wished I could call Abby in on that first day and talk to her—
tell her everything. If I had just been honest in the first place . . .

But whenever I started the "if I had just" game, I started drinking again and fell into the same never-ending circle.

One day that week, who knew which one, I woke in the living
room and heard Jackson on the phone.

"I don't know, man," he was saying. "I thought he'd be better
by now. He's just . . . not."

Silence as the other party on the phone spoke.

"I don't want to bring Mom over; that would just make it
worse," he said. "And he won't talk. I don't know what to do,
Todd. He just stares into space or drinks or sleeps."

Silence again.

"Who?" he asked. "Hold on." I heard him move to the table by
the couch and pick up my cell phone. "Paul, you said?"

Fucking hell.

I reached for the glass I knew would be by my side and let the
alcohol do its trick.

"Nathaniel Matthew West," a fierce, strong voice said, hours,
maybe days, later.

I pretended not to hear. I had been having the most wonderful
dream. Abby had been there; she'd been—

"I know you heard me," the voice said. "Wake up."

I rolled over. I was in bed. Always good to know where you
were. Bed was good. You could sleep in bed. "Go away."

There was light when I woke up again. I didn't like the light.
The darkness was better.

"I told Jackson you're not allowed any more alcohol."

The voice was starting to piss me off. Why wouldn't it leave
me alone?

"Fuck off," I told it.

"I have some nice coffee brewing downstairs—"

I pulled the sheets over my head. "Don't want coffee."

"Get your sorry, good-for-nothing ass out of that bed right this minute."

Damn. He wouldn't shut up. "You don't tell me what to do, Paul."

"Someone damn well better."

"I'm not a child."

"Then prove it," he said. "And speaking of children, I left my newborn son and sleep-deprived wife to be here with you, so you better get out of that fucking bed before I drag you out of it."

I thought about my options for less than five seconds and then sat up. "I don't remember you being this much of a pain in the ass."

Paul smiled. "Then you don't remember me very well."

Sitting in the kitchen over the next few hours, I told him everything. All about Abby and how I knew of her, had watched her, then lied to her. I even told him about the ridiculous safe word. He knew, of course, how I'd treated her badly after her first punishment, so I glossed over that part. I went on to tell him how I'd fallen in love with her. How she'd fallen in love with me.

He nodded solemnly as I detailed our final night and the fateful morning I pushed her away.

"Dug yourself quite a nice hole, didn't you?" he asked finally.

I wrapped my hands around my coffee mug and let the warmth seep into my fingers. "Yes."

"So, what are you going to do about it?"

I looked up at him. Was he serious?

"I mean it, Nathaniel. Are you going to sit here and moan and groan about everything you did wrong, or are you going to be a man and do something about it?"

"She's gone. What else is there to do?"

"You've got bigger problems than Abby."

"What?" What was he talking about? Abby was the center of everything.

"You've got to fix yourself before you can fix things with Abby." He got up and washed his cup.

"There's no fixing anything with Abby." I glared at him. "I just told you she left me."

"With good reason, too." He turned away from the sink and faced me. "But the start of your Abby troubles wasn't your deception. The start of your Abby troubles was you. How you feel about yourself."

What the hell?

"Now, I'm no expert, but I know you have a strong and wonderful family who would do anything for you. Do you even know everything Jackson did while you were incapacitated? How scared he was for you?"

I shook my head.

"You're a selfish little boy trapped inside the body of a frightened man." He pointed at me. "It's time you grew up and faced the facts. So I ask you, Nathaniel. What are you going to do about it?"

I dropped my head and looked at the table—struck through the heart by the conviction of his words.

Knowing what I had to do, I reached for my phone and called Todd.

"Todd?" I asked when he picked up. "Can you give me some names? I need help."

Chapter Thirty-three

Todd worked his magic and set up an appointment for me with a highly regarded psychiatrist for the next day. I returned home from the consultation feeling better than I had in a long time. The hole in my heart was still there and it still ached, but just the freedom of talking with someone felt good.

I walked into my foyer, eyes avoiding the plush bench—there were some things I wasn't ready for yet. While I might have been feeling better about myself, I knew there was much to do where my actions toward Abby were concerned.

I threw my keys on the kitchen counter. Paul sat at the table, talking on the phone. "I have a flight scheduled for the day after tomorrow," he said. He must have been talking with Christine.

He looked up as I walked in and winked at me. I went to the refrigerator and pulled out a bottle of water. I hadn't had a drop of alcohol in almost twenty-four hours, and even though my head still hurt like the devil, my vision and mind were sharper.

Paul probably wanted privacy, I thought, so I started to leave the room, but he waved for me to stop.

"When I get home, I have diaper and nighttime duty for a week?" he asked.

Damn it. I hated that my behavior had taken Paul away from his son.

"Of course, love," he said, laughing. "As soon as I learn how to lactate."

The intimate tone of his voice made me uncomfortable. I thought about leaving and waiting for him in the living room, but I could tell the conversation was almost over.

"Give my boy a kiss from Daddy." His lips curved into a smile. "I love you, too," he said, and hung up with a sigh.

"I'm sorry," I said, leaning against the countertop. "Christine must hate me."

"She did say to fear for my life if I didn't make it home soon."

I sat down at the table. "Is that weird?"

"Is what weird?"

I thought the question obvious. "For your submissive to talk to you that way."

"She's not my submissive twenty-four hours a day, seven days a week."

I shrugged. "I just think it would feel strange."

"Because you haven't done it."

"Maybe."

He raised an eyebrow. "Are you ready for this? We can have this talk if you think you are."

"What talk?"

"I'm an eternal optimist and I'm thinking positively. Even if you and Abby never work out, maybe one day you'll find someone else."

"Damn it, Paul." I ran my fingers through my hair. "I can't think about that right now."

"Maybe not. But if you'd been prepared, you might have done things differently with Abby."

"I can't imagine being with anyone other than Abby, and I don't think she'll ever take me back."

"You said she loved you. If that's true, maybe she'll give you a second chance."

It hurt too much to hope. To allow myself to think that one day I might be at a place to work things out with Abby. That she might be at a place to talk to me. Hell, at this point, I'd be happy if she'd just look at me one day. Of course, we'd have to be in the same room for that to happen, and that wasn't looking likely.

"Tell me how you two do it," I said. "How it works for you."

"We tried the twenty-four-hour, seven-days-a-week thing in the beginning, and I won't lie—it was hard." He looked at me as if gauging my reaction. "It was hard for me because I never felt like she could be completely open and honest, and it was hard for her, because she never felt like she could be completely open and honest."

I thought back to the times I'd desperately wanted Abby to talk to me. I remembered the night of the black-tie benefit, how difficult it had been for her to tell me what kind of wine she wanted. "I can see that."

"So we went to weekend play." He smiled. "That worked out better for us. The trick is finding what works for you. What works for your submissive. It has to work for you both, if it's going to work at all. I know people who play only once every few weeks." He shrugged. "Again, it's what works for you."

"And it's never interfered with your marriage?"

"I'm not saying it's perfect, but what marriage is? We still fight. We still make up. Is it work? Yes, but that's life. And it's always changing. We had to regroup when Christine became pregnant. I'm sure it'll be weeks, if not months, before we can get back into the playroom, but that's okay. It's what works for us. And we love each other. We want what the other person wants."

I shook my head. "I don't know. There are a lot of people who think it isn't BDSM if romantic feelings are involved."

He looked taken aback for a second, started to say something and then stopped. Finally, he spoke. "Usually, when someone tells me what Christine and I have isn't real, I invite them back to my playroom so I can show them just how real it is. But you've been in my playroom, so I won't do that." He paused. "My other reaction is to knock the shit out of anyone who dares to call my wife a fake submissive."

I held up my hand. "I wasn't calling her fake. I was just repeating what I've heard."

"I know, and you've had a rough week, so I'm going to go easy on you." He sounded like he didn't particularly want to go easy on me.

"I appreciate that," I said wearily. "But what do you say to those who think you can't call it BDSM?"

He leaned across the table and held my gaze. "Does it fucking matter what you call it?"

"What?"

"If you and your submissive are getting what you need physically, does it matter that you're getting it with someone you have an emotional connection with?"

"But is it harder?"

"Was it harder when you punished Abby?" he asked, instead of answering.

"Yes."

"Then there's your answer. But I ask you, was it better when you held her? When it was you bringing her pleasure? When it was her bringing you pleasure?"

"Oh hell, yes."

"So yes, it's harder," he said. "But it's also better. At least in our case. The important thing to remember, Nathaniel, is that I don't have all the answers; I only know what works for Christine and me. I can't answer for everyone else, but then again, I don't expect them to answer for me either."

"So it doesn't matter to you what other people call it."

"Not in the least," he said. He must have noticed my confusion. "You're not completely ready for this yet. I might have been a bit premature in bringing it up." He patted my hand. "Listen, when you're ready, you call me."

I put my hand on top of his. "Deal."

He stood and walked to the door, but before he left the room, he looked back over his shoulder. "And, Nathaniel," he said. "When you and Abby get back together—bring her to visit Christine and me."

My mouth dropped, but he just laughed and walked out.

When he left two days later, he repeated his request. I just smiled and nodded. I mean, hell could freeze over. Who was I to deny the possibility?

Two weeks later, I had finished seven counseling sessions and, emotionally, I felt better. I talked to Paul several times during those two weeks and even spoke to Christine once. I'd been hesitant when Paul suggested I talk with his wife, but afterward, I was glad I did. Christine was charming and vivacious and gave me an insight into how BDSM worked in romantic relationships— from the submissive's point of view.

I still couldn't sleep in my bedroom and I'd yet to enter the library, but things were getting better.

Slightly.

There were times I walked into the kitchen and felt certain I smelled the floral scent of her body wash. Times when I took a shower that I'd think I heard something and I'd turn to see if it was her.

I picked up my phone to call her several times. Once, I even brought her up in my contacts list, my finger hovering nervously right above the call button.

What was she doing? Would she hang up on me?

I couldn't bear it if she did.

Jackson still came by my house almost daily. Not long after

Paul left, I finally got around to properly congratulating him on his engagement. He was almost sheepish when he asked me to be his best man.

I tried not to think about the fact that Abby would more than likely be Felicia's maid of honor. The wedding was in June. Four months. Would I be ready to see and talk to Abby in four months?

I had no choice.

I picked up the mail from where the housekeeper had set it on the foyer table and walked into the living room. I sat down and flipped through the stack. Now, why would I get a copy of *People* magazine? I thumbed through a few pages, not understanding. My gaze fell on a picture of Jackson and Felicia.

Oh, the engagement. Jackson probably had one sent to me.

I started reading the article.

Seconds later, I threw the magazine across the room and picked up my phone.

"Jackson Clark," I said when he answered. "Who the fuck told *People* magazine Abby and I were linked romantically?"

"That might have been me," he admitted.

"Why? Why would you do that? She probably thinks I had something to do with it." Or maybe, I thought, maybe, she wouldn't see it. Maybe she would never know. I could only hope.

"I thought you two would eventually get back together," he said.

"You what?" I yelled.

"Okay, here's the thing," he said, using the same voice I remembered from the countless nights he tried to keep me away from the brandy. "Mom's throwing Felicia and me an engagement party."

Engagement party. Okay. I could handle that. It would be when? May?

"So," I said.

"So, we want it in March."

"March? Like one month from now, March?"

"Yeah."

"Fuck."

"I thought by now Abby would have gotten her head out of her ass——"

"Stop it right there."

"I mean, I know it was hard on her. Felicia said it was. But if she'd just call you, you know, try to work it out."

"I never expected her to," I said quietly.

"I sure as hell did."

"Why?"

"She had to have known how it would hurt you when she left. I don't get it. I know she misses you," he said. "She should call you. Or, and I'm just throwing this out there, you call her."

She missed me? She missed me?

My brain belatedly caught what else he had said. "I can't call her."

"Why not? I bet she'd listen."

"She won't. Our breakup was all my fault."

"But you said she left you."

"Because of me. Because I made her leave."

"What? On purpose?"

I nodded, even though he couldn't see me. "On purpose."

"Man, you were more fucked up than I realized."

"I know."

"Guess it's you that needs to get your head out of your ass," he said with a little laugh, but he was timid, as if he didn't want to push me too far.

"Guess it is."

"Are you?" he asked, all seriousness again.

"I've been trying," I said. "I thought I had until June. Then you tell me Linda's throwing a party a month from now." But that could be good. Maybe it would force me to face my demons sooner rather than later. All my demons. "It's okay, really. I'll be fine. It's a good thing."

I hoped it was a good thing. If I told myself it was a good thing often enough, maybe I'd eventually believe it.

Jackson let out a sigh of relief.

"You still coming by this afternoon?" I asked.

"Wouldn't miss it."

We hung up and I walked over to the desk in the living room. One month. One month before I saw Abby again. My heart pounded and I closed my eyes to calm down.

I took a seat and started working, immersing myself in schedules and e-mails to keep from thinking about the party. I replied to Yang Cai and started planning a trip to China for July. Now that the entire spring and summer stretched out empty and alone, I saw no reason to put off the visit. I'd probably need a distraction after the wedding anyway. Another e-mail asked me to present at a conference in Florida in October. Why the hell not? I'd fill up my fall schedule as well.

One week before the party, I sat down and wrote out everything I wanted to say to Abby. Every lie explained. Every deception brought to light. I laid out every penalty against me. Not because I had any hope of getting her back; I simply wanted to explain, to own up to my mistakes. I was still in therapy and it was helping. I was stronger emotionally, but talking to Abby would test my progress.

Once, I actually stood in front of my mirror and practiced what I would say, but I looked stupid, so I stopped. Instead, I transferred everything I wanted to say onto index cards and kept them in my pocket. Every once in a while, I reached down to touch the cards. I brushed my fingers over them and whispered my apology to Abby.

A few days before the party, Elaina called while I stood in my closet, trying to decide what to wear. I'd talked to Elaina a few times since the split. She had always been short—she knew, even without me saying anything, that it was all my fault.

"Hey, dipshit," she said.

I smiled. Elaina never changed. "Elaina."

"You ready for this weekend?"

No, but I might as well be. There was no stopping it.

"I spoke to her," she said, not waiting for me to answer.

My heart pounded. "You did?" I asked. "When?"

"Last time was yesterday, but I'd spoken to her a few times before then."

The question danced on my tongue. Did I want to know? Yes. I absolutely had to know. "How . . . How is she?"

She sighed. "How do you think she is?"

Angry. Upset. Pissed. Sad. Confused.

"I don't know," I said. "I want . . ."

What did I want? I wanted her to be happy. I knew in that second, though, no matter how much I'd avoided saying it, or even thinking it, I wanted her back.

I blinked back the tears that sprang to my eyes. Counseling had made me so emotional lately. Emotional or not, there was the truth—I wanted her back.

"She wants to kick you in the balls," she finished.

I bit back a laugh. "I deserve that."

"I know you do." I heard the smile in Elaina's voice as she talked. "I told her as much myself."

"Thanks."

"She wouldn't let me give her a gown for the party. She wants to do this her way."

That sounded like Abby. Her way. Her move. She probably wanted nothing to do with us now. She might not even show up at the party.

No. She would go for Felicia. That was the kind of woman she was. Even though it would make her uncomfortable, she'd go for her friend. And since she would be there, I'd talk to her. Finally.

If she listened, she listened.

If she kicked me in the balls, she kicked me in the balls.

The lights of the penthouse glowed through the windows. After giving my car to the valet, I stood and stared at the front of the building. Abby was on the other side of those doors.

I took five steps toward the doorway and stopped. Then I turned and took four steps back to the valet.

Story of your life, West. Two steps forward, one step back. End it. End it here.

End it now.

So I turned, but stood unmoving, watching the door. It opened, and Jackson came out. He jogged down the walkway to me.

"What are you doing?" I asked.

He grinned sheepishly. "Thought you might need a little pep talk."

"Pep talk?"

He threw an arm around me and we started moving forward. "I know it's my fault you're here tonight, and I wanted to give you some moral support." He stopped, turned toward me, and put his hands on my shoulders. "You're a good man, Nathaniel West, and there's a good woman waiting for you inside. Now, I don't know what happened between the two of you, and I really don't care. What I care about is the two of you working it out, okay?"

I crushed him to my chest. "Thank you, Jackson. I owe you a lot."

"I guess maybe we're even."

"I guess maybe we're not," I said, and I knew that even though his chest muffled my voice, he could still hear me. "I owe you

more than I can ever repay. If you hadn't found me that day . . ."
I shivered, not wanting to think back.

He pulled back. "But I did, so no worries."

I clapped his back. "No worries."

We walked together through the door.

Once inside, Jackson trotted off to find Felicia. Todd met me at the entrance, pushing through a crowd of people.

"Hell, I don't even know most of these people," he said as he finally made it to me, straightening his jacket.

"How's it going?" I sounded calm, but my voice cracked at the end, and I broke out in a cold sweat just thinking about moving into the main room.

"Good," he said. "Listen, Melanie's here. I don't think she's going to do anything to embarrass you, but I wanted you to know. I'm sure she knows who Abby is."

Fuck. Melanie. I hadn't thought about her being here.

"Don't worry," I said. "I'm going to go straight to Abby and ask her to talk."

That was my plan. I could do it. I would do it. Walk straight to Abby. Ask her to talk. My fingers danced over the cards in my pocket.

I'm sorry, Abby.

Todd smiled. "She's right inside. Talking to Linda."

I gave him a quick hug, straightened my shoulders, and made my way into the main banquet room.

Damn, I thought as I entered. Todd hadn't been kidding. Who were all these people? My eyes scanned the faces before me.

Where was she?

"Nathaniel!"

"Hey, Nathaniel."

All these people I didn't care about and didn't want to talk to came up to me, slapping me on the back, wanting to chat. I shook hands but kept moving.

Find Abby. Had to find Abby.

I shook someone else's hand.

She hadn't left, had she? Heard I'd entered the room and left through the back door?

"Looking good, man," someone said. "Haven't seen you around lately."

I might have answered him.

My eyes swept the crowd again.

There! Standing beside Linda, just like Todd had said.

She looked beautiful.

In all my dreams, she'd never looked more perfect. I could barely take her in—her upswept hair, the shimmery silver gown, the way she worried her bottom lip. The entire room faded away and it was just me and her.

I couldn't get to her fast enough.

And still, it took forever to cross the room.

She didn't move away from me. She simply waited, her eyes thoughtful and searching.

"Hello, Abby," I whispered when I stood before her.

If my use of her name surprised her, it didn't show.

"Nathaniel."

Okay. This was good. I said something; she answered. Progress made.

"You look well," I said. She looked much better than well, but I didn't want to come on too strong or too desperate. Although I was certain she could see right through me.

"Thank you."

There was a small room off the main hall—I remembered from looking over the facility's layout. I needed to get her somewhere private so we could talk.

I moved closer. "I wanted to tell—"

"There you are."

I looked over.

Melanie?

"Melanie, this is not a good time," I said, anxious to get back to Abby.

"You must be Abby," Melanie said, holding out a hand for Abby to shake. "It's nice to finally meet you."

Fucking hell. What was she going to do? Carry on a conversation?

Like, right now?

"Melanie, I——" I started.

"Nathaniel!" someone said. I looked over my shoulder. It was the man who had asked me to present at the convention in Florida. "Just the man I've been waiting for. Come with me. I need to introduce you to some people."

What? No? I wanted to stay and talk to Abby.

But Melanie stood there, a little smirk on her face, and there was no way I was talking to Abby in front of Melanie.

The party would last a few hours—I had plenty of time.

I'd find her later.

Except I didn't.

I always found a reason not to talk to her—she was with Felicia; she was talking with Elaina; Linda was introducing her to someone.

The pittance of courage I'd built up over the last few weeks left me. I'd had one shot and Melanie had ruined it.

I kept telling myself the party wasn't over yet. I still had time. I just needed to gather my courage together, find her, and ask her to talk. Simple. Very, very simple.

I'd just do it later.

I looked down at my watch—eight o'clock. I bet the party

wouldn't even end until midnight at the earliest. I stood with a group of Linda's colleagues, listening as they rambled on about some new hospital something or other, but watching Abby—she was hugging Elaina.

"What do you think, Nathaniel?" one of them asked.

Why was she hugging Elaina?

"Nathaniel?"

Was she leaving? Why was she walking toward the door?

Oh, God. She was leaving.

She was leaving and I wouldn't see her until June.

NO!

"Abby," I called, but of course, she didn't hear me. "Abby," I said louder, but all the damn people were too loud.

I turned and my eyes fell on the deejay booth beside me. I pushed the man out of the way and hit the off button on the mixer. I wasn't even thinking as I jerked the microphone from his hands.

My eyes never left her back.

"Don't leave me, Abby."

She spun around.

"I let you leave once and it almost killed me. Please," I begged. "Please don't leave me."

Chapter Thirty-four

She just stood there.

Stood there and looked at me for what had to be the longest seconds of my life.

Would she leave? Would she shout at me? Would she stay? Finally, she walked to me. It had worked. She wasn't leaving.

Of course, she didn't look entirely pleased to be staying. Especially when she ripped the microphone out of my hands.

"What the hell do you think you're doing?" she asked, eyes lit with fire.

I glanced around the room.

Shit. What had I done? Everyone stared at us, like we were the star attraction in some weird freak show. Someone I didn't even know elbowed the person beside him and jerked his head toward me.

Well, this was embarrassing.

"I'm sorry," I said. "But I couldn't let you leave. It was wrong for me to go about it like this, though." I'd let her leave. Again. It'd destroy me, but I'd do it. "Let me walk you to your car."

"I'm here now," she said. "You may as well go ahead and say what you wanted to."

She blew a strand of hair out of her eyes and I shoved my hands in my pockets. Wouldn't do to reach out and tuck the strand behind her ear. She'd probably slap me.

This would have been so much easier if I'd been able to talk to her earlier. Then she'd looked amiable. Now she looked pissed.

I took a deep breath. "There's a small room in the——"

"Ladies and gentlemen," the deejay said. "The best man and maid of honor—Nathaniel West and Abby King!"

Jackson.

I recognized the song from my first, and only, dance with Abby. Jackson would have known that song, remembered it. Damn fool never forgot anything.

Which meant I was supposed to dance with Abby.

"Ah, hell," I said, wondering just how long he'd been planning this.

I'd kill him with my bare hands.

I looked over to Abby.

She was still angry.

Maybe she wouldn't turn me down in front of all these people. Of course, if she did, I deserved it.

I held out my arm. "Will you?" I asked, almost not wanting her to answer. What if she said no?

But, miracles of miracles, she put her hand on my arm.

My stomach did a complete flip-flop.

I collected my courage, pretended it was no big deal she'd just taken me by the arm, and led her to the floor. I caught Jackson and Felicia kissing out of the corner of my eye. Then we made it to the middle of the floor and I had eyes only for Abby.

I stood and let her make the first move.

She reached out and put a hand on my shoulder. My stomach flipped back over.

"I'm trying to decide how this could be more embarrassing and failing," I said, because out of all the scenarios I'd imagined, talking to Abby in the middle of a crowded dance floor had never been on my list of possibilities.

I placed my arm around her waist, and it might have been my imagination, but I thought she took a step closer to me.

"I blame you completely," she said. "If you had just let me leave, this wouldn't have happened."

But then she would have left—didn't she see that?

"I went about it all wrong," I said again, being completely honest. "But if I had let you leave tonight, I'd never have forgiven myself."

"If you felt that strongly about it, then maybe you should have tried calling me sometime in the last month."

"I wasn't at the place I needed to be, Abby."

"And you are now?"

"No, but I'm coming closer."

I took a deep breath, and her scent worked its way into my soul once more. I never thought I'd have that scent around me after she left. I knew, even if I never held her again, that I'd forever have this moment, this night, this song, to remember.

Tonight was not the time to talk. The important part had been accomplished—I'd talked to her, she'd listened and not run away. Maybe, if I was honest with her, she'd agree to meet me later.

"It was a mistake to think I could do this tonight." We were still in the middle of the dance floor, but no one was watching us any longer. I stopped dancing and she didn't drop her arms from around me. "I have no reason to hope you'll agree and I'll understand if you won't." *Give her an out*, I heard Paul's voice say in my head. "But will you meet me tomorrow afternoon? To talk? So I can explain?"

I braced myself for her to laugh at me.

"Okay."

"You will?" I asked, unable to contain my surprise. "Really?"

She smiled. "Yes."

She smiled at me. My heart raced. "Should I pick you up? Or would you feel more comfortable meeting me somewhere? Whatever you prefer." Her choice. Her decision. Her way.

"The coffee shop on West Broadway?"

Perfect. "Yes. One o'clock tomorrow?"

"One o'clock will be fine."

The song ended and I had no other reason to hold her, so I led her off to the side. "Thank you, Abby. Thank you for the dance and thank you for agreeing to meet me tomorrow."

She surprised me by not leaving immediately, but staying longer. Felicia went over to her shortly after the dance ended and they talked, quite animatedly, I might add, for a few minutes. Abby looked up and caught me watching her. I smiled.

Flowers. I should send her flowers.

I wondered briefly where to find an open florist. It was New York; someone had to be open.

I glanced over at Abby again. Elaina joined the group and hugged her. Probably asked why she hadn't kicked my balls.

She needed more than flowers.

My eyes fell on the caterer discreetly checking the hors d'oeuvres.

She needed cans.

Cans because she'd been the one to show me I could be so much more than what the world thought. We could be so much more than what the world thought.

My feet nearly flew over the floor in my rush to get to the caterer. "Excuse me," I said, holding out my hand. "Nathaniel West, best man and cousin of the groom. I wonder if I could bother you for a small favor . . ."

Once the box of label-less cans was safe in my car, I wrote a simple note:

> To Abby,
>   For being right about the labels.
>
>   Nathaniel

I ducked back inside the building. Todd stood waiting.

"There you are—I thought you ran off," he said.

I glanced over his shoulder—Abby was still inside. I could see her dancing with Jackson.

While she was in the same room, I wouldn't leave.

"Todd, can I ask you a favor?" Last time we talked, he'd told me he owed me for what he felt was his role in my breakdown. I argued with him, but if he really wanted to help . . .

"Sure. Anything."

"I have a box in my car—can you drive it to Abby's apartment and put it outside her door?"

He raised an eyebrow. "Nathaniel?"

Damn it. He probably thought it was some stalker thing. "No," I said. "It's not like that. I want to send her a little thank-you for agreeing to meet with me tomorrow."

"She agreed to talk with you?" His eyes lit up. "That's wonderful."

"I hope I don't screw it up."

"Do you know what you're going to tell her?"

I brought the cards out of my pocket. "Wrote it all down."

"Sounds great. Looks like you've got everything covered. Just promise me one thing."

"Sure, what?"

He pointed to the cards. "Don't show those to Abby."

I got to the coffee shop an hour before we'd planned to meet and used my free time to call Paul. He helped me calm down a bit and reminded me what today was about—Abby needed to get how she felt out in the open. I needed to hear and understand firsthand how my actions made her feel. Then, and only then, could I try to explain myself.

After our call, I took the cards from my pocket and read them one last time. I finished and blew out a deep breath. I hoped she would listen. I hoped there was still a chance of us being . . . something, at the end of the day.

I saw her approach the coffee shop. She wore a pair of jeans and a light blue sweater; her hair was pulled back into a sloppy bun with a few loose tendrils. In other words, she looked gorgeous—as usual.

I still couldn't believe she'd agreed to meet me and sat stunned as she approached the table.

Manners, West.

I hopped up and pulled out her chair for her. "Abby. Thank you for meeting me. Can I get you something to drink?"

She sat down. "You're welcome. And, no, I don't want anything to drink."

Of course not. She'd agreed to meet me in public not because she wanted to have coffee or eat with me, but because she thought it would be safer somehow.

I had asked her to come and I would start. Todd had told me not to bring out the cards, so instead, I took a napkin—anything to keep my hands busy. "I don't know where to start, really. I ran this through in my head a hundred times. I even wrote it down so I wouldn't forget anything. But now . . . I'm at a complete loss."

I had to get this right. This was my one shot.

"Why don't you start at the beginning?" she offered.

I dropped the napkin. I had lived through my pain. Had started the process of facing my demons. But now . . . now I had to face her pain. To fully understand what my behavior had cost her.

"First of all," I said, for this was the most important, "I need to apologize for taking advantage of you."

She cocked a delicate eyebrow. Was it possible she didn't know?

"I knew you had never been in a relationship like ours before and I took advantage of you." There was no other way to explain it. I wouldn't even try. "The safe word, for example. I told you the truth when I said I'd never had a sub use her safe word before, but beyond that, I didn't want you to leave. I thought if I made the safe word a relationship ender, you wouldn't leave me. Of course, that backfired on me, didn't it?"

"It was your fault."

Yes. It was. It was all my fault—every word a lie, every action a deception, every denial a sham that served no purpose but to drive her away.

"Yes, it was," I said. "You gave me your trust. Your submission." But there was something even more important—the part that cost her the most. "Your love. And in return, I took your gifts and threw them back in your face."

She didn't acknowledge what I had said or agree with me. Her eyes caught hold of mine and I saw the pain she'd been living with.

"I handled everything you gave me physically," she said. "I would have handled *anything* you gave me physically, but emotionally, you broke me."

I broke her.

With my actions. With my words. With my betrayal.

The sharpness of her pain struck me, and it was worse, so much worse, than my own.

"I know," I whispered.

"Do you know how much that hurt? How it felt when you pretended that night meant *nothing*?"

I knew—it was so much more than nothing. I *knew*. And I'd lied to her.

She hit the table, shocking me. "It was the most amazing night of my life and you sat at that table and told me it was a *scene*. I'd have been better off if you'd plunged a knife in my heart."

Yes, because physical pain was bearable. Emotional pain hurt so much worse. I should have known that—I'd lived with it my entire life.

"I know. I'm sorry." I wondered if she could even hear me. "So very sorry."

"I want to know why," she demanded. "Why did you do it? Why couldn't you just say, 'I need time to work this out,' or, 'We're moving too fast'? Anything would have been better than what you did."

Again, she spoke the truth. But she didn't know. She still didn't know the entire truth.

"I was afraid," I said. "Once you found out . . ."

"Once I found out what?"

I had to tell her. I had no other choice.

"Our relationship was a house of cards I'd built," I said. "I should have known it wouldn't take much to bring it down."

I watched her uneasily. Would she leave after I admitted what came next?

"It was a Wednesday," I said. "Almost eight years ago. I was—"

"What does eight years ago have to do with anything?"

"I'm trying to tell you," I said. "I was meeting Todd for lunch on campus. He wanted to meet at the library." I wondered if she even remembered that day. Probably not. "I saw a woman running up the stairs. She tripped and fell, looked around to see if anyone was watching. I went to help, but you made it to her first."

"Me?"

Okay, she didn't remember. I suppose I never really expected her to. Who would remember a stumble from almost eight years ago?

"Yes, it was you. You knew her, and you both laughed as you picked up her books. There were several people nearby, but you were the only one who helped." I picked the napkin back up. "I made sure you didn't see me and I followed you into the library. You did a group reading of *Hamlet*. You read Ophelia."

Her jaw dropped open.

"I stayed and watched," I said. "I wanted more than anything to be your Hamlet."

The boy reading Hamlet was no match for her. No one deserved to be Hamlet to her Ophelia.

I looked up—she still watched me in amazement.

"Am I making you uncomfortable?" I asked.

"Go on."

"I was late meeting Todd. He was upset." An understatement. *Do you know how crazy my schedule is, Nathaniel?* he'd asked. *I gave up meeting Elaina to have lunch with you.* "Then I told him I'd met someone. It was only a little lie."

There is no such thing as a little lie. All lies are wrong.

"Why didn't you come up to me?" she asked. "Introduce yourself? Like a normal person would?"

Like a normal person? Was she serious?

"I was already living the lifestyle of a dom, Abby, and I thought you were a young, impressionable coed. In my mind, there was no way we would have worked. I had no idea of your submissive inclinations until your application crossed my desk." I wondered briefly if I'd have done anything differently if I'd known. No, I decided, not since I'd been in a committed relationship. "Even if I had known, I had a collared submissive at the time, and I am always monogamous once I collar a submissive."

"My submissive inclinations?"

She didn't know? How was it she didn't know? The truth hit me then—it was because we'd never talked. About anything.

I leaned toward her. "You're a sexual submissive, Abby. You have to know that. Why do you think you hadn't had sex for three years before you were with me?"

"I hadn't found anyone who . . ."

Ah, she understood. Finally.

"Who would dominate you the way you needed," I finished.

She dropped her head.

"Don't be embarrassed," I said gently. "It's nothing to be ashamed of."

"I'm not embarrassed. I just hadn't thought of it like that before."

The puzzle pieces started falling into place.

"Of course you hadn't," I said. "Which is why you were so angry when I suggested other dominants for you."

A flash of anger shot through her eyes. "I hated you for that."

As I suspected. "I was very much afraid you would take me up on it," I said, wanting her to know how painful those words had been for me to say. "I searched my mind trying to find someone I thought would suit you. But I just couldn't bring myself to imagine you with someone else. I would have done it if you'd asked, though. I would have."

"You were thinking of me and what I needed when you suggested other dominants?" she asked, and I knew she was still having a hard time understanding my offer.

"I knew you had asked specifically for me, but after actually being a submissive, I knew you would need to do it again. Then I saw how you reacted, so I'm sorry for that as well." Because as her dom, it had been my responsibility to make her understand, and that was just one more way I'd failed her.

I'd failed her. That was the truth.

"Jackson keeps saying you should have done more," I said. "Tried harder to get through to me. But he doesn't know the details. What I did. It's easy for him to place blame. He doesn't understand there was nothing you could have done that would have changed my mind that morning. Nothing would have changed the outcome. Don't blame yourself."

Because it was all my fault.

"I pushed," she said. "I shouldn't have expected so much so fast."

"Perhaps not, but you could have expected more than I was

willing to give you." Anything but my rejection of the love you gave so freely. "Instead, I shut you down completely."

She nodded.

"But there's more," I said.

"Todd?"

Elaina still didn't know, Todd had told me. Which meant Abby still didn't know about Tampa.

"I didn't pursue you, but I couldn't let you slip away either. I would watch you at the library, hoping to catch a glimpse of you. He knew I was watching someone, but I told him I was working up the courage to speak to you."

"He believed you?"

Smart woman, that Abby. Even she didn't believe it.

"Probably not, but he knew I wouldn't do anything improper." Without realizing it, I reached across the table toward her. I wanted so desperately to touch her. I caught myself just in time and pulled my hands back—she still wouldn't want to touch me.

"And I didn't, Abby. I promise you. I saw you only at the library. I never attempted to find out any more about you. I never followed you."

"Except the morning I left you."

So she knew; she'd noticed me on the road behind her. "It had been snowing and you were upset. I had to make certain you were safe."

"So when you saved my mother's house—you knew who she was? You knew she was my mother?"

Maybe she hadn't figured that one out when I thought she had.

"Yes, I did it for you. I knew your name from the library. It was on the bank paperwork as well. You were the goddess I longed to worship. My unobtainable dream. The relationship I could never hope to have."

I peeked up at her, wondering if she remembered the words

she'd said right before I kissed her. How she'd called herself a goddess.

"When we were in Tampa, after we played golf, Todd joked with me about the library girl from all those years ago. Dinner the night before had jogged his memory. I told him it was you and he got angry."

She nodded absentmindedly.

"*A relationship like yours demands complete truth and honesty.*" I ripped the napkin in my hands apart as I quoted Todd. "That's what Todd told me. And I was not being truthful in keeping my past knowledge of you a secret. He wanted me to tell you, and I agreed. I asked for three weeks. I thought that was enough time for me to plan how to tell you, and he thought that was reasonable."

"But we never made it to three weeks."

"No. We didn't. I would like to think that if we had, I would have told you. I had every intention of doing so. But then that night happened and I was afraid you would think I had tricked you or somehow manipulated you."

"I might have."

Tell her.

My heart thumped.

You have to tell her.

"I've never felt for anyone the way I feel for you," I said. "I was scared. You were right about that. I thought it would be easier to let you go, but I was wrong."

It hadn't been easier, not for me, and more important, not for her.

She didn't say anything, so I continued. "I'm in therapy now—twice a week. It feels strange saying that. I'm working through things. Your name comes up often."

She gave a small laugh.

"I haven't allowed you a chance to get a word in, but you

haven't run off screaming," I said. "Dare I hope any of what I've said makes a little bit of sense?"

She inspected her nails. "I need to think," she said finally.

She wanted to think—maybe that meant she would want us to talk again. She didn't say anything else, but simply rose to her feet.

I stood with her. "Yes, you need to think things through. It's more than I could hope for."

It was probably crossing a line, but I couldn't help it, I had to touch her. I took her hands and pressed my lips to them.

"Will you call me later this week?" I asked. "I want to talk more." Not once, in all our time together, had she ever called me. Would she this time? "If you want to, that is." Because again it was entirely up to her. Everything, this time, would be up to her.

"I'll call you," she whispered. "I'll call you regardless."

Chapter Thirty-five

On the way home, I called Paul.

"How did it go?" he asked.

"I think it went well," I said, remembering the conversation. "She talked and I listened. I talked and she listened. She said she'd call me. I hope she does."

"From what you've said about Abby, if she said she'd call—she'll call."

I merged onto the highway and headed to the estate, barely noticing the traffic I passed.

"She'll call," I said. "I just hope . . ."

"What?" he asked after several seconds.

"It's just—" I forced myself to acknowledge the truth. "I want it all. I want to take her to dinner, ask her what her favorite meal is, what she wanted for Christmas when she was twelve. I want to take her to my bed and keep her there all night." I paused. "And, God help me, Paul, I want her in my playroom."

He laughed softly. "Got it all planned out, have you?"

"Most of it depends on her."

"All of it depends on her," he corrected. "Every step from here still has to be up to her. Take it slow. Get to know each other. Build her—"

"Trust in me. I know. I know. You've told me."

"Just making sure you listened."

"I did."

"Good," he said. "Because if you bring up the playroom too soon, you'll scare her. And before you even *think* about returning to the playroom—"

"We have to talk," I said, finishing his sentence. "Safe words, our new arrangement. We've gone over and over this, too."

"I know we have. I just can't emphasize enough how important it is for the two of you to talk this time."

"This time," I scoffed. "You say that like it's going to happen."

"I think it will," he said. "Eventually. Eternal optimist, remember?"

"Hmmmp."

From his end of the phone came the unmistakable sound of a baby's howl.

"Oops," he said. "Naptime's over. Christine's out shopping. Girl time, you know?" The howling got louder. "Call me after you talk to Abby."

We disconnected, and I spent the rest of the drive home in silence, reflecting on my talk with Abby. When would she call? Would she want to meet again, or would she tell me to leave her alone?

But she'd let me kiss her hand—surely she wouldn't have let me do that if she planned on telling me to leave her alone.

I brought my hand to my nose to see if any of her smell lingered on me.

Maybe.

For once, silence wasn't my enemy. It was a friend—allowing me time to reflect and think. I smelled my hand once more, certain I could catch her scent and letting myself ponder Paul's optimism.

When I arrived home, Apollo rushed to me and sniffed me all over as soon as I entered the foyer. I squatted down and he licked my face, whining. Occasionally, he looked back to the door as if expecting Abby to enter.

"I know. I know you miss her."

He whined again and pawed at me.

"Soon maybe," I said, hoping for both of us that I was right.

She didn't call on Monday. I spent the day in my office with my cell phone on my desk, waiting for it to ring, and I gave Sara explicit instructions to let me know the second Abby called.

It was okay, I told myself. She needed time. She had to think.

Kyle called and invited me to attend the high school play he was in the coming weekend. I agreed to go and ran over and over in my mind whether or not I should ask Abby to go.

Yes. No. Maybe.

I slept restlessly that night.

Tuesday wasn't any better. I went home that afternoon feeling a bit dejected, knowing every day that passed meant either she wouldn't call or else she'd tell me she didn't want me around when she did call.

My phone rang right after I'd eaten a quick dinner and was getting ready to take Apollo out for the night.

Abby King, the caller ID said.

My heart thumped madly, and I hit the connect button with a trembling finger.

"Hello," I said.

"Nathaniel," she said, voice crisp and no-nonsense. "It's me."

I know, I wanted to yell. I know, trust me.

"Abby," I said instead. Tuesday night was good, right? It was a good sign. Tuesday would be much better than Thursday or even Wednesday.

"There's a sushi bar down the street from the library," she said. "Will you meet me there for lunch tomorrow?"

"Of course," I said. She wanted to meet, talk, and have lunch. That had to be good. "What time?"

"Noon."

"I'm looking forward to it."

That settled it—Tuesday was my most favorite day of the week.

I arrived at the restaurant at five to twelve and looked around for an empty table. Then I found the most wonderful surprise— Abby was already there, had a table, and was waiting for me.

Waiting for me.

I straightened my tie and walked directly to her. Her eyes followed me the entire time, and my heart leaped when she smiled at me.

Fucking lucky-ass bastard.

"Abby," I said, sitting across from her.

The corner of her mouth lifted. "Nathaniel."

I smiled even brighter. So far, so good.

The waiter walked up to our table and took our orders. Abby knew exactly what she wanted and ordered her rolls with an air of authority.

I took a deep breath after handing the waiter my menu and looked at her. "It's going to be a beautiful spring."

"I can't wait for the cherry trees to start blooming. They're my favorite."

See? I told myself. You can do small talk.

"I have a few at the house. Apollo loves to roll around in the blossoms once they fall."

She laughed. "I can see him doing that."

"It's a sight to behold," I said, but I wasn't talking about Apollo. I was talking about her. Her sitting across from me, chatting easily, laughing. Looking beautiful.

"Apollo's one of a kind."

"That he is."

"How's work?"

"Just me doing my part to save the global economy. How's the library? Anything exciting happening?"

She sat up straighter. "I'm organizing a poetry reading. Classics—Dickinson, Cummings, Frost. You know, all those boring things no one ever reads?"

She was teasing me.

I loved it.

"Then you do the people of New York a great service by ensuring the poetry greats are kept alive."

"I don't know about that, but it's really fun."

"Do you read them all at the same session?" I asked, having never been to a poetry reading.

"Sometimes," she said. "But I've decided to split this one up. We'll give each poet their own reading, taking place over the next few weeks. Dickinson's up first—next Wednesday. I might even be able to drag Felicia along this time."

"Felicia," I said. "Jackson talks of nothing else. How is she?"

"Fine. I decided to let her live, even though she embarrassed me by playing that song at the party."

"Very cordial of you."

"After all"—her eyes sparkled with amusement—"she wasn't the one who called my name in front of hundreds of people."

She was still teasing me.

"In that case," I said, "I commend you once more on your cordiality. This time for allowing me to escape with my life."

"It was nothing. I'm rather glad you did it. *Now*, that is."

The teasing tone had all but left her voice, and I knew it was time to talk about more serious matters.

"Before we talk about anything else," I said, "I need to tell you something."

"Okay," she said warily.

"I need you to understand that I am in therapy to work on my intimacy issues and my emotional well-being. Not my sexual needs."

My doctor, along with Paul, and to a certain extent, Todd, had helped me see my lifestyle was completely acceptable. Why I needed that assurance, I didn't know, but I felt better having it.

"I am a dominant," I told her. "And I will always be a dominant. I cannot and will not give up that part of me. That doesn't mean I can't enjoy other . . . *flavors.* On the contrary, other flavors make for good variety." I wanted that variety with her. "Does that make sense?"

"Yes. I would never expect you to give up that part of yourself. It would be like denying who you are."

She understood. She got it.

"Right," I said.

"Just like I can't deny my submissive nature."

She really got it.

I smiled. "Exactly."

The waiter interrupted us briefly to deliver our teas. I felt better getting that part out, knowing we were both on the same page, that if we ever did get back together, she knew what to expect.

Yet there was still one puzzle piece missing . . .

"I've always wondered, and you don't have to tell me," I said, "but how did you find out about me in the first place?"

She glanced down at her tea.

What? It was a reasonable question, wasn't it?

At once, she looked up and waved her hand. "Oh, please. Everyone knows about Nathaniel West."

She didn't want to tell me something. That called for drastic measures. "Maybe," I said. "But not everyone knows he shackles women to his bed and works them over with a riding crop."

She choked on her tea.

"You asked for it," I said.

"I did." She wiped her mouth. "Completely."

My swift response relieved the tension somewhat, but the question remained.

"Will you answer?" I asked.

She took a deep breath. "I first took real notice of you when you saved my mother's house."

So my actions had not gone unnoticed. I felt positively delighted.

"Until then, you were only a man I read about in the society pages," she continued, "a celebrity. But then you became more real."

The waiter brought our food and I felt annoyed at his interruption. Abby had just admitted that she had known of me and followed me in the papers for years. I needed more from her, had to know the details. The information shocked me. Was it possible she'd been waiting for me nearly as long as I'd been waiting for her?

She prepared her soy sauce as she talked. "Your picture was in the paper for something not long after that—I can't remember what for now."

Who cared what my picture was in the paper for? My picture was always in the paper. How had she found out about me? About my lifestyle?

"Anyway," she said. "My friend Samantha stopped by while I was reading the paper. I made some comment about how nice you looked and wondered what you were really like."

She had? From a picture in the paper?

"She got all edgy and shifty," she said.

"Samantha?" I asked. I thought back quickly, but couldn't remember a Samantha in the community.

"An old friend of mine. I haven't talked to her in years."

I ran through my memories again, but still couldn't place a Samantha. How had she heard of me?

"She went with her boyfriend to a party or a gathering or

something, I'm not sure of the proper name, for dominants and submissives. They were dabblers."

Of course—a play party.

"Ah," I said. "And I was there."

If this Samantha knew who I was, I must have been a participant or instructor. Apparently she had not wanted Abby to get involved with the likes of me and felt so strongly about it that she'd broken confidentiality. Ordinarily this news would have made me furious, but under the circumstances, I suppose now I should probably have thanked her for the introduction.

"Yes," she confirmed, "and she told me you were a dominant. She said she shouldn't tell me and swore me to absolute secrecy, and I haven't told anyone—well, except for Felicia, when I had to. But Samantha didn't want me to get some romantic Prince Charming fantasy going with me as your Cinderella."

All those wasted years. All those years I'd longed for Abby and, miracle of miracles, she'd been longing for me.

How was it possible?

"Did you?" I asked, needing to know exactly what she thought of me.

"No," she said offhandedly. "But I did fantasize about being shackled to your bed while you worked me over with a riding crop."

Holy fucking hell.

Now I was the one choking on my tea.

She looked at me with innocent eyes. "You asked for it."

I laughed. Abby wanted me. Had wanted me for years.

And she was teasing me about it.

"I did," I said. "Completely."

Completely and one hundred percent asked for it.

"I didn't do anything but fantasize for a long time," she said.

Fuck. She'd fantasized about me. For years. I couldn't wrap my brain around it.

Her eyes dropped to her plate.

"Then I asked around. Several of Samantha's friends still live in the area, so it didn't take long to find Mr. Godwin. I held on to his name for months before I did anything."

The timing had been perfect. Had she talked to Godwin earlier, I would have been with Melanie and her application would have been ignored. I sucked in a breath at the realization of how close we'd come to never meeting.

She shrugged. "I eventually knew I had to call him, though— anything was better than . . ."

"Unfulfilled sex," I said, still thinking about Melanie.

"Or just plain unfulfilled in my case." She looked up as if needing reassurance. "I couldn't have a normal relationship with a guy. I just . . . couldn't."

Of course, I knew exactly what she meant. Thankfully, due to my talks with Paul, I could help.

"I believe there are varying degrees of *normal*, Abby," I said. "Who really gets to define what normal looks like anyway?"

Because never again would I let anyone else define me. Not even myself. I refused to allow Abby to have the same doubts I'd struggled with for so long.

"Frankly," she said, "I've done what's normal in the eyes of everyone else and it's boring as hell."

"Different flavors, and they can all be delicious when tasted with the right person." *I want to taste them all with you.* "But yes, one's natural tendencies do have a way of defining what one sees as normal."

"You tried a so-called normal relationship once. With Melanie."

Yes, if we were going to have a relationship, I had to talk about Melanie.

"Yes." I took a bite of a roll and chewed it while I thought. "With Melanie. It was a miserable failure." I flinched, remembering how I'd hurt Melanie. Not as badly as I'd hurt Abby, but I'd still hurt her. "We failed for several reasons—Melanie is not a natural submissive, and I couldn't repress my dominant nature." I thought back to the night she found me in my playroom. "But she didn't want to admit we couldn't work. I never understood that."

Never understood why she had to go crying to Todd and Elaina. Why she felt the need to interrupt what I was trying to tell Abby at the engagement party.

"For what it's worth," Abby said, "she seems to be over you now."

I wondered again what the two of them had talked about at the party. However, if Abby thought Melanie was over me, it really didn't matter.

"Thank God," I said.

I girded myself and asked, "Are you?"

She looked at me with the most beautiful longing in her eyes. "No."

Relief, excitement, anticipation, and hope surged through me.

"Thank God," I answered again simply.

I reached across the table and took her hand. "Nor I, you," I said, because it wasn't enough for me to know how she felt—I had to be honest with her. Let her know how I felt.

Our eyes met, and I felt the chains of my past start to loosen. If we had made it this far, perhaps we could make it a little bit farther.

"I'll do whatever it takes to earn your trust back, Abby. For however long it takes." I took a deep breath and forced out my next question as I stroked her knuckles. "Will you let me?"

"Yes."

I felt like jumping onto the table. Instead, I squeezed her hand and let it go. "Thank you."

We were going to do it. We would work through this and find our way—together.

I wanted to talk to her for hours.

The damned waiter came back to the table.

"Have you ever made sushi?" Abby asked.

Okay, we could talk about sushi.

"No. I never have, but I've always wanted to learn."

The waiter took my glass and refilled it. "We have classes. Next Thursday night. Seven o'clock."

Abby looked at me.

Should we? her eyes asked.

Like a date? A regular date? To get to know each other?

Yes, of course. Anything to be near her. I almost said as much, but then I heard Paul's voice in my head: Every step from here still has to be up to her.

I raised an eyebrow at her. *Your call. You decide.*

"Let's do it," she said.

She agreed. She wanted to try. I decided then and there to ask her to the play on Saturday.

My opportunity came as we were leaving the restaurant.

"Abby," I said, helping her with her coat. "Kyle's in his school play. Opening night is Saturday and he asked me to attend. Will you come with me?"

I tried to read her expression, but couldn't decide what she thought.

"What time?"

"I can pick you up at five," I said. "We could have dinner before the show?"

Before today, she hadn't wanted me to pick her up or meet her at her apartment. Had our conversations and confessions changed that?

"Five it is."

After she left, I called Sara and told her I'd be working from home the rest of the afternoon. I drove to my estate with one purpose and, after dealing with Apollo's neurotic sniffing once again and letting him outside, I walked down the hallway.

I stood outside the double doors and closed my eyes. It was time. It had been long enough. The past was the past and today was the day I would leave it behind for the last time.

I took a deep breath, opened the doors, and stepped into my library for the first time in weeks.

Saturday finally arrived following what had to be some of the longest days of my life. I wondered if Felicia would be around, but Jackson told me she'd be at his place for the evening.

I ignored his "I told you so" attitude.

The date with Abby could not have gone better. She was beautiful, enchanting, and quite the conversationalist. She invited me to the Dickinson reading and I accepted without thinking twice.

For the record, her favorite meal was braised leg of lamb, and when she was twelve, she'd wanted a bike for Christmas.

I knew Kyle wouldn't have a huge part in the play, but when he stepped out on the stage for the first time as a chorus member and saw me sitting in the audience . . . words couldn't describe the pride I felt. He'd come so far from the sickly boy I'd met not too long ago, and he'd worked so hard to have an active life.

I tried my best all night not to accidentally touch or brush against Abby. In keeping with what Paul said, I wanted her to dictate our physical relationship. My only moment of indecision came when I dropped her off at her apartment. Should I try to kiss her?

"Thank you for inviting me," she said as we stood at her door. "I had a really nice time."

"I was glad to have you with me. The evening wouldn't have been the same without you." I couldn't help myself—I took her hand. "I'll see you Thursday night."

I looked into her eyes. *May I kiss you?* I wanted to ask.

Not yet. Let her make the first step.

But what if she doesn't?

She didn't.

I smiled at her and turned to leave.

"Nathaniel," she said after I took a few steps away.

My heart pounded, but I turned to face her. She walked to me and I stood still, waiting, unable to keep my eyes from the vision approaching me. Did she want . . . ?

Would she . . . ?

Then she stood before me and touched my face. The touch of a goddess, the feel of her fingers as they traced my jaw and worked their way into my hair—how had I lived without her touch?

I hadn't.

"Kiss me," she said. "Kiss me and mean it."

And mean it, she asked. Show me how you feel and don't take it back.

Never, I knew. I would never again deny my feelings for her.

"Oh, Abby," I said. I could live for three hundred years and would still not begin to understand the forgiveness she offered me.

I slipped my fingers under her chin and lifted her face. My eyes closed as I brought my lips to hers. I felt her need as soon as our lips touched. Felt her longing. How delicately it balanced and mirrored my own. Yet I took my time and savored the feel of her—her softness, the way she moved with me.

She stepped closer, and I drew her nearer. I parted my lips under hers as she deepened the kiss.

In that kiss, I told her everything. For once, I held nothing back, and in return, I felt her give herself once more to me. It was a gift I didn't deserve, and I would treasure it for as long as she allowed. I would treasure her. Make her feel wanted and needed and loved.

I felt my body stir at her nearness, at her continued touch, and I pulled away. I didn't want her to think I expected anything tonight. To be allowed to kiss her was enough.

I sighed against her lips. "Thank you."

Thank you for your acceptance, your forgiveness, your willingness to allow me back in your life. Thank you for not giving up on me, on us, even though I had.

She looked up at me while I still cradled her in my arms. "You're welcome."

Chapter Thirty-six

I sat in the last row of the room, watching as she led the Emily Dickinson session. She mesmerized me as she read—poems on death, loss, and life. One in particular, "Come Slowly, Eden!" held me in a trance. She read it in a low, sultry voice, looking back at me as she spoke the last line.

> " 'Come slowly, Eden!
> Lips unused to thee,
> Bashful, sip thy jasmines,
> As the fainting bee,
>
> Reaching late his flower,
> Round her chamber hums,
> Counts his nectars—enters,
> And is lost in balms!' "

Who knew poetry could be such a turn-on?

I shifted in my seat as the reading ended. My plan to allow Abby to dictate our physical relationship felt right, but I wasn't sure how much longer I'd last if she kept throwing things like that my way.

Still, when I left her for the evening, all I gave her was a soft, chaste kiss.

We learned how to make sushi the next night. I thoroughly

enjoyed standing by her and learning something new. She stayed so near me, I could smell her light Abby scent. But more than that, we simply enjoyed being together, laughing when one of us messed up, delighting when it turned out correctly.

Our kiss that night was more passionate.

Jackson asked if we'd like to double date with him and Felicia the next weekend, and we hesitantly agreed. All four of us had a great time. Felicia talked warmly to me, and I saw her shooting Abby smug glances a few times. When she caught me looking, Abby simply rolled her eyes.

Apollo grew more and more agitated whenever I arrived home after being with Abby. I wanted badly to ask her to my house, but worried she might think I expected something physical from her.

Finally, about three weeks after we'd been to see Kyle's play, I dropped by the library on a Thursday afternoon. I picked Thursday because I didn't want to stop by on a Wednesday—too many memories for both of us.

Her eyes lit up as I walked into the library. "Nathaniel!"

I leaned across the desk and gave her a quick kiss. "How's your day?"

"Good. Yours?"

"Better now."

I couldn't help but smile at the way her cheeks flushed slightly. I cleared my throat. "I wanted to see if you would mind coming to my house for dinner."

She didn't say anything.

"To see Apollo," I said. "He misses you, and when he smells you on me—"

She held up her hand. "I understand. I would love to come over for dinner and to see Apollo. I've missed him."

"Thank you." She didn't think any less of me for inviting her to my house—she'd accepted. Apollo would be so happy.

Although not as happy as I was.

Apollo was psychic—I was almost positive. He refused to stay in the house the next night. Instead he waited outside, practically dancing in his excitement. When Abby pulled up the drive in Felicia's car, he started spinning in circles.

I hurried outside, leaving my post at a front window. "Apollo, please," I said. He practically knocked her over in his quest to lick her all over. "You must forgive him, Abby. He's been excited all day."

She rubbed his head, and he stayed by her side as she walked up the stairs. "That makes two of us."

I gave her a kiss when she reached me.

Afterward, she pulled on the towel in my hand. "What are you cooking?"

"Honey-almond chicken," I said. Same as the first time.

"*Mmm*. My favorite."

I remembered.

I opened the door. "Come inside. It's nearly ready."

We ate at the dining room table. I tried not to concentrate on how right it felt to have her in my house again. How she breathed life into the dark, dead spaces. I pondered again how I'd ever thought letting her leave would be the best course of action and gave silent thanks for her forgiveness.

Apollo, of course, sat on her feet throughout dinner.

I thought it would be a bit uncomfortable, eating at the table, as if the past would somehow steal away what we'd both been working so hard to build over the last few weeks. It wasn't, though. I'm not sure we stopped talking at all the entire meal—it was a wonder we ate anything.

What was even more surprising was the fact that I could carry on a conversation at all after she licked her lip to catch a bit of sauce. What had I been thinking? I wanted to ease her back into my house, into my realm, not spend the entire meal thinking about her lips.

A movie, I decided. We should watch a movie. That way, we could sit together on the couch; maybe I would slip an arm around her. She'd snuggle close . . .

I jumped up to clear the table after we finished eating.

"Let me help," she said, getting up to join me.

"I can get it."

"But I don't mind."

I put the dishes in the sink. "I wash and you dry?"

She nodded and picked up a towel.

As we worked, it struck me how well we fit together. Even doing mundane things such as the dishes. We were a team. We belonged together. Surely she knew.

But I couldn't assume she knew anything. I had to tell her.

Yet I still argued with myself.

After the movie. If you tell her before, she might think you want sex.

No, after the movie, she'll think you want sex. Tell her before.

After would be better.

After is just you procrastinating again.

My hand trembled as I gave her the last dish. She dried it quickly and put it in the cabinet, then returned to place the towel beside the sink.

Now, West.

I took a deep breath. "Abby——"

"Nathaniel——" she said at the same time.

Our gazes locked for a second and we both laughed.

"You first," she said.

I took her hand. "I just wanted to say thank you for coming tonight. Apollo hasn't been so calm in months."

Damn it. That hadn't come out right.

"Well, I'm glad for Apollo." She gave my hand a gentle squeeze. "But he's not the only reason I came over tonight."

I know. Thank you.

Stop thinking it. Say it.

I rubbed her knuckles, stroked the soft skin of her hand. "I know."

A small smile lifted the corner of her mouth. "Trust me. I'm a pretty selfish creature."

Selfish? Abby? How could she even think that?

I traced her jaw. "You're not. You're kind and loving and forgiving and—"

"*Nathaniel.*"

I needed to tell her. Had to tell her. Now.

I placed a finger on her lips. "Stop. Let me finish."

She didn't say anything else.

I stared into her deep, wide eyes and gently cupped her face. "You've brought my life so much joy; you've made me feel complete." *She needs the words. Give her the words.* "I love you, Abby."

She sucked in her breath.

"Nathaniel." She leaned her cheek into my palm. "I love you, too."

I felt certain my heart would explode. She loved me.

She loved me.

She.

Loved.

Me.

"Abby." I sighed, pulling her into my arms and kissing her. It was the only way I knew to show my feelings. She parted her lips under mine.

Oh, God. Her taste.

She pulled me closer and ran her fingers through my hair as she kissed me harder and deeper.

Forget the movie—I wanted her.

Let her lead.

I broke the kiss, dragging my lips up to her ear. "Tell me to stop, Abby." *Please don't tell me to stop.* "Tell me to stop and I will."

And I would. I didn't want to, but I would. Anything beyond this point was up to her.

"Don't," she said.

Fuck. She wanted me to stop.

"Don't stop," she said.

Yes.

My fingers skimmed her arms. I needed to make certain she was sure. "I don't want you to think I brought you here for this." I tasted the skin of her ear, unable to hold myself back. "I don't want you to think I'm pushing you."

Because, as much as my cock wanted to disagree, a movie and cuddles on the couch would be fine.

She pulled away from me and smiled.

"Follow me." She held out her hand.

Huh? Follow her? I'd follow her anywhere.

She took me out of the kitchen, down the hall, and into the foyer. I still had no idea what she was doing.

She started up the stairs.

Holy fucking hell. She was taking me upstairs and down the hall into my bedroom. Which I still hadn't moved back into.

I stood in shock as she led me to the foot of the bed and turned.

I cupped her cheek. "Abby. My beautiful, perfect Abby." I dropped my head and kissed her again. When I felt her breathing change, I pulled back, then drew her close, kissed her neck, and murmured into her skin, "Let me love you."

Tonight was all about her—making love to every single part of her.

I carried her to the bed, laying her on her back. "I'll start with your mouth."

In all our time together, starting from the first day she walked into my office, I had cheated us both by not kissing her. For the next several minutes, I did my best to make up for it—teasing her, teasing us both, with soft nibbles and gentle, sweet kisses.

Finally, though, I couldn't hold back any longer. I framed her face and kissed her long and slow and deep and filled with all the passion I could.

She arched her back, brushing her chest against me, and I pulled back. "I could kiss your lips for hours and never tire of your taste"—I took in the sight of her lying in my bed—"but the rest of you is so damn delectable."

I unbuttoned her shirt, taking my time, wanting her to know what I was doing. Still wanting to give her a chance to back out. She didn't move from the bed, though. Her eyes watched me as I slipped the shirt from her body.

"I can feel your heart racing." I ran my hand down her arm and captured her hand in my own. "Feel mine," I said, placing her hand over my own flying heart.

She took her hand out of mine and dragged my shirt over my head. I heard her sigh as she ran her hands over my chest and down my arms. How good they felt on me.

Heaven.

But I wasn't anywhere near finished. I trailed my lips downward—over her collarbone, across her shoulders.

"An often-neglected body part is right here"—I took her arm—"the crook of the elbow." I kissed her there. "It would be an unpardonable sin to overlook this tasty delicacy." She tasted so delicious when I licked her, I took a gentle nibble.

"Oh, God," she moaned.

I lifted my head. "And I've only just started," I said, because I had to taste the other parts of her—starting with her sweet breasts. I worked my way over to them, kissing and tasting as I went. I did away with her bra quickly, eager for the feel of skin-to-skin contact.

I leaned over and felt her nipples brush against my chest, barely able to contain the moan threatening to escape from me. I cupped one breast in my hand. "Your breasts are perfect. Just the right size, and when I do this"—I took a nipple between two fingers and rolled gently—"your body shakes with anticipation."

A shudder overtook her.

Perfect.

"Do you know how sweet your breasts taste?" I asked, teasing myself as much as her, for I was anxious to get my mouth on her again.

"No."

"A shame, really." I sucked her into my mouth. Mmmmm. Her taste. So much better even than I remembered. I couldn't help myself—I sucked her even deeper and bit her the way I knew she liked.

She rewarded me with a moan.

I released her from my mouth and blew on her other breast, watching as her nipple hardened. Her skin was so responsive. I took my time tasting the other breast, starting at its base and working up. I tested its weight in my hand. Perfect.

"And this one?" I asked. "Just as fucking sweet as the other." I licked my lips and tasted it.

Her hands dug into my hair, holding me close as I continued my rediscovery of her body. She felt so right under me, so perfect in my arms. I took my time, wanting to drive her into a frenzy of pleasure. We had all night, and I planned to enjoy every second.

Her hands grew more urgent as they danced across my back, and she pulled me up toward her—kissing me soundly and deeply.

Fuck. I'd never get tired of this woman.

Her hips lifted, circling and searching for my own.

"Wait," I said, breaking the kiss. A reminder to me, really. "I haven't gotten to the best parts."

But I gave her what she wanted, moving my hands lower to stroke the slope of her belly. I hooked my fingers into the waistband of her jeans and pushed them as low as I could.

"Another overlooked body part," I said before licking her belly button.

She gasped and tightened her grip on my hair.

"Do you know how many nerve endings are found here?" I asked. I pulled back slightly and watched her skin respond as I blew on her, now wet from my tongue.

Beautiful.

I took the clasp of the jeans and undid them, drawing them slowly down her hips, trailing my thumbs lightly across her skin. I slid back as I undressed her, exposing the tiny bikini briefs she wore. My cock throbbed, but I shoved my needs to the back of my mind and focused on her.

She had other plans. As soon as I threw her jeans from the bed, she pushed me onto my back. "My turn."

She undressed me, taking my pants and boxers off at the same time, running her hands all over me.

Her hands felt so good.

"Abby," I groaned when her hands stroked my cock.

"Roll over," she said, and I turned onto my stomach.

She straddled me, sitting on my butt and running her hands over my shoulder blades, then down my spine. Her lips followed, ending right at the small of my back, and she then licked her way up again. I pushed my hips into the bed, desperate.

Fuck. I needed to get my focus back on her, so I turned over, grabbing her and rolling her underneath me.

"I forgot where I was," I said, trailing my eyes down her body. "Now I have to start all over."

Because starting over would give me time to calm back down, to bring her back to the edge and heighten her pleasure. I kissed her—parting her lips with my tongue, savoring her taste.

"We discussed your mouth," I said, when we were both breathing heavily. "And your neck," I said, working back over her delicate skin. "Your overlooked elbows and belly button—and I definitely remember these." I kissed her breasts, rolling first one nipple and then the other between my lips, tickling her with the tip of my tongue.

"Ah, yes," I said, when her body trembled beneath me. "I remember now." It was time to drive her completely mad, for she thought she knew where I'd go next. I slid down her body. "Right. About. Here," I said, coming to rest between her legs, ignoring where she really needed me and taking her knee in my hand.

She lifted her head and stared at me.

"The knee is an erogenous zone for many people," I explained.

Her head fell back to the bed.

I played with her knee—kissing and caressing it. I gently lifted her and tasted the skin behind her knee before switching to her other leg.

"Nathaniel. Higher."

I know. I want it, too.

Instead, I slipped lower, coming to rest at her feet. I took one in my hand, examining the curve of her arch. Then I kissed the inside of her ankle, and ever so gently, placed a soft kiss on the bottom of each foot.

She was indeed a goddess.

Who needed to be teased more.

"Now," I said, raising my head. "I feel like I forgot something. What was it?"

But I'd forgotten how sinfully she could tease me.

"You're a smart man." Her legs shifted, then parted and gave me a perfect view of her silk-clad sex. "I'm sure it'll come to you."

A growl ripped from my throat—if that's the way she wanted it, I was more than ready. I crawled up to her and ripped away the silk that stood between my goal and me.

I lifted both her legs and slipped under them. I licked her gently, remembering how tentative she had been the first time I did so. She was not tentative now—she lifted her hips to me, trying to get closer.

"Now, right here is an important spot," I said. "Because, this"—I ran my tongue over her again and again, in between my words—"is pure, unadulterated Abby."

"Dear Lord."

Just you wait, darling vixen.

"And after I spend hours kissing your mouth"—I spread her with my fingers and her wetness coated me—"I could spend hours kissing and licking and drinking from your sweet"—my tongue dipped into her—"wet"—I licked her again—"pussy."

I set my mouth on her and thrust my tongue inside. I sucked her clit gently and pushed my tongue deeper. She let out a small gasp and her muscles tightened around me. As her orgasm subsided, I continued to kiss and stroke her folds, wanting to keep her sensitive, knowing how it would intensify her second release.

When her body relaxed, I slipped out from under her and set her legs on the bed.

"Now"—I moved up her body—"let us continue."

She stretched under me as my weight came to rest on her. I spread her legs with my knees and placed my cock so it just brushed her wet entrance. I wanted a deep emotional connection this time, so I took her hands and intertwined our fingers.

"Abby," I said, because her eyes were closed and I wanted them open and watching mine. She opened them, and the love and wonder I saw shining back at me stole my breath.

"This is me, Nathaniel," I said. I pushed partly into her, wanting her to know, to feel, the truth of my words, of my actions. "And you, Abby." I slipped deeper inside. "Nothing else." No scene. No trickery. No deception. Just us.

"Nathaniel," she said.

Just love.

I kissed her long and deep, bringing our hands over her head as

I pushed even farther inside her body. She groaned, and I rocked my hips to slip all the way inside. Then I pulled back to look into her eyes again as I starting moving within her.

I took my time, holding her hands and her gaze as we slid together. I kept my thrusts slow and purposeful, wanting us both to feel every inch of our skin touching, wanting to draw out every minuscule pleasure possible from our joining.

She arched and lifted herself to me, wanting more, wanting faster. My body begged for the same, but I forced myself to hold on to the control, to cherish this moment.

"Nathaniel. Please."

I obliged, moving a bit faster, giving us both a taste of what we wanted. It still wasn't enough. She wrapped her arms and legs around me, meeting my thrust with her own. Still, I kept my pace slow and steady.

"Damn it, Nathaniel. Fuck me." She bit my earlobe.

Her words shot fire through me and I no longer wanted to be in control. I wanted to let myself feel. To let my body and my need take over. I pulled back and started a new rhythm, driving into her with faster, deeper thrusts.

I grabbed her hips and jerked them upward, so I hit deeper within her.

"Nathaniel!"

Fuck. Yes. Shout my name.

But as I had discovered once before—as much as she was mine, I was also hers. The feel of her—her under me, her surrounding me—proved it.

"Oh, God, Abby!"

She started to tense around me, and I dropped my hand to rest between us, making sure I hit her clit with each thrust.

"I'm . . . I'm . . . I'm . . ." she said.

Let go. Give yourself to me.

She screamed through her orgasm, but I kept my rhythm

going, knowing she had more. A minute later, another spasm ran through her body and I knew I couldn't hold my own release at bay any longer.

I thrust again and held deep inside her as my own climax ripped through me. I felt her muscles clench around me a third time as I released into her.

I rolled us to our sides, not wanting to crush her, but not willing to let her go just yet, and kept my arms around her as our breathing slowed.

I lifted my head, kissed her. And as I held her in my arms, I knew what I wanted. Knew I wanted her to stay with me all night. It only made sense that my first night back in my bedroom would be with her by my side. She would probably turn me down, but I still had to ask.

Of course, even if she didn't stay, she didn't have to leave quite yet. I slipped out of her arms and walked to my dresser. From the top drawer, I took a handful of candles and set them out, lighting them as I went.

When I returned to the bed, she rolled onto her back and I gathered her in my arms. We sat silently for a few minutes, simply enjoying the moment. I ran my hand across her shoulders and kissed her forehead.

"I didn't plan for this to happen tonight," I said. She lifted her head and I kissed her lips softly. "Truly, I didn't."

"I'm glad it happened, though." She sighed and nuzzled my chest. "Very glad."

Again we sat silently, and I thought about how much I wanted her body against me all night.

Ask her.

I swallowed. "Abby? I know you didn't bring anything, but would you stay with me tonight?" I pulled back and met her eyes. "Here. In my bed?"

A lone tear trickled down her face.

"Please." I brushed the tear away with my thumb. "Sleep here. With me."

She pulled out of my arms, and I looked at her, confused. She wasn't going to leave, was she?

"Yes," she said, and kissed me. "Yes, I'll stay."

Before I could tell her how happy I was, she pushed me onto my back and straddled me. "But we have *hours* before it's even remotely time to think about something as mundane as *sleep*. So for now"—one of her fingers traced my lips—"let me start with your mouth."

I slept with her in my arms all night. Unlike the last time, I felt only contentment and peace—all was right, in both of our worlds. I didn't even try to stay awake, but drifted off to sleep shortly after she succumbed to her own dreams.

Of course, I woke at my usual five thirty. I stayed where I was, though, enjoying the feel of her—how her body fit against mine, how her head rested on my chest, her hair cascading around me.

She stirred two hours later, waking and stretching lazily against me. I ran a hand down her back, and she lifted her head and smiled.

"Good morning," I said.

"'Morning."

"I'd go fix you breakfast or coffee, but I'm not willing to leave the bed just yet."

She arched her back against my hand. "Breakfast and coffee can wait."

I couldn't agree more. "Sleep well?"

"*Mmm.* Best sleep ever."

I kissed her forehead. "Thank you for staying."

It meant so much that she'd stayed with me all night in my

bed—it was another little step confirming what we had, what we could be, confirming our future together.

"Thanks for asking me."

"Oh, no. The pleasure was all mine."

She giggled. "I'm not sure it was all yours."

I laughed along with her until she reached out, cradling my jaw in her hand, and kissed me.

She pulled away and sat up. "Can I ask you a question?"

"Anything."

"The whole no-kissing rule," she said. "Was that a rule with all subs or just me?"

Not exactly the morning-after conversation I wanted to have. I had to be honest with her, though.

"It was just you, Abby," I said, stroking her hair.

"Just me? Why?"

Honest. You have to be honest.

"It was a way to distance myself," I said. "I thought if I didn't kiss you, I wouldn't feel as much." *Idiot. What were you thinking?* "I'd be able to remind myself I was just your dom."

She pulled back slightly. "You kissed your other subs," she said under her breath.

Fuck.

"Yes," I said. No matter what, be honest, Paul had told me.

"But not me," she said, eyes downward, expression a bit crestfallen.

How could I make this right? What could I do? How could I convince her that our past was past and our future would be so different?

"You know what this means, don't you?" she asked, before I could decide what to say.

"No," I said, not sure where she was going.

She moved up my body and whispered in my ear, "You've got a lot of making up to do."

Okay. I could deal with this. I gave her a tentative kiss. "A lot?"

"*Mmm*," she said, and I kissed her again. "With interest."

Oh, she was teasing again. I smiled. "Interest?"

"Lots of interest," she said in her vixen voice. "You better get started."

My cock twitched at her words. "Oh, Abby," I said. "I always pay my debts."

"Nathaniel," she said that Sunday afternoon. We were sitting on the couch at her apartment, sharing the newspaper. I set down my section. She looked nervous.

"Yes," I said.

"I was thinking." She didn't say anything else, though, and I started to get worried.

I scooted closer to her. "Is something wrong?"

She shook her head. "I don't want to assume anything." She played with a loose thread on the cushion. "It's just . . . I was wondering." She looked up at me. "When will you collar me again? I mean, you will, won't you?"

I placed my hand on the side of her face and lightly stroked her cheekbone. "Is that what you want?"

She nodded. "I want all of you. Every part."

My thumb traced her lips. "And I want every part of you that you'll give me."

I had wanted her to bring up the collar first, to make sure it was what she wanted. Even then, I had never expected the topic to surface so soon.

"You should know . . ." I started, trying to find the words. "I've been a lover and I've been a dom, but I've never been both to the same person before." She had been so honest. I needed to do the same. "I don't know how to do it. How to be both to you. I'm so afraid I'll mess up." She started to say something, but I stopped her. "I will mess up, Abby. I know I will."

She placed her hand over mine. "You don't have to be an expert at everything."

I looked into her beautiful eyes. "I'd never forgive myself if I hurt you—"

"You won't hurt me."

"I'm not just talking physically. If I hurt you emotionally again—" I shook my head, unable to go on.

"We'll do it together." She looped her arms around my neck. "You and I. We'll work it out. Together." Her lips brushed my ear. "I want you. As my lover and my master. We can do it."

"But if—"

"I told you once before you thought too much. It's still true. You need to stop. We can be beautiful."

Hearing her talk, I felt my confidence grow and I drew her closer. "You're a very smart woman, Abby King. I should listen to you more often."

She gave a low, sultry laugh, her lips inches from mine. "I'll remind you of that."

"You better."

Her hands untucked my shirt. "Don't worry. I will."

"Before we do anything, we need to talk."

"Later," she said, unbuttoning me. "Felicia's coming for dinner in two hours."

"Tomorrow night," I said in between kisses. "My house. Kitchen table."

"Right now. My apartment. Bed."

I swept her into my arms and carried her down the hall.

Chapter Thirty-seven

She looked up in confusion when I set the papers in front of her the next night.

"What's this?" she asked.

I gave her a pen, took my own papers, and sat down across the table. "I want us to redo our checklists."

"Us?" She smiled, eyes dancing wickedly. "Why? Did yours change?"

I returned her smile with one of my own. "Mine? Not so much, but I think yours might have. In one or two areas, at least."

She took the pen and filled out the header. "I can mark a few more things as experienced."

I checked off the first few items on my list. "I suppose you can."

"You're still out of your mind if you think long-term sexual deprivation is ever going to fly with me."

I chuckled. "Just fill out the list, Abby."

For the next few minutes, only the sound of pens scratching paper filled the kitchen.

"You know," she said, "I don't think you had kissing listed as a hard limit."

Damn it. I thought we'd already discussed that.

I pretended not to hear her. "Hmm?"

"If I'd looked at your list after you collared me, you might have had some explaining to do."

I looked up at her so she would know the truth of my words. "Had you questioned me on anything, I would have had some explaining to do."

"You're the dominant; it's not my place to question you."

I set my pen down and took her hand, needing her to know how much this meant. "I was wrong, Abby. And yes, it is your place to question me. Why do you think I told you to speak freely at the kitchen table? Why do you think I gave you the library? In the future, please tell me what you feel in those places, okay?" Her eyes went wide with understanding. "I want to know. I need to know. We'll never grow if we don't talk."

Her thumb stroked my knuckle. "Okay," she said, but I knew we had more to talk about.

"Let's finish the checklists and we'll talk some more."

I finished my checklist quickly and watched as she filled out hers. Every so often, she would nibble her bottom lip, start to mark something, and then tap her pen on the table before making a decision.

She's so inexperienced. You can't fuck this up again.

"Okay," she finally said. "I'm done."

We exchanged lists and I read over hers, comparing it in my mind to the one she had filled out before. Some of her limits had changed and some hadn't. I looked up to find her running a finger over my list, probably trying to line it up with hers.

"Do you have any questions?" I asked.

"I don't know where to start."

"Should I go first?" I asked and, at her nod, I continued. "You should know, I will never violate your hard limits, and I'm not trying to get you to change them, but I have to ask—what's your problem with canes?"

"Are you asking because you have it marked as"—she looked down at my list—"*like it a lot?*"

"Yes, and I want to understand why canes are a hard limit, when so little else is."

"There was a case I read about one time, in Singapore. You know they cane people there?" She didn't wait for me to respond, but continued. "It's for punishment. It sounds frightening. It bleeds and leaves scars."

I stared at her, confused. "You think I would beat you until you bled, leaving scars, and enjoy it?"

"No." She shook her head. "I just . . . didn't want to try it."

"Didn't?" I asked, picking up on the operative word.

"I need to know more about them first."

"Okay. We'll leave it as a hard limit for now. See if we can find a way to teach you more."

Fucking hell. I was shaken that she thought I could use her like that. I needed to think about how to introduce canes to her so she wouldn't find them so scary.

"Breath play?" she asked, looking down my list. "Hard limit?"

"Yes. Always has been. Always will be." While my hard limits had changed over the years, controlling someone's ability to breathe, to choke them, was something I'd never do.

"I just wondered what it would be like."

"It's too dangerous. I don't feel comfortable doing anything like that." But there was more, and this was a perfect opportunity to talk and show my new honesty. "Beth wanted to try breath play, so I read up on it, spoke to a few dominants, even watched a scene once." I looked up and caught her eye. "I know my limits, though—I just couldn't . . . I can't take that kind of risk. I'm sorry, Abby."

She shrugged. "No big deal."

"It is a big deal," I countered. "After my failure with Melanie—"

"Wait a minute." She held up a hand. "What's this about your failure with Melanie?"

"I failed her. I couldn't be what she wanted."

"Look at me, Nathaniel," she said, and her eyes were livid. "You didn't fail Melanie. Why do you think it was all on you? No, you couldn't be what she wanted, but she couldn't be what you needed."

"If I had just tried harder."

"You both would be miserable to this day," she said, and the wicked sparkle returned to her eyes. "And where would that leave me?"

The corner of my mouth lifted. "Where, indeed?"

"No more talk of failing Melanie," she said, picking up the papers and tapping them into a stack. "Now, where were we?" She looked over the list again. "Oh, yes. Breath play. Won't ever happen. Any more questions about my list?"

We went over a few more things, not so much to change anything, but to get a better understanding of why certain things had been marked the way they were. I explained the reasons for my hard limits and she talked about things she wanted to try.

There was still so much to talk about, but after going over the lists, I drew her into my arms and took her into the living room to watch a movie.

It felt odd.

It felt strange.

It felt good.

The next night, we regrouped at the table to discuss the whens and hows of our relationship. I started by telling her I had no interest in her being a submissive seven days a week. I wanted her as my lover just as much.

"Can we do the weekend thing again?" she asked.

It had been what I wanted to try, and I felt relieved she had suggested it herself. "I think that's a wonderful idea."

"And during the week, we're Nathaniel and Abby."

"I like it, but it's going to be hard. Going from Nathaniel and Abby to dominant and submissive." I had spoken to Paul earlier in the day about what he and Christine did. "I think it would work best to have set start and stop times and rituals for when I collar and uncollar you."

"Collar and uncollar? Why would you take your collar off me?"

"Because we're just us during the week," I said, repeating her words. "I could collar you every Friday, let's say at six, and take the collar off Sundays at three."

"I wore it every day last time."

"But things have changed."

"I'm not arguing with that, but by wearing it every day, I would keep that connection between us."

My heart swelled with pleasure at her words, but it wouldn't be a good idea for her to wear the collar during the week. I had seen firsthand how she acted wearing the collar, and I didn't want her to be in that frame of mind during the week.

I lowered my voice. "I understand why you want to wear my collar every day, but will you listen to some advice? From someone who has more experience?"

Her eyebrow shot up. "Are you going to play the experience card often?"

I swallowed my laugh. I had lived the lifestyle of a dom for more than ten years and she wanted to know if I would play the experience card?

"Yes," I said simply.

She huffed and sat back in her chair.

"Abby, listen. Whether you admit it or not, the collar puts you in a certain frame of mind and I don't want you in that frame of mind during the week." I had wanted her in that frame of mind during the week before, but not now. Not this time. "If I ask if you want peas or carrots for dinner on a Tuesday night, I want the answer to come from Abby, my lover, not Abigail, my submissive."

"I know, but . . ."

I had her. I could see it in her eyes. "I'm not giving you a meal plan or an exercise routine or stipulating sleep, or—"

"Thank goodness for that. Because insisting on eight hours of sleep would severely limit our weekday activities."

Fuck yes, it would, and I planned on a lot of weekday activities.

"Agreed," I said. "But to get back to what I was saying, if I want to have sex on a Wednesday and you're not in the mood, I want you to feel free to say so. The collar"—I shook my head—"it will limit you. Even though you think it won't."

"Okay, weekends only." She leaned forward in her seat. "Now, what was it you were saying about rituals?"

I talked to her about how a ritual would help get us both in the necessary frame of mind for Friday night and how it would ease the transition back to everyday life on Sunday afternoons. Repeated enough, Paul told me, it would become a signal we would learn to respond to.

"Are you sure you want to play the entire weekend?" I asked, once we'd agreed on times and rituals. I wanted to offer her options. "Maybe we could just scene a few times. That way you wouldn't be serving me the entire time."

"You mean, like cooking and waiting on you?"

"Right. If you don't want to do that . . ."

I would try. It would be completely outside of what I was used to with my submissives, but I would try. For her.

"I don't know," she said. "I rather like doing things for you. It's actually quite the turn-on."

My cock hardened at her words. "Really?"

"*Mmm*," she replied.

Well, okay, then. If she liked it, we'd do it. And if it turned her on . . . I'd have to give some thought as to how to work with that one.

Later, though. We had more to discuss tonight.

"We need to set up safe words," I said. "I always used yellow and red in the past, and I think those are good choices for you. When—"

"Two? You're giving me two safe words?"

"It's a commonly used system."

"But last time—"

"I already explained my error in the way I set things up last time, Abby. I won't have you walk out on me again."

She took my hand. "I'm not leaving. I just don't know why I have to have two safe words."

"Because we'll be pushing your limits," I said, thinking back to the things she wanted to try. "If you say *yellow*, I know I'm pushing, but can continue. *Red* stops the scene completely."

"But you've never had a sub use a safe word before."

"I have now." I kissed her hand. "And I want you to feel completely safe and secure anytime you're with me. Even when I'm pushing you."

"Yellow and red." She thought them over. "Like a traffic light."

"Exactly," I said. "And since I'll be pushing your limits, the safe words will also help me."

"You?"

"I can push, knowing you'll say *yellow* if I need to slow down," I explained. "You trust me, and in turn, I trust you'll use your safe words if I push too hard, too fast, or too far. It gives me peace of mind."

"I never thought about you needing to be safe."

"I know. I want to set things up correctly this time." I stopped for a second, knowing there was more. "I was also wrong when I punished you." She looked up in surprise. "Not so much for punishing you, but for not providing any aftercare."

"Aftercare?"

"I should have come to your room that night. Talked. Held you. Made sure you were okay. Checked your skin. Made you sit down the next morning instead of waiting until lunch. Anything."

"Oh."

"I was so wrapped up in my own feelings that I didn't give you the attention you needed." I held her gaze. "It won't happen again."

She didn't say anything.

"If I have to punish you again—*when* I have to punish you again," I corrected. It was inevitable. It would happen. "I want you to understand that it'll be different."

We spoke more about aftercare and what she should expect. We went over what would result in a chastisement and what the various penalties would be.

When she didn't have any more questions, I put an end to the discussion for another night and we took Apollo out for a walk. I showed her the cherry trees, pointed out where flowers would be coming up soon. As we walked, I reached for her hand and our fingers intertwined.

My phone gave a low double beep.

"Yes, Sara?" I looked at my watch and smiled. Five forty-five. I should have guessed she'd show up early.

"Ms. King is here, sir."

"Thank you. Send her in at five after six. Once she comes in, you can go ahead and leave for the night."

"Yes, sir," she said and hung up.

It was a Friday night. Abby had told me she wanted to resubmit her application to Mr. Godwin and come back to my office for an interview. I thought it damn near the craziest idea I'd ever heard and told her no, but she persisted. After some discussion, I saw her point of view—it would make things more official, and Godwin knew better than to question any orders I gave him.

"You want me to forward just Abigail King's application to you?" he asked. "No one else's?"

"That's right. Only hers."

"I have a new one here. Looks promising. She asked for you."

"Not interested. Call and tell her I'm not available. Indefinitely. And that goes for anyone else who asks."

Abby had requested I recollar her that weekend. We talked about timelines in detail. I told her there was no rush—I'd even questioned her about it that morning in the shower—but she had been insistent.

I looked at my watch again.

At three minutes after six, I turned back to my computer and started typing.

Damn fucking lucky-ass bastard.

The door opened and closed. Abigail—Paul had told me it would be easier to keep in role if I thought of her as Abigail on the weekends—walked across the floor and stopped in the middle of the room. I peeked up and looked at her—head down, arms to her sides.

Whatever you did to deserve to have that wonderful creature in your life, I don't know, I typed.

Damn fucking lucky-ass bastard.

Coming back to your office, giving you a second chance to be her dom.

Loving you even though you were such a fuckup.

Loving you, period.

Damn fucking lucky-ass bastard.

In the history of damn fucking lucky-ass bastards, you, West, are the luckiest damn fucking lucky-ass bastard.

Now, go give her what you both want.

I stopped typing.

"Abigail King."

She didn't move. Didn't acknowledge me.

I pushed back from my desk and walked behind her. I stopped for a second and smelled her. Delicious. I took her hair in my hand and gave a twist.

"I was *easy* on you last time," I said, because it was the damn truth and she knew it. She also knew I would not be easy on her this time.

I pulled her hair, and she worked to keep her head down. Excellent. I had not yet given her permission to look at me.

"You told me once you could handle anything I gave you physically," I said. "Do you remember?"

She didn't speak—I had not given her permission to do so.

I jerked her hair. "I'm going to test that theory, Abigail. We'll see just how much you're able to handle."

I let go of her hair and moved to stand in front of her. "I'm going to train you. Train you to service my every need, desire, and want. From now on, when I give a command, I expect you to obey immediately and without question. Any hesitation, raised eyebrow, or disobedience will be dealt with on the spot. Is that understood?"

She still didn't speak.

"Look at me and answer," I said. "Do you understand?"

Her head lifted and her eyes met mine. "Yes, Master."

Yes, *Master*? She called me *Master* before I collared her?

Again?

"Tsk, tsk, tsk." I'd known she would mess up. Expected it, even. But I had not thought it would happen in my office. "I thought you learned that lesson last time."

She looked completely confused.

"How do you address me before I collar you?" I asked.

"Yes, sir."

"I let that mistake slide before," I said, and walked to my desk. Could I do this? "But like I said, I won't be as lenient this time around."

I had to. To show her I meant it when I said I was easy on her last time.

"Lift your skirt and put your hands on top of my desk," I said.

My penalty for improper forms of address varied depending on what the violation was and when and how it occurred, but I had nothing down for failure to use the proper name before collaring.

"Three strokes," I said as she positioned herself. "Count."

My first smack landed on the fleshy part of her right butt cheek. "One."

The second landed on the left.

"Two."

My strikes were strong enough to color her ass—she needed to feel them—but not hard enough to leave any lasting mark. The final one landed on her sweet spot.

"Three."

Just like that, it was over. I felt better. We were going to be fine. I rubbed her gently, noting she didn't wince or shy from my hands. I smoothed her skirt down. "Go stand where you were."

She walked gracefully back to her spot in the middle of my office.

"Do you remember your safe words?" I asked.

"Yes, sir. I remember the safe words."

"Good." I opened a drawer, took out a box, and lifted out the collar. "Are you ready, Abigail?"

A smile lit her face. "Yes, sir."

I went and stood in front of her, collar in my hand.

"Kneel."

When she dropped to her knees, I fastened the collar around her neck.

Mine.

"I'll put this on you every Friday evening at six o'clock," I said, repeating what we had agreed to, "and take it off Sunday afternoons at three."

The collar looked so fucking good on her.

She would take me in her mouth now—it was the next step in the ritual we had decided on—but first, I had to do something . . .

"Stand up," I said.

She rose to her feet, obeying, even though I knew she didn't understand.

Every time I'd collared her in the past, feelings of possessiveness had overwhelmed me. The joy of seeing her in my collar, the sheer animalistic nature it released in me, was staggering. Every time before, I had wanted to kiss her.

"You look so fucking good wearing my collar."

This time, I would.

I slipped a hand under her chin and brought her to me, crushing her lips under mine. Showing her with my kiss how she affected me. How the sight of her wearing my collar affected me. She was tentative at first, but responded at my urging.

I finally broke the kiss and pushed down on her shoulders. "Back to your knees."

She dropped back into position and licked her lips. "Please, Master, may I have you in my mouth?" she asked, as we had agreed. I would put my collar on her, but in return, she would ask to serve me.

"You may."

I closed my eyes as she unbuckled and unzipped my pants. Over the last few weeks, she had given me oral sex, but it had always been in bed and never on her knees. I'd wanted to save that for when I recollared her.

I took her hair in my hands and, when she tried to ease my cock into her mouth, forced myself in. Showing her I was in control. She belonged to me. All of her. And I'd use her mouth in any way I desired.

For that was the gift she gave me.

And that was the gift I accepted.

I thrust in and out of her mouth and she worked herself on me. Running her tongue along me, sucking me deeply. I hit the back of her throat and still she took all of me, using her teeth, the exact way she knew I liked.

"Fuck," I groaned.

I tightened my grip on her hair and thrust harder. Fuck, she felt good. My balls tensed up, and I knew I wouldn't last much longer. She recognized I was close and grabbed on to my thighs in expectation.

I pushed my cock to the back of her throat and groaned again as I filled her mouth. She swallowed around me, drawing me deeper down her throat as she did so.

I slipped from her mouth and slowly untangled my hands from her hair. I ran my fingers over her head, stroking her scalp, hoping to soothe away any pain.

"Buckle my pants, Abigail."

Once she obeyed and my clothes were straightened, I told her to stand.

I cupped her chin and lifted her face so she looked at me. "I'm going to work you hard tonight. I'm going to bring you to the edge of pleasure and leave you hanging. You will not release until I give you permission, and I will be very stingy with my permission. Do you understand?"

She was silent.

"Answer me."

Her eyes shone dark with desire. "Yes, Master."

Very good.

"I'll be home in an hour. I want you naked and waiting in the playroom."

To be continued . . .

Abby and Nathaniel's story reaches its enticing
conclusion in the final instalment
of Tara Sue Me's explosive trilogy,

THE TRAINING

Coming in October 2013

The drive back to Nathaniel's house took longer than it should have. Or maybe it just felt like it took longer. Maybe it was nerves.

I tipped my head in thought.

Maybe not nerves exactly. Maybe anticipation.

Anticipation that after weeks of talking, weeks of waiting, and weeks of planning, we were finally here.

Finally back.

I lifted my hand and touched the collar—Nathaniel's collar. My fingertips danced over the familiar lines and traced along the diamonds. I moved my head from side to side, reacquainting myself to the collar's feel.

There were no words to describe how I felt wearing Nathaniel's collar again. The closest I could come was to compare it to a puzzle. A puzzle with the last piece finally in place. Yes, for the last few weeks, Nathaniel and I had lived as lovers, but we both felt incomplete. His recollaring of me—his reclaiming of me—had been what was missing. It sounded odd, even to me, but I finally felt like I was his again.

The hired car eventually reached Nathaniel's house and pulled into his long drive. Lights flickered from the windows. He had set the timer, anticipating my arrival in the dark. Such a small gesture, but a touching one. One that showed, like much he did, how he kept me firmly at the forefront of his mind.

I jingled my keys as I walked up the drive to his front door. My keys. To his house. He'd given me a set of keys a week ago. I didn't live with him, but I spent a fair amount of time at his house. He said it only made sense for me to be able to let myself in or to lock up when I left.

Apollo, Nathaniel's golden retriever, rushed me when I opened the door. I rubbed his head and let him outside for a few minutes. I didn't keep him out for too long—I wasn't sure if Nathaniel would arrive home early, but if he did, I wanted to be in place. I wanted this weekend to be perfect.

"Stay," I told Apollo after stopping in the kitchen to refill his water bowl. Apollo obeyed all of Nathaniel's orders, but thankfully, he listened to me this time. Normally, he would follow me up the stairs, and tonight that would be odd.

I quickly left the kitchen and made my way upstairs to my old room. The room that would be mine on weekends.

I undressed, placing my clothes in a neat pile on the edge of the twin bed. On this, Nathaniel and I had been in agreement. I would share his bed anytime I stayed over Sunday through Thursday nights, but on Friday and Saturday nights, I would sleep in the room he reserved for his submissives.

Now that we had a more traditional relationship during the week, we both wanted to make sure we remained in the proper mind-set on weekends. That mind-set would be easier to maintain for both of us if we slept separately. For both of us, yes, but perhaps more so for Nathaniel. He rarely shared a bed with his submissives, and having a romantic relationship with one was completely new to him.

I stepped naked into the playroom. Nathaniel had led me around the room last weekend—explaining, discussing, and showing me things I'd never seen and several items I'd never heard of.

At its core, it was an unassuming room—hardwood floors, deep, dark brown paint, handsome cherry armoires, even a long table carved of rich wood. However, the chains and shackles, the padded leather bench and table, and the wooden whipping bench gave away the room's purpose.

A lone pillow waited for me below the hanging chains. I dropped to my knees on it, situating myself into the position Nathaniel explained I was to be in whenever I waited for him in the playroom—butt resting on my heels, back straight, right hand on top of my left in my lap, fingers not intertwined, and head down.

I got into position and waited.

Time inched forward.

I finally heard him enter through the front door.

"Apollo," he called, and while I knew he spoke Apollo's name so he could take him outside again, another reason was to alert me who it was that entered the house. To give me time to prepare myself. Perhaps for him to listen for footsteps from overhead. Footsteps that would tell him I wasn't prepared for his arrival. I felt proud he would hear nothing.

I closed my eyes. It wouldn't be long now. I imagined what Nathaniel was doing—taking Apollo outside, feeding him maybe. Would he undress downstairs? In his bedroom? Or would he enter the playroom wearing his suit and tie?

Doesn't matter, I told myself. Whatever Nathaniel has planned will be perfect.

I strained my ears—he was walking up the stairs now. Alone. No dog followed.

Somehow, the atmosphere of the room changed when he walked in. The air became charged and the space between us nearly hummed. In that moment, I understood—I was his, yes. I had been correct with that assumption. But even more so, even more important, perhaps, he was mine.

My heart raced.

"Very nice, Abigail," he said, and walked to stand in front of me. His feet were bare and I noted he had changed out of his suit and into a pair of black jeans.

I closed my eyes again. Cleared my mind. Focused inwardly. Forced myself to remain still under his scrutiny.

He walked to the table and I heard a drawer open. For a minute, I tried to remember everything in the drawers, but I stopped myself and once again forced my mind to quiet itself.

He came back to stand at my side. Something firm and leather trailed down my spine.

Riding crop.

"Perfect posture," he said as the crop ran up my spine. "I expect you to be in this position whenever I tell you to enter this room."

I felt relieved he was satisfied with my posture. I wanted so much to please him tonight. To show him I was ready for this. That we were ready. He had been so worried.

Of course, not a bit of worry or doubt could be discerned now. Not in his voice. Not in his stance. His demeanor in the playroom was utter and complete control and confidence.

He dragged the riding crop down my stomach and then back up. Teasing.

Damn. I loved the riding crop.

I kept my head down even though I wanted to see his face. To meet his eyes. But I knew the best gift I could give him was my absolute trust and obedience, so I kept my head down with my eyes focused on the floor.

"Stand up."

I rose slowly to my feet, knowing I stood directly under the chains. Normally, he kept them up for storage, but they were lowered tonight.

"Friday night through Sunday afternoon, your body is mine," he said. "As we agreed, the kitchen table and library are still yours. There, and only there, are you to speak your mind. Respectfully, of course."

Both of his hands traced across my shoulders, down my arms. One hand slipped between my breasts and dropped to where I was wet and aching.

"This," he said, rubbing my outer lips, "is your responsibility. I want you waxed bare as often as possible. If I decide you have neglected this responsibility, you will be punished."

And again, we had agreed to this.

"In addition, it is your responsibility to ensure your waxer does an acceptable job. I will allow no excuses. Is that understood?"

I didn't say anything.

"You may answer," he said, and I heard the smile in his voice.

"Yes, Master."

He slipped a finger between my folds and I felt his breath in my ear. "I like you bare." His finger swirled around my clit. "Slick and smooth. Nothing between your pussy and whatever I decide to do to it."

Fuck.

Then he moved behind me and cupped my ass. "Have you been using your plug?"

I waited.

"You may answer."

"Yes, Master."

His finger made its way back to the front of me, and I bit the inside of my cheek to keep from moaning.

"I won't ask you that again," he said. "From now on, it is your responsibility to prepare your body to accept my cock in any manner I decide to give it to you." He ran a finger around the rim of my ear. "If I want to fuck your ear, I expect your ear to be ready." He hooked his finger in my ear and pulled. I kept my head down. "Do you understand? Answer me."

"Yes, Master."

He lifted my arms above my head, buckling first one wrist and then the other to the chains at my side. "Do you remember this?" he asked, his warm breath tickling my hair. "From our first weekend?"

Again, I said nothing.

"Very nice, Abigail," he said. "Just so there's no misunderstanding, for the rest of the evening, or until I tell you differently, you may not speak or vocalize in any way. There are two exceptions—the first being the use of your safe words. You are to use them at any point you feel the need. No repercussions or consequences will ever follow the use of your safe words. Second, when I ask if you are okay, I expect an immediate and honest answer."

He didn't wait for a response, of course. I wasn't to give one. Without warning, his hands slipped back down to where I ached for him. Since my head was down, I watched one of his fingers slide inside me and I bit the inside of my cheek again to keep from moaning.

Shit, his hands felt good.

"How wet you are already." He pushed deeper and twisted his wrist. Fuck. "Usually, I would taste you myself, but tonight, I feel like sharing."

He removed himself and the emptiness was immediate, but before I could think much about it, I felt his slippery finger at my mouth. "Open, Abigail, and taste how ready you are for me." He trailed his finger around my open lips before easing it inside my mouth.

I'd tasted myself before, out of curiosity, but never so much at one time and never off of Nathaniel's finger. It felt so depraved, so feral.

Damn, it turned me on.

"Taste how sweet you are," he said as I licked myself off his finger.

I treated his finger as if it were his cock—running my tongue along it, sucking gently at first. I wanted him. Wanted him inside me. I sucked harder, imagining his cock in my mouth.

"You will not release until I give you permission, and I will be very stingy with my permission." His words from the office floated through my mind and I choked back a moan before it left my mouth. It would be a long night.

"I changed my mind," he said when I finished cleaning his finger. "I want a taste after all." He crushed his lips to mine and forced my mouth open. His lips were brutal—powerful and demanding in their quest to taste me.

Damn, I'd have a stroke if he kept that up.

headline
ETERNAL

FIND YOUR HEART'S DESIRE...